The
Big
Ballad
Jamboree

THE
BIG
BALLAD
JAMBOREE

A NOVEL BY
DONALD DAVIDSON

Afterword by
CURTIS W. ELLISON AND WILLIAM PRATT

UNIVERSITY PRESS OF MISSISSIPPI

JACKSON

99 98 97 96   4 3 2 1

The paper in this book meets the guidelines for permanence and durability of the
Committee on Production Guidelines for Book Longevity of the Council on Library
Resources.

Library of Congress Cataloging-in-Publication Data

Davidson, Donald, 1893–1968.
    The big ballad jamboree : a novel / by Donald Davidson ; afterword by Curtis W.
Ellison and William Pratt.
        p.   cm.
    ISBN 0-87805-853-2 (alk. paper)
    1. Country musicians—North Carolina—Fiction. 2. Country music—North
Carolina—Fiction. 3. Country life—North Carolina—Fiction. I. Title.
PS3507.A66B54   1996
813'.52—dc20   95-25543
                                                                          CIP

British Library Cataloging-in-Publication data available

The
Big
Ballad
Jamboree

TIME: The summer of 1949.

PLACE: Carolina City—in southwestern North Carolina—and nearby Beaver Valley, a mountain cove almost depopulated by modern improvements. Carolina City is a typical small city of the Southern uplands, but is not found on any present-day map. Station WCC, in Carolina City, will naturally not be listed in any radio guide—or was not listed, in 1949.

CHARACTERS: All fictitious—but since they must behave as if they were "real," they do know and make mention of certain well-known personalities in "hillbilly music"—later more euphemistically known as "country music."

THE PATH WAS IN THE GULLY

We came to the edge of the big woods, and, for all Ed Cooley's grumbling, I found the path in no time. Soon as I could look down and see the beech trees beginning, I knew where we were. All day we had been in the high hills back of the old MacGregor Place, Ed Cooley and me, like old times, fishing or pretending to fish, and though the woods had changed a lot, I could still pick up the landmarks, and proud to think I could, after so many years. That is something you have in your bones, or not at all—the way you just know the lay of the land by the feel as much as the look. It's not anything you do with your head.

It was the short cut back over the ridge we were taking, like I planned, not fishing Hurricane Creek along the north side of the ridge and all the way to the big road before coming in, the way we used to. But I don't really know to this good day why I planned it like that. Something must have told me to do it, but it was not anything I could explain to Ed Cooley or, for that matter, to anybody.

"Even if you do have the car parked at the spring," Ed Cooley said, "it's jest a little piece from there to the house, and what's the gain? Climbin' one more ridge, and that the steepest, after climbin' ridges all day. And after circlin' all through the high hills, and gittin' directions all caterwampused, how will you ever hit the right place in the woods?"

"I'll hit it, all right," I told him. And I did. Though it must have been ten years, no less, since we'd come in that way.

On the south side of the ridge between Hurricane Creek and Beaver Creek there is a considerable rise, almost a knob—though some folks might call it a point—and that was what I aimed to hit after we crossed the ridge. At the foot of that rise the big woods start to thin out. Right on the brow of the ridge a deep gully begins and runs on down into a little hollow—a high hollow that overlooks the MacGregor Place. Beech Hollow, that was

Grandpa's name for it. It's mostly beech in there, a fine stand of old beech, and not cut over, right down to the spring where the farm road ends. Where the path comes near the edge of the slope there's a good deal of rock and you can stand there and see the old MacGregor Place rolled out before you, and all the country around it.

Maybe that was in the back of my head all day—to stand on a rock and stick my thumbs in my belt and look down from Beech Hollow and say, "It's mine now." Near to set of sun, with the shadows stretching and cattle grazing all one way and smoke rising from the chimney, all mine and no man to say me nay. But night would be coming on, and there'd be no time to tarry on the porch after supper. Back in Carolina City, that's where I had to be, picking a guitar and stretching my neck to the mike. Not quite like common, though, because the year was over and Cissie would be back. Not that she had told me, but the word was out. Maybe that was what brought me over the ridge no matter what.

Still, we had not reached the lookout place. Where a spot of pasture used to be, the blackberries and wild plums had come in thick. You could not see the path. Ed Cooley would call it "lost."

"There's the gully!" I told Ed. "It must have been a road once. Now it's jest where you find the path!"

"I be dogged! Ain't that a place for a path?"

"That's the way things are, these days. This is where we come out, and it ain't but a little stretch to the car."

On the edge of that gully, flatfooted and panting, Ed looked big as a bear and mighty nigh as rough. He was sweating and puffing from coming over and down, with his little string of fish and his big lot of fishing tackle that he just would bring along.

"If you'd been a disk jockey instid of a barber, you might have more wind," I said.

Ed twisted the bandanna out of his hip pocket and wiped the sweat out of his eyes.

"Then you never would have me in the high hills, to carry a load and back you up."

I thought I'd give Ed time to ketch his wind, but Ed never did need that kind of wind. He went right on talking.

"Hit's a shame not to fish Hurricane Creek, but I know you have a date tonight—and not jest with Rufus."

"I don't know what you're a-talkin' about."

"Well, ever'body in Carolina City does."

I pulled a sassafras leaf and chawed it and said nothing.

4

"Didn't I read in the paper that Miss Cissie Timberlake, former star of the Turkey Hollow Boys show, was comin' back from New York? And that she would be guest singer tonight, on the program Rufus is puttin' on for the Future Farmers' convention?"

I kept on chawing sassafras.

"Well, I know why you're climbin' ridges and takin' short cuts. But why did you take to the bushes in the first place? Why ain't you back in town, primpin' and gittin' ready? And you need a haircut, by the way."

"That's too late to explain to a barber, this late in the day."

"But that's what the paper said, wa'n't it?"

"That's what it said."

"But that ain't all you know about it, is it?"

"That's all."

I took a quick run down the bank, wrastled through some bushes, and put my feet on the path. Ed was still on the edge of the gully, and still talking.

"I don't believe it. Didn't she even send you a postal card? I wouldn't give a copper for a gal like that." He was shouting into the gully now. "You ain't the least part of a man if you let Cissie treat you that way."

She hadn't sent me so much as a postal card, not lately. And I truly didn't know why I took to the woods that day, except that I couldn't bear to wait around Carolina City. But even if I could explain it, nobody would understand my explanation unless he had been a hillbilly radio singer and courted Cissie Timberlake.

"Come on, Ed, if you're comin' a-tall!" I pushed along. Behind me came a big noise in the brush.

"I'm right with you. Whurever MacGregor goes, Cooley'll be right behind."

Then, after a stretch of quiet, "She shore did treat you rough. But I look for a change."

I could smell the beech woods now, all about where the path took us close to them; and I heard a squirrel bark. It was getting on late afternoon, and the squirrels were moving along towards home, like us.

"Keep quiet, Ed," I called back. "We might git us a squirrel or two for supper."

"Whut with? Hook and line?"

"My rifle's in the trunk of the car."

"Hit'd be a waste of bullets. This is your lucky day. Jest knock 'em out with a fishin'rod."

As far as fishing went, it had been my lucky day, though it was the first time I'd been out with Ed in many a month, and the first time in years on the old MacGregor Place, often though we had talked about doing it. Either Rufus had us on the road, or the weather turned bad, or I was helping Old Man Parsons with the fences and the cattle, trying to get the place back in shape. Much as I had wanted different, and figured different, I couldn't live at the MacGregor Place or even sleep there overnight more than once in a while. So far, it wasn't even a good picnic spot, but just business and worry. Not so much worry, though, since I had moved the Parsons couple into the old cabin to be my tenants. Moved them in from high up in Beaver Valley where they'd been living with a granddaughter after the government took their own place and run them out. I fixed up the old cabin, put running water in it, and a telephone. It was the first time they'd ever had a telephone in a house where they lived. Maybe the first time they'd ever talked on one, for all I know. Anyhow they soon learned about answering the telephone, and they already knew all there was to know about shooting varmints, and about keeping the cattle in and the strangers out.

Grandma's room was the only room I had been able to clean up and use in the big house since I finally bought the place back from the trashy fellow that Ellie May sold it to. When Ma died, we all agreed that Ellie May was to have the place because she was the only one of us that could farm it, right then. But when the war come on and the Army took all her boys, she couldn't farm it. That was soon after I was discharged and started in being sideman for Rufus, and I didn't have much cash. She knew I aimed to buy it. I told her we ought to keep it in the family, and why couldn't she hold on till I got enough for a down payment and the financing? But she claimed she needed the money, and I couldn't stand in her way. My other sisters all said sell, and she sold out.

Now I had it, rundown though it was, and money to meet the payments. Ellie May let me have the old cannonball bedstead, the big wide one that Grandma's Uncle Clisby made her out of wild cherry for a wedding present.

And that was where Ed and me slept, the night before, with the moon shining in and the whippoorwills going strong. Mrs. Parsons got us early breakfast, down at the cabin, and we were in the high hills soon after daylight. Little though I cared, it seemed like I got a bite every time I threw out my line, but Ed had only middling luck.

Now my head was crisscrossing with thoughts like pig tracks in the barn lot. It was hot there in the brush, where you could hardly see anything except the blackberries that would soon be ripened, above the clusters, the tops of beech trees on both sides, with the sun already coming level and yellow under the down-slanting limbs and the little quiet leaves.

6

I stopped to listen. There was no sound of Ed. I gave him a holler. He didn't answer, and I hollered again. Then I heard him, coming slow, and singing:

> It will be some day in June
> I'll travel back and say:
> "Don't claim I was false-hearted
> Just because I went away."

I could see the weeds moving. He picked up the chorus:

> Some day in June, some Carolina day
> I know you'll love me better
> Just because I went away.

When Ed came in sight, he had his head down and was dragging his feet.

"What's the matter, Ed?" I asked him. "Are you singin' to keep up your spirits?"

Ed reached out and jabbed a finger at my chest.

"By no means. I'm a-singin' to keep up *yore* sperrits. I'm a-thinkin' about you and Cissie."

"Well, think about somethin' else. Somethin' cheerful."

I turned to go on, but Ed grabbed my arm.

"What about tonight? Better do some thinkin' before night."

"I've had nothin' to do but think for a whole year."

"Hold on jest one minute and answer me one question. If Cissie is a-goin' to sing tonight, what will she sing? Regular old hillbilly songs? Or that new stuff she has been studyin' up in New York?"

"I don't know but one thing, and that is that Cissie ain't been studyin' any new stuff. You're mistaken, Ed. She's been studyin' the oldest stuff there is—ballads, folk songs. I told you about it."

"I don't rightly know what you mean. But Cissie is smart, and if she is singin' ballads and folk songs, that's what you'll be singin', and Rufus will be singin', before long."

"Rufus won't stand for it. I have done tried him."

"Then Rufus is as big a fool as you are, Danny. Here we are in 1949 and hillbilly music is tops. But where will you be in 1950—or '60—if you don't keep up? If it's somethin' to study in New York, it'll be somethin' for the radio, sure."

I turned away, and meant it. We moved along fast, and came to the brow of Beech Hollow, and stopped, looking down.

"Mighty pretty!" Ed Cooley said, as if to himself. "Mighty pretty—if you can pay the taxes, and I reckon you can."

Now the light was coming golden from the west, the shadows of the trees were lying long across the grass, and the big shadow of the hills would soon be creeping in. It was the way I liked best to see the MacGregor Place. The ridge sloping sharp from Beech Hollow to the spring. The field road beginning in the grass just beyond. The clump of old beech trees at the spring—and my car under the beeches. Follow the field road on down—it runs close to the branch all the way—and you come to the first gate. To the right of it is the water gate over the branch. I could see ten head of my steers near the water gate, and the rest must be close behind the brush and trees along the branch. But right then I wasn't thinking about cattle, and my eyes went on beyond.

Beyond the first gate, the field road turns up to the old MacGregor house, but the branch runs off more to the west and finally across the road to Beaver Creek. The house stands on the rise, the way a house ought to stand, and it faces west because Grandpa built it that way—the porch on the west, and the south end of the house to the road. You won't find many like that, because most folks build 'em to face the big road, as close to the road as they can crowd and still have a front yard.

Grandpa built it so he could sit on the front porch after supper and look to the mountains, same as he did when he lived in the cabin on the slope below and sat on the steps of the dog-run. Grandpa was born in that cabin and wouldn't tear it down like nearly everybody did. "No," he said. "Leave it. I like it whar it is. Hit's not in my way. And leave the corncrib and the old log barn. I like them too, right whar they be, and we might need 'em some day, no tellin'." That's what Grandma told me he said, and she let him have his way. And as to the big house—the new house, it was then—Grandpa said, "No white pillars for me. I done seen enough big white pillars, all about, too many, with the paint peelin' off and nobody to clean up the bird droppin's. And woodpeckers drillin' into 'em. Or maybe jest white pillars only, standin' with no house behind 'em, like I seen in Georgia, when I was lumberin' down there. Make it anyway you want," he told Grandma, "but no white pillars."

So they made it a two-story house with a one-story porch and plenty of bay windows. That was the style then. No looks much, but real comfortable. An ell running back for the dining room and kitchen, and a porch all latticed up between them and the main house. The new barn and smokehouse farther back, and always a big woodpile convenient.

And though Grandpa wouldn't stand for white pillars, he graded out an avenue, all the same, down the far slope to the main road, and set it out on both sides with oak trees. No pines for him, he said. He was tired of looking at pine trees.

Now the late sun was full on the house. And smoke going up from the cabin below where Mrs. Parsons was cooking supper. And Old Man Parsons was chopping wood. I couldn't see him but I could hear the ax strokes, slow and steady.

Beyond the road, on the other side of Beaver Creek, the ridge was turning deep blue, but from where we stood you couldn't see the big mountains to the west. It was a fine thing to look down and see the whole place and not mind the weeds and gullies because you didn't notice 'em much, from up there, and in that light.

The big road goes on to the west, up Beaver Valley and into the big mountains and the high hollows. Up there, the folks I used to know had mostly gone. The government had come in, or the power company, or the State of North Carolina, and bought them nearly all out, or just chased them out one way or another. Or they moved off to work in the mills. The Timberlake place, up the road a piece, was state forest now. And that was what sent Cissie and her old mother into Carolina City. Only a few of the old families had held on—folks that didn't have much the government wanted, like the Kennedys and the Ritsons and old Aunt Lou Watkins.

And I was the only one that had tried to move back. If I hadn't caught on to what pickin' and singin' would do, I never could have come back, either. It was a rundown place, but I had a start on the fences and the cattle, and somebody to help. You could call me lucky. I would have called myself lucky if Cissie and me hadn't broke up. That left me empty as a gourd.

I didn't say a word. Neither did Ed, for a change. Maybe Ed was thinking about his own folks. They used to live beyond the Timberlakes, but not one Cooley was left in Beaver Valley that I knew about. Without a word between us we walked down to the car.

I had forgotten about the squirrels till I put my hand on the door handle. Then a big gray squirrel ran down a limb right over my hand. Time I got my rifle, the squirrel was on the other side of the tree, all set to jump for the next tree. I could just see his bushy tail among the leaves. It was a long shot, but I brought him tumbling. That stirred up another squirrel high up in the same tree. I shot quick and got him too. He fell close to the tree trunk, and at first I thought he would lodge, because he hit limb after limb, falling down slow. Then I heard the thump on the ground, and Ed said, "Two tries, no misses. It's better to be born lucky than rich." He picked up the two squirrels and came bringing squirrels and fish, all together.

"If we have squirrel for supper, whut you goin' to do with all these-here fish?"

"Give 'em to the Parsons—or take 'em home yourself."

Then we heard the farm bell ringing.

"What's that for?" I asked Ed. "She can't be ringin' the old man home for supper. I heard him choppin' wood."

"He must want you, quick," said Ed Cooley.

I fired two shots into the air to let him know we heard. The bell stopped, and we jumped into the car.

I took the road up to the house in fast second, bumps and all, then angled across the grass to meet Old Man Parsons. He was coming over the stile, bareheaded and grand with his white hair and long whiskers, like somebody out of the Bible except that he was wearing ragged pants. He was telling me before I could get out of the car.

"They want you." He was waving his hand in the direction of Carolina City. "I told 'em I didn't know whar to seek you but I'd keep ringin' the bell."

"Is it a telephone call, Mr. Alex? Did you get the number?"

"Yes-siree, it's that-air telephone. It's Rufus Whitthorne. Been ringin' off and on, all day. He didn't like it when I told him you'd be here when you got here."

Old Man Parsons laughed a deep belly laugh. His cheeks were rosy as a boy's, and he wouldn't take backtalk from no man. I wished I could have seen Rufus' face when he had Old Man Parsons on the telephone.

"I told him you was somewheres up Hurricane Creek, singin' to the fishes," said Old Man Parsons, and laughed again as I started for the house. "And he said, 'Well, ain't that jest like a MacGregor?'"

Ed said, "I'll lock up the house and get our clothes."

When I reached the door Old Man Parsons had thought of something else. "Hold on," he shouted. "There's a union in it, too. It's Rufus and the union. On that telephone."

Inside the kitchen Mrs. Parsons was at the table rolling out biscuit dough. "He's mixed up," she said without even looking at me. "Thar's a Western Union call too. I answered the telephone twicet myself. It's Rufus callin' and it's Western Union callin'. He's always gittin' mixed up."

When I finally got Rufus I could almost see him red in the face and the freckles popping out.

"Danny, what the hell do you mean by runnin' off to the woods when we have a big night comin' up?"

"Go right ahead and tell me what. I'm a-listenin'."

"Danny, you ain't got a minute to lose. Git right out to the airport and meet Cissie Timberlake at the plane. She wants you."

"You don't mean me, Rufus. You better send somebody else."

"Yes, I mean you, and she means you. You are sweet Danny ag'in and no foolin'. Cissie 'phoned me from New York this mornin'. She wants *you* to meet her and nobody else. And she wants you to play for her tonight."

I could hardly hold the telephone to my ear, but I managed to say, "Why didn't she let me know before this?"

"Danny, you big fool, she's been tryin' to reach you and that's why she called me, when you couldn't be found."

"But what is she goin' to sing?"

"Git on out to the airport and ask her. Hit don't matter. Any of them songs you used to do, like 'White Roses on My Mother's Grave.' You and Cissie got to make them Future Farmers weep. Goodby and get along."

I said, "I'm gittin'," and he hung up, sharp. I couldn't wait till I got Western Union and the operator began to read the telegram. It said about the same thing: "I WANT YOU TO PLAY FOR ME TONIGHT. PLEASE MEET PLANE FIVE-FORTY-FIVE. LOTS TO TELL YOU. CISSIE."

Ed Cooley already had the car turned around and pointed towards the avenue when I came out, and all our stuff piled in the back. Old Man Parsons was sitting on the stile, holding the squirrels by the tails. As soon as Ed saw my face he knew what was going on.

"What did I tell you?" he said. "You better listen to me when I advise you."

"I've got to meet Cissie at the airport in half an hour."

"If you drive fast you can make it."

"I'll have to drop you up town," I said. "I can't take you home."

"That's all right," said Ed Cooley. "Me and the fish will take a taxi."

"Will you be back for supper?" asked Old Man Parsons.

"Not tonight," I told him. "Not very soon."

And I put the car in gear. We hit the avenue fast. Ed Cooley was quick to open the big gate and shut it again. When he got in the car again he said, "You better think what you are goin' to tell Cissie. Cissie is a smart gal."

"I won't have time to think. Or even to change my clothes."

"Well, you can practice thinkin' for the next thirty minutes," said Ed Cooley. "You can practice on me. You never did explain what really happened."

I already had the car up to sixty or better, and my eyes on the road, but what I was really seeing was Cissie, in a green-checked gingham dress and the guitar slung over her shoulder, and a little smile coming as she bent over towards the mike and begun to sing.

"I thought it was jest a notion," I said out loud, but I was talking partly to myself. "It was after she started to teachers college and turned ag'in the hillbilly music . . . It's the old songs . . . Nothin' suits her anymore unless it's been moulderin' in the grave for at least a hundred years . . . She's a fool about ballads . . ."

The needle on the dial moved up to seventy. Now the gullies were all on the side, and my path between them, hard asphalt and meant to stay. I could hear the voice of the Western Union operator and see the words like they were printed big on yellow paper. I WANT YOU TO PLAY FOR ME . . . LOTS TO TELL YOU . . . CISSIE.

It didn't go with what had happened before.

Maybe Ed Cooley was right, and it was time to start thinking.

2

THE TROUBLE ABOUT THE BULL FIDDLE

There's money in the new songs if you are willing to put on a hillbilly outfit and stand up to the mike and do what Rufus tells you. And go where he books you, Saturday nights and other nights and noons, even early mornings if Rufus says go. Look like you're pleased to be there, too, and having a big time singing, no matter how you feel. It wouldn't work any other way, and, truth is, you do have a big time. It's the music does it. It's the world's wonder how it takes hold of you. Pay $25 or $30 for a shirt, maybe $200 for a whole outfit—they all come from somewhere out in California. But that's just chickenfeed once you're in the money. Keep making records that'll sell—don't forget that. And don't forget the little fifty-cent song books with your picture on the cover. And by all means don't forget to have a kind word for the disk jockeys when they come around telling you about some song they've written and the little band they've started at a place you never heard tell of. That's how Rufus made his pile, and for all I know it might be a million.

If you are a band leader like Rufus, you'll have a Cadillac, custom-built the way you want it. Nothing less will do. Rufus has his Cadillac even though he's still a long ways from the top. If you are Hank Williams or Carl Smith you can be pretty independent, and get your dates arranged by the Artist Service Bureau like the one up in Nashville. Rufus don't have to work so hard at that since he got his own manager, but still he has to watch his chances. If you are a sideman in the band, like I am for Rufus, you won't make as much money, but you'll make a right smart. And the main part of the money comes from the new songs. You got to keep making up new songs for your own crowd, and you got to know the new songs that others make up and that are ketching on. You got to know what folks will like before they know it themselves. And you got to like it yourself, too, else you won't have no heart to sing it.

But of course the old songs are the best. I knew it all the time, down deep inside. The trouble is, they don't hardly ever ketch on in the record shops or amongst the jukeboxes.

I sung "Gypsy Davy" once on a program we were trying out for Kurly Krisps. It was soon after Cissie broke up with me and went off. I got to thinking about her that morning in the studio, up there in Carolina City, while we were waiting to go on the air. It just floated into my head all of a sudden:

> What made you leave your house and land?
> What made you leave your money?
> What made you leave your own true love
> To go with a Gypsy Davy?

I ought not to a-done it, but the devil got in me. To begin with, the commercial set my teeth on edge: *Start the day with Kurly Krisps! Kurly, Kurly, Kurly Krisps! Sweet and crunchy! Good and munchy!* Rufus had us sing it loud and fast, and make a sort of joke out of it. Then he let out a big turkey-gobble—that's our trademark—and after Kelly Warlick snatched out a fiddle tune and the Cory sisters droned out a lonesome song, he said: "And now here's the wildest young gobbler and the redheadedest redhead of us all—Danny MacGregor—and goin' to sing a good ol' sweetheart song! Whut you got for us, Danny?" And I said, "Hit's a regular ol' sweetheart song named 'Gypsy Davy,'" gave my guitar a slow roll, and set in. By that time Rufus couldn't do a thing but look surprised and get red around the ears.

I sung it the way I learned it 'way back yonder. Not all of it. Only the best and saddest parts, about how the girl heard the gypsies singing and ran off with 'em; and her sweetheart, or maybe her husband, followed and tried to get her back. He asked her a lot of questions about what made her leave him. Then he had to give up:

> Take off, take off those fine kid gloves
> All made of Spanish leather,
> And give to me your lily-white hand
> And say farewell forever.

Time we got out of that studio, the station manager was hot after us. "Cut out the long-hair stuff!" he said. "We want real hillbilly music." He was already getting complaints.

I didn't know what they were complaining about till it was explained to me. But that's what he said: "Cut out the long-hair stuff!" Meaning they didn't want no poetry. The Kurly Krisps advertising man was listening, and no telling who else. They thought it was poetry.

Rufus grabbed me and mighty-nigh tore a piece out of my shirt. His eyebrows moved up and down, and every freckle on his face stood out.

"Whut you pullin' on us, you redheaded stringbean? Why didn't you sing 'Tell Me Goodby Again' like we agreed? Want to make us lose a contract, do ye?"

"What was good enough for my old grandmammy is good enough for Danny MacGregor," I told him, and snatched my shirt away. "And it ought to be good enough for all them red-toenailed women that's a-settin' around listenin' to the radio. It's a real old hillbilly song, Rufus, and you know that as well as I do."

"You are right," said Rufus. "But there ain't no money in it for Rufus and his Turkey Hollow Boys."

I knew he had me there. So I tucked in my shirt and went home without another word.

Now, most of a year had gone by, and I was hitting seventy on the Carolina City road with Ed Cooley wanting me to explain it all over. I could tell him about it, but I couldn't explain it. All Ed would say was: "There's just about room for a pin to get between a woman's yes and no."

"Maybe so," I said, "but when Cissie puts her mind on it she can make a pin behave like a crowbar."

But at least she did send me the telegram.

Some time back, if any living man had told me that we would break up on account of "ballads," I would have laughed in his face. I wouldn't have realized what he was talking about, even though I could sing what they call ballads. And it was the same with Cissie up to the time when she got it into her head to study music on the side at the state teachers college, and then took the notion of going the whole route and getting herself some degrees. Till Cissie went to college I don't reckon she knew any more'n I did that there was any old books with our songs in 'em, or anything to study about 'em except just to learn 'em the way we did long ago from Grandma and the old folks. And Cissie never really got her head set ag'inst me till she begun to call them old songs "ballads." Up to then, she was crazy about hillbilly music, and the fact is she just about put herself through college and supported her old mother to boot, singing with me and the others for the Turkey Hollow Boys.

It was the State Teachers people that learned her different. She begun to go around with a book under her arm and talk about folk songs. Sometimes she would talk to me about it but I didn't ketch on. I ought to a-took warning when she begun to mention Dr. Hoodenpyl, like he was Jesus Christ. But how could I know? I was simple as a hog in the pen just before hog-killing time.

Even when Cissie won a scholarship and decided to go to New York, we didn't really break up at first—though it's true she kept holding out ag'inst gitting married. She wouldn't name the day. Yet maybe I might have gotten a promise if I hadn't made one big mistake.

"Wa'n't it somethin' about a bull fiddle?" Ed Cooley asked me. "And for God's sake don't try to pass that truck on this hill!"

I eased up on the accelerator. "It ain't safe to talk about bull fiddles if you are goin' to ride with me."

But it helped to talk about it, all the same.

It was the last part of that summer, and, so happen, the evening before Cissie left for New York. We were having a practice spell in Studio B, after the Friday evening crowd had gone. We were spread out comfortable on the front row, trying out the new song Rufus had made up.

The song was about a pore one-horse farmer that never could raise but one bale of cotton. But he believed in cotton and was bound somehow to git his one bale ginned and hauled to town. Then he would sell it and pay off the crop loan and pretty soon borrow ag'in so he could raise another bale o' cotton next year. All the way to town he kept meeting up with trouble. Started out with chillun in a quarrel, no meat in the smokehouse, no flour in the barrel. One jump from the sheriff and plain starvation; old woman scoldin' like the nation. But he was a believin' man and kept travelin' on to more trouble.

Rufus took the story part, singin' it fast and snappy, in that screechy voice he uses for comedy songs. The rest of us backed him up and come in on the chorus. We put in all the noises: horse pullin' foot out of mud, jackass brayin', pigs squealin', old woman scoldin'. And Cissie was there, too, listenin' to us practice.

Now Cissie has a natural way with almost any kind of musical instrument. Kettledrums to fiddles, there's hardly a thing she hasn't set her hand to, though what she does best is straight singing.

When Rufus gave us a break, the others all went out, but I stayed to have a Coca-Cola right there with Cissie. Time was short and I didn't want to waste a minute of it. But she didn't seem to want to talk. She just sat there wrinkling up her forehead and drinking Coca-Cola. All of a sudden she picked up Ozro's bull fiddle, and derned if she didn't start in on the cottonbale song. "Ridin' on a Cottonbale"—that's what Rufus named it.

Cissie ripped off Ozro's solo part for the bull fiddle, slick as if she'd been practicing it a month. It's the kind of solo part Ozro is so good at. Comes between the verses with the guitars and little fiddles backing up the bull fiddle. And Ozro had made it up to come after this verse:

Came to the river and I didn't have a boat;
I can't fly, but cotton will float.
So I hitched me a rope to an alligator's tail
And I rode the river on my cotton bale.

Then the bull fiddle comes in big and bold with the tune, like it might be an ol' alligator humpin' along, and bellowin' too. Cissie did all that part from the umpa-umpa in the verse right on through the bass solo. I never saw a prettier sight in my life than that little girl wrestlin' that bull fiddle, high heels scotched well apart, skirt up to her knees, yellow hair flyin', and long white fingers jumpin' all over the fiddle, right hand pickin' the strings like Kingdom Come. She puckered her mouth now and then, to make the notes come better, and the more she puckered, the more I twanged all over. When she finished, Cissie flung her hair back over her shoulder and stood there looking at me, still puckering her mouth a little as if she wanted to smile but wouldn't, and the big bull fiddle nudgin' up ag'inst her yellow sweater and blue skirt as if it knowed what Heaven was like. That was when my crazy idea hit me, and who could blame me?

"Let's do it ag'in, Cissie," I said, and grabbed my guitar. We heard a big laughin' and clappin', and Kelly and Elmer started in to sing and play with us as we swung into the tune once more. Then Cissie saw Rufus and Ozro comin' in at the back. She broke off, right in the middle of the tune. She propped the bull fiddle up in its place and sat down, cool and sweet as if she had never run that alligator down the river.

"Don't turn loose," said Ozro, in his wheezy stage voice. "You got that-air alligator right by the tail."

Rufus was looking Cissie over, the way he would look over a horse he might be thinkin' of buyin'. His eyebrows were shootin' up and his scalp of sandy hair was movin' above his big ears. But his gray eyes were as cold as he can make 'em when he starts figurin'.

"Ozro," he said. "Looks to me like you mighty nigh lost your job."

"Oh, I always likes to see the women do my work." Ozro was shovin' the bull fiddle at Cissie and grinnin' like a lazy old 'possum.

"I'd be ashamed to take the money for what work you do," Cissie joshed him back. "You and the bass fiddle." She stood up and smoothed her skirt, prim as a March lily in a patch o' thistles. Ozro whinnied like a horse, that's his common answer on the show. He unjointed himself, all six feet two of him, and doubled up in his chair.

But Rufus was not joking. Square in front of Cissie he was standing, straddle-legged and playing with his tie that has the turkey-gobbler hand-painted on it. Rufus and his tie looked mighty nigh ready to strut.

"I'm talkin' business," he was saying, "and talkin' business is talkin' sense. How about it, Cissie? Better change your mind and hang around with us folks that know you. Ozro and that bass fiddle ain't much for looks, and besides, he likes his banjo better. You do the bass fiddle of 'Ridin' on a Cottonbale,' and we'll make it a smash hit. Soon be on the Grand Ole Opry at Nashville for regular, not jest once in a while. It would set us up, and it would set you up."

Kelly had been tuning his fiddle, but now he stopped, and we all stopped whatever we were doing. Cissie stood looking at the floor, not even switching an eyelash, and we all looked at Cissie like she had the key to the gate of glory right there in her little blue purse.

"I been talkin' to their man," Rufus said. "No tellin', we might git us a spot on one of the big shows, any time."

Still she didn't answer. Rufus thought he had drove his nail and was all set to clinch it. He dropped into a wheedlin' whisper and said:

"Better listen to ol' Uncle Rufus, Sugar! Might be Carter's Champion Chicks! Might even be the Royal Crown Cola show!"

He might as well have tried driving nails. At "Carter's Champion Chicks" Cissie flinched three times, as if ever' word was a thorn-prick, and when he rolled out Royal Crown Cola, she took three steps back, and I wondered whether she mightn't haul off and slap him, right there. But she didn't. Unless a smile that's not meant is a slap, and a voice all sweet and creamy.

"You are mighty good to me, Rufus," she said, "and I'd sure like to keep you for an Uncle. But I've promised. I've done promised to take the scholarship." She took another step back and knocked over an empty Coca-Cola bottle. It kept rollin' and rollin' like it never would stop and Cissie watched it over her shoulder till it bumped a chair leg and quit. Then: "I thank you kindly. A woman better not try the bass part. I was just relaxin'."

Rufus grabbed his fiddle, for he knew when he was whipped. "Well, as the old Dominecker rooster said to the little Guinea hen, it was sure good scratchin' while it lasted. Scratch it out, boys!" He hit his fiddle a lick and struck out a piece of tune—

> If you don't—want me—a-followin' after,
> Why are—you always—smilin' back?

And as we begun to j'ine in and back him up he shouted over the music, still fiddlin', "But there ain't no law ag'inst my bringin' this up once more, is there? You might change your mind!"

And Cissie shouted back, all smiles, like talkin' on the show, "If there is a law, I know you won't rest till you break it."

We laughed, and bore down hard on the tune, and went on practicing. But, fool that I was, I couldn't get the bull fiddle out of my head. I couldn't truly see, any more than Rufus could, what Cissie was reachin' for.

Not that she hadn't explained it to me, several times. And after she started working with that man over at the College—that Dr. Hoodenpyl—it was her main subject for talk, and ever'thing from politics to kinfolks ended up in ballads, ballads, ballads. And ever' time Cissie cocked her head and asked me, "Danny, don't you think that's the best thing for me to do?", I would knuckle under and say, "If it's good enough for you, it's good enough for me."

But I didn't half-know what she meant. It was just words to me—all she told me about "model scales" and "gapped scales" and the two kinds of singing that she called Homy Phony and Polly Phony.

I made it a principle not to argue. If Cissie had asked me, "Don't you think the best thing is for me to run for President?", I would a-shouted "Yes, Lord!" and got ready to stuff the ballot box.

And so would any man—with Cissie Timberlake leaning up to him and batting her eyelashes. Any man would have thought, just like me, that it was all a gal-notion, and she would get over it and settle down, after a while.

So—when we were having late supper that night at the Dixie Grill, Cissie had a good time telling me, all over ag'in, about what she was going to study in New York. Should she study Elizabethan music, the lute and flute?

I hadn't give Cissie nary nay, all evening, nor Cissie said nay to me, until I made my big mistake, and 'twas Cissie that got me into it, when she said, "And the wonderful thing about the old tunes is, how they stand up even under mistreatment, like that tune Rufus is using for the cottonbale song."

That was about the time we had gotten to the apple pie and ice cream, and, without thinking much, I said:

"You call that mistreatment? I don't know what you mean."

"Oh, Danny darlin', you do know what I mean. I've told you before. Too noisy. Just whangin' and bangin'. You could sing it five times better'n Rufus, anyhow. You have a better voice and a better manner. Half the time, Rufus just screeches."

Then I made my mistake. I said: "Well, anyhow, I liked you and that bull fiddle mighty well. It was a sin the way you made the alligator roar."

Cissie gave me one quick look and kept on eating apple pie and ice cream, like she hadn't heard. It was the first time that evening that her hearing had failed, and I ought to have took warning. But I couldn't see the sinkhole for the bushes. I walked right into it.

"Rufus don't miss a thing. He's right about you and that bull fiddle. What he don't know is what you and me could do together—once we got started on our own."

Cissie put down her fork and h'isted her red flag.

"Danny," she said, "what are you lettin' out your tongue about?"

I saw the red flag and slowed up a little. Not enough, though.

"Well, I reckon you would look even prettier pickin' a guitar. Or just singin'. But you know how it is—a pretty Carolina girl playin' the bull fiddle. The crowds like it. I don't know why I forgot you could handle a bull fiddle."

Cissie put up the hurricane signals and got ready to turn on the siren. "If you are goin' to draw out that subject, you can just drive me home, right now."

She threw her napkin on the table and picked up her purse. That was as much as to say she'd scratch my eyes out. I caught on, but it was too late.

"I won't draw out no subject if it frets you. Go on and tell me some more about ballads."

But all I could get out of her was, "I'll wait till you finish your dessert." It looked like she was ready to cry and was only being polite about it because we were in the restaurant.

Sure enough, no sooner were we in the car than I could tell Cissie was crying, though she didn't make a sound.

How do you go about comforting your sweetheart on the main road at night, with the trailer-trucks snorting destruction in your face and the wild teenagers leap-frogging the trucks with their jalopies, just to prove the undertakers' ambulance signs belong right where they are?

I don't truly know. But I made my try.

"Honey, I didn't mean to make you mad. And I don't rightly know what you're mad about. But if it's the bull fiddle, I'll take it all back, and sorry I mentioned it."

There was not a sound but the blast of the diesels and the whoops of teenagers. I reached over, but Cissie moved away. It was nothing but her hand there, and it cold as a frog's back.

Finally some words came out in a sort of choked-up way: "Go on. Talk about the bull fiddle. It's just as well. Shows what you really think of me."

I tried to laugh, even if it was only put-on, and at the first good place I pulled off the road and stopped the car.

"Time's gittin' along," I said, "and why should we be bound to Rufus for what's left of it? Let's forget about bull fiddles, but let's look ahead. You can pick and sing, and I can pick and sing, and when you come back, a year from now or whenever it is, we ought to be ready to go on our own. With all you know about music, we will soon be out in front, and who will there be to ketch up with us? Trouble with the Turkey Hollow Boys and all sech bands, they don't know enough about music."

It wasn't quite true, the way I put it, but I was bound and determined to meet Cissie halfway.

But she was set to be contrary.

"They know more about music than some stuck-up people think. You don't mean a word of it. Drive on!"

"Forgive me, Cissie. Hit was a honest mistake."

"It was no mistake. It came from deep down. You don't care nothin' about music, really. All you want is to put on a show. And sing commercials. And make records. And rake in money. Like the other hillbilly howlers!"

"Now Cissie, hit jest ain't so."

"'Tis—and all too true! And why don't you stop sayin' *hit* when you mean *it*? Makes my flesh crawl to hear you."

That wasn't the first time Cissie had corrected me, and I had been trying to mind what she told me, and talk better, without getting mad. This time it stung me.

"And who are you, I'd like to know, to talk about sayin' *hit* for *it*?"

She didn't answer. I let her have it again.

"And why did you pick up that bull fiddle and play it, in the first place, if you don't like playin' the bull fiddle?"

Cissie straightened up, there in the dark of the car, and begun to talk in an entirely different voice. She talked like I might be some stranger.

"It was the tune I was checkin'. I wanted to see what Rufus had done to it. It's amazin' how he can take a perfectly good old tune and make it sound corny. But the bass part somehow brought out the antique original . . ."

"Hit's a fine tune—I mean *it's* a fine tune."

"Yes, but it's no tune Rufus could make up."

"He made up the song, didn't he? He said he did."

"I'll give Rufus credit for the words—but not the tune. He stole the tune. Borrowed it if you want to be polite. Of course even the greatest composers do that. Rufus would have remembered it if he ever once heard it, back in the mountains somewhere. Rufus has a good memory."

"Cissie, I don't know jest what you mean."

"I know you don't. And that's what hurts. Because I have been tryin' so hard to make myself believe you understand. Now I'm afraid you never will. You won't know what I mean—but Rufus' new tune is just an old, old Irish reel. You can get Petrie's *Irish Airs* out of the library and look it up for yourself."

"I don't see what difference all that makes."

"No difference to you, but a lot to me. It's no use to keep explainin'. I know what you really think of me."

"Cissie, I think the same as ever. I don't change."

"Yes, Danny, you don't change. You keep on thinkin' I'll give up everything I'm interested in just to get up before the mike with a gang of hillbilly singers, and call it 'country music.' If it brings in money, you'd be pleased to have me on the Grand Ole Opry stage in a short skirt and a fake country costume, straddling a bass fiddle and showin' my legs. That's what you keep thinkin'."

I tried to get in a word, but she wouldn't let me.

"I ought to have known it all the time. But because I thought so much of you, I wouldn't quite believe it till tonight. I saw the way you was lookin' at me—just like Rufus did—and the others. I never was so ashamed!"

She started to cry again.

"I didn't mean it that way, Cissie. I was just thinkin' about what we always planned—I thought you promised me . . ."

"I know, Danny. But you're like all the men though I dreamed up you was different. We'd sing around awhile, and then you'd have me out at the old MacGregor Place raisin' a passel of children. Raisin' your children and lookin' after your fat cattle. All them dumb old Hereford steers and them foolish old Hereford cows that ain't even got enough sense to lick their own calves. No thank you, Danny."

She had turned her back to me by this time and pulled out her little handkerchief. I could see it in the dark. I put my hand on her arm and she jerked away. "Just take me home," she said. "Please start the car."

"But Cissie, what are you goin' to do if not what we talked about? How will you make the money? There ain't no money in ballads."

She turned her face to me just as a car passed, and I could see the tears on her cheeks and her eyes swelled up.

"I'll study some more," she said, as if she had a hard time getting it out. "I'll study till I can make a good salary teaching. Dr. Hoodenpyl says I can get more scholarships—and some grants. Then I'll get a teaching job. It won't be big money, but it'll be enough to keep Ma and me. It's what

I told you before. And I never did promise you anything else for sure, did I?"

She had told me before. And it was true. She never did promise anything else for sure, though I thought it was as good as a promise. You might say we had been raised together, almost, and sweethearts all the time, one way or another.

But now the bull fiddle had done the damage. There was nothing more for me to say. Not right then. I started the car.

When we drove up to her house, I saw the porch light go on. That meant Mrs. Timberlake was waiting up for Cissie. Cissie was out of the car before I could open the door for her. I caught her at the front gate and held her one more time.

She fought me for a minute, pulled clear away, and shut the gate against me. Then all of a sudden she turned back and kissed me once, with the gate between us, leaning over the gate and holding me by the arms and crying.

"I don't want to be a sorrow to you, Danny," she said. "Don't let me be a sorrow to you."

She took a few quick steps away. The porch light, coming through the moon-vines, made shadows across the lawn, and her face was in the shadows. I couldn't tell now whether she was laughing or crying, but she was saying, "Go on and sing the hillbilly music, Danny. Sing it to 'em good." And for one blessed minute there was not another sound in the whole world but Cissie's voice.

Then she ran all the way to the front door and never once looked back. I was gripping the top of that gate like a man trying to stop a runaway horse, but it didn't do the least good. The door closed, and I flinched as if she had shut it in my face. That was the last I saw of Cissie for just about one eternal year.

Naturally, I didn't tell Ed Cooley that last part and only enough of the rest for him to get the general idea of what it was all about. At first he didn't say a word. We were coming into Carolina City, the west part, on the high ridge road, butting into heavier traffic every minute. Finally Ed busted out laughing.

"Danny," he said, "I always knowed you was a fool, but I never knowed how big a fool till now."

Ed Cooley laughed some more and slapped me on the leg.

"That's all right," he went on. "I always did enjoy helping a man make a fool of himself, 'specially if he's a good ol' friend o' mine."

"You git out o' this car before I kick you out. Here's your stop, Ed. Main Street and Rutherford."

Ed hopped out on the sidewalk with his fish and fishing tackle.

"You need a shave, Danny," he yelled over the traffic noises. "Shave and a haircut."

"Shut up. I'll shave myself." I slammed the door.

"Don't forgit to put on your cream-colored pants," Ed was shouting, as I shot back into the traffic. The drugstore clock said 5:40, and I had just time to make it if I cut through the back alleys and my luck held out.

3

I MEET CISSIE—AND EVERYBODY ELSE

When I steamed into the airport, I'd a-vowed luck had left me. Cars parked everywhere—even outside the entrance gate on both sides of the pavement. And inside—cars piled up, cars overflowing the white lines onto the circle drive. There was a state policeman at the gate. When I hesitated, he shook his head, waved me on, and yelled, "Keep movin'! Can't stop here!"

So I sashayed right on till I saw a line of about a half-a-dozen cars, all decorated with streamers and flags, parked in the reserved space right square in front of the main building. At the back end of that line there was a motorcycle policeman resting on his machine, but he had left just enough space ahead of him for one car. Big as Ike, I whipped into that space without asking; and as I wrestled the steering wheel I caught sight of the Carolina City High School Band just ahead, all in formation and ready to go, with the sun flashing on the shakoes and brass and on the silk shirts and bare legs of the little drum majorettes. The car in front of me, I noticed, was one of the Sheriff's cars, and when I slid out, one of the deputies stepped up to me—he was a fellow I knew—and asked: "Are you on the Reception Committee, Danny?" "Why, yes, I am, Will." I barefaced lied to him. "She sent me a telegram. Hope I'm not too late."

"Naw, you ain't. The Big Boy is jest now gittin' off the plane. I'll put a sticker on your windshield."

He pulled something out of his pocket, and I could see the print: FUTURE FARMERS OF AMERICA: KEEP GROWING. I started for the waiting room door. Will yelled, "Hey, don't you want a badge?"

I hesitated only a second. "I'm a Future Farmer, all right, if there ever was one. Do you think I need a badge, with these whiskers and these-here brogans?"

"The badge would look better," said Will, "if you had on your cream-colored pants. But you can stick it in your pocket."

I took the badge, and as soon as I ran through the waiting room and saw the crowd and the banners on the other side, I was glad I had it. I had plumb forgot it was an election year and time for the politicians to make hay. When I saw the banners reading BE READY WITH REDDY, I knew who was on that plane besides Cissie; and I knew who had turned out the crowd. It was Carlos B. Reddy on that plane, with his Hollywood coonskin cap and all. And it would be Sheriff Looney that had turned out the crowd of office-holders and ward-heelers and their folks. Sheriff Looney would be snuggling up to the big politicians, and most of all to Carlos B. Reddy, who, I finally remembered, was speaking on that same Future Farmers program that Rufus had us dated for. He was running for re-election to Congress, and would never miss a chance to be seen and heard at any big meeting. His motto was "Always Be Ready." He said it was because his Mamma had named him Carlos B. on purpose, and told him it meant "Carlos Be Reddy," but folks from his home town said no, that wasn't right; his Mamma's maiden name was *Bee* and she was kin to the man that first named Stonewall Jackson "Stonewall." Anyway, Carlos B. Reddy was always ready—especially when it came to getting elected, and he sure was good at that.

I bulled my way through the crowd and showed my badge to the airport attendant. He said, "Go right on, Danny. They are just starting." But I said, "No, I believe I'll wait right here a minute," stepped through the gate, and stood watching the show.

At first I couldn't get sight of Cissie. She was lost somewhere in the Reception Committee. A lot of Future Farmers were lined up, convenient to the steps of the airplane, and for every Future Farmer there must have been two or three politicians standing right behind him and playing Uncle to him. Carlos B. Reddy was coming down the line, shaking hands with every Future Farmer; and the political Uncles—some of them were Aunts— were reaching their hands over the shoulders of the Future Farmers. A newspaper photographer was running backwards in front of Carlos B. Reddy, crouching down like a Russian doing a Cossack dance, and trying to get angle shots. Flashbulbs were going off, and right in front of me at the gate, where a microphone and loudspeaker had been rigged up, a Station WCC radio reporter was droning away: "Mr. Reddy and party have just gotten off the plane . . . Now he is shaking hands with the Future Farmers Reception Committee . . . Just a minute and we will have Mr. Reddy at the microphone . . . Stay tuned to WCC . . . Mr. Reddy is looking very happy . . . There are two ladies with him . . . I'll find out in a minute who they are . . . He is smiling at the pretty blonde on his left. I wonder who she can be . . . We'll find out . . . Oh, now I recognize the other lady with

Mr. Reddy. She is Mrs. Eccles, whom I think you all know—Mrs. Jethro Z. Eccles, prominent clubwoman and civic leader . . . But I want to find out who that pretty girl is with the yellow hair. Congressman Reddy likes her and I don't blame him. He is smiling at her again and she is smiling back. Oh, boy . . . Now Mr. Reddy is coming to the microphone . . ."

Mr. Reddy was coming, all right, because the tall woman in black-rimmed spectacles, the one the announcer called Mrs. Eccles, had the honorable Congressman by the arm and was simply bringing him. But he was dragging his feet a good deal because the pretty girl on his left was Cissie and he just plain meant for her to come along too. I got a notion that he was looking for a chance to slip his arm around her in a fatherly way. But he was right in public view and had to make a speech. So he stepped up to the microphone like a good boy.

What Carlos B. Reddy said in the first part of his speech I don't know. I forgot about him, and I forgot about not being shaved and dressed up in all that fancy crowd. For Cissie was there before me in a neat gray-blue suit that sure was made for her lines, and just the littlest excuse of a straw bonnet on her yellow hair. I thought she was a little pale, but her chin was up and her eyes were sparkling as she looked over the crowd. No doubt she was searching for that hillbilly hat and shirt that I didn't have on to go with the cream-colored pants that I didn't have on either, for she didn't pick me out till I wigwagged our old salute. Then Cissie waved at me and began to shape words with her mouth behind the Congressman's back. I couldn't read her lips, but I nodded my head anyhow.

There was a kind of a break in Carlos B. Reddy's speech and a lot of clapping and yelling. Then he reached for Cissie and said, "Come here, young lady!"

The radio announcer started for the mike too.

"Stand back, young man," said Carlos B. Reddy. "I want to take your place for a minute and interview this beautiful young lady. You young fellows get plenty of chances to interview the pretty girls in private. Only chances I get are in public, but I'm not going to miss one, all the same. My motto is Always Be Ready. And I AM READY."

The crowd busted loose. The radio announcer scratched his ear.

"Ladies and gentlemen," said Carlos B. Reddy, "our grand old state is rich in everything that is good and fine and beautiful. She is rich in tobacco and corn, rich in textiles and manufactures, rich in her fair women and brave men, rich in scenery, rich in history and traditions. She's rich in everything that's any good to the human race. But until I got to the airport at Washington today and met this lovely young lady on the plane, I had forgotten how rich we are in ballads and folk songs. Coming down here on the plane I had the privilege of sitting by this lovely young lady. I had a talk with her. I found out about the great work she is doing. And she has convinced me, my friends—I'll say she convinced me in five minutes—that our ballads and folk songs are just about the richest crop we grow. You already know her. You have heard her on the radio, many times. But I'm proud to stand before you here today and start my visit to this noble city by introducing Miss Cissie Timberlake of your own Carolina City—and God bless your souls, she's a honey!"

The crowd whooped. Cissie made a pretty bow. So far it had been all speech and no interview. But Carlos B. Reddy was going to have his interview.

"Now I understand, Miss Timberlake," he said, "you are planning to collect a lot of our old ballads and put 'em in a book, so we can all learn what we don't already know. You are going to print the words and the music too? Is that right?"

"That's exactly right, Mr. Reddy," said Cissie, in her sweetest voice, leaning right up to the mike. It was her natural voice, not her stage voice, and it sounded good to me.

"Well, Miss Timberlake, I want you to know and I want all who are listening to know that your humble servant and the people of this great state are right behind you. We are right behind all this ballad collecting."

"Thank you, Mr. Reddy."

"And now, Miss Timberlake, I am going to ask you about a song. I am going to ask your opinion as an expert. I want you to tell us if this song is a ballad."

Bless my heart if Carlos B. Reddy didn't start singing into the mike, while the radio announcer, and the Future Farmers, and the politicians listened with their mouths open, and the tall woman in black-rimmed spectacles looked like sour persimmons. Carlos Reddy had a right good baritone. He put feeling into it, and the song he sang was—

> Some day in June, some Carolina day,
> I know you'll like me better
> Just because I went away.

I couldn't hardly believe my ears. But much more I couldn't hardly believe my eyes. Because Carlos B. Reddy was taking advantage of his position. He was taking advantage of me and every man there. He was drawing Cissie up to the mike to sing with him, and, just like I thought he would, he was putting his arm around her—in a fatherly way. But the crowd liked it.

They were egging him on, laughing, yelling, clapping, and singing. "Look at him," I heard a young feller say, right behind me. And another young voice, "I'd give a million dollars to be in his place." And then somebody growled, "Oh, why don't he quit clownin' and let us go home?" but he got shushed mighty quick. When the next round of applause was over, Carlos B. Reddy took off his coonskin cap, wiped his forehead with his handkerchief, and said:

"That's the kind of song I like. It's one of my favorites. And it fits the occasion because, Miss Timberlake"—he still was holding her hand—"we do like you even better because you went away. Now is that song a ballad?"

Cissie was on the spot, but she had her answer ready. "Not yet, Mr. Reddy. Up to now, it's been just a good old hillbilly song, and Rufus and the Turkey Hollow Boys got it started on the radio. But now you've got it started and I think it'll turn into a ballad in no time."

"Well, it's a fine song, and Rufus and the Turkey Hollow Boys are fine singers, and you have a lot of fine singers and fine folks here in Carolina City. We are right behind them all. And you are going to sing for us tonight, aren't you, at the Future Farmers celebration?"

Cissie put on her best hillbilly radio voice. "Yes, Mr. Reddy, if the creek don't rise and the stars don't fall, I'll be thar ridin' side-saddle on my one-eyed mule, with the little fiddle and the big guitar, a-bringin' you songs from near and far. But mostly up from Turkey Hollow way, where the folks all work on a six-hour day, 'cause the sun don't rise till ten o'clock, and it sets at four behind solid rock."

"That's fine! That's just fine! And I'll be there, and I'll be ready because Carlos B. Reddy is ALWAYS READY. And don't forget, friends, that I'm always ready to serve you up there in Washington. Yes, I'm there to shake up the bureaucrats and see that you get every bit of what's coming to you from FHA and all the other A's and B's and all the way through the alphabet to Z and Ampers And. Take it away, young man!"

He waved to the announcer. The tall woman in spectacles was on him in a flash, steering him right past me through the gate as he bowed right and left and waved his coonskin cap. The procession of Future Farmers and political Uncles marched right behind in close order like they had drilled. I dived for Cissie, and she was diving to meet me halfway. She gave me both hands and came up close. Maybe she only meant to whisper something private in my ear—but anyway she put me in a position to take advantage of my position. And I did. Then she wasn't whispering, she was leaning up to my ear and shouting, over the noise of the loudspeaker and the yelling, "For God's sake, get me out of this quick, Danny!"

"Cissie, I'm the very man to do it." I showed her my badge. "We are goin' to town right behind the sirens and State Police and Carlos B. Reddy."

I had her captivated with one arm and shoulder and shoved at the crowd with the other. "Good Lord," she said, as we battled ahead, "do we have to stay with that man? Danny, I'm fit to perish. I'm airsick, almost, and twice as sick from having to put up with Carlos B. Reddy all the way from Washington."

"Leave it to me. I'll fix it."

"And where is your nice suit, Danny? Where have you been? You're not on any Reception Committee. You're a fraud—the same old blessed fraud. And you smell like fish."

"I'll explain—you jest wait."

The band had picked up a cue. It was lighting into "Some Carolina Day," and doing it in march time, with lots of trombone. We got through the waiting room and out to the parking circle. On that side was another mike and another radio reporter with his mouth glued to the mike and his eyes rolling. The roar of the band music, caught and reflected under the overhang of the entrance, sounded like Niagara Falls with bass drums and cymbals added. The little half-naked drum majorettes were twirling their tasselled sticks and twisting their hips as they marked time. Carlos B. Reddy was still shaking hands. Sheriff Looney, tall and dignified, was walking the line with a deputy, trying to get the Future Farmers and the political Uncles into the cars, so the parade could start. It would be just like all the parades for the Big Boys. The band would lead us down to the entrance while the crowd stood bug-eyed, all wanting to rush for their own cars. Then the band would do column-right out of the way, and countermarch and play "The Stars and Stripes Forever" till we had passed by and they could pick up their own bus transportation and highball after us. Then the motorcycle police would throw their sirens wide open. Sheriff Looney would throw his siren wide open and start his red light winking. They like their sirens, the Big Boys and police do. If it wasn't for sirens, maybe you couldn't hire a policeman for love or money, or a politician either. And the sirens would scoot us right into town at not less than 60 M.P.H. That was a parade. I'd seen plenty of 'em.

"My baggage, Danny! Are you forgettin' my baggage?"

"Right here, Miss Cissie—ready to go."

It was Will, the deputy. He was rolling the baggage truck himself.

"Sheriff told me to hurry things up. Can't wait on the airport people."

"That's mine!" said Cissie. "And that! and that!"

She had one small regular overnight bag—and two other square chunky pieces. I lifted them into the car. They were heavy as a load of brickbats.

"Must have books in these, Cissie?"

"Oh no. The big one is a tape recorder, and the other is a special portable battery set. I looked all over New York for that combination. Isn't that wonderful? Aren't you glad for me?"

"I'm glad as a fox in a hen house. Bet they cost you some money."

There was a lot of noise. I thought she said, "Money, yes, and more besides." But a police whistle was blowing. Cissie slipped into the low front seat of the car while I held the door. And in my old sassy way, I reached down and tucked in her skirt for her, to keep the door from ketching it. And she laughed back at me, in her old sassy way. I felt gay as a cricket. I jumped in and started the motor. Cissie moved over close to me. She leaned against my shoulder and put her lips right to my ear. "I'm not tellin' what they cost me, not all of it. But I don't mind if you'll help me work it out. If you'll stand by me . . ."

The snare drums began to roll, louder and louder. I glanced ahead. Far down the line the baton of the leading drum majorette was pointing to the sky.

"I'm standing by you. Here I am. Satan himself couldn't break me loose."

Cissie's eyes were shining, and she was just about to say something more. But the whistle blew sharp again. The baton came down—*smack down*—and blasted all loving and kissing and everything else in creation right into the trombone-trumpet-tuba middle of the "The Stars and Stripes Forever," and I hated John Philip Sousa for all I was worth.

We began to roll. Cissie straightened up. She smoothed out her skirt and began to talk more in the way of conversation.

"I had to have the tape recorder, and I knew it would cost every bit of $400. And the special portable battery set would be a whole lot extra. But I was out of money. So I just telephoned Rufus, and he was very kind. We fixed it up at the bank, too. He is startin' me in with this engagement tonight, and there will be at least five or six more. Then I'll see what next. Meanwhile, I'm all set to start collectin' ballads and begin my thesis."

"Ta-de-ta, tum-te-ta, tum-te-ta, ta, ta-a-a!" said the Carolina City High School Band. The well-drilled cohorts of Sheriff Looney and Carlos B. Reddy were roaring and clapping as loud as the band. Cissie had to raise her voice considerable to make me understand.

"That'll be—for my M.A.—THESIS," she screamed. "But it MIGHT— LEAD to—a Ph.D., too!"

"M.A.?" I screamed back. "Ph.D?"

"DEGREES! Don't you understand? Just like a UNION CARD! Help me get a JOB! Don't I look like a SCHOLAR?"

"PRAISE HEAVEN, NO! How could a scholar have that figure?"

We were right at the entrance gate. The band was doing column-right and playing the trio, with the horns turned away from us.

"In fact, I may get a chance to teach this summer, right here at State College. Dr. Hoodenpyl has to go to Washington, part time."

The band was countermarching in the open space where their buses were parked. I felt like they were countermarching through my skull.

"Mrs. Eccles is very much interested too. She got still more interested when I talked to her at the Washington airport, and she found out I am from the mountains and can sing ballads myself. She is an enthusiastic booster of folklore."

"Mrs. Eccles?"

"Yes, Danny, you saw her right there with Carlos Reddy. That big woman. She is president of I-don't-know-what-all, and secretary of a lot more. She is strong for regional culture. Knows a little music, too."

We were passing the band. The drums and trumpets had just finished sounding ruffles for Carlos B. Reddy and the flag.

"Mrs. Eccles. Carlos B. Reddy." She was ticking them off on her fingers. "And I'll count Rufus and his whiny songs too—even though he is nice. That's part of what it's costin' me, Danny." Cissie shook her fist at the parade ahead. Then she laughed and eased back in her seat. "But it's worth it— every bit. To be back here. Just to be here. Not be pushed around and regimented. Clear away from the city mess and the noise."

The police sirens opened up and said it wasn't so. She shook her head and flapped one little hand helplessly. We zoomed right up to sixty before we hit Cherokee Boulevard, and held it there. It was all I could do to stay close up, watching the car ahead and keeping both hands on the steering. Cissie slipped across the wide seat, close to me and began to talk into my right ear, while the only answer I could give her was out of the side of my mouth.

"And you are goin' to play for me tonight, ain't you, Danny? I couldn't explain it all in a telegram. I haven't hardly touched a guitar in weeks."

"Um-m-m, yes."

"We can run over the songs at my house. I wish I could show you a smooth arpeggio accompaniment that I've worked out for 'White Roses.' But there won't be time, I reckon. So we'll just use the old chords. And let's do it in E-natural."

"Uh-m-m-huh! When do I eat? I'm a starvin' man."

"Ma will fix that. You got to get out of this parade somehow. We'll go home—and use my old guitar. We can practice while Ma is ironing my dress."

32

"When do I shave and fix up? I been in the woods all day."

"Well, I'll phone Rufus to pick me up, so you won't have to come back for me. There'll be time. We might even try the tape recorder. I want to explain about that. Of course I *could* notate the ballad tunes straight from the singer. I've learned how to do that, Danny, and you'd be surprised to see me work it. But the recorder is the new thing. I can record, then play back and notate at home till I get the tunes just right. But the field work—that's the big thing, and it's where you come in."

"'S that so? How I do come into it?"

"Like everything. There's only one Danny."

We hit the first traffic circle outside Carolina City and slowed down a little. I watched for my chance and eased to the right, out of line, then shot off on a side street. Carlos B. Reddy and the Future Farmers would never know the difference. I throttled down to an easy forty and began to ravel out the side streets to Cissie's house. I took one hand off the steering wheel and reached for Cissie.

"Now ain't you glad, Cissie, that I got on that Reception Committee?"

"You heard what I said. Why do you think I wired you?"

"Ain't it a shame we have to work tonight?"

"Hadn't you better watch that steerin'?" she said. But not very stern.

4

WE MAKE THE FUTURE FARMERS WEEP

A State policeman flagged me, soon as I hit the main gate of the high school campus. "Take the left-hand drive, Danny," he said, when he saw the gobbler on my car. "Bear around the tennis courts and park behind the gymnasium."

"And follow that noise?" I asked him.

He liked the idea. "Follow that noise and save the Future Farmers if you can. It's Carlos B. Reddy."

Cars were jammed everywhere. The gymnasium windows were open, and Carlos B. Reddy was coming through strong over the loudspeaker. The air was sticky and heavy, and there was a little smell of magnolia fighting a hopeless battle with asphalt, dust, and gasoline. It felt like a thunderstorm. I picked my wide-brim hat, my Turkey Hollow coat, and guitar off the rear seat and lit out. I had on my cream-colored pants and thanked the Lord that pants and coat were Palm Beach.

My crowd was in the basement—in the locker room where the sign said "Visiting Team." If I thought I'd get a private word with Cissie before the show, that was just another one of my big mistakes. She was over at the far end, where they had an electric fan in a window. Rufus was on one side of her and Uncle Dock, our announcer, on the other. To look at her, you'd never dream it was a hot June night with us waiting in the locker room where the fragrance of departed football players by no means bowed and stepped aside. The dress Cissie's mother had ironed was just a sweet old-fashioned white dress—I'd call it school-girly—with hardly any sleeves. And a ribbon around her neck and her hair tied up somehow in the back and partly hanging down. She looked about sixteen. Cool as the North Pole—and just about as far away. The boys were scattered all around on the locker benches, tuning their instruments or just smoking and talking. Kelly and Jake were standing up, their heads and their fiddles close together, practicing the opening bars of "Black Mountain Rag." Soon as I saw all the boys were in their shirt sleeves, I put my hat on the nearest locker and started to hang up my coat.

"Don't forget where you hung that coat," Rufus called to me across the room. "You may need it, quick."

Uncle Dock came to me, and Rufus and Cissie right behind him.

"This is the layout, Danny," said Uncle Dock. He had something that looked like a script in his hand. "Like Rufus says, you may need that coat any minute. You'll wear hats and coats for the entrance and for the first number, no matter if it is 100 degrees, because the full regalia is part of the show. Then take off hats and coats and be comfortable for the rest. They've got some fans rigged up on the temporary platform. I don't think it will be too bad."

The sweat was popping out on Uncle Dock's rolypoly face and dripping on the script while he talked.

"This ain't a script," he said. "You know we don't need that. It's just the evening's program for the whole thing, and I've jotted down a few things to help me. Lucky we are not on the air, and there's no commercials. Just the regular show—anything Rufus and you boys want to pull off." He glanced at Cissie. "Except for the special numbers—our lovely former member that's come home to us."

I nodded and tried my guitar.

"I've got an extra mike hooked up back of the platform," said Dock. "They can't see it from the floor. You start the fuss back there and come right on stage, the regular way. The stage steps are there by the mike. You know . . ."

I nodded again. My guitar was in tune all right. What Uncle Dock was telling me was an old story. We had played together so much that all we needed was for Rufus to give the sign. We never let the show get cut and dried. So the beauty of it was, we always seemed to be just picking and singing for fun. And so we were though we knew it all by heart. Any other way would kill it. And that was why the imitation hillbilly stuff was so dead—the stuff the Tin Pan Alley people did when they tried to horn in on the big money.

By this time Kelly and Jake were going right on through "Black Mountain Rag," and I couldn't help putting in with them on the guitar, and Ozro was coming with the bass—and so were the other boys. Cissie was patting her foot, with her arm over Rufus' shoulder, and smiling as she talked something very private into his ear. And he was nodding his head up and down and grinning. It was hot in that locker room, but what we were feeling was the music.

Our manager, Bob Greenhow, stuck his head around the door and yelled: "You better line up pretty soon. Carlos B. Reddy is through at last. And Mrs. Eccles is reading off the winners in the cooking and sewing contests." We stopped the music.

"Will we have time to try 'Barefooted Gal' just once?" Rufus called back.

Bob looked at a paper in his hand. "It's a fairly long list," he said. "And she sure is a talkin' woman. Go ahead but don't take too long. I'm givin' you first call." His head disappeared.

"I'm shore glad to have our sweetheart back with us ag'in," said Rufus, with his big hairy hand on Cissie's. "Makes me feel like a young bachelor startin' on his first courtin'. I've got Cissie dated up for six appearances and tryin' to get more. But lo and behold, she's up to somethin'. She's out to do some tradin'."

Rufus looked at me and scratched his head.

"Looks like she's tryin' to trade me out of a redheaded guitar-picker. And she's a hard trader."

Cissie was not looking at me. She was smiling at Rufus, like it was all a gag and she was waiting for her cue.

"Only she don't want him for a guitar. It's somethin' else, and she won't tell. What d'ye say boys? What do I make her pay for a rawboned, redheaded, wamperjawed guitar-picker like Danny MacGregor—and no extra charge for that cowlick?"

I strummed my guitar.

"Full time or part time?" asked Ozro.

"Can't use a sideman full time," said Cissie. "Part time only."

"In that case, Rufus," opined Ozro, "I think we could release Danny for the movie rights of what goes on when Cissie works him part time." He made a sound on his bass fiddle. "Um-m-m—yum! We'd all git rich!"

They all stood up and roared.

"Part time or overtime," I said, "it'll be time well spent."

"Hush, boys, you're talkin' foolish," said Rufus. "I got to trade close with this gal. I want to keep this gang together for the big chance." He pulled some letters out of his pocket. "Here's the letter from the WSM man, and we're bound to git that audition for the Grand Ole Opry before this summer is over."

Rufus waved the letters. "We'll work out somethin'," he said, and I thought he sounded a little anxious. "Now come on and let's take a few licks at 'Barefooted Gal.'"

He grabbed up his fiddle and tried the tuning. Cissie looked across at me behind Rufus' back, and I swear to God she winked at me. And the next minute she was standing up on a locker bench singing, and we were tearing into that song:

> Walking down the road with a barefooted gal,
> Sunday morning and summer weather;
> Get religion and love together
> Walking down the road with a barefooted gal.

We liked that song so much that we almost didn't notice Bob at the door. "Second call! Second and last call!" he was saying. "Get goin'. She's reached the end of the list."

We scrambled into line. My place was next to Cissie for the show and this time she couldn't get away from me. On the concrete steps, going up, it was hotter than in the locker room. The sweat was running down my chest inside my shirt and coat and piling up above my hatband. But back of the platform, in the shadow, where one low-watt bulb marked the extra mike, you could feel the electric fans, and it was better. I managed to get my hat off and mop the sweat away. A big woman's voice was putting a heavy load on the loudspeaker and giving the high steel beams of the gymnasium roof a real workout. "And now," the big voice was saying, "before we turn to the musical entertainment, let me once more remind you, the Future Farmers of America, that you, too, have a part in this great modern task of world leadership . . ."

Cissie leaned over and whispered, "That's Mrs. Eccles. She's right behind me, just like Carlos B. Reddy. And she's right behind you, too, only she don't know it yet. You'll have to meet her, some time."

"Will she make a world leader out of me?"

"If she does, just go along quietly. Never try to argue when you get arrested."

The big voice was racketing on, but I could hear chairs rattling and feet shuffling on the front side of the stage. " . . . And as our great President has so eloquently said, 'We cannot live alone in a world of fear and . . .' "

I leaned up to Cissie and slyly took her hand. "Tell me what it's all about," I whispered. "Are you buyin' me from Rufus? Or just rentin'?"

"Don't you understand, Danny?" she whispered back, and her cheek was almost against mine, and her heart beating against my arm. "It's the ballads. It's my thesis. You promised to stand by me."

"Cissie, what *are* you gittin' us into?"

"I didn't try to explain everything to Rufus, but he did agree to some things. He wants to keep me on a string; but I mean to keep him on a string. It'll be late August before he can get the audition at WSM, and we'll have that much time to try out ballads. You'll have some free time, and I'm countin' on you."

The applause was starting, and I could tell it was more relief than pleasure.

"When can I have a date?" I said right quick.

"S-h-h-h!" said Cissie. "Bob is turning on the extra mike." Then close to my ear. "Pretty soon."

"Cissie," I mumbled—as much to myself as to her, "this is *some* game of marbles. I'm goin' to have to risk my best taw."

In our radio shows we do all the starting noises right in the studio. But for these special shows, when we are not on the air, we handle it backstage, then make an entrance. So when some kind of chairman had made his little speech about the musical treat they had in store, wild cheers and clapping went up in waves and I began to realize what a big audience was out there, though I hadn't yet seen it. Uncle Dock took over the stage mike and made his regular spiel about Rufus and the Boys of Turkey Hollow—comin' down the road, home from the hunt, guitars behind, and fiddles in front, ready to fight or ready to love, pickin' and singin' like Heaven above.

We had done it hundreds of times, and you might think I'd be sick of it. But there was something about it that always made the hairs on the back of my neck stand up and thrill. As if, sure enough, we had just come down through the mountains and back to the settlements. So it did, once more. Maybe it was just partly the excitement of the crowd that I could hear rustling and stirring and even yelping a little on the other side of the stage.

There was one second of dead quiet. Then, to perfection, like always, Rufus broke out his wild turkey gobble.

"Putt-tt! Putt-tt! Putt-tt!" went Rufus. Then—"Gobble-gobble-gobble-gobble-gobble!" Magnified on the loudspeaker system, it seemed the whole air was full of turkeys gobbling. And we all, the way we knew, made answer with all the clucking and calling sounds that a flock of turkeys can make. Then Rufus broke in with his long, long woods holler; and we answered that. And Ozro fired two shots with his stage pistol. And we were off, mounting the stage, Rufus leading, fiddles in front, guitars behind, picking and singing "Turkey Hollow Strut," just like Uncle Dock had said it—

> Ready to fight
> Or ready to love,
> Pickin' and singin'
> Like Heaven above.

And there we were, all in line before the audience, with everything clicking perfect, and Cissie not forgetting to make her little separate entrance, almost a dance, in front of the line, and a sort of country curtsy. It makes a picture, if you see it from the audience side, with or without scenery.

And that audience, it must have been a thousand strong, mostly young fellows and teenagers with their folks, was standing up, on chairs, or on the tables where they had the banquet, giving us a big hand and not caring for the heat or future farming or anything but hillbilly music. Up front, near the stage, was a passel of boys, I don't know how many, that had brought guitars and were trying, some of them, to follow us. Carlos B. Reddy had a front seat too. He had on his political smile, but the boys with guitars were pretty near crowding him off his dignity. The Eccles woman was there. She seemed to be looking straight at Cissie and me, not pleasantly either.

"I don't like the way that woman looks at me," I said behind my hand to Cissie while Rufus was filling in at the mike and we were getting settled in our regular places back of him. I didn't see how Bob managed so smooth, but in spite of all the big goings-on, our chairs were where they belonged, also the table and speaker for the steel guitar, and everything else.

"It's a chance I had to take," whispered Cissie, eyes straight ahead and smiling at the audience. "To be seen here with you. She don't like hillbilly music."

"—and we air shore glad to be here," said Rufus, "and bring you some of the good old hillbilly music. Some calls it 'country music,' but that's like puttin' sugar in cornbread—"

"Maybe she won't hold it against me," Cissie went on, "but she thinks it represents a cultural regression."

I made out like I knew what Cissie meant. "Jest put plenty of expression in the regression," I said, "and we'll wipe that sour look off her face."

Rufus was working into his regular "Way Down South" talk. Only he made it "Way Up in Turkey Hollow." And we were all ready to come in with the sounds and the comedy.

"Way up in Turkey Hollow," he was saying, "we-uns likes to sleep late of a Sunday morning. Especially when we has been to a big barbecue and been swingin' the gals at a dance the Saturday night before.

"But me—I'm a real Future Farmer. And on this Sunday mornin' I riz up before sunrise to git my yardstick and measure how much my years of hybrid corn had growed endurin' the night. And I wanted to see whether my gover'ment potatoes was grumblin' about bein' too crowded in the hill—"

"Paint 'em blue!" yelled somebody far back in the crowd, and there was some laughing.

"Oh no," said Rufus. "That comes later. First I was goin' to explain to 'em about our new housin' projick—

"But as I was sayin', I riz up airly. And as I was tiptoein' down the stair-steps from the left, I could hear my dear old Pappy right below me, hard at work on his music."

Rufus gave a deep bass snore, and Ozro followed up with some noises on the bull fiddle.

"And right beside him my dear ol' Mammy was carryin' the treble—"

He gave a high snore with a squeak at the end. And Kelly and Jake carried it on out with the fiddles.

"And up above me in the loft, there on the corn-shuck mattresses, my six big brothers and my seven pretty sisters were all comin' in strong on the chorus."

We were ready with the jug band, and we gave them the chorus with about thirteen different roars and whistles and gurgles. Cissie had not forgot her part, and gave a real female whistle with her fingers in her mouth, but she said to me, while the audience was curling up with pleasure, "It's even cornier than I remembered," and I said back to her, "You hold on tight."

"But me—" Rufus went on with the build-up—"I am the seventh son of a seventh son. And I can hear the wool growin' on a sheep's back. I understand the language of the birds—all but the turkey buzzards and I don't want to l'arn that. I know jest what the ol' cow means when she says, 'Mo-o-o-o!' and what cusswords the ol' bull is usin' when he goes aroun' mumblin' 'Bo-o-o-o! Bull-loo-loo!'

"So I stepped around behind the house and hid in a clump of jimsonweeds to see if the birds could tell me anything about the United Nations on that fine Sunday mornin'.

"But all I could hear was the crows over in my hybrid cornfield!"

Kelly and Jake were right on the ball with their crow calls. Far off, you could hear the cawing, then nearer and louder.

"Up over my head, where the chickens was roostin' in the branches of my biggest peach tree, my ol' Dominecker rooster waked up. And he heard the crows too.

"First he stretched his neck to see whether anybody was awake and stirrin' in the big house. But all he could hear was what I heard. They was still busy at their music. Pappy was bass, Mammy was treble, and the boys and girls was weavin' out the chorus."

We followed the cues and put in the sounds.

"So the ol' rooster thought he'd better break the bad news and git 'em up.

"He flapped his wings, he did! He stretched his neck, he did! And he told 'em: 'The crows are EATIN' up ALL the CAWN-N!'"

"Nobody stirred. The crows heard him but they didn't care. They answered him back: 'CAWN! CAWN! CAWN!'

"The ol' rooster moved along the branch nearer to the house and made another try: 'The CROWS is E-EATIN' up ALL-L-the CA-A-AWN-N-N-N!' And the crows answered: 'CAWN! CAWN! CAWN!'

"Still nobody riz up. Nary door or winder cracked.

"But he was a good ol' rooster. He knowed his duty and he done it. He tried once more. He flapped his wings six times harder, he ruffed up his neck feathers, cleared his throat, got up on his tiptoes, and screeched: 'The CRO-O-O-OWS is eatin' UPPP ALLLL the *cawn!*' He almost broke down on the last *cawn* because his voice give out. Then he looked around to see what would happen.

"About that time my ol' turkey gobbler that had been peckin' aroun' the yard begun to notice. He swelled up his neck, he reddened up his wattles, he cracked his tailfeathers, spread out big as a balloon, smacked the ground with his wings and said: 'WHUT-T-T? WHUT-T-T? Whutt-the-heck-you-gona-do-about it? Whut-the-heck-you-gona-do-about-it?' "

The crowd boiled up with shouts. Rufus had 'em going, for sure. But he held them down with a wave of his fiddlebow. He pointed the fiddlebow right at Carlos B. Reddy and sounded off:

"All of us Future Farmers—we have a good friend right here in the front row that knows what to do about it. That's our friend at Washington, Mr. Carlos B. Reddy. If we git in trouble with the corn crop, he will shore fix us up on corn loans. Then we kin sleep late ever' mornin' in the week and let the gover'ment do the work."

That got another big round. And Rufus went right on, quick.

"But right now—right now—what we are a-gona do about it is to sing a song you all know, and it's Mr. Reddy's favorite song." He struck a lick on his fiddle. We all came in with the lead, and that was the way we sang "Some Carolina Day," with Rufus doing the chorus, then one verse; then he waved to the boys in the front seats, with their guitars, and they did it, singing sweet with their young voices, then everybody joined in till the windows rattled, and if the thunder was muttering I didn't hear it.

And so we came by the regular route, everything timed very pretty, closer to Cissie's numbers. Rufus was holding her back till near the last. It was an expert job, and some would call it almost too slick. But I don't know. If you feel the music all the time, and believe in it, I don't know how it hurts it any to do it right—to have that know-how and give it that extra touch that only the old hands can give the hillbilly music. Cissie might call it "corny" and some would even say "trashy," but when the fiddles are bowing fast and full, with the strong beat of the guitars and bass bearing them up, and the voices coming in, it goes right to the marrow of the bone, it just gathers you up, and I don't see how man or woman can stand out against it. No matter what Cissie might say, I could see out of the corner of my eye that she was patting her foot all the same, just like the rest of us. Maybe that straight-ahead smile she had on was only a stage smile. I didn't know how much she had changed. I couldn't quite figure out what she was up to, and Lord knowed when she would give me a chance to ask her. And I was beginning, at last, to feel tired. It had been a long day, and still not over. But the steady beat of the music was gathering me up. I hoped it was working on Cissie too. I figured it was on my side, no matter what she figured.

We don't give the audience a chance to ketch their breath, hardly, on a stage show like this one. Just hit 'em from all angles, changing from fast to slow, from slow to fast, and they can't get wearied. Everybody gets his turn, everybody pulling for the other fellow, live and let live, free and easy and have a big time out of it. Get stuck on yourself, they unstick you mighty quick—laugh you down, freeze you out, it must be turn and turnabout. And Lord, it helps not to do the commercials, not to be on the air. That meant, like on this evening, that Rufus or one of us was at the mike with comedy or what-have-you, and no announcer breaking in.

So when Ozro did his "Slewfoot Sal," his best banjo piece, picking and singing, and exploded at the end with his whinny, I picked up on the heels of the handclaps and took them off in another direction with "Tennessee Waltz," for we always do some of the new hits along with our own stuff, and before they could get through remembering the night and the Tennessee Waltz and how much they had lost, with as much redheaded tenor and good guitar as I could put into it, Rufus was edging up to the mike to begin his talk for "Ridin' on a Cottonbale," and we were getting ready and getting our breath too.

It was then Cissie pinched me and whispered, "Who is that man?"

It was a man with a polka dot tie. He looked more like an automobile salesman than a Future Farmer or a political Uncle—a middleaged man, he was, with no expression on his face, just a blank. What marked him was that good-sized bow-tie with good-sized polka dots on it. Where he came from, I don't know. He was just there, as if he dropped from the roof, and it must have been pre-arranged, for a boy on one of the front seats got right up and gave the stranger a place. Mr. Polka Dot Tie sat there and looked at us like we were horses for sale and he was tired of looking at horses but maybe he would buy if he could figure close.

"Must be a gypsy horse trader," I told Cissie. "Look at his tie." And that was all I could whisper before we were off into the big riot of "Ridin' on a Cottonbale," and coming to the top of the program fast.

When we ended there was thunder in the air, and it wasn't all hand-clapping. Maybe it was just dry thunder, maybe a storm coming. I wondered if the folks would begin to drift out and see if they left their car windows open, and some of the old folks did. But not a Future Farmer or Farmerette budged. We still had them sitting on the edges of their seats and calling for more.

The clock on the side wall of the gymnasium said 10:24. Rufus was at the mike again. Even with the fans going, the sweat was beginning to come through on the back of his shirt. He was telling what a pleasure it was to have Cissie back again on the home team. I touched my guitar lightly to check the tuning. Little "E" was a shade flat, and I put it up. It was feeling the weather, and so was I, but Cissie was leaning toward me and smiling. "You know the way, Danny," she whispered. "Take it easy and don't crowd me," and I nodded silently, wishing I could read her eyes along with her smile.

"She's been up thar in New York," Rufus was saying. "Up thar in New York for a whole year, a-studyin' music, all the kinds of music thar is in the world, especially the kind they have in books and operas, I reckon. I don't doubt it's fine music, and furthermore I don't doubt that if anybody could carry it all off in his head, that person is Cissie Timberlake. But the p'int is, don't you see, she knew that if she wanted to graduate in the music of the heart, she'd have to come back to us, and here she is, for our guest singer tonight, and I hope to keep her interested. And another fine thing is, it brings together ag'in one of the finest teams on the Turkey Hollow show, and one you'll all remember, for Danny MacGregor is going to play for her—by special request. And Cissie is going to do one of the old heart songs you all know, 'White Roses on My Mother's Grave.' It was one of our own boys that composed it, you remember. A boy we all loved, like we love the song."

The crowd was very quiet. Rufus dropped his voice and became solemn. "That was our own Tom Granberry. The late Tom Granberry. He was the Jimmie Rodgers of our part of the country. Lots of you must have knowed him. 'Wild Tom,' some folks called him. Because he was a roving boy from the time he was sixteen. And sorry for it, later. They telegraphed him his mother was dying. He didn't get home in time, but he remembered something she had said, and that's what the song is about. You can see the roses to this day in the old family cemetery. But Tom was killed on Normandy Beach. He left us this song, and hit's his best one, and I don't know anybody that can handle it better than our own CISSIE TIMBERLAKE—"

The crowd roared and many of them stood up as Cissie walked up to the mike.·

"And our own DANNY MACGREGOR—"

I got a hand, too, but I knew it was all part of Cissie's welcome. I rolled a chord, and they were all perfectly still. I floated the first few notes of the tune, with the spotlights on Cissie and me and the notes going sweet enough into the lights beyond and all the faces. I rolled another chord and came in light and easy as Cissie began—

> I never knew, dear Mother, when I left you,
> I'd drift too far away to say goodby;

"Goodby" comes on a long note that she holds while the guitar repeats. She was all of a sudden an old-fashioned little girl in a white dress—and her voice was a white rose growing right up out of the guitar music, climbing and blooming on the notes of the strings, the same voice I'd known, but somehow different.

> That your one parting kiss would be the last one
> Or that I'd plant white roses where you lie.

Another long note, and the key changed and went into a minor. She sang a little faster, and bolder too:

> The great world won me far too early, Mother.
> It taught me to forget the love you gave.
> But one thing that you wanted I've remembered,
> And now white roses bloom above your grave.

The tune slows on that last line. And Cissie's white rose voice brought every word to bloom while I pushed music up against them, a chord for every word, and rolled the last chord, then caught her voice on the uptake for the chorus and followed with steady beat:

> White roses on my Mother's grave,
> White roses slipped from buds her own hands grew.
> Now you sleep forever on the hillside,
> White roses bring me back at last to you.

The tune goes up, slowly, on "Now you sleep forever," and when the voice climbs to "hillside" you are right at the little cemetery; but the voice takes you up further to a high note, the highest, on "roses," and then lonesome

44

chords and voice move down till you are there with the lonesome boy bending over his mother's grave. Almost like the chariot swinging low.

I could not see the faces anymore, and hardly knew where we were. I seemed to be alone with Cissie, walking up the hillside in the second verse of that song, along an old mossy stone path, down by a spring house with a tree shading it, and out along a grassy path to a broke-down wall with a gate in it. She was leading and I was walking on guitar notes right straight into the white roses, not looking at my guitar at all, just watching her lips and throat till we came to the highest place and voice and strings and white roses brought me back at last to the ending chord. I touched it softly, just once, and stood there in the complete silence of the family cemetery.

Then I woke up, and it turned out to be the complete silence of the Carolina City High School gymnasium, me with a guitar slung in front of me and Cissie beside me and both of us about a mile from our chairs. I couldn't hear a sound, and I thought, "Could we have missed entirely?" Cissie took me by the hand to lead me back to the chairs, and as we turned, the applause broke at last. I don't think I had ever heard anything like it, but I was too dazed to care. They had almost paid us the compliment of not applauding. We had made the Future Farmers weep, like Rufus asked us to. We took some bows, because we had to, and I did notice a few things. Mr. Polka Dot Tie was beating his notebook with his hand, and he was standing up. Carlos B. Reddy was waving his hat. Mrs. Eccles had taken off her glasses and was wiping them carefully. The Turkey Hollow Boys were looking solemn and glad at the same time, and Rufus was blowing his nose with a red bandanna. I thought he looked a little scared. But no matter—he was on his feet in another second, in control again, and I was up there with Cissie once more, leading the whole gang in "Barefooted Gal," which goes fast and lively, and answering her singing questions in the verse as if I had never been mixed up with white roses. But I don't really remember much of that. The next minute we ended the program on "Black Mountain Rag," and the thunderstorm broke right in the middle of it. Then there was the usual scramble. The Future Farmers were mobbing the stage.

Cissie had me by the arm and was pulling. "Come on, Danny, I can't stand any more. Get me out of this."

I put my arm around her and pushed at the crowd. It seemed to me they were all yelling and patting us on the back. Rufus came in between and stopped us. "Hold on," he said. "There's somebody I want you to meet." Cissie pulled my arm. "I've got to get Danny home," she shouted back at Rufus. "He's tired out." And to me she said, "I think that man is a WSM talent scout—that man in the polka dot tie. I don't want to meet him, do you?" I said, "Well, why not?" but I followed Cissie. All the same Rufus caught us at the steps. "Here they are," he said and grabbed me. "I want you to meet Mr.—(he named the name, but I lost it)—Mr.—. He's down here from WSM." "I'm glad to meet you, Mr.—," I said, and was so confused I almost said "Mr. Tie," but the Lord was with me. The man had put his horse-trading face back on. "It was good," he said. "It was damned good. It was too damned good for a hillbilly show." "She can break the sobs into it if you want it that way," said Rufus. Cissie was smiling and pulling my arm. "I'll see you later," she said. "Got to get this hillbilly singer home. He's had a hard day."

Thunder, lightning, and rain were coming strong. I cased my guitar and Cissie found her coat. I had no raincoat. We dashed for my car. It was only a few steps but I was drenched. The rain was solid on the windshield but I started anyhow and bulled past the timid drivers and ahead of the crowd.

"You really are tired, aren't you, Danny?" she said. "I ought not to have made you do it."

I slowed at the entrance gate. She was patting my cheek. "You were good, Cissie," I told her. "Like the man said you were too damned good. You nearly had me down."

"It is almost a folk song, isn't it? Right now I don't really know why it isn't."

"What is almost a folk song?"

"It's something I'll have to take up with you." Her voice was very soft. I liked the sound of it, that way. "What about startin' tomorrow? Ma could put up a lunch, and you could pick up me and the lunch and the tape recorder and—"

"And drive out to the MacGregor Place?"

"I wondered if you would ask me."

I shot ahead of a line of cars. The lightning flashed bright as day. It seemed like I could look clear over the city to the mountains. I put on speed.

"It suits me," I told that girl. "It suits me fine."

5

CISSIE'S POINT FOUR

"You know I could never trade Rufus out of anything. It's Rufus tryin' to trade me."

I was starting my new life, but it was at a mighty steep angle. We had spread our picnic dinner at the spring below Beech Hollow, then walked back to the house. I heaved the recording machine and the battery set out of the car, lugged them up to the front porch, and got a table out of the house to put them on. We were sitting on the porch steps smoking and enjoying the breeze and the shade. What I was really thinking was how Grandpa had figured it just right to have that porch catch the western breeze and the shade of that big oak to fall at this particular moment out of all time on my pretty sweetheart and me and how tickled the old man would be if he could know how it worked out. I could see him rubbing his knotty hands together and saying, "Wa-al, I declar', it's Danny and Cissie." That was what I was thinking, but what I said was just something ornery and plain about how if she was going to trade with Rufus for me, I wished she had done bought me long before now and not throwed away a whole year. That was the wrong way to put it.

"What have I got to trade with? I'm seven hundred dollars in debt, right now," she said. "Not counting what Ma let me have out of savings. And you ought to be ashamed to talk about me throwing away a whole year."

I thought she was really mad. She flung her hair back, turned her head away, and looked off towards the mountains.

"I didn't mean it that way. I just meant this is the first time in a whole year that you and me have been together away from the crowd and outside an automobile."

It was a good speech, for a fellow like me. But I might as well have been talking to the breeze. She wasn't taking notice of my speech, or me. I don't think she even heard me. She was looking at a paper that she took out of her purse.

"Now, let me see," Cissie said, wrinkling her forehead, "there's old Mrs. Rountree—she's too far off. And the Kennedy place—I don't think so, today. And Aunt Lou Watkins—maybe we could see her if we start in time. And who did you say you've got livin' in the cabin here?"

"The Parsons couple. You remember Old Man Parsons."

She threw away her cigarette, grabbed for a pencil, and wrote something.

"We could start with them, maybe. They're sure to have something if I can just get it out of 'em."

"Aunt Lou Watkins lives five hundred yards straight up a steep mountain," I reminded her. "You'll have to climb. You can't get there in an automobile. Not in my automobile!"

"Oh, yes," she said, and kept studying her paper. Then she stuffed it in her purse and laughed out loud. Before I could defend myself she was up on her feet and gave me two hard punches, one on the chest, and the other on my leg muscle.

"Gittin' soft, are you, Danny? Can't do nothin' but drive automobiles!"

I was right after her as she ran to put the table between us. Her yellow hair was flying. She laughed in my face and said, "Can't do nothing but drive automobiles and stand up to the mike."

"All right," I said, as I caught her. "I'll climb, I'll fetch and carry. But what do I get out of it?"

"That's for you to figure." She was impudent as a hornet and knew where to pop that stinger. But I was stronger. She couldn't get away. I held her tight, with her back to me and her arms pinned. She was warm and trembling like a young rabbit caught in the fence corner.

She looked back at me over her shoulder. "Calm down, Danny. We are in plain public view."

"I reckon it's my house." I let her go. "Yours, too, if you like it."

"You've got to learn to act like a ballad collector. Not like the foreigners that teach music up in New York." She was fixing her hair. It was a very fine western breeze that knew so well how to play with her hair and her blue skirt and mould the thin yellow blouse close.

"Stop makin' passes," she said. "Learn to be academic. Haven't you got any chairs?"

I gave up and brought the chairs. "Is this academic?" I said, and held the chair for her, very proper.

"Yes, if you'll take your seat and pay attention. Plug in the battery." She was opening the tape recorder. It was a very fine tape recorder, I could see right away, and it took a seven-inch reel. She had the reels already set and was beginning to warm up the machine.

"Machines," I said. "That's somethin' I can handle. But what you want with a portable battery set? These days, ever'body has electricity."

"Not everybody. Not even in this house of yours. And I'll start with you. I want you to sing into my machine." She handed me the little microphone.

"I didn't bring my guitar, Cissie."

"Please forget about guitars. I just want the pure ballad. Now let me see—" Cissie wrinkled up her forehead and studied a little.

"Let me see—I believe I'd like to get your version of 'Little Musgrave and Lord Barnard.' "

"Don't know any such song, Cissie."

"Yes, you do. But I forgot—you would call it something else. 'Little Matty Grew,' maybe. I know it, but I think you know more of it than I do."

"That song, Cissie? You shorely don't mean it?" I won't deny I was surprised. Here she was, looking me right square in the face, and I couldn't so much as touch her, yet she was begging me straight out to sing that song.

"Yes, I do mean it. What's the matter? Pitch in. Go right on."

"Good Lord, Cissie. Of course I know it, but how can I sing it—with you settin' right there before me—and—and—" I was plumb embarrassed. I didn't know what excuse to make. "And the Parsons might hear, if they are listenin'." I dropped my voice to a whisper.

"Why, Danny, I do believe you are blushin'. But that's the ballad I want. I was thinkin' about it, comin' down on the plane."

"Cissie, I hate to think what you've been studyin'. They'd cut me off the air right now if I sung sech a song as that on the radio."

"This is not for radio, Danny, just for me. Don't be so modest. Go ahead."

I hadn't thought of that wicked old song in a long time, and I don't reckon I had sung it since they brought the whiskey out at the lumberman's barbecue, some years back, and called for something spicy. True enough, Cissie and me used to sing it together, in times past, before we growed up and went to school and learned better. But it ain't by no means the kind of song you would sing for your own sweetheart, when she's just come home after a year and you are trying to gain back some lost ground. But there I was. She wanted the song, and there was nothing for me to do but to light in and sing it. So I started, kind of slow and careful, and ashamed to look Cissie in the face while I was singing:

> It was on one day, it was on one day,
> The very first day of the year,

> Little Matty Grew rode into church
> Some holy words to hear.

Right there she cut the switch and stopped me. "Hold on, Danny. That's not quite right. That's not what I remember."

"Whut's wrong?"

"Didn't you always sing, '*Hit* was on one day'?"

"Name of Heaven, Cissie! Ain't you told me a thousand times never to say *hit* when I mean *it*?"

Maybe you'd think Cissie would be flustered, getting caught like that. But you don't know Cissie. She just smiled and corrected me like I was some little pupil stuck at the foot of the class.

"Polite conversation is one thing. Ballads are another. This is a ballad, and it is literature. Besides, if Queen Elizabeth could write *hit* for *it*, and maybe say *hit*, for all I know, who am I to deny you the right? You must sing the ballad exactly, word for word, the way you remember it."

I was getting mighty confused, but I had decided to go her pace, whatever it might be.

"All right, then. You want me to sing every bit of it—the way I know it? It's mighty rough in places."

"I want you to sing it through—every bit." She didn't blush or even smile. She just looked like plain business.

So I set in and sung it. Every bit. All that wicked old story about how Little Matty went to church, but Lord Dan'l's wife put her eye on him and asked him to go home and stay the night with her while Lord Dan'l was away. And how a little footpage was a-standin' by and run through the creeks and freshets to bring Lord Dan'l the bad news and he started gallopin' back home with all his men. Then how they was lyin' in bed and Little Matty thought he heard a horn blow but no, the lady said, "It's only the shepherd boy a-blowin' the sheep from the fold," and he had better turn over and "hug my back from the cold." Then Lord Dan'l rushes upstairs with his sword, throws back the covers, and catches 'em, right there. And Lord Dan'l says—

> How do you like my blankets,
> How do you like my sheets,
> How do you like my pretty lady
> That lies in your arms and sleeps?

Lord Dan'l lends Little Matty one of his swords because he don't want it said in old England that he slew a naked man, and they fight. It's a terrible battle. Little Matty wounds Lord Dan'l, first lick, but Lord Dan'l cuts him down, and he dies right there on the floor of the bedroom with the lady vowin', all the same, she loves him better than her own husband. So Lord Dan'l makes one more swipe with his sword and splits the lady's head clean to the neckbone. No sooner has he done that than he's sorry of it. The old fellow admits Little Matty was pretty much of a man, after all, and he tells his bunch of men to take the lovers out and bury them decent.

I remembered it all pretty well and didn't make but one or two little slips. And Cissie—she didn't move a hair. She just patted her foot and looked over a book she had with her, and seemed right pleased. When I got through, she cut off the machine and stood up.

"It's a terrible off-color thing, Cissie—and bloody too. I don't see what you want with it. Of course it's sort of pitiful in a way. But it never could happen these days. The whole thing would be settled in a court at Reno or somewhere, and the lady would find some way to nick Lord Dan'l for alimony on the grounds of mental torture."

She was still looking at her book.

I kept talking just to be talking and get it out of my mind. "Split her head right down to the neckbone," I said. "What a way to treat a woman! Do you think he really did that?"

"It's a fine old ballad. You sing it well." Then she hesitated a minute. "In this seventeenth century version the injured Lord treats the Lady even worse."

"My God, Cissie, what could be worse than splitting her head?" I was all on fire to know.

Save grace, she was blushing a little. "I could tell you but it might embarrass you. You can read it for yourself."

She put her finger on the verse, and I read it. Near as I could make out, it said that this Lord cut off the woman's breasts and her heart's blood ran trickling down her knees.

"God-a-mighty, Cissie, what kind of a book is this? Why they could hardly print this stuff in the tabloids, much less sing it on the radio."

"I've tried to explain to you before, but you never would really pay attention. Now you just look over that ballad and see if it isn't the same one you were singing. It was first printed in 1658, but the ballad is older than that. I think the version you and I know is older."

It took a minute to look over that thing. Sure enough it was pretty much what I had been singing, except that whoever printed it was even a worse speller than I am. All the way through he had *lye* for *lie* and *tinny* for *tiny*. And I knew better than that.

It was a hard jolt for me to take. But I tried to take it quiet. I sat in the split-hickory chair, holding the book in my lap, and Cissie bending close, looking over my shoulder.

She was being very patient and sweet, like I was her slow pupil in the First Grade.

"This book has 305 ballads in it, all of them handed down from long ago, maybe centuries ago: *English and Scottish Popular Ballads*. It's part of what Francis J. Child spent most of his life collectin'. Kittredge brought out this short edition after Child died. The big edition is bigger than that tape recorder."

Cissie yanked up another chair and sat beside me. She leafed over pages of that book with one hand, and the other was on my shoulder, pulling me to her, and pulling me deep into that book. She put her finger on page after page and showed me. I stared at the book where her finger pointed, and every time she was right: it was an old song I knew or had heard some time, maybe not quite the same words, but it amounted to the same story. And I felt like Cissie was running far ahead of me, with her hair streaming and her feet flying. I would never ketch up unless I could make her slow down and look back.

"Three hundred and five ballads! You've got to learn 305 ballads—less what you already know?"

"Oh, no—not learn them to sing, not all of them. That's not the idea. The idea is to study 'em and know about 'em so that I'll recognize the ballads when I hear them, even if it's only a couple of lines. This is the book the professors use for a guide; and so will we when we go collectin' ballads—old ones or new ones, but mostly the old ones like Child collected. They are the best. Maybe we can find some versions that have never been printed. They are always changing."

"Well, Cissie, if this feller went out and got 305, and they are the best—what is left for you? He's done got ahead of you."

Cissie began to squirm in her chair. "Mercy sakes, I don't know where to begin with you. You'd have to study the whole thing. But anyhow, nobody much has collected ballads around here."

"You'll git folks to sing into this machine? Then you'll write down the words and tunes and print 'em in a book—even if they are the same ballads Child has already put in his book?"

She laughed in a bothered way.

"It does sound a little crazy. But that'll be my thesis. That'll be research—in the field. Child worked mostly in the library, and didn't collect tunes. See, the book don't have music."

It didn't have music. Just words. A lot of words I didn't know. Even some letters not in my alphabet.

"Now the big thing in these times, Danny, is to get tunes *and* words both. Get 'em fresh—right from the singers—folks that never learned ballads from books and maybe can't even read. That's the real thing—the pure ballad. Somethin' you can't learn from books. That's what the professors rave about."

"You mean these college professors rave about 'Little Matty Grew' like I sing it—the way I never learned it out of a book?"

She nodded, and smiled till her dimple showed.

"Great Jehovah! You ought to make something out of that, sure enough. But why are you goin' to put 'em in your book if the finest thing of all is *not* to have 'em in a book?"

She zipped out the dimples. She put both hands to her forehead, leaned back in her chair and kicked her heels on the floor. Then she rested her chin in her hand and moped.

I saw it was time to break out a pack of cigarettes.

"It's all right," I said. I laid the book on the table. "Whatever you and Child say is all right with me. A good rooster can crow in any henhouse."

Cissie giggled and looked relieved. "Hard head, soft mind," she answered back. "If I can only knock it into your head, I reckon it'll stick. Now listen. First—"

She balanced her cigarette on the edge of the table. She held up one hand and counted off fingers with the other hand.

"First, Danny MacGregor, I'm a-goin' out through Beaver Valley and all around and gather in these ballads. Because I want to do it. That's a good reason.

"Second, I'm a-goin' to print 'em in a book, if I can, because that's what the college professors want, and that's how I get a degree and a job. That, Danny darlin', is what is called 'the scholarly attitude toward the material.' It ain't a scholarly attitude and it ain't scholarship, no matter how much you know, unless you put it in a book. They've been collectin' ballads and puttin' 'em in books for two hundred years, and still—"

"Two hundred years!" I broke in. "Cissie, you are teetotal ruined. That must make a million ballad books already. Who would want—"

"Don't interrupt!" She shook her head mournfully. "That just shows how ignorant you are. The more books there are, the more scholarly that makes me—and my book. If I was the *first* one to try to print a ballad book, they'd laugh in my face—they'd kick me right off the campus. But if I add *one more* book to all the rest, that'll make a respectable woman out of me, after bein' nothin' but a tired-out, lowdown, hillbilly radio singer. Don't you see, they like to keep startin' all over again. And then the American material hasn't been fully explored yet."

The cigarette had burned nearly to the table edge. She picked it up, took one draw, and tossed it into the bushes.

"You mean these perfessors have been puttin' our old songs into books and studyin' 'em all this time—and we never knowed a danged thing about it?"

"That's right, Danny. Our own schoolteachers didn't tell us. And don't you remember the new teacher that came into the eighth grade and tried to start us on Russian folk songs? 'Pull, brothers, pull,' and all that? She said we ought to be a-learnin' folk songs. She didn't ask us if we knew any already. But I want to go on to Number Three—"

She held a finger up to my face and turned it down slowly.

"Three is art. Little as you think it, Danny, ballads are art, too. Art music! The art singers are singin' ballads at concerts and on the radio. They are makin' records and record albums—"

"Now you are talkin' sense. Do their records sell?"

"Oh, yes. Certainly. There's Richard Dyer-Bennett and John J. Niles and Susan Reed. You might not know about them. But there's Burl Ives . . ."

"Burl Ives can't hold a candle to Hank Williams—"

"Don't be low-minded. I'm talkin' about art, Danny."

"Or to any of the top hillbilly singers. They can outsing Burl Ives any time. They can make up their own song hits, too, and their record sales run into the millions. Are you a-goin' to make records and sell 'em?"

"Well, if you want to talk *money*. I do have some ideas along that line. But I won't go into it now. I want to make my fourth point."

"Go on."

She wiggled a finger right under my nose.

"Point Four. My Point Four is Danny MacGregor. The famous hillbilly radio singer. And the best sideman in the business. He is a key figure. He is a point all by himself. I didn't exactly *trade* with Rufus. I just sort o' let him figure out that I couldn't take on any engagements beyond six or seven, maybe, unless I got some help on my own project and got through with it—some new musical stuff I was workin' out. Rufus got the idea without any trouble. What he said was, 'Want me to loan you my best man, do you?' And I said, 'Would you call it a loan?' And he asked, 'What about rentin' him—for a consideration?' and I said, 'Hadn't I better try him out first? Then we can talk.' Rufus laughed, and 'Don't you forget the consideration,' he says, and that's the way it stands. Didn't he mention it to you?"

"Only what you heard—that night. What ever'body heard."

"It's his jokin' way, don't you think?"

"Yes, and jest as good as a contract."

Cissie turned a switch on the tape recorder and began rewinding the tape that I had sung onto. I remembered Ed Cooley's big round face, that day when we were coming through the bushes, and what he said about Cissie. And he was right, I told myself. I think I see what she's up to, and I better humor her.

Cissie's slim hand was on the switch, and her eyes were watching the tape. She stopped the reel with a bang and a flutter and looked up at me with a smile that an angel would swear was honest.

"It don't matter about Rufus and me," I said. "But if you're a-goin' to roam the country and ask folks to sing songs like 'Little Matty,' you'll need me. Point Four is ready to go."

She turned the honest smile into something sweeter.

"A good sideman can do almost anything, can't he, Danny?"

"Yes, he can make a jaky singer sound like Caruso if he puts in the right background."

"That's it, I want that right background."

"And a good stout back, too, for this stuff?" I tapped the machine.

"Yes, and always a scholarly attitude toward the material." She was laughing, very sassy. "And an academic manner."

"Well—"

"I'll play back your ballad in a minute, Danny. But I want to tell you more about Point Four. The real point of Point Four is that maybe it's a way to get our feet back on the right path. You and me both. There's somethin' partly phony about the hillbilly radio stuff, you can't deny there is. You make money, and you have fun, but where does it take you in the end? Just to the same hullabolloo, with more singin' commercials and salesmanship comin' in all the time, and the songs gettin' more and more corny because there just can't be enough good ones for the demand. I think it's got too much phony in it, and it's the wrong path. And I was thinkin' how it would be if we could go back to the songs we used to know—and the folks we used to be. Find the place where we got off the right path, and start over. I was thinkin' you might like to try that."

"Go on, Cissie. I might."

"I found out, it seemed to me, that that old path was the only really new path left to take. And I'll tell you when I found out. It came to me all of a sudden, last spring, before Rufus thought up the cottonbale song, and we were sort of goin' round in circles. Remember?"

"Yes."

"Up till then, I just thought ballads were somethin' to study, and hadn't caught on. But one day, in Dr. Hoodenpyl's class, he brought in a little old brown-eyed woman to sing ballads for us. A little old wrinkled woman, and she didn't have a good voice any more. He got her out of a mill town, maybe, a broken-down old woman. But she had a dulcimer with her, and sang to it, and the thing was, she meant what she was singin'. It carried me back."

Cissie began to sing:

> Last night I dreamed a weary dream,
> It filled my heart with sorrow.
> I dreamed we pulled the leaves so green,
> Up on the banks of Yarrow.
>
> Oh, true love mine, stay here and dine
> As you have done before, O,
> And we will pull the leaves so green
> Up on the banks of Yarrow.

She sang it slow and sweet, in a minor key it was, her breast and white throat hardly moving as she breathed, her forehead lifted to the floating summer clouds as the song come up from the red lips and carried us both out along the green stretches of pastureland where the road led through the trees to the cool, high valleys.

She sang that much, and said: "It was somethin' the Doctor couldn't ever understand, for he's not our folks. But while the little old woman was singin', and the dulcimer twangin', I could remember your grandma walkin' between us, you on one side, me on the other, when we went to gather laurel that was bloomin' on the banks, where the path went steep along the rocky stream. Your grandma was singin' that song. And we were singin' with her."

I was choked up and couldn't speak. I nodded that I remembered.

"And then"—Cissie said—"somehow I knew my feet were on the wrong path, and I wanted to take that other one. That's the only way I can explain it. Do you understand?"

I cleared my throat, and nodded again. "You don't need to say a word more."

Then, just as I feared she would bust out cryin', Cissie began to chatter, very bright and peart, about her work, and the work at teachers college, that summer. It was all planned. She would help Dr. Hoodenpyl in his ballads course, maybe even teach it some, if he was called away, and wouldn't it be splendid to get that experience? But the main thing was to drive out along the highways and byways, and chase ballads. And me drive the car and tote the machine, I mighty quick realized, but we didn't talk about that. Cissie suddenly turned on the playback of my ballad.

So there was the machine singing me myself back to myself while I sat on my own front porch with my sweetheart.

"Wouldn't it be better with a guitar?"

She shook her head and cut the switch.

"No, it's right as it is, and you sing it well—except that your manner is too polished. Too much radio singin'." She closed the machine and snapped the fasteners. "Let's go and see Mr. and Mrs. Parsons. Lucky I brought my ballad checklist."

My car was a strange thing to see, parked near the old iron hitching post and block. But the stones between the front steps and the gate were not strange—gray and cool as ever, with green moss in the cracks. The overgrown boxwood gave out a faint smell. Cissie stepped light ahead, heels clicking on the stone, and I came behind, toting my load.

Cissie turned through the boxwood to the old calacanthus bush and came back with a late bud crushed against her nose. She stood with her eyes closed, breathing the spicy smell.

"Like home," she said, blue eyes looking at me above the almost black-red flower. "It's what I remember."

She walked on slowly, rolling the flower in her fingers. "We better take the car down to the cabin," she said, over her shoulder. "You have a load."

6

YOU CAN'T TALK BACK TO MOSES

Two or three mornings later I was in Ed Cooley's barber chair, having the works. "Ever'thing you got, Ed—haircut, shampoo, shave, massage, tonic, and especially the tonic. Turkish bath would be good if you had it. Rub the back of my neck, too. Got a crick in it. Been walkin' the tightrope with a pretty girl hangin' on one shoulder and a recordin' machine on the other. I'm foundered like a horse that witches been ridin'."

"Jest ree-lax, Danny. I'll be the doctor."

It was relaxing and cool just to be in Ed's barbershop. On the street outside, it was already moving up to ninety in the shade. The barbershop was a cave away from the blare and the glare—a place for men to hide out from the women for a change. Ed wouldn't run a beauty shop on the side, like a lot of barbers. He had some modern improvements, linoleum on the floor, lathering machines, air conditioning—but he kept the golden oak barbershop furniture and even the rack for the old-fashioned shaving mugs with the shaving mugs still in it. He picked up some money on the side selling the mugs to antique hunters and always kept one or two in the window for bait. Ed, with his round good-humored face, was comfortable like his barbershop, and in his white coat he looked like an old-fashioned doctor that had learned to expect a little but not too much from people going and coming.

'Twasn't long till Ed had snipped and lathered and hot-toweled some of my story out of me. He didn't seem surprised. "Tape recorder, eh? Git 'em to sing in it. Works fine, I'll bet. Didn't I tell you? She's a smart gal. You go right ahead. Whut's a little thing like a crick in the neck. Bet your feet hurt, too, don't they?"

"Um-m-m," I said, through that sizzling towel.

"I thought so. Well, there's a chiropractor and a corn-and-bunion specialist right here in this same block if you need 'em. But when a man is courtin', it don't pay to be discouraged. Jest go ahead and humor her and take the consequences.

"If you git in trouble—well, I jest downright know you will git in trouble. The MacGregors always do. When you git in trouble, I'll help you out. But I don't want to fool around with some little ol' measly trouble. Wait for hit to grow some. Hit will, shore. Is that towel enough?"

He pressed the towel down tighter and made sure I had the smallest possible crack to breathe through.

"Now when I was courtin' my wife, she was crazy about religion. So I had to go to church Sunday mornin', Sunday night, prayer meetin', Christian Endeavor, box suppers, memorize the Golden Text, go to Sunday School, read the Bible ever' night, think about my sins and try to be sanctified. Nothing else for me to do because that was what she wanted to do. And I was crazy about her like you are about Cissie."

Ed took off that hot towel and slapped on another one twice as hot.

"That ain't too hot, is it? If you had been around, you would have noticed I was a changed man, and you could have helped me out, but you was gittin' started with Rufus and I didn't bother you. Anyway, I shore am glad Elora didn't join the snake-handlers church, because if she had done that, I would have had to go right in amongst the rattlesnakes. Yessir, if that idea had tuck her, I would have jest blind-fool gone to rattlesnake church too. If that girl had said to me, 'Take that ol' swamp-rattler by the gullet, raise him up, and look him in the eye,' I would have done it. And if she had said, 'Now, Ed, tetch him to your forehead,' I would have done it if I died for it, and thought it was worth it. I was that crazy."

He snatched off the towel and began to rub in the massage cream.

"But Elora didn't go in for the rattlesnake style of religion, and that was lucky for me. Bad enough, though, as it was. Worst part was when a travelin' preacher named Crossno come to town and I had to go to revival meetin' three times a day for two weeks. Elora thought Brother Crossno tuned the angels' harps and combed God Almighty's whiskers. I thought he was a pale, puny, belly-achin' wether-sheep of a man, but I didn't tell Elora that. She went in the choir, I went in the choir. I held the book for her and sung out strong on 'Jesus is tenderly calling for you, Calling you home, Calling you home.' Elora went down amongst the sinners, whisperin' in their ears to come to Jesus and prayin' for their souls to be saved. So I follered right after and whispered and prayed like a real soul winner. Ol' Jim McCloskey, remember him?—he was one of the first sinners I tackled—a hard case too, settin' on the back row of the tent spittin' tobacco juice between his feet. I kneeled by him in prayer, but before I could whisper anything to him he said, 'Ed Cooley, what the hell are you doin' here?' I said 'God bless you, brother!' and went and found me a pretty girl to kneel by—which was a mistake because Elora caught me at it. But anyway, I said my Amen to ever' one of Elora's Amen's. If she shouted, I shouted. She cried, I cried. I was a purty hot Christian and soul-saver for them two weeks. It wore me out. I lost fifteen pounds in two weeks—that's over a pound a day. But it paid off."

He was rubbing my face. Between rubs I got in a word.

"Paid off—how?"

"Well, Danny, not to go into all the dee-tails, you wouldn't be int'rested in that—just the technique. Hit was a fine moonlight night when we got through that revival, and I walked home with Elora. She was feelin' mighty happy over savin' so many souls, and I jest up and tuck advantage of her. I said, 'Elora, narrow is the path that leads to salvation, and few there be that kin walk straight upon it. But broad and slick is the road that leads to hell, and many there be that skids to perdition. Elora, my soul is saved but if you want it to stay saved you better marry me before I backslide. Furthermore, it is written, Pluck a brand from the burning, and if you are goin' to pluck me, for God's sake go on and pluck before I fall back in the fire ag'in.' She said, 'Ed Cooley, it's the God's truth,' and she plucked me right then. We went right from the revival tent into holy matrimony."

"Ed, if I could get through it in two weeks, but Cissie—"

"Then jest take the punishment. A man's got to take his punishment when he goes a-courtin'. You got a ballad-chasin' sweetheart—well, chase right along with her. Mighty light punishment, I'd call it, compared to singin' 'Jesus is calling' three times a day for two weeks straight and bein' a strict Christian. It was hard on me but I got over it."

"Got over bein' a Christian?"

"I wouldn't say that, Danny. You know I'm a good Christian. I'm talkin' about the fury of it and the punishment. Funny thing is, we don't go to church much, any more. Elora says she don't like the preachers we have now. They don't preach the Bible like Brother Crossno. So we mostly stay at home Sunday mornin's—read the paper and maybe listen to the radio."

He flicked powder on my face and jerked off the cloth.

"Feel better now, don't you? Jest take your punishment and watch your chance. And remember, the more she punishes you, the more she loves you. It's a sure sign."

Ed took my money and rang the cash register.

"I do feel better, Ed, thank you. And I thank you for the Sunday School lesson. It's almost as good as a Turkish bath. But danged if I know what it has to do with a ballad checklist! Can you tell me?

"You'd be surprised at the mileage a ballad checklist can put on a car. And the places it takes you to. And the people. If we just had a sound truck to go with the tape recorder, I could imagine I was running for Sheriff."

Ed called out "Next" and turned to his next customer. "I'll be seein' you," he said.

"You'll be seein' me, all right. I can feel that trouble comin' on."

I could hear him saying "O.K." as I opened the door and stepped into the heat of the sidewalk. That afternoon I'd promised to meet Cissie and drive out to the Kennedy place. I didn't like the idea at all, but Cissie said she had already written Buck Kennedy a card and made a date. And so we had to go, she said. But first, all I had to do was go by the WCC office and get my mail; then go to the Piedmont Harmony Studio and meet Rufus and one or two of the boys, to work out the background for a new record he was making for the Dover Sisters—that's what a sideman is always having to do: put in the hard licks and somebody else rake in the credit. There was our regular Friday half-hour morning program at Rufus' Own Record Shop. And after that, some practice—till I had to go to Kiwanis for lunch and wear my button and eat my cold mashed potato as if I liked it. Then I had to hump over to WCC and put in my own five minutes on a Neighborhood Store program. That was all till I got my car and met Cissie— Station WCC, the sideman stuff, Rufus' Record Shop, Kiwanis, Esso, Neighborhood Stores, Piedmont Hotel Features, Lumbermen's Mutual, fan mail, requests, practice—that was my old life. The ballad checklist—that was my new life.

The ballad checklist was just two or three pages of song titles Cissie had typed off and carried with her all the time. I called 'em song titles—she said they were variants of ballad titles and explained that the same ballad might go under any number of different names. "It's just my reminder list," she said. "Nothing you have to worry about."

But you better look out when a woman starts making a list. It means some man has got to sweat.

It was like hunting a fox in fifty different woodlots, and in every different woodlot the owner would have a different name for a fox, and you wouldn't find out till too late, maybe, what name his fox went by. You'd ride up and say to the farmer, "Where is that fox?" And he'd scratch his head and say, "Never heerd of sech a thing!" Then you'd ask him if anything had been stealing his chickens, and you'd try him on weasel, squirrel, otter, wolf, polecat, and rabbit. And when you come to "rabbit" he'd say, "Oh, yes, now I know what you mean. There is a big red rabbit with a long brushy tail around here, and I think he's been stealin' my chickens."

It sounds crazy—but that's what a ballad checklist is, and that's about the way Cissie worked it.

But it didn't do her much good, that first day, after I had sung "Little Matty Grew" and we rolled down to the cabin to practice recording ballads on Old Man Parsons and his wife. No wonder, though. Old Man Parsons is a hard man to master.

It'd take more than a ballad checklist or even a Sheriff's warrant to get him over the stile, once he's decided to go some other way.

"Do you suppose they are taking their afternoon nap?" Cissie asked me, as we walked down the path to the cabin between the rows of cosmos Mrs. Parsons had planted and stepped into the dog-run where the potted geraniums stood to take the sun and morning glory vines were climbing on both sides. "I wouldn't want to disturb them."

"Lord, honey, you forget. They think you are liable to consumption and water on the brain if you sleep in the daytime. If he ain't readin' his Bible, he'll be plaitin' a whipcracker or smoothin' a axe handle. No, hold on." For I could hear a tapping sound. "He must be cobbling a shoe."

That was it. They were both busy. Little Mrs. Parsons had her sewing in her apron when she came to meet us, and Mr. Alexander Campbell Parsons, in all his glory, had an old shoe on the last and was patching the sole. He carefully took the tacks out of his mouth and welcomed us. It was like being welcomed by Moses and the Ten Commandments. You saw the long nose standing like a rock above the flowing white moustache and beard, the wide-open blue eyes looking over into the Promised Land, the forehead high and grand, and the white hair long and shaggy at the back—and right away you began to worry about the last time you sneaked in a visit to the Golden Calf. Whether or not he was wearing his black string tie, you couldn't see, on account of the whiskers, but his white shirt was very clean, and he had on black suspenders.

"What a wonderful coverlet you have!" said Cissie, stopping by the bed to admire.

Um-huh, I thought, she's going to creep up on him from the distaff side. Nice plan if it works—but I bet with myself it wouldn't work. I put down the machine and battery set and made myself comfortable. Mrs. Parsons just said, "Yes'm, thank ye," and began to thread a needle. She didn't look at all like the mountain women they are always putting in the movies and the magazine section of the Sunday newspaper. She had on a neat green-check gingham dress that I guessed was store bought, and a pretty little flowered apron. But for the black eyes, she would have been a good deal like my Grandma, with her gray hair drawn back in a roll, and her easy, quiet way.

"It's so nice to be in this good old log cabin house again," said Cissie. "After being in New York. I'd forgotten how nice it is."

"Hit's easy to take keer of," said Mrs. Parsons. "Just sweep the floor and go around with the feather duster. But I do enjoy the telephone and electric lights."

"Cain't git any good shoe leather any more," said Mr. Parsons. "Mout as well be calf hide, what they call cowhide these days. Goin' to tan me some cowhide myself, next time you slaughter, Mr. MacGregor."

He was pecking away at the shoe sole and talking at the same time. Cissie didn't know quite where to take hold, but she wouldn't give up. She decided to work on Mrs. Parsons. She had already admired the coverlet. So now she went on and admired the sewing and asked Mrs. Parsons about the pattern. Then she admired the old clock on the mantel and the dog-irons in the fireplace and the hearth rug and did her best to make conversation. She had the ballad checklist out of her purse already, but she couldn't find a good place to bring it in. And all the time Mr. Parsons was tapping at the shoe sole.

It was the sleepy time of afternoon, with the women talking and the old man tapping his hammer, and I just about dozed off, sitting with my head against the high back of the rocking chair. The room had that old-fashioned smell of wood ashes and hickory smoke. Many's the time I had roasted sweet potatoes in the ashes of that fireplace. It was big enough to cook in. There was the same old crooked crack in the hearthstone that I remembered. There ought to be a vase full of paper squills on the mantel, for Pa to light his pipe, and a gun in the corner. No, there were three guns, by George—an old muzzle-loader, a shotgun, and a Winchester rifle. Old Man Parsons was well provided. I could almost dream Cissie and I were shelling red and yellow ears of popcorn into a skillet, and I was raking the coals out of the glowing fire and the popcorn was beginning to pop— pop—pop—beneath the lid—

But no, it was the shoe-hammer, and Cissie wasn't a little girl with a pigtail down her back. She was a very peartly dressed young lady, sitting in a cane-bottom chair with her knees crossed, and saying, "Danny, Danny. I do believe he's gone to sleep. Wake up, Danny, and set up the machine."

"I jist had my eyelids closed," I said. "I wa'n't asleeping."

The two women were laughing at me. Mr. Parsons was not noticing. He had the shoe off the last and was feeling the sole inside.

"Mrs. Parsons has a dulcimer," Cissie was saying. "And she is going to show it to us. If we can just persuade her to play it, too, and sing—"

"Hit's in the loft. I ain't tetched it since we moved."

"Danny and I were wondering," said Cissie, "whether you or Mr. Parsons would know some of these old songs we are trying to find. We know some of them, but we want to get the words and the tunes straight. Get the whole thing right from the folks that really know. Like you and Mr. Parsons."

The only table in the room was small and it had a large family Bible on it. I started to set the machine on top of the Bible, then decided that wouldn't do. I stood looking for a place to put the machine. Cissie came over.

"What a very fine old Bible this is," she said. "Do you mind if I lay it on the bed and use this table?" She lifted the Bible, and I moved the table in front of the fireplace. The old couple said nothing. Old Man Parsons sat stroking his whiskers. His blue eyes glittered.

I opened up the machine and connected the battery. Mrs. Parsons was standing close behind Cissie, peeping at the machine around her shoulder, looking guilty and excited at the same time, like the married folks do when they pass the Hula-Hula Dancer sideshow on the way to the big tent. The main thing was, how was Cissie going to get them to sing without insulting them. Old Man Parsons still said nothing. I laid low.

Cissie was fingering the knobs and switches one after another and putting up a hand now and then to push back her hair. She decided to open the attack with some big college words. "It's a kind of conservation of resources," she said. "Like the conservation of natural resources that you hear so much about—the coal, and iron, and oil, and the wild life and the forests. Only this is something we are not letting the government do. These old songs are our treasures. We don't want to let them pass away. I want to get them in a permanent form before they are lost—lost and forgotten. Get them to study myself, and learn them, and teach them to other people—"

"Will you put them on the radio, Miss Cissie?"

Little Mrs. Parsons put her hand over her mouth as if what had popped out of it scared her and she didn't mean to do it again. Cissie looked startled. Her eyebrows went up. Old Man Parsons stroked his whiskers and said nothing. I laid low.

"I hadn't really thought about that yet, Mrs. Parsons," said Cissie. "It's a possibility of course. But won't you get your dulcimer? I have my checklist here, and we can start in."

Mrs. Parsons threw another anxious look at the old man. "'Twon't do no harm to git it and look at it," she said. "Even if I can't sing—" She started for the door. "I don't know how good them strings is." And she went out.

"I'll be glad to show you how this machine works, Mr. Parsons," said Cissie. "The tape recorder is a very new thing. Almost like magic, the way it puts the song on this little tape."

Mr. Alexander Campbell Parsons rose up and came to the table. It was like Moses coming down from Mt. Sinai. He tapped the machine with one long bony finger.

"They are the abomination of Babylon. They are Sodom and Gomorrah and the trick of Satan. And they do be the ruination of the world."

Cissie didn't have a chance to answer. You can't talk back to Moses. She stood by her machine, with her hand on the switch, looking up into Mr. Parsons' face. All she could do was dodge, if he threw the Ten Commandments at her. Or grab the machine and run.

"For don't the Bible say," he went on, "that where your treasure is, there will your heart be also? That's Luke, the 12th Chapter and the 34th verse. And don't the Bible say, in the 16th Chapter of Luke, when Jesus is rebukin' the Pharisees for lovin' Mammon, 'Ye are they which justify yourselves before men; but God knoweth your hearts; for that which is highly esteemed among men is abomination in the sight of God'?"

I heard a little quiet humming sound. Cissie had turned on the machine. Alexander Campbell Parsons was being tape-recorded, but he didn't know it. He was bringing out the ram's horn. He was blowing down the walls of Jericho. Cissie was smiling in a stiff way. And I was still laying low.

"Now I know you air a clever young lady, and you kin justify this-here machine and all other machines before men. But can you justify 'em in the sight of God? That's what I'm axing ye, Miss Timberlake. I'm glad to have ye here in my house, and I want you to be pleased and comfortable. But I also want to tell you that I don't put no faith in machines, I don't care how pretty they make 'em.

"Three-score and ten years, jest about, I've lived in Beaver Valley. I kin remember back to the time when we didn't have no machines a-tall in Beaver Valley unless maybe it was a coffee grinder. I've seen the machines come, and I've seen the people go. And the better they make the machines, the worse they make the people.

"That's because they put their treasure in the machines, and don't the Bible say that where your treasure is, there will your heart be also? And don't that mean their hearts are not with God? And it means, too, that their hearts are not with their own folks and not with the land God give 'em to live in.

"My Pa owned 300 acres of good mountain and valley land in Beaver Valley. Most of it come down in our family from the Revolution. Now I don't own an acre. I'm jist here in the evenin' of my days, workin' on shares with Mr. MacGregor, and glad to have the chance. What done it? I kin tell you. Hit was the sawmills and lumber companies; hit was railroads and autymobiles and then trucks; and finally hit was them conservation people that you was talkin' about that come in and took what was left of the land. They surveyed it, and they condemned it. They condemned me, and put me out. I had a house once; now I'm back in a log cabin like my great-grandpa built and glad to have a roof over my head. And why? You can't say they done it for the good of the people and the glory of God? No, they done it because they loved the machines better and because they'd rather feed the machines than have the people feed their own selves.

"Now I want to ax ye three questions. Then I'll go my way, and let you go your way, and I'll let Lula take care of you, and it's all in good will I'm a-axing, and you'll have my blessin' because Danny MacGregor likes you and you must be all right."

"She's Cass Timberlake's granddaughter," said Mrs. Parsons. She had come back and made no more noise than a shadow. Now she was in her chair again, holding the old dulcimer in her lap. "I thought you knowed she is Cass Timberlake's granddaughter."

"Nobody named hit to me, so I didn't know. That makes it still better. Cass Timberlake was a friend o' mine, and now I can see you favor him some.

"But I want to ax you the questions—and you ain't the first one I've axed 'em of, and if you miss, you won't be the first to miss. But I won't take off yore head for missin', and you won't take off my head for axin', nuther.

"Now the first question is out of the Old Testament: 'Wherefore do the wicked live, become old, yea, are mighty in power?' Answer me that—why do the wicked prosper?"

I felt sorry for Cissie, standing there, like a poor little sinner dragged into judgment. I bet with myself that she hadn't read the Bible in many a year. But she looked him in the eye and didn't flinch.

"I wouldn't remember the text, Mr. Parsons, but my Ma taught me that the Bible says we can't understand the mind of God. And the wicked will be punished."

"That's a good answer," he said, and his voice was softer. "For the Holy Bible does say, 'Shall any teach God knowledge?' And them that thinks to teach God are reserved for everlastin' punishment. And now my second question is out of the New Testament, and it is, 'Who will overcome the great dragon that deceived the whole world?' Answer me that."

Cissie was frowning, and I knew she was digging in her memory, and didn't want to be outdone by the old man. I thought I could answer it, but maybe not in the right words. She almost had the very words.

"I think the great dragon is Satan, and only God can overcome him, through Jesus Christ our Lord. That's what I was taught."

66

"And it is right, it is shorely right. For the Book says, 'They overcame him by the blood of the Lamb, and by the word of their testimony.' I can see you was raised right, young lady. But you may not remember the answer to my third question, and since you have been talkin' about songs, it is: 'What songs is most pleasin' to God Almighty?' Answer me that, and I'm through."

"I couldn't quote the Bible on that, Mr. Parsons. But it would have to be sacred songs—spiritual songs."

"I'm glad you said 'spiritual songs,'" the old man said. "Because I don't hold for what they call gospel hymns, and the py-anner banging out like they was dancin'. No, I want the old songs, out of 'The Sacred Harp,' with the old shapenotes and no py-anner. They are all accordin' to Scripture, and don't the Good Book say that the redeemed will stand on the sea of glass, with the harps of God in their hands, and sing the song of Moses the servant of God, and the songs of the Lamb?"

Mr. Parsons turned and took his black hat from a nail on the wall. He put it carefully on over his white hair. The brim drooped in front till it almost covered one eye. He took a stout hickory walking stick from the chimney corner and struck it thunderingly on the wide planks of the floor.

"The day is gittin' on," he said. "Lula will take keer of you."

Cissie had cut the switch and was looking at her checklist. Mr. Parsons took it from her hand and squinted one eye, while he held it at arm's length and read it from under the droopy hat brim.

"I used to know some of 'em. Before I knowed the name of trouble. They air all worldly songs."

"But all of them, Mr. Parsons," said Cissie, "came before the machine age, and that's the main reason why I want them. The only reason I use the machine is that it's easier. I could write them down in pen and ink."

"Lula can sing 'em," he said, handing back the list. "Hit would choke me in my throat to do it. And remember them times."

He was at the door, his broad back turned to us. "Standin' on the sea of glass," he repeated to himself, "with God's harp in hand. Singin' the songs of Zion." He struck the floor again with his stick and was gone.

"He's mixed up," said Mrs. Parsons. She was tuning the dulcimer, softly, using a ten-penny nail to turn the wrought iron keys that stood straight up from the head. She put the nail through a hole in the keys and twitched the corners of her mouth as she turned and listened. It was a very old dulcimer, I could see, not made like any I could remember, because it had an extra soundbox raised above the tapered body, and the strings ran along that on to the fretboard, where the frets were just pieces of wire, set in somehow. And it was a four-string dulcimer, and all the strings were fretted, none open. The head of the instrument ended in a carved scroll, very lovingly whittled out and finished.

Mrs. Parsons passed her right-hand fingers across the strings a few times, while with her left hand she touched the fretboard. But I could see she was fretting only one of the four strings. A little lonesome tune was shaping up on that one string, above the humming and twanging of the other strings that backed it up. She knew how to play a dulcimer, and I began to be right interested. Cissie was sitting with her chin in her hand and not a word to say, just dreamy-looking and pleased, letting Mrs. Parsons go her gait. The pleasant humming sound went with the little old woman and the smell of wood ashes and the turkey-feather duster that hung by the fireplace. It seemed to explain everything and somehow to lift us up to where we could look down on trouble. Mrs. Parsons strummed and plucked, trying the strings, and went on talking.

"Yes'm, he's mixed up. He ain't been the same man since the gover'ment moved us out. Back yonder, when our chillun was little, he was a mighty man, and a gre't hand for ever' kind o' singin', and dancin' too. Now all the time I tell him what is to be, will be. But he is onreconciled in his heart and stubborn in his head. Don't take no pleasure in anything but readin' the Bible and thinkin' about the Day of Jedgment. Sometimes, if we kin ketch a ride with anybody I git him to go with me to a Sacred Harp singin' somewheres, even if it's way over in Rabun Gap. He likes that pretty well— to sing the spiritual songs all day, and dinner on the grounds, and seein' the folks. He likes to sing bass in songs like 'Marchin' to Zion' and 'Alabama.' But the good don't last. We git back home, and he's right back at the Day of Jedgment ag'in. Says hit's comin' soon. And that thing the gover'ment is makin', hit's a sign."

"You mean the atom bomb?" asked Cissie. "I read a lot about it while I was in New York."

"I don't rightly know what they call it. But they air makin' it. And folks do say hit's strong enough to blow up the world. Alex says that's the sign. Hit's the openin' of the seventh seal."

She looked around uncomfortably. The dulcimer kept trying to slide off her lap.

"We could just as well put the recorder on the floor," Cissie said. "And Mrs. Parsons could rest the dulcimer on the table."

I began to make myself useful again. Cissie was looking at her list. "I don't recognize that tune you were playin'," she said. "It's a sweet tune."

Now you're on the right road, lady, I thought. No more Bible texts.

"I thank ye kindly," said Mrs. Parsons. "I ain't much of a singer. But I do like to be thinkin' about the old times and the stories about 'em that's in the songs. It helps some. But I don't sing 'em when he's around." She lowered her voice. Outside, Mr. Parsons was cutting wood. The chopstrokes of his axe came slow and steady, muted by the log walls. "Unless the grandbabies are visitin'. Then he don't mind."

She looked up at the ceiling, then down at the dulcimer. Cissie motioned to me with her head, and I flicked the recorder switch. Mrs. Parsons was singing in a thin, high old woman's voice that quavered just enough to blend right with the dulcimer.

> It was on a summer's morning all in the month of May
> Down by the Banks of Claudy I carelessly did stray.
> And there I heard a pretty maid, in sorrow did complain,
> All for her absent lover that sailed the ocean main.

She stopped suddenly and looked a little alarmed, and I thought she was blushing as much as a nice old woman can blush. "Is that the kind of old song you meant, Miss Cissie?" was her shy question. I almost cut the switch, but Cissie frowned at me not to do it.

"Go ahead, Mrs. Parsons. It's beautiful. It's what I want."

"Hit's a story about a lovin' couple," Mrs. Parsons said. "Lak Alex an' me, when we was young folks." She laughed a low laugh. "Hit was a long time ago. He sailed the ocean main sure enough, Alex did. When he volunteered and went to the Philippine War—and all them places far over the sea. He wanted me to marry him before he left, but my Pa said I was too young and he didn't trust Alex to support me, he was so hasty in all his doin's then. Two year he was gone, and wrote me some letters. But there was a long time, just before he come back, when there wa'n't no letter. So one summer's mornin', like the song says, I was walkin' along the high waters of Beaver Creek, lookin' for wild strawberries, and I heard a noise in the bushes behind me. I looked around, and it was a soldier in a blue uniform with a old brown hat on his head, and I was scared to see a stranger behind me there. Then he said, 'Lula, don't you know your own sweetheart?' And it was him. 'Twas Alex, come back from the war. I'll sing you the rest—"

> I stepped up to that fair-pretty maid and gave her a surprise:
> You see she didn't know me, for I was in disguise.
> I said, "My fair-pretty maiden, my joy and my delight,
> Why do you roam so lonesome upon this weary height?"
>
> It's on the Banks of Claudy, if you should want to know,
> There roams a fair young maiden who knows not where to go.

"I'm lookin' for a young man, and Johnny is his name,
But on the Banks of Claudy no more does he remain."

"It's two long years or better since your lover left the shore,
A-crossin' the main ocean where the salty billows roar,
A-sailin' the main ocean for honor and for fame,
But they say his ship was wrecked and lost all in the wars of Spain."

Oh, when he told the grievous news, she fell in dark despair.
She cried and wrung her lily-white hands, she tore her golden hair.
She said, "If Johnny's drownded, there's no man I will take.
All on the Banks of Claudy I'll wander for his sake."

Oh, then he stepped up to her, no longer could he stand.
He took the maid into his arms, saying, "Darlin', I'm the man.
I've sailed back o'er the ocean to end your grief and pain,
And on the Banks of Claudy we'll never part again."

The golden light of afternoon was striking level through the windows, and the dust in the rays from the windows was golden, all around Cissie's head and on the wrinkled forehead of the singer. The chopping had stopped for awhile. Now it began again, slow and steady.

"That's him, right now. Happen he was a-listenin' and ashamed for us to know. He ain't the man he was, neither be I the gal I was, but we make out. And ready for the Jedgment Day if hit comes to that."

Cissie said: "I never heard the song to that tune before. It's beautiful, Mrs. Parsons. And now I want you to hear how beautiful it sounds on the machine."

She leaned over, ran back the tape, and started it to playing. On the first try she missed. What came out of the machine was Mr. Parson's thundering voice: "But can you justify 'em in the sight of God—" Cissie stopped it quick and jumped the tape ahead. Mrs. Parsons looked bewildered. But when Cissie picked up the ballad, her face changed. She sat amazed, with her hands in her lap, her head high, her eyes on the slowly turning tape, to hear her voice and the dulcimer blending on "It was on a summer's morning all in the month of May." She had a voice that recorded well, and you might have thought it was a young girl singing in an old-fashioned way. Cissie played it through. At the end Mrs. Parsons sighed. She looked younger and brighter. "I didn't know hit would sound like that," she said. "Why, hit's—hit's almost like the radio, ain't it?"

Cissie was busy with her checklist again.

"Now, we'll go right ahead with other things you know, Mrs. Parsons." She began calling off titles. The two women had forgotten all about me. Each one, now, was playing to the other.

"If you don't need me, Cissie," I said, "I'll go and see Mr. Parsons about some things."

She looked up, hardly noticing. "That's all right, Danny. I'll call you."

As I closed the door behind me I could hear her checking 'em off. "Do you know 'The Devil's Nine Questions'? 'Lady Isabel and the Elf Knight'?"

I walked over the place with Mr. Parsons till the sun was low.

7

BEWARE OF A FAIR-SPOKEN MAN

"**I**t's a gone country, Cissie. No doubt about that. It's gone."

The blacktop road ends at Pegram's Crossroads, six or seven miles west of my place, and that was where we first stopped next morning on the way to collect Aunt Lou Watkins. It was a part-cloudy day, with a thin skim of white high up and darker, heavier clouds beginning to boil across the mountain ridges to the west. And across that thin skim of white cloud was a vapor track drifting like a chalk mark that some giant had drawn carelessly across the sky from southeast to northwest and left to slide. A high-flying military plane, I told myself, from Florida or maybe Fort Jackson.

And on the ground at Pegram's Crossroads, not a soul in sight but us. On the door and all across the front of Pegram's Store, election handbills were tacked—LOONEY FOR SHERIFF—with his picture, and a lot of others. That was about all the store was good for any more. Planks were nailed over the windows. Empty beer cans were lying all around, at the side of the road, on the porch of the store, and on the bench where the loafers used to play checkers. When parties drove out late at night from Carolina City, they would see only dirt road ahead, and would decide to drink their beer and go no farther.

There was nobody to pick up the beer cans after them, next morning. Nobody to care whether the beer cans were picked up or not. Around the store and the blacksmith shop, the rank dogfennel was taking hold. Sweet clover, horseweeds, jimsonweeds were banking up against the square front of the blacksmith shop. Above the door was the sign that had been there ever since I could remember: CHEW BATTLEAXE TOBACCO. Along the side wall I could see what was left of a circus poster. A woman in tights was floating down from a high trapeze, but of the man who had to catch her, nothing was left but two naked arms.

There wasn't any blacksmith at Pegram's anymore. There were hardly any wagon tires to put on anymore, or plow points to sharpen, or horses and mules to shoe. There wasn't any little auto repair shop, either, or even a gasoline pump. There were not enough folks left in Beaver Valley to support anything but their own selves. They had had plenty of practice in doing that. They had to be tough to stay.

"It's worse than I remembered," Cissie said gloomily. "Pegram's Store was open when we were last here. The old man sold us Coca-Colas."

"The wholesalers closed him out. He's gone to live with one of his daughters, I heard."

"Then we'll have to work fast to get the ballads before the rest move away. And before the old folks die. I don't like to think about it. It's sort of—ghostly."

"It's still worse at Big Cataloochee and Little Cataloochee, where the Smoky Mountains Park came in and moved them all out. Nothin' left but tombstones. If it was TVA land, there wouldn't even be tombstones. TVA moves even the dead folks, they tell me. Then puts water over empty graves."

Cissie shuddered. "Don't talk that way. Makes me feel like somebody's walkin' on my grave. Let's go."

"All right. Aunt Lou ain't ghostly, the least bit. We turn right and drive to the last place where I can turn the car."

The narrow dirt road was hardly more than a winding track. Till you got to the ridge, it was mostly bottom land, but not an acre was being farmed. Sage grass had come everywhere, and field pine crowded into the sage. Blackberries, sumac, pokeberries, and all kinds of brush had crowded into the road shoulder. They slapped the car fenders and jabbed into the windows. When we hit the ridge and came into thick woods, the road was wider, but steeper and much rougher. I watched the high middle for rocks, and drove slow.

At last I came up a steep rise that put me into second, then down a slope between high clay banks.

"Down yonder is where we git out and walk. It's the last place to turn—if that feller will let me—"

At the foot of the slope the road crossed a small branch. A black Model-T Ford had stopped there, rear wheels in the water, headed towards us. The driver was talking to a towheaded boy on horseback. The boy turned in his saddle to look at us, then kicked his horse, splashed through the branch, and disappeared up the steep road beyond.

"There goes our messenger," I told Cissie. "I bet that boy's one of Aunt Lou's tribe. He'll tell her."

I eased down the hill. The Ford pulled out of the branch and a little to one side, then stopped. The driver was holding out his arm, waving me to stop. As I came closer, I saw the old Ford had a courthouse license number and a Red Cross sticker on the windshield, and the shiny black paint was new. I put on my brake and hopped out. A blackheaded boy with spectacles on was grinning at me from the driver's seat.

"Hello, Mr. MacGregor," he said. "You better not try that road on the other side." There was a middleaged woman with a sharp nose and not much chin in the seat with him. She just stared and looked sour.

"You better turn around here." The boy got out. He was wearing a Carolina City High School sweatshirt. "The road's too bad for your nice car. I got up as far as the old chestnut grove and decided to stop and turn around in the ditch."

"That's all right," I said. "We aim to walk up. Thank you just the same."

He was a nice boy, all grins to see us, and he wanted to talk. "I'm Tom Bolling, and I'm drivin' for Miss Slemmons. These old Fords can go anywhere." In the back seat of the Ford I could see what looked like a broken-up spinning wheel.

"If you'll just pull up a little," I suggested, "I'll turn around and park." Tom Bolling shuffled his feet and looked at Cissie. "I just wanted to tell you—" Cissie was smiling, across the seat of the car, and Tom Bolling was red to the ears. "I just wanted to tell you that I liked your song, the other night. 'White Roses'—it's the best. And I'm learning it on my guitar."

Cissie was out of the car, and shaking his hand, thanking him, and I thanked him again and shook hands. "I just wanted to tell you," he said. He jumped back into the Ford, and soon chugged off up the hill.

"He jest wanted to tell you," I said to Cissie, as solemn as I could. "You can't get away from it." And after a lot of work with the clutch and wheel, and Cissie watching the back end, I got the car turned and parked, and heaved the machine and battery set out on the bank of the branch.

The branch looked lots wider than it had looked from the top of the hill, and I was sure it had a mud bottom. There was one big rock in the middle, and a man might make it across in two jumps if he didn't have anything to carry and nothing slipped. But I would have something to carry. So I opened the car trunk and got my fishing boots.

"Where is the footlog?" Cissie was asking. She was stepping among the wheel ruts at the water's edge. "There ought to be a footlog."

I was leaning against the car, slipping on my boots, peeping at her around the car fender.

"It's washed downstream somewheres by this time—if there ever was a footlog. I'll carry the machine and battery acrost first—and try the bottom of this branch—and then—"

"Couldn't you back the car across and park there?"

"Oh, no, Cissie. We'd stick in the mud."

"I reckon we might."

I waded across with the machine and battery. It was a mud bottom, and the mud was every bit as deep as the water was high above it. Then I stepped back across, tied my shoes together, and flung them over my shoulder.

"Now, Cissie!" I said, took a good hold, and lifted.

"Don't you slip," said she, close to my ear.

I took my time crossing. She rested light in my arms and didn't move. And I took my time in putting her down again.

"Don't tease. Take a professional attitude. You promised." Cissie smoothed her skirt and poked at her hair while I changed back into my shoes and hid the boots in some bushes.

We started the long climb. Cissie looked at me rather sweet and said she'd better carry the battery a while. At first I wouldn't give in. Then I felt her hand warm on mine. When she had the battery, she seemed suddenly very happy, and began to hum "The Banks of Claudy." I told her we better go slow, and rest every hundred yards maybe. It was a right stout climb, with a load.

The second time we rested, I took the battery again.

"What do you think that woman was doin' up here?" she asked.

"I think she's one of the courthouse people. Some kind of social welfare work. And I'll bet she's usin' a county car, now and then, to do some little things on the side. You saw that spinnin' wheel."

"I can imagine. But just so long as she's not collectin' my ballads."

"Don't worry. That's not what she's after. But we better save our breath."

We climbed silently up. It was fine and airy and cool in the mountainy woods, there in the deep shade, walking slow with Cissie, no matter how heavy the burden got. But pitiful and ghostly when we came through the chestnut grove, and saw the old bare chestnut trees, green giants once, now long dead from the blight, and the sun coming down cruel on their white limbs and the trashy second growth around them.

Up and beyond, the little rocky road took us into good timber, a stand of tall pine and a few oaks, close by running water where the stream made a talking riffle over mossy rocks, with laurel overhanging and a feel of mountain country. Cissie ran down to the stream to dip her hands in water and cool off, and, she said, the hearts-busting-with-love might be growing there. I kept hinting we should tarry, but she said, "Don't you be a-tollin' me back to the Banks of Claudy," and handed me the battery set again.

We wrestled the road, then, up and on, and come to the open where the breeze freshened us, and saw Aunt Lou's big old frame house on the flat above us, snuggled into a good place on the mountain shoulder, the two tall poplars over it and the clearing around, and smoke going up from somewhere behind, like it might be brush burning. And the whole valley, reaching into the far mountains, laid itself out before us, as we inched step by step and raised far peak after far peak, with my burden pulling me back and Cissie plucking me on, along the up-slanting gullied road that seemed to end in nothing but sky.

But it turned, as the breeze broke the clouds and the sun bore down hot, and it ended in Aunt Lou Watkins' front yard. The dogs began their yowling and barking before we could see them, and tore down the path to exterminate us right now and have it over with before we could find a tree to climb or even a good-sized stump. Black dogs, yellow dogs, little spotted fices, and rampaging hounds with long ears. They all had their hackles up and swore, Aye-Gad, they didn't like our smell. Up at the house I couldn't see nobody stirring but I could hear a phonograph playing.

"Just walk straight ahead," I told Cissie as she edged close to me. "Hit jist means 'Welcome stranger.'" But they were walking stiff-legged and looking mean, and I was afraid one of the fices might nip her from behind.

Then Aunt Lou came out and made the biggest noise of all.

"Elmer! Roscoe! Mary Lou! States Rights! Joe-Bob!"

She was standing at the top of the steps, waving her stick.

"You triflin' rascals, whur be ye?" She beat a loud tattoo on the porch railing with her stick. "Stop that danged phonygraph. Come and he'p the company."

The phonograph cut off. A crowd of younguns boiled out of the front door and from around the house. Those that came down the steps skillfully dodged Aunt Lou's stick as she swung at their legs.

"Kick them low-down curs out o' the way," Aunt Lou was shouting. "States Rights, Elmer, take their grips."

The towheaded boy we had seen at the ford reached us first. In one single motion he booted a large tan-colored hound out of the way, grabbed the machine and battery out of my hands, and said, "Hidy, Mr. MacGregor, I'm States Rights, walk right in and set down." The swarm of younguns mixed with the swarm of dogs. The dogs began to wag their tails and loll out their tongues. The younguns grinned. There were more children and one or two grown folks banking up behind Aunt Lou at the head of the steps. It was always that way at Aunt Lou's. Her kin never left her lonesome, and at the side of the house and scattered under the barnyard locusts I could see their rigs—an old Ford, a buggy or two, and a wagon with chairs in it.

"Cissie, honey," shouted Aunt Lou, coming down a couple of steps, "I been dyin' to see you ever since I got your note. And States Rights said he seed you-all at the ford. And Danny, God bless ye." She hugged us both as we surged up to meet her on the wave of younguns and dogs.

"It's long-looked-for come at last." Aunt Lou was leaning on her stick, looking Cissie over from head to foot. "I war as hot waitin' to see you as if I had a bellyful of yellow jackets. But I knowed you'd be takin' yore time, comin' up the hill. Lovers' walkin' is half talkin', and weddin' without courtin' is like vittle without salt. Look at her, Danny! She's red as a pokeberry. But ain't she purty? That blue skirt is mighty becomin' to her, ain't it? Matches her eyes and brings out her shape nice, don't hit? See there, Mary Lou? D'ye see, Katie May?"

Aunt Lou waved her stick at two teenage girls that were standing with their arms around each other. One had on faded blue jeans with white shirttails hanging over, the other red slacks. They were chewing gum and staring at Cissie.

"Mary Lou is Sarah's gal," said Aunt Lou. "And Katie May is Walter's oldest. And that's what they l'arn, a-goin' to high school. How to wear pants and paint their fingernails, and the county court a-raisin' my taxes to teach 'em to act like trash and trollops. Look at Miss Cissie, ye frousty little fools and l'arn the lady's fashion."

Aunt Lou stopped for breath. Her eye fell on the machine. She poked it with her stick.

"Well, take a cheer and rest your legs. And open up that machine. I'm a-dyin' to see how it sounds. We all heard tell about yore new kind of phonygraph."

"Why, how did you know, Aunt Lou?" asked Cissie, and Aunt Lou settled herself in her big rocking chair, and said, "Oh, the news gits around. Ever'body's talkin' about it and waitin' for you to turn up. Bring me my snuff, Mary Lou. No, I have it." She hauled a box of Bruton's Snuff out of a deep pocket in her skirt, removed the top, then put it back on. "No, I won't dip. You said you'd be wantin' me to sing."

I took one of Aunt Lou's big potted ferns off a table and made a place for the machine, close in front of her chair, in the middle of the porch where she could see it and everybody could watch. On that long, deep porch that ran the whole width of the house, there was room and to spare for children, grown folks, dogs and ballad collectors. Aunt Lou's house was a house, no mountain cabin. That porch, like the house, was weatherboarded with planks of heartpine, pit-sawed long ago by the Watkins men when first they took up that land; and the ceiling of the porch the same, and the floor. Aunt Lou's potted ferns and plants were on tables and small benches, on the floor of the porch, and the ends of step-planks. Two homemade swings hung by chains from the ceiling, one on each side of the door. Aunt Lou's tribe were in the swings, or in the split-bottom chairs, or on the floor and steps, or standing—whispering to one another, or just silently waiting. There were no older men-folks, only boys mingled with the numerous girls of all ages. One pretty young woman, with flaxen hair and with eyes and complexion no Hollywood star could touch, had a baby in her lap. Another woman peeked at us through the screen door.

And Aunt Lou, in her rocking chair by the front door, where the breeze was best, and her eye could sweep the road and barn lot, commanded them all like a general in his headquarters. Winters, the rocking chair set by the fire, where she could look out of two corner windows, front and side, and rule the kingdom good as a queen. She carried the hickory stick for mastery, not because she needed it to help her strong, stocky body. How long she'd been a widow, I didn't know, nor how old she was, nor how she had held out on a lonesome mountain farm and no good road up to it. Only that it was what she liked, and what Aunt Lou liked, she would have, and neither Saint nor Devil could say her nay.

Nobody ever saw Aunt Lou in anything but a good humor. She knew everything that went on in Beaver Valley and a good deal of what happened in Carolina City. She knew everybody's kinfolks, back to Adam, who married who, and their children on down. Not a marrying or a courting but what she had the inside of it before anybody else. It was most of all the lovemakings that she doted on, and could call even the younguns' sweethearts' first names before they hardly realized they were in love.

And there she sat, rocking gently, her stick on the floor by her chair, her bright hazel eyes watching us at the machine. Her white hair was neatly combed, her wrinkled face was gay as a girl's, and if she had false teeth you'd never notice it, the lips were full and so ready to laugh. Her fresh-ironed light cotton dress of a nice green color was no longer than Cissie's skirt above her feet that were just as small as Cissie's, and I would have sworn Aunt Lou was wearing nylon stockings. And as she rocked, she talked, and nobody else talked much, except when she threw the ball to 'em.

Cissie began her ballad spiel, carefully not saying anything this time about conservation of natural resources, but she didn't get far before Aunt Lou snatched the ball from her and was off again.

"If it's songs you want, you've come to the right place. You won't have to send to the hollow, as the sayin' is. We've got it right here, and whut I cain't remember the younguns can. There's States Rights with his banjo, too. He's been devilin' me for money to buy a guitar so he can sing and play like Danny. And Elmer plays the fiddle. And Virgie over there, with the baby—she sings, and that new baby of hern is already cryin' in tune. Day or night, the music never stops around this place, if it's nothin' but Roscoe or Mary Lou or somebody playin' the same hillbilly record over and over.

"No, we don't hardly need to be invited, when hit comes to singin'. And you might have knowed. You didn't even need to ask, whyn't you jest come on?

"Like that story, about back in Carpetbagger times, after the Confederate War, when the Democrats was comin' back. There was a man runnin' for some office on the Democrat ticket, and he knowed it would be close, so he decided to go to see ever' single voter, no matter where. He saw most ever' voter in the district, but there was one man livin' back in the hills that he hadn't seen, and he didn't know how that feller lined up and couldn't find out. So he told himself, 'Well, I cain't afford to let that one vote go for lack of tryin'. Hit might be the winnin' one. I'll have to see that feller.' So he saddled his horse and asked the way and rode out.

"Finally, this candidate come to the right house, he did, after takin' the wrong turn half-a-dozen times and swimmin' his horse over the creeks only to land in somebody else's barnyard and havin' to swim right back again. 'Twas a fur piece in the backwoods, that voter's place was. And when he come to it, 'twas a house off the big road, like this, with an old apple tree in the yard and boy-chillun climbin' it and fightin' and wrastlin' all around. He hollered 'Hello the house' till they hyurd him, and a woman come out on the steps. He tipped his hat polite and ast if that was Mr. So-and-So's place, and she said, yes, it was, but Mr. So-and-So was back up in the hollow burnin' bresh and clearin' some land. The candidate said, 'Well, I'll ride up thar and talk to him if you'll p'int the way.' But the woman said no, 'I'll send to the hollow for him, and you light and come in.' Then she grabbed a broomstick and lit into them boys.

" 'Beauregard,' she yelled out. 'You git right down out of that tree, and hitch this gentleman's horse. Robert E. Lee, you stop fightin' Jefferson Davis this minute, and you and Nathan Bedford go and ketch up old Stonewall. Ride up in the hollow and tell yer Pappy there's a gentleman here to see him.'

" 'That's all right, ma'm,' said the candidate, 'you don't need to send to the hollow. You've done told me all I wanted to know.' And he tipped his hat and rode off."

Cissie and I laughed, the girls laughed, the boys yelled, the baby crowed on his mammy's lap, the dogs barked and milled around, and Aunt Lou looked pleased with herself.

"So you don't have to send to the hollow to ask," Aunt Lou repeated. "Because I know you, and I've knowed you both since you was lap-chillun. Now if you was somebody like that woman that was here, that Miz Slemmons or whoever it was, hit would be different.

"She's an antiquer, that woman is. Almost thought I'd have to invite her to leave, or sic the dogs on her. Come here sayin' she was workin' for the county health and the Red Cross and all that. But it turned out that my rockin' cheer and clock was really what she was after. I turned her off, polite. She said she'd look around the place if I didn't mind. I said, 'Look all you want, but don't ax me to sell nothin'.' All the same, she came right in agin. She'd been up in the barn loft, prospectin' around, and she saw my coffin boards. That's my good black walnut coffin boards. I been savin' up, twenty-five year and more, for when the time comes. And she had the gall to try to trade me out of 'em. That's the way they are, them antiquers. Pull the featherbed from under a dyin' man and offer his widder fifty cents, they would. Finally I remembered and had Roscoe git down them pieces of broke-down spinnin' wheel on the rafters of the smokehouse, and I give her that to git shut of her and the Red Cross and the county health. 'Twan't none o' my spinnin' wheel, noways. Belonged to Jim's first wife."

Aunt Lou stopped for breath again. Then she said, "All right Cissie, honey. Play the new phonygraph some. Let's see how it sounds."

"Well, Aunt Lou," said Cissie. "I didn't bring any recording along much. I was intendin' and hopin', you see, to get—"

"I see whut you mean," said Aunt Lou. "But cain't you play something anyhow, so we can see how it's gonter sound, when we sing into it?"

"All right, Aunt Lou. Let me see—I don't know just what's on this reel, but I'll try it and—"

She reversed the reel, started it back, tried it, got it a twangy note or two, jumped ahead, then let it go, and the recorder said, in Aunt Lou's very voice: "—stop fightin' Jefferson Davis this minute, and you and Nathan Bedford go and ketch up old Stonewall—" and then right on through the end and the laughs and yells and dog-barking.

Aunt Lou grabbed her stick and got up to look at the machine. She fished her spectacles out and looked at it close. The recording of the dog-barks and boy-yells started more dog-barks and boy-yells. The teenagers in slacks giggled. The baby began to cry. The youngest children jumped up and down and rolled on the floor. Aunt Lou waved her stick and the young riot stopped.

"Good God, Cissie," said Aunt Lou. "What kind o' thing—?" She stopped and laughed and put her hand over her mouth. "Is hit workin' now?" she whispered. "Is hit—?"

"No, ma'am," said Cissie. "I've turned it off. But it is a good machine, isn't it?"

"'Taint safe to have around the house, is it?" said Aunt Lou.

"Buy one, Granny, and put it in the girls' room at night," yelled a boy's voice. Then, in a painful tone, "Make Katie May stop pinchin' me."

"But hain't you got no music in it?" asked Aunt Lou.

"That's what we came here for," explained Cissie. "And if you'll start singin', I'll play your own songs back to you, and you can hear yourselves. How you sound to other folks."

"Well," said Aunt Lou, "hit serves me right for talkin' so much. I've heard tell you cain't teach an old dog new tricks, but this is gonter be a new one. Come on, now, let's begin."

"All right, Aunt Lou." Cissie was pulling out her ballad checklist. She began to read. "'The Devil's Nine Questions.' 'The False Knight on the Road.' 'Lady Isabel and the Elf Knight.' 'The Douglas Tragedy.' 'The Soldier and the Lady.' 'The Two Sisters'—tell me if you know any of these—'The Cruel Brother.' 'Lord Randal'—"

"Hold on, Cissie," said Aunt Lou. "I cain't keep up with you. But I think them's all mean and bloody ones, ain't they. I've hyurd 'em sung, but I never could norate 'em. I like the lovin' ones better. That's the kind I always l'arned easy. Like Mr. Weatherburn and the pretty lady he kidnapped."

"Oh," said Cissie. "That's 'Captain Wedderburn's Courtship,' by the common name. Go right ahead, Aunt Lou."

Cissie gave Aunt Lou the mike, and almost before she could turn on the recorder, Aunt Lou started, in a very low singing voice for such a talking woman, but a very husky positive manner.

> Oh, there was a pretty young lady,
> Was a-walking down the lane,
> She met with Mr. Weatherburn,
> The keeper of king's deer.
>
> He said so she could hear him,
> 'Oh, it is ag'inst the law,
> But I'll have that maid in bed with me,
> And she'll lie next to the wall.'

"I don't edzackly know what that means," Aunt Lou broke in, talking, "that about lyin' next to the wall. But thar wa'n't no doubt about his intentions, war there? Hit's a right lovesome tale."

Cissie said nothing. Aunt Lou went on. "But she was a right clever gal, and knowed how to handle a man. She give him some hard jobs to do."

And she sang some more. At first I didn't catch on. The tune seemed familiar, but I had never heard the part of the song Aunt Lou started with. I thought, well, if the women can stand it, I can. Then Aunt Lou got on to what I remembered, and I knew what that song was. What the lady tells the man he has to do, before she'll consent:

> First, I want a cherry,
> A cherry without a stone,
> And next my love must get for me
> A chicken without a bone,
>
> And last my love must catch me
> A bird without any gall
> Before I'll ever bed with you
> And lie next to the wall.

She went on with the rest, not stopping to talk any more. About how the man says that's easy, and he answers her riddle. But then she asks him questions six—six more questions—that is, six more big jobs for him that he could never do without knowing the answers. But that lucky fellow, he knew the answer to every one, and so Aunt Lou went on to the end—

> This couple they got married,
> So why not you and I?

Aunt Lou was thoughtful when she finished. "Seems like thar's a verse left out. Somethin' I cain't quite remember the words for it, but only the sense. But I'm shore that he stold her away. Grabbed her and put her on the horse, before she started axin' him questions." She was humming the tune under her breath, trying to remember.

"That's right, Aunt Lou." Cissie was looking at her encouragingly. "He did carry her off. It's a bride-stealin' ballad. Sing that part, too."

"No, I jest plain cain't remember that part. But she was a clever gal, and that's the way to manage a man. Ax him some hard questions. Give him some hard jobs. Hear that, Katie May? Air ye listenin', Mary Lou, and you gals? Make your sweethearts work for you. See if they're any good. Like Miss Cissie is makin' this-here Danny-boy work for her. I bet she can ax him some hard questions."

The little girls were giggling and whispering. The boys were looking hacked, trying not to seem interested. Cissie was busy with her list, pretending not to notice.

"You are gittin' mighty personal, Aunt Lou," I said. "Now if I was like that Captain Weatherburn, and knowed the answers ahead o'time—"

"You better know 'em," she said. "If you don't know, you better study in yore head and l'arn 'em. She is a clever gal, but don't you let her fool you. Don't let nobody steal her away."

"Don't you want to sing another ballad, Aunt Lou?" asked Cissie, very pointed. "Then I'll play back some of it."

"That's edzackly what I mean to do," went on Aunt Lou. "But hit's in my thought to speak a warnin' to these triflin' granddaughters o'mine. They ain't really triflin', they air smart as any, but the school, hit makes 'em triflin', and their Ma's air ever too busy at jobs to tell 'em what a woman ought to know. Now, gals, you hear me. You open them lazy ears."

Aunt Lou picked up her stick and rapped it on the floor. "Come here to me, Mary Lou. Come here, Katie May." The two girls in jeans and slacks came obediently and sat on the floor in front of Aunt Lou. They had stopped giggling, and looked close at Aunt Lou with their big hazel eyes that were much like hers, but they had their blonde hair in horsetails not like any way Aunt Lou ever fixed her hair. "And you littlest ones, too. You might as well start l'arnin' even if you don't understand." Others came, in all sizes, and Aunt Lou had a regular congregation of young females on the floor in front of her chair.

"I ain't worried about the boys. They can fight their way out of trouble. Or go to court. But it's different with a woman.

"Now you pretty gals—hold on a minute." Aunt Lou turned and looked at the machine. "You ain't puttin' this on that machine, air you, Cissie. Hit's jest all in the family."

"Oh, no, Aunt Lou. It's turned off." Cissie had her ballad checklist out still and was trying not to look distressed. I knew she was wondering how she would get Aunt Lou back on the ballad track again.

"Well, no tricks now. I'll sing some more in a minute. We got all day, hain't we?"

"No tricks, Aunt Lou. I'll just sit and listen."

And she sat down on the floor herself and put her arm around one of the youngest, a little blue-eyed thing with a curly head.

"Now all you pretty gals," continued Aunt Lou. "Take warnin'. That is to say—beware. You all get to ketch a husband some time, and I know you will, for thar never was nary Watkins gal that failed with the men, far as I kin remember, and I kin remember far back. But I'm tellin' you like I've told all the rest before you—beware. Beware and beware. You don't need to let him know it, but beware jest the same. Beware and beware, but most of all beware of a fair-spoken man. I don't mean to say to hold it ag'in him that he's a fair-spoken man, if he's solid besides. But if he's fair-spoken and not much else—Beware."

Aunt Lou suddenly pointed her stick at Mary Lou and Katie May.

"Now thar was little Omie Wise? What happened to her? Tell me."

The two older girls looked at the floor. There was silence.

"Speak up," said Aunt Lou. "Don't tell me you don't know. You are jest ashamed to say."

Finally the little blue-eyed curlyhead piped up. "She got drownded." And laughed out loud. And they all laughed.

"'Taint much to laugh about," said Aunt Lou, and pounded her stick. "And tell me, honey, how Omie Wise got drownded."

"She promised to meet him at the spring," said the little one, "because he promised her money and fine things." She was almost singing it. "And they got on a horse, and away to Deep River did ride. And he *throwed* her off the horse, and she drownded in Deep River."

"That's right, Annie, honey," said Aunt Lou. "And what kind of a man was he, that man?"

Little Annie shouted the answer: "He was a fair-spoken man, he was."

"And what ought Little Omie to ha' done, before she got on ary horse with that fair-spoken man."

"She ought to BEWARE," Annie sang out in a high scream. The girls laughed, the dogs barked, the boys looked sheepish, and Aunt Lou laughed and shouted loudest of all.

"That's hit! Beware! You ought to be ashamed to let Annie remind you. And now let's git the bad taste of it out of our mouths. Roscoe, bring your fiddle. States Rights, where's your banjo? Let's give Cissie some real music to put on that machine."

But Virgie, the young woman with the baby, who had left us and returned once or twice before, now came to the door.

"Some of these girls got to help put on the dinner," she said. "It's nigh ready."

"Hit can wait five minutes," said Aunt Lou. "Turn on that machine, and we'll knock some music into it."

Cissie was at the machine, shaking her head mournfully at me, and winking at the same time, while there was a great scampering around, and Aunt Lou began to dip snuff, not in the nasty white trash way of pouring it from the can into the lower lip, but in the old genteel way of dipping with a little soft twig brush and rubbing it very carefully into her gums.

"You got to help me get her away from the crowd," Cissie whispered. "Else I'll never get her ballads. Can't you draw 'em off somehow?"

"If I'm still able to walk, after dinner," I whispered back. "Can't you smell that ham? And I think fried chicken too."

But States Rights was already plunking with his banjo, and fiddle-scraping Roscoe was coming in with "Leather Breeches." Two of the other boys were shuffling into a breakdown in a far corner of the porch, and the little girls were patting their feet and reaching for partners. The smell of fried ham was coming stronger every minute, but it looked like that crowd would rather dance than eat.

Aunt Lou stomped to the edge of the porch and spat over the railing. She wiped her mouth with her handkerchief and shouted, "Hold thar a second. I forgot. Play my song-ballit, Cissie. I want to hear some noble thing before I set down to my dinner."

So the shiny machine, the neat reels turning slow, gave back the old song, while Aunt Lou stood square in front of it, watching it suspicious-like, both her gnarled hands resting on the crook of her stick. I couldn't tell how she was taking it, except that her knuckles whitened as she gripped her stick. It was a good recording, but Aunt Lou's husky voice was bolder, not soft like Mrs. Parsons' voice, and what you noticed most in the song was how Aunt Lou was having a good time with the story, especially the part about lying in bed next to the wall.

When the song came to the part about "a cherry without a stone," Cissie began to hum the tune with the machine, and the others picked it up with her, while she turned up the volume, and soon all were singing together, the littlest with the biggest, and it carried me away too till I was telling the mountains about it with the rest of 'em, not thinking any more but just singing. And Aunt Lou was nodding her head and patting her foot, with her head bowed over.

"Hit's the world's wonder," she said, and laughed faintly, when the tape had run. "Jest to think thet all I could remember of singin' and tellin' back through the years—thet Cissie could take it and put it on thet little string." She was quiet for a second, then made the regular comment. "And hit's almost like listenin' to the radio in town, ain't it? But—" she went on rapidly—"it put me to thinkin' about my man Jim Watkins, and how he come ridin' through the woods and out into the brushy pasture one mornin' when I was out lookin' for Old Sukie that was always strayin' off. And took me up behind him to save my feet from the dew, he said. And that was after his first wife died, and the first time I ever seed him."

"Was he a fair-spoken man, Granny?" said a boy's voice, speaking sly.

"You hush, States Rights! If Jim Watkins hadn't rid through that pasture, thar's some of you wouldn't be here today."

Aunt Lou brandished her stick at States Rights. "Never mind. Let's change the tune. You gals start up and sing once before we go in to dinner. Sing about the kind o' man you're a-goin' to marry. Come in on the fiddle and banjo, boys. Come on—I would not marry a blacksmith—"

They picked it up and sang, very lively, and I knew Cissie would be turning the switch again.

> I would not marry a blacksmith,
> He smuts his nose and chin.

And on the chorus—

> Soldier boy, soldier boy,
> Soldier boy for me.
> If ever I get married,
> A soldier's wife I'll be.

Soon we were at the long dinner table, where there was room for nearly all except the smallest children, who had to wait; and where everything in the house there was to cook had been cooked and put on: fried ham and chicken, string beans with onions, early peas, black-eyed peas from the dried stock, hot biscuit and hot cornbread, pear preserves and blackberry jam in covered glass dishes, buttermilk and iced tea to drink, two or three kinds of dessert, all of which you had to try—chess pie, peach pie, pound cake—a regular old-fashioned country dinner, with Aunt Lou at the head of the table, talking all the time and yet watching to see that the girls kept our plates full.

When I staggered away from the table, and while Aunt Lou was busy commanding the clearing of dishes, Cissie came at me again with her whispering.

"You got to toll 'em off, somehow, Danny. I can't afford to lose the rest of the day with talkin'. Do your part, now."

I was full as a tick and hardly able to think, but my eye fell on States Rights, who was hanging around sort of pitiful, with his banjo tucked under his arm.

"Come on, boy," I said. "Come on, the rest of you. Let's git off under the locusts and try some new chords on that banjo."

They joined me with a whoop, and I tolled them off into the barn lot, where the noise wouldn't carry on to the porch, and for the rest of the afternoon I kept most of them away from Cissie, fighting off my sleepy feeling and going crazy thinking up tunes, stunts, songs, and games. I turned myself into a babysitter, a gal-nurse, a boy-hero, and a playground supervisor, all rolled into one. We worked on the banjo, and we worked on the fiddle. We walked to the spring and back, looked for eggs, and upset the setting hens. Then we played games—games I hadn't played since I was in school: foot-and-a-half with the boys till my back and legs ached from jumping and I hoped I wasn't ruptured; mumble-peg and jacks and marbles when I got too tired to run; Chick-o-My-Craney-Crow, Club-fist, Fox and Geese, Old Mother Hobble-Gobble, Here Come Three Dukes A-Riding, and I don't know what else.

The big question was whether my memory checklist of games, riddles, and hillbilly radio songs would outlast Cissie's ballad checklist. Come to the lean shank of the afternoon, I was flibbity as a dishrag. Just as I was about to give up hope and sing 'em "Rockaby, Baby," I heard Cissie calling me from the corner of the front yard. And I joined her there.

"Is it three hundred ballads in your book? Or is it three thousand?"

She was fingering the blooms of the red rambler roses that were growing along Aunt Lou's picket fence and looked pleased and satisfied as if she had a million dollars in the bank.

"You were wonderful to help me, Danny. I couldn't have done it without you."

"I can't put in many days like this."

"It has been a day, hasn't it? But here's somethin' to remember it by."

I felt her fingers pressing mine, and what she left in my hand was a red rosebud. She gave me one quick sidelong look and ran to the porch.

Aunt Lou was still in her chair, and still in good humor, but she looked tired. "I'm as empty of songs as a straw stack is of wheat," she said. "That gal has done run me through the thrasher."

But she got up, to tell us goodby, and began to talk again. She walked down the steps with us, still talking, and halfway to the front gate, before we could make our break. Then she made us wait until she could call up States Rights and Roscoe from the barn and order them to help me carry the machine and battery down the hill.

I let them start. We walked down the road in the level afternoon light. There was not a cloud in the sky. We walked in the shell tracks, Cissie in one, I in the other, the two boys behind us, and dogs all around. I was over the tired feeling and beginning to think about crossing the ford again, and how it would be if I could just get rid of the boys. I hoped nobody had come along and picked my boots out of the bushes. There was a summer smell of clover and dust, and it was a lightsome thing to see Cissie stepping along, pulling a long grass stem now and then, or a daisy flower.

When we came into the cool of the woods, I thanked the boys kindly and told them goodby—I could do the rest of the totin'. They seemed surprised and a little stubborn, but I sort of urged my goodbys on them. Finally they got the point, whistled to the dogs, and set off. We watched them moving into the shadows, waving one more goodby.

One old hound dog was slow in following them. He stood in the middle of the road, watching us out of yellow eyes, nose up, sniffing the air.

"Go along, feller," I said to the dog. "Go home, git!"

The big dog didn't budge. The hair begun to rise along his backbone. He growled a little.

"That dog is suspicious of somethin'," I said. "I wonder if there's a varmint around." I picked up a rock.

"He's suspicious of a wildcat varmint named Danny," said Cissie. "And so am I!"

I was so surprised, I threw the rock before I thought. The old hound gave one woof and then a yelp as he loped off.

I turned, and Cissie was laughing quietly. "Three's a crowd even if it's a pore ol' houn' dog," she said, and came nearer to me. Through the cool afternoon shadows we walked down to the ford, and crossed over the way we had come, me with Cissie in my arms and nobody but the birds to see.

8

BUCK KENNEDY AND THE BALLAD ABOUT THE NAKED WOMAN

That was how we got started on the ballad collecting, in the hottest part of June, and the weather coming on drier every day. After the first few tries, Cissie improved her technique and learned better how to creep up on the right side of the singing folks, and feel her way along into whatever they had to give her. She didn't memorize her ballad checklist, exactly, but she knew it well enough to keep it in her purse until she got a singer started and full willing to go the route. Sometimes she wouldn't even bring in the machine at first, but would just leave it in the car until we had passed the time of day and worked the talk around to the right place. And she just about entirely gave up any set spiel about conserving natural resources and preserving the oral tradition and that sort of college talk.

And she took pity on me, and borrowed the college machine, that works on AC, to use wherever they had electricity in the house. That helped, but even so, there was plenty of sweat and plenty of trouble. The battery for her own machine was always running down; and I had to rig up a connection for recharging it with the car motor when we were off in the far hills and had a long day of recording. Those were the days when I worked hardest at fetching and carrying, up and down hill, and splicing tape when we had breaks, and recharging. Other times it was easier. I just parked in the shade while Cissie went in alone, and maybe read one of Cissie's books a little, or just dozed and dreamed, till she came back.

It was more and more a surprise to me how many of our old songs had already been printed, but Cissie kept insisting that it didn't make a whit of difference, there were plenty that hadn't been printed since our foreparents first came to the country; and that was her thesis, just to set them down, transcribing tune and words from the tape, just like she found them, and no matter if they were only a little different from what had been printed.

I could sing a good lot of 'em myself, but it was not my singing that Cissie wanted. "I can get your songs any time," she said. "Besides, you don't know many that I don't know. We learned them together, didn't we?" And when it came to practicing for Rufus, she wouldn't stand for more than a lick and a promise, maybe only a half an hour before we joined up with the Turkey Hollow Boys, on the days when she was due to sing. Nor would she stay, very much, for any of our little jam sessions and practices—not any more than she could help doing, and still draw her pay from Rufus. "The fiddle tunes are all right," she would say. "But I can't take much of that tacky cowboy stuff. And the steel guitar just naturally sets my teeth on edge. Besides, I've got to work on my thesis. I've got to bear down on the real folk songs, and the transcribing and annotation and collation." So she would slip away, making up a nice smile for Rufus, and never failing to whisper me some second and third reminders to pick her up after breakfast for the next jaunt into the hills. It made many a long day for me, but all I could do was hope for the best, and lay low.

All the same, it was right amazing, the way she could stir the old folks up to sing. She would stand there with a little white hand fluttering over the knobs and switches, cut her eyes around, cock her head on one side, and smile as sweet as sugar pie, and say:

"Mr. Bobo, I'd just love to hear that song you know about the old man from the northern sea. Tillie told me you used to sing it for her when she was little. I want to get it on this machine so a lot more folks can hear it and learn it."

And Tillie, the granddaughter, would be a-standing around somewhere close by, all lipsticked and frizzly-headed, trying to decide whether to look ashamed or pleased, and his old woman would take a dip of snuff and look like nothing at all. The old fellow would clear his throat and gaze up from his rocking chair like a dying calf. And Cissie would say:

"Just hold this in your hand while you sing." And she would give him the little portable mike and fold his old brown hairy fingers around it. "Danny and I are ready when you are. You know how it begins, 'There was an old man by the northern sea, Bow-ee down.'"

Then she would smile again, and tuck in a lock of hair, absent-minded-like, around her pretty little ear. And before he knew it, the old fellow would be singing, shaky-like at first, but getting stronger all the time, as if something warmed up inside when she touched him, and with his eyes rolled up towards Cissie like he wished he was young again.

Afterwards, she would always play some of the recording back to them. They were pleased with that as a sick kitten setting up to a hot brick, and it generally ended up with somebody asking if she was going to play the song on the radio, and if she did they wanted to be sure and hear it somewhere. That was always a hard one for Cissie to handle, and it gave me the dry grins to hear her try. She would laugh and begin to talk fast and promise to let them know if that ever happened, and pretty soon would give me the sign to pick up the machine and go.

As the days went on, it began to get more wearisome, yet I didn't really mind, long as Cissie was taking songs from old withered-up farmers like Tom Bobo, or the old grannies, or the girls at the Mountain Weavers Craft Shop, or folks like that. Sometimes I felt sorry for her, too, like when she tried to get ballads from the retired school-teacher woman who wanted to play accompaniments on her old piano; or when she ran into religious folks that thought it was a sin to sing ballads; or the young crowd that only wanted to pick and sing, hillbilly radio style, and asked her where they could get a second-hand steel guitar, real cheap.

That was all a part of ballad-chasing, I found out. I could stand it if Cissie could—and she could. But when she finally got around to Buck Kennedy, that was different. I was troubled in my mind, and I had a right to be.

Now I won't deny that Buck Kennedy knows as many of the old songs as the next man, and maybe more, as Cissie claimed. And he sings 'em in a rousing way, even if it is a sort of a bull-bellowing bass. My worry was, I knew too much about Buck Kennedy. I remembered how he had been all roundabout the world too much, in too many kinds of rough places. His raising was none too good to start with, though his Ma was a church member and I know she died in the arms of Jesus. But Buck was just a gangling young sprout when she died; and when the old man married again, Buck soon fell out with his stepmother and his Pappy, and he left home.

Some say Buck ran off with Ringling Brothers Circus. Others say it was some cheap street carnival show. I don't know about that. But I do know for positive that he worked a spell for Goodyear, up in Akron, Ohio, because Ike Summers told me he saw Buck there when he went to Akron with some other boys from the neighborhood. He said Buck was making a lot of money at tire building—and throwing it away as fast as he made it, if I know him. He didn't come back to the house in Beaver Valley till his old pappy died, about ten years ago. Then he started to live on the old Kennedy place, all by himself at first. There was nobody left in the family, not around here anyhow. Buck raised a little corn and some hogs, and I expect he might have done something else with the corn than feed it all to the hogs. He never married. Finally his sister Ola came to keep house for him, for a while, after her husband died. Buck could have married, ten times over, for he was always a handsome man, and no woman ever found it easy to turn her back on him. But Buck is the kind of man to go after a good time—and then shy off. So no woman ever quite hooked him. The older Buck got, the more it seemed he liked the young girls. Went to all the dances and parties and made a point of honeying up to the prettiest one, and most especially when he thought he could take her away from some young feller who was hot in love with her. The big wonder was how the pretty girls fell for Buck, every time, even though they knew he was just about as rundown as the old Kennedy hill-farm, and no telling what he would be up to next.

Cissie knew Buck's reputation as well as I did, but when she goes out a-hunting songs, Cissie don't hold back for reputations. Fact is, I soon found out, Cissie would walk right into the jailhouse and get a song from some popeyed old drunkard just as quick as she would from a gospel preacher. I almost think she would rather seek out the old drunkard. That's what the professors taught her, I reckon.

"What do I care how mean they are?" Cissie would say. "If they know any ballads, I'm a-goin' to have 'em. You explain to me, Danny MacGregor, how it is that the meanest ones know the best songs."

"Am I one of the meanest, then?" I would answer. "I know some right good songs."

"Hush up, Danny," she would say. "Hush up and come on. And as for Buck Kennedy, I can handle him. You can worry about his reputation. What I want is his songs and I aim to have 'em."

"Well, Cissie," I told her, "it's a good thing you'll have me to go along and watch Buck's reputation. I still have time to do it, before Rufus starts our swing into South Carolina. But—"

I stopped and scratched my head because I had a sudden idea, and yet for some reason was almost afraid to spring it.

"But what? Don't start holdin' out on me."

I knew she would worm it out of me, sooner or later, so I let her have it. "I don't see why you keep traipsin' around to all these people. Takes too much time, and wears you out, and I can't go around with you the whole endurin' summer. Why don't you make 'em come to you? Record 'em at your house, where you can be comfortable. Or at the college. It would be safer, too. And they would like it."

Cissie looked me over, to see if I was up to tricks. It was a pretty cool look, and what she said was like figuring on paper. "It's an idea. You do have ideas sometimes, Danny. I'll think about it. For it is true I've got to start teachin' soon. And I'll have less time for travelin', with Dr. Hoodenpyl away."

So right about the last of June, after I had stepped out of Ed Cooley's chair, for that was the very day, and after I'd gone my rounds thinking all the while, as Ed Cooley had said, about taking my punishment, I met Cissie as usual, and we left Carolina City and the hot asphalt behind, and we were on our way to the old Kennedy place, following the old creek road in the sultry afternoon, way up in Beaver Valley. We passed the old Timberlake place, all growing up in sage grass and brush, and my Pa's old house, which was even worse, and saw the government signs that marked the boundaries and the surveyors' stakes that marked where the new highway would take the front off both places and leave 'em perched on a clay bank. Neither one of us wanted to stop. It was better just to keep moving on the creek road.

After we had crossed the creek road four or five times, over the rickety old bridges, and moved up in the deep shade, hairpin turn after hairpin turn, skidding around on the gravel, and high up, we came to the forks of the creek where you have to cross and take the steep branch road to the Kennedy place. There was grass growing on the turn to the bridge. That road hadn't been used much of late, I could see. I stopped the car and went to look at the bridge. There was a litter of dead sycamore boughs and twigs on the approach to the bridge and on the bridge itself. The cross planks of the bridge were rotting out, and even the big planks on the wheel track didn't look good. To my right I could see auto tracks going down the bank to the ford; but the ford looked deep. I went back to the car and spoke my piece.

"Cissie," I said, "I think we better walk the rest even if I do strain my shoulders once more with that machine."

She began to frown, and I added, right quick, "We can walk the bridge. You follow me."

So I led, and we walked the bridge, stepping carefully on the main sills. It seem like nearly a quarter of a mile up the hollow to the Kennedy place, and every step of it was work for me.

The house is nothing but an old log house that old man Kennedy started to weatherboard over, a long time ago. He never got beyond the front side and one end, and he never painted the weatherboarding. Buck closed in the dog-run and built a porch on the front, which is the high side of the house and faces southwest, looking down the hollow.

Time we got up the slope to the front gate, the machine and battery set were really dragging my shoulder sockets.

"Isn't it a wonderful view Mr. Kennedy has?" Cissie remarked, right when I was in the middle of my sweating.

It is a wonderful view, all right, once you get up a ways from the bridge. The house sets on a knob, with its back to the ridge. You can look out along

Beaver Valley and see the Cowee and Fishhawk Mountains and many more all day long—if you are a Kennedy. But I was no kind of Kennedy, and in no kind of humor for scenery.

"No better'n at my place." I slung the words at Cissie, who was ahead of me and up to her knees in grass and rabbit tobacco. "And you don't have to scratch for fleas when you sit on my front porch."

Right then Buck's dogs caught wind of us and ran out from behind the house, barking their heads off. Buck come to the door and whistled 'em back, but just as if to spite him, that old yellow bitch of his led the pack under the porch and chased out a couple of shoats that had been lying there in the cool.

"Git ready to scratch," I called out.

"Shame on you," said Cissie. "Here comes Mr. Kennedy."

Yes, she called him *Mister* Kennedy. And it was Buck all right, stepping right to her down the walk and making out as if he couldn't hear the squealing of the shoats and the yapping of the dogs.

"How about gittin' the squeal on the machine while you are here?" I asked her, and it was the *Mistering* made me do it. "And Buck's hog calls and dog calls? This is your chance."

"You shut up—before I mash your mouth," Cissie flung back at me, forgetting her college manners, but under her breath because Buck was right at hand.

He was slicked up, more than I had ever seen him. Shoes blacked, clean shirt and tie, even had a haircut and shave. I'll have to admit Buck made a right handsome figure of a man, stepping out bold in the June sun, with his hair turning a little gray above his bright black eyes and a face like a politician's above his broad shoulders. Looked like he belonged in Congress, more than Carlos B. Reddy. Handsome sure enough if you didn't notice the veins in the big nose and the bushy eyebrows and forget that forty-some-odd beltline.

"Good evenin', Miss Timberlake," said he, polite as a picture. "Come right up on the porch. I been expectin' you."

"Howdy, Buck," I said.

He hardly more than nodded me a quick glare. "I see you have a helper. If I'd a-knowed you had all that heavy stuff, I'd a-met you at the crossroads with my jeep."

So that's it, I told myself. I bet he's a-making it and a-running it out in a jeep. I squinted across the barn lot, and there was the jeep. I could see the back end of it, over by the log corncrib.

Buck took Cissie by the arm and helped her up the porch steps, paying no more attention to me than if I'd been a baggage porter. It fretted me, just to be around him, but I had no grounds for argument. So I sweated up the steps behind 'em, meek as Jesus, and bound not to let him know how I felt, though I could guess right away what was in his head. I set up the equipment on an old kitchen table he had out there, and we tested the machine, and pretty soon Cissie was going to it in the regular way without losing much time on politeness.

Twenty times or more I had been through it all, and I had heard the old songs sung into the machine so much that I'd almost begun to get weary on the job. Besides, I kept telling myself, I know most of the ballad songs better than the broken-down old folks—anyway, as well as Buck Kennedy did. Of course no two people ever sing 'em exactly the same. They know a few words different here, and they forget some other words there. Sometimes they leave out whole verses or maybe sing different verses. The bother about my listening was that I was always filling in to myself, when they forgot, or saying over in my mind what I knew that was different.

So it was a pain, like when you listen to a preacher reading out of the Bible, and he can't pronounce the hard words, and you want to speak up and help him but you can't because you are a-settin' there on a bench in a starched collar and have to remember you are a sinner and keep quiet. I would try not to pay too much attention while the recording was going on. At the same time I had to look interested and make up a face, because Cissie was as hot about the ballad songs as a coon dog on the trail, and just as crazy to record "Barbary Ellen" the twentieth time as she was the first, even if it was the same old cruel "Barbara Allen" with only a few words changed.

Yet when Buck Kennedy started singing, I own up that I didn't have to strain and pretend. I always listen hard when a real good singer is rocking along with a good tune and making it ring—and making the story come out clear, the way it ought. Buck was doing just that. He truly surprised me, though he sung too loud most of the time.

All the time, Cissie was smiling and looking pleased, full of compliments too, and patting her foot softly on the old strip of carpet, there on the porch, while Buck ripped along through all the common things like "The Miller's Two Daughters" and "The Hangman's Tree" and "The Brown Girl"—and "Barbary Ellen" of course, which he sung very pretty in his bass voice, and looked at Cissie mighty hard, too, like he might have some notion of playing Jimmy Grove himself and dying for love. I watched him close, every minute I wasn't changing the reels or mending tape.

Cissie had her checklist, there on the table. She didn't need to look at it, hardly, but just called off what she wanted under the different names. She went back over the first part of it to be sure she wasn't missing anything.

"Do you sing 'Lady Isabel and the Elf Knight'?" she asked Buck. Then, over her shoulder to me, " 'Child Number 4,' you remember, Danny!" That was just to show off and set me back. She knew I couldn't remember the numbers of 'em even though I had been reading in her book now and then.

"Whose child did you say?" asked Buck. He hadn't seen the inside of a book, I reckon, since he quit school at the fourth grade or whenever it was.

"Never mind," said Cissie. "Maybe you know it under a different name. Do you know 'Pretty Polly'?" Buck said he did, and started singing, but it wasn't the right one.

Cissie tried him on "Saltwater Sea" and a few other names, but still he couldn't remember. So she began with her trick of telling a little of the story. "You must know it, Mr. Kennedy. The one where the girl steals her father's horse to run off with a man, and they ride till they come to the sea, and he tries to kill her—"

"Oh, yes," says Buck, opening his black eyes wide and sitting up straight. Then he squinched his eyes and gave Cissie a sly sideways look. "Oh, yes. That's whut I call 'Six King's Daughters.' But it ain't a nice kind of song. Are you sure you want me to sing it into yore machine?"

"I sure do, Mr. Kennedy. It may not be very nice in some parts, but it's a real old song, and I want it for my collection."

"Well, I think I know it. But I better go and look in Maw's old shoebox and see if there's a ballit wrote out. I might not be sartain of some verses."

Buck went into the house and stayed a considerable spell. While he was gone, Cissie got out her notebook and began to write in it. I had noticed she was beginning to get restless. She reached for her ankles now and then, and she kept squirming around in that old split-bottom chair. I knew what was after her. The same as was after me. I blew cigarette smoke at the ceiling and said nothing.

When Buck came out again, he had the old shoebox in one hand and a Flit gun in the other. His eyes were a brighter black, and as soon as he got near, I knew he had tuck time to wet his whistle.

Cissie grabbed the shoebox right away. It was full of old paper, wrote in pencil. "Oh, what a treasure, Mr. Kennedy! May I look over these?"

"My Maw, she wrote 'em out," said Buck. "She was a singin' woman, and always writin' 'em down. Excuse me while I shoot some of this around yore feet. They don't bother me much, anymore, but I keep this handy for visitors."

He sprayed all around our feet and over the strip of carpet and sat down by the mike again. He looked through some of the ballads with Cissie and took one of them out to sing from. But as soon as he started to sing he laid it down on the bale. Cissie picked it up and followed him from the paper.

Buck sung along right well through all the part where the girl took one of the horses thirty-and-three and they rode off, the man on a brownie bay and girl on a dappled gray, because the man had promised to take her to bonnie Scotland and marry her. They rode through the lonesome woods till they came to the deep blue sea—and Buck was right with 'em, all the time. But when he came to the next part, Buck began to hesitate—the verse, you know, where this man, who was a robber man, tells the lady to take off her clothes:

> Take off, take off those fine clothing,
> Take off, take off, said he,
> For they are too costly and too fine
> To be rotted in the sea.

Cissie didn't move a muscle. She kept on reading the paper ballad. I blew smoke at the ceiling and watched Buck. Buck darted his eyes at Cissie, to see how she was taking it, then stared right into the mike and went on singing, kind of too careful, what the lady says to the robber:

> Oh, turn your body round and about
> And view the leaves on the tree,
> For it is not fitten a villain like you—

Then he sort of swallowed for a second and ended the verse:

> A pretty woman to see.

Buck didn't stumble any more. He went through the rest at a gallop, about how she seized him tight in her arms so white and drownded him in the sea, and rode back home. He got through quick, as if he was glad to be shut of the whole thing.

Cissie was blushing up to her hair, but she didn't flinch. She was bound to be scholar, which was a mistake if she was around old Buck Kennedy, but she let him have it all the same.

"Mr. Kennedy, there was one part you didn't sing the way it is in your Mother's ballad sheet. See here!" She put her finger on the place, and I knew what place it was.

I reckon it was a real surprise to Buck Kennedy, but he didn't take it in a good spirit. He put the wrong meaning on it, and me right by him all the time. The liquor was working on him—the liquor and Cissie's finger pointing to the words.

"Shore enough," he says, bobbing his head up and down too many times. "That is Maw's handritin', and I can read it: 'It is not—fitten—a villain—like you,—A *naked* woman—to see.' Want me to sing it over again?"

Derned if he didn't have the impudence to wink, a sort of halfway wink, anyhow. Still, I held back. I might have just thought he was winking, I told myself.

"No, we won't make another recording, this time," Cissie said. "But if *naked woman* is what you remember, that's what you ought to sing. I'll make the change in my transcription." She wrote something in her notebook.

" 'Pretty woman' is right," I put in. I couldn't stand it no longer. For though I knew naked woman was right, it never would do to encourage Buck Kennedy to go around singing about naked women. " 'Pretty woman' is what I remember. That's what my own Granny taught me."

I was lying, but I aimed to do all I could to stave off trouble. Cissie wouldn't even look at me. She acted as if she didn't hear me, and grabbed up her book.

"Look here, Mr. Kennedy." She leafed over some pages. "Here it is in an old Scottish version of your song. Just the same as in your Mother's ballad sheet."

Then she read it right out of the book to him, like she would read a newspaper story. And Buck Kennedy laid his finger to the side of his big nose and tucked the thumb of the other hand under his suspenders and looked as devilish as he really is.

"Well, ma'am," said old Buck Kennedy. "I was jest wantin' to be polite to the ladies. Course I know the old folks back yander didn't make no bones about singin' out sech things, but I thought now that we have Sunday School ever' week, and settlement work down yander in the cove, us rough fellers ought to take keer about our language in public. But if it kin be printed in a book, then I reckon it kin be sung for all to hear."

"I would be very dishonest if I didn't record the old songs exactly as they are remembered. Every single word," said Cissie. "Now wouldn't I?"

"Yes'm, Miss Timberlake. You shore would. And if you wants sech honest old songs, I know a lot more. Let me see. There's 'Little Scotchy'—that's a rare un. And 'Little Matty Grew,' and—"

I don't know how long it would have gone on, with me a-setting there, itching where the fleas were crawling up my pants leg, and burning inside to think how my poor foolish Cissie was leading Buck Kennedy on to devilment. But the fleas were beginning to get a little limp and dizzy with the DDT or whatever was in that spray. They had begun to come out for fresh air. I saw one drop off my shoe top onto the carpet, hopping rather weak. Then I saw one crawl right out from under the hem of Cissie's skirt, just below her knee. I could see it plain ag'inst her stocking—a big old fat hog flea, sort of gasping, just barely holding on. And Buck Kennedy had his black eyes on the same spot. Before I could knock his hand away, he reached right over, said "Excuse me," and picked that flea right off Cissie's leg, cracked him with his nail, and threw him over the porch railing, all in one motion, as if he had well practiced.

Next thing, I had my fist one inch from Buck's nose.

"Cissie and me will thank you, Mister Buck Kennedy, to keep your hands to yourself. Crack your own damn fleas if you want to crack fleas."

But Cissie was down on me with her coldest, most schoolteachery voice.

"Cissie will thank you, Mr. MacGregor, to sit down, and let us finish the recording."

Buck Kennedy laughed in my face. I thought his full red lips, drawn back over his crooked white teeth, were the sorriest sight I ever saw. But I didn't hit him. And I didn't sit down either.

"The sun is gittin' low," I said, not daring to look at either Cissie or Buck Kennedy. "We better leave this place." Then I took the bull by the horns and just plain began to close up the machine.

Cissie didn't object, after all. "Will you let me take the shoebox with me, to copy your texts, Mr. Kennedy?" she asked him.

I didn't mind that. But the next thing Cissie said nearly killed me. She was taking the words right out of my own mouth, and me a big fool to have thought of 'em.

"And since Danny is so uncomfortable on these trips, and so busy with the radio and all, I wonder if you would mind coming to my house some time and letting me record the rest of your songs? You sing them so well, Mr. Kennedy."

Buck was willing as a hog at the trough. "You kin have my Maw's texts to keep if you want 'em," he said. "And I'll be tickled to death to come to yore house. Any time you say. I have my jeep."

That was it. He had his jeep. Next thing I knew, Buck was offering to take Cissie across the ford, and she was all smiles about it. While I was wrastling with the equipment, Buck brought the jeep around to the steps. He helped Cissie into the front seat before you could say scat, resting his hand on her arm in a way I didn't like. There was nothing for me to do but shove the machine and battery into the back and crawl in with them. And take the bumps, too, down that hill and through the ford, holding on to the seat with one hand and the equipment with the other. If Cissie hadn't been there on the front seat with him, I guess Buck would have tried to tip me out. As it was, I was the one that caught the splash as he ripped through the creek. And while I was reloading the equipment in my car and wiping muddy water off my face, Cissie was giving old Buck Kennedy the sweetest goodbys and thank you's I had heard her give anybody.

But for me, nothing. Not even a thank you. The minute we got on the road again, Cissie had her loose-leaf notebook on her lap and was flipping through it and raving about Buck Kennedy's songs. A perfect example of the true folksinger, she said. The genuine article, unspoiled by civilization. Wonderful Dorian and Mixolydian tunes, and she didn't have anything else in her book as good. A big discovery, he was, and too bad she couldn't get to him sooner, but she could handle that, if she didn't have to work too hard at the college. And it was a good idea, to get Buck Kennedy and some others to come in town for recording. For that idea, when she got around to it, she was, after all, much obliged to me.

I let her talk and swung the car around the hairpin turns fast as it would take them. The tires screamed and the back end skidded some, but I didn't care. The turns were well-banked, and I could see ahead. Cissie shut up her notebook, quit talking, and held on tight.

When we leveled out on the creek road I slowed down and eased the car through the shallow fords.

"Cissie," I asked, "what church do you belong to?"

"Are you tryin' to scare me, Danny? Why do you ask?"

"No matter why. What church?"

"Oh, you know. Methodist, I reckon. I s'pose my letter is still in First Methodist. But I don't know whether I'm a member in good standin'."

"That don't matter. Just so you're not thinkin' about j'inin' the rattlesnake handlers' church."

"No, Danny, don't be a fool, and what are you drivin' at?"

"Well, that's good, I'm shore relieved to know you don't like rattlesnake church. But tell me, what do you think of a travelin' tent preacher named Crossno?"

"Never heard of him, and I don't like tent preachers and revivals."

"That's fine, Cissie. That makes me feel a lot better."

"Danny, you are poutin' about somethin', and don't you be a-talkin' to me that-a-way, in strange tongues."

"I'm not poutin'. I'm jest studyin' in my mind. I'm studyin' punishment, and how much a man has to take from a woman that he—"

I didn't finish the sentence. I just stepped on the clutch and brake a minute and put my eye right on her. Then resumed speed.

100

"A woman that he faithfully promised to help," she filled out, "a pore little ballad collector and ex–hillbilly artist."

"I don't like the 'ex' part. And I wouldn't like it if you told me to pick up an ol' swamp rattler by the gullet and tetch him to my forehead. But if you said so, I reckon I would."

She laughed out loud. "Cheer up, Danny, the worst is over. If I hadn't thought it would do you good as well as me, I never would've asked you in the first place."

Cissie reached across the steering wheel and took my cigarettes out of my lefthand shirt pocket.

"If you want to take somethin' by the gullet, you can practice on Buck Kennedy, for all I care." She lit a cigarette and offered it to me. "Just be downright certain that I get his songs first."

I took the cigarette. But I feared the worst was not over.

And it wasn't.

9

MRS. ECCLES PUTS BUCK KENNEDY ON THE AIR

Out of sight, out of mind, is what the old folks say. But next morning when the Turkey Hollow Boys rolled out of Carolina City, bound for Augusta, Macon, Atlanta, and other points west, I told myself it might work different. An old sack takes a lot of patching! Maybe I was just an old sack to Cissie from being around too much. Anyhow, it was a three-weeks tour, and Rufus was counting on me.

At first it seemed like a relief to be with Rufus and the Boys again, in his Special Cadillac, away from women and trouble. We had good crowds at Augusta—a lot of G.I.'s there. They went wild about "White Roses." But they liked everything we did. And so it went all along the route.

Pickin' and singin' begun to get into my bones again. The guitar and me, we thrummed together, and we begun to think Cissie surely must be wrong. For a while the commercials didn't seem to bother. I stepped over them like puddles. The hillbilly music couldn't be so bad, if all these folks took it so serious and if it all seemed fresh and fine to me once more. I wondered if I had been making my neck too limber, carrying Cissie's yoke. Wouldn't her ballad fever soon be over—like a mule's gallop? But when we had hit the one-night stands for ten or twelve nights running, and had fought the trailer-trucks along the two-lane, winding Georgia roads, I had some other thoughts. When I begun to notice the commercials again, I knew I was on the ragged edge. Working for Rufus? Yes, I was—and for fertilizer firms, drugstores, overall factories, purgatives, cosmetics, dog-biscuit companies, till it wore me out.

I could hear the adding machines clicking underneath my guitar frets.

The only relief I got was in feeding quarters and dimes into the pay telephone to call Cissie three or four times a week. Not that I could get much sweet talk out of her—only how the thesis was moving along and

Mrs. Eccles had some big schemes. But I made a date with her for the Saturday night when we would be back. Or so I thought.

That afternoon, soon as we got in from our Spartanburg broadcast, I called Cissie. Her mother answered.

"I'm glad you're back in town, Danny," she said in her slow, mournful way, as if there'd been a death in the family and she hated to tell me. Mrs. Timberlake mostly talks like that.

"If you're a-callin' Cissie," she went on, "it's jest too bad. Cissie's at the beauty shop. She jest left five minutes ago. She's havin' her hair set."

Mrs. Timberlake made it sound like Cissie had been taken off in an ambulance, and all the friends and relatives had better gather around if they wanted to hear her last words.

"That's fine," I said. "Then I reckon she's expectin' me tonight after our show is over."

"Ye-es, Da-an-ny," she answered kind o' sad. "Ma-aybe she i-is. Bu-ut you—be-et-ter ta-alk to Cissie about tha-at. The-ese da-ays, she's ri-ight—busy."

I thought it was just Mrs. Timberlake's regular way of talking and nothing out of common. It was already after four o'clock, and we would have to go on the air at six, the first time that Saturday evening, and later on, at 9:30, we'd have the stage in Studio B—the big one. So I decided to step around to Ed Cooley's even if it was Saturday afternoon, and freshen up. It would rest me, and, besides, Rufus won't stand for you to be looking woolly around the ears when he's putting on a stage show. You've got to be dry-cleaned and wet-cleaned, pressed and barbered. So, since time was short, and I didn't have my car, I got the hotel to let me have a room to change, sent my suit out to press, and turned up at Ed's place. Luckily I didn't have to wait long for his chair.

Ed was looking solemn, and there was a wicked cut in his eye. He just said "Hidy" and nothing more till he begun snipping. Then he opened up.

"Been out o' town, ain't you, Danny?"

"Yes, on the Georgia swing, and back home through South Carolina."

"Put on some good shows?"

"Good as ever. You know Rufus."

"Feel like huntin' some, for a change?"

"'Tain't the huntin' season, Ed. You know that."

"Well, for a fact, most folks are out fishin', right now. All the same I thought you might be goin' a-huntin', and take me along. I wouldn't want to miss it."

"Squirrels, you mean?"

"Naw, I thought you and me might git us a buck!"

"Ed, you know there ain't no deer much in these parts. If there was, we'd git arrested for huntin' 'em."

"Well, maybe we would git arrested but I don't think so. Don't a man have a right to hunt a buck if the scoundrel gits into his own garden patch?"

"What are you talkin' about?"

"Don't matter whut I'm talkin' about so much as whut ever' body's talkin' about!"

"Tell me what you mean, Ed, and quit foolin'."

"I mean Cissie and Buck Kennedy, that's whut—hold still, you nearly made me cut your ear."

I nearly jumped out of that barber chair—because, till Ed mentioned him, Buck Kennedy had just about slipped out of my mind. I settled back. "What's goin' on?" I asked Ed. And he told me, while he finished up feather-edging, lathering and shaving.

It was Buck Kennedy's jeep, parked at Cissie's house, three or four days of every week, and sometimes at night. Folks had noticed it, Ed said. The talk of the town was that Buck Kennedy was beating my time with Cissie.

I was worried, but didn't want to let on how much.

"Oh, no, Ed. It's not what you think. Cissie's writin' her thesis. She is jest crazy to git them old songs on her tape recorder. That's all."

In the mirror, straight in front of me, I could see Ed's face. He was frowning. The corners of his mouth were pulled down. And he was holding his razor in the air, behind my back, like he would just as soon scalp me as not.

"Don't git excited, Ed," I told him. "It was my idea in the first place. I told Cissie she better make the singers come to the house. Or else to the college. I couldn't bear for her to be goin' out to Buck Kennedy's house, all alone. But I didn't put it to her quite that p'inted."

Ed reached for his soft brush and began dusting off the loose hair around my neck and face.

"Well, it's your funeral," he said. "And Cissie's. I'd a-thought she knowed about Buck Kennedy."

"She knows, all right. But he can sing a lot of ballad songs, and she's bound to have 'em. That's all there is to it."

"I don't think that's all." Ed sounded like he was gritting his teeth.

"What else, then?"

Ed bent over and put his lips close to my ear.

"Buck's been drivin' Cissie around in his jeep, here, there, and yonder," he said in a low voice. "And she's a-takin' him around to sing for the school-teachers and the children. And even the Kiwanis Club."

I could feel the blood rushing to my face, and a tingle running along my bones. But I said: "Well, what's the harm? And how do you git so much information, anyhow?"

Ed was whispering again. "I don't want to tell you here. You step back into the dressing room and I'll tell you."

"I got to telephone Cissie first."

"All right, you telephone Cissie. You'll find out somethin', I'll bet. Somebody's hat's been on the rack where yore hat ought to be."

He switched off the cloth, and in another minute I had dropped my nickel in the telephone at the back. It was already after five o'clock. This time Cissie answered, and I thought I would melt when I heard her voice.

"Hello, Cissie, I'm all set to take you away from that thesis tonight."

"Danny, I'm so glad you called at last. Mrs. Eccles and Mr. Kennedy are coming out to the house tonight, and—"

"So you forgot our date, Cissie? I wouldn't a-thought it."

"Please, Danny. I didn't really forget, but this new project came up all of a sudden—and how could I get word to you when you were barnstorming around South Carolina? You said you'd call me from Spartanburg—"

I did try to telephone her from Spartanburg, and couldn't get her before we left. But I passed over that and cut right in.

"What new project?"

"Oh, Danny, *dear*. Don't be mad. Buck Kennedy has turned out to be a *great* discovery. Not only the ballads he learned in the mountains, but in all his travels. Mrs. Eccles is strong for him, and Dr. Hoodenpyl says he is the most wonderful discovery he has heard of anywhere. So we have been using Buck in—some experimental concerts. And tonight we are GOING ON THE AIR!"

"What time?"

"Eight o'clock. And the teachers association and the Chamber of Commerce are *both* sponsoring us. That's Mrs. Eccles' work."

"I'll be at your house right after we finish our first broadcast," I told her.

"There won't be much time," Cissie protested. "We'll be rehearsing."

"That's all right. I'll just drop in for a minute."

She didn't refuse, and I hung up the receiver. Before I could turn around Ed had left his customer and was pushing me into the little dark dressing room. "D'ye see now?" he asked. "I know from the look on your face. Didn't I tell you?"

One low-watt bulb hung from the ceiling. The barbers' coats and ties were on a row of hooks. Ed's heavy hand was on my shoulder and he was squeezing hard.

"You see, Danny, hit's serious. You cain't jest brush it off."

"Of course," I said, "the Chamber of Commerce and the teachers association wouldn't know about Buck Kennedy. They are city folks. But you are right. Cissie ought to know better."

"Yes, Danny, you and me know better, too. And so does Wallace Exum."

"You mean the Exum boy that's disk jockey over at WCC? How does he come into this?"

"Don't forget, he's my nephew. My sister Mattie's son. And the Exums are some kin, too. And I don't have any chillun of my own."

I looked at Ed and began to remember things. Ed went on talking quiet, like he was thinking out loud and remembering too.

"Now Wallace is taking some summer courses over at State Teachers College. Usin' his G.I. money, I reckon. And he's in that man Hoodenpyl's ballads course—the one Cissie is helpin' teach and goin' to take over, if she hasn't already done it, while Hoodenpyl goes off to Washington or somewhere. Maybe she told you."

"She mentioned it. Go on, Ed."

"Now I get my dope from Wallace Exum. He's been tellin' me, and I'm tellin' you. Hit's a bad thing for Cissie to have Buck Kennedy messin' around. Hit looks bad, and it *is* bad. But it ain't goin' to be healthy for Buck Kennedy, either, if he keeps turnin' up where he ain't got no business to be. It ain't goin' to be healthy, I'm tellin' you. Cooleys don't have no use for Kennedys, and I reckon you remember why."

Ed took his hand off my shoulder. He turned and spat into the toilet bowl, then faced me again. The veins stood out on his forehead.

"Well, do you remember, or don't ye?" His voice was rough.

I looked Ed right back in the eye. "I remember what my Grandpa told me. And my Pa. No need for you to ask."

"I can remember cl'ar back to my Great-Grandpa," Ed said. "That's when hit started. And hit never has stopped."

I knew what he meant. The Cooleys and the Kennedys were not shooting at one another any more. Not exactly. But they were as far as folks can be from shaking hands, and yet not shoot. The Kennedy that was Buck's Great-Grandpa went over to the Carpetbaggers after the Confederate War. The Cooleys stayed on the Confederate side. And that Kennedy tried to work a slick trick. When the Carpetbag government put the taxes up, and the Cooleys couldn't pay their land tax, this Kennedy bought it for the taxes. Not only bought it but tried to take it. And that was when the war started between the families. The Cooley men took down their guns, and a lot of good folks helped them. Ever since, there had been bad blood, and some killings, back and forth.

"Did your Great-Grandpa go with the Ku Klux—or was it that other crowd? Those Guards, or whatever you call 'em?"

"Well, Danny, I wouldn't never tell ye, if ye wa'n't my best friend. But I'll tell ye. After the first shootin', the Kennedys went and got the soldiers. They burnt our barns, and ever'body else's barns that stood with us. Then my Great-Grandpa went over into Rutherford County and joined the Constitutional Union Guards. But hit don't make no difference. Same thing as Ku Klux—the old Ku Klux."

"Ed," I said, "this is somethin' I got to think about. It will take some thinkin', too, because I don't want no public trouble, and Cissie mixed up in it."

"That's right. We don't want no public trouble. We'll act private."

"I aim to look before I leap."

"Don't you look too long. Can't stop to dig a well if the house ketches fire. But, from what Wallace says, there's a way of fixin' Buck's clock right now, and no harm done to Cissie. He's doin' some business on the side, Buck is. If we can't git at him, the law can."

I nodded, and Ed began to look more cheerful.

"Oh, hell," he said, and laughed, "I ain't goin' to be drawin' a bead on Buck Kennedy tonight. You're a-sweatin' to see yore gal, I know that. So git along. But remember, you've got a new quarrel with Buck, on account of Cissie, and I got an old one. So yore quarrel is my quarrel, and Wallace's too, when you're ready. And I got more to tell you about Buck. You can't trust him."

"I'll be figurin' on what you told me."

"Don't you take too long figurin', or you'll never git a shot. Call up the dogs and light out. That's better than figurin'."

Ed barged through the door to his customer. I highballed to the Piedmont, changed into a fresh shirt and the new-pressed suit, gobbled a sandwich and milkshake, and as soon as our half-hour program was over, grabbed a taxicab and went on out to Cissie's, guitar, big hat, cream-colored pants, and all the fixin's. Sure enough—there was Buck's jeep parked in front of the Timberlake house, and a big new Buick too.

The moon was overhead, and bright as day almost, but with the porch light on, the vines arching over the front steps made a dark lacy pattern against the gray weatherboarding of the wall. I stopped a second at the gate, thinking how Cissie said, right there, the year before, "Danny, don't let me be a sorrow to you!" and I remembered what my Pa used to say, when I was downhearted: "I never tell my sorrow to any coward man, but only to my fiddle. Then I can ride out singing." And a man's voice, inside, was beginning on "Barbara Allen," as I walked softly to the door.

It was airly in the month of May
When green buds, they was swellin',
Poor Jimmy Grove on his deathbed lay
For the love of Barbara Allen.

Mrs. Timberlake let me into the hall. Buck Kennedy's voice was movin'
along with Barbara.

Mother, mother, make my bed,
Oh, make it soft and narrow.
Sweet Jimmie dies for love of me;
I'll die for him tomorrow.

"S-s-s-h!" whispered Mrs. Timberlake, and motioned with her finger.
Though her face is wrinkled some, she is a lot like Cissie, especially in her
way of smiling. She was smiling, yet she was whispering in her usual slow
moan, like somebody grieving for the dead. "They air goin' over the script.
She is a-timin' it once more, before they go to the radio station."

I stepped to the parlor door and peeped in just as Buck finished burying
the lover.

Mrs. Eccles, in her black-rimmed spectacles and a fancy hat, was in the
old Morris chair by the golden oak table, reading from a script. Cissie was
on the piano bench, with another script propped in front of her on the
music rack of the old upright piano. Buck was leaning against the piano,
mopping his face with a blue handkerchief and looking pleased and scared
all at the same time.

"And now, friends of the radio audience," said Mrs. Eccles in a big bold
contralto, "we conclude our first program of ballads and folk songs, given
under the sponsorship of the Morgan County Teachers Association and
the Carolina City Chamber of Commerce. We invite you to listen again
at this same hour next week, when we will offer our second program of
the summer, with Mr. Buck Kennedy of Beaver Valley as our singer. May
I once more remind all of our listeners, as I said at the beginning of this
broadcast, that Miss Cecily Timberlake will be glad to hear from anybody
who knows old songs of the kind Mr. Kennedy has so beautifully sung for us
tonight. Miss Timberlake is making a collection of the ballads and folk songs
of western North Carolina, and I am sure you will want to help her make it
completely representative of our ancient and rich traditions. Send your copy
of the song to Miss Cecily Timberlake—C-e-c-i-l-y, Cecily Timberlake,
care of WCC, or see Miss Timberlake at Dr. Hoodenpyl's office, State
Teachers College. And now, as President of the Western North Carolina

Folklore Society, I wish to thank Miss Timberlake and Mr. Kennedy and bid you all—goodnight."

"Exactly twenty-nine and a half minutes," said Cissie, glancing at her wristwatch. "That'll be just right for the announcer to take over."

"Splendid! Splendid!" said Mrs. Eccles. They all looked at me, and Cissie said, "Mrs. Eccles, this is my friend Mr. Danny MacGregor." And I saw I was about as welcome as a horse doctor at a birthing.

"Why don't you give Buck a good guitar to sing by?" I burst out, kind of ruffled. "He don't stay square on the tune when he gits excited."

Mrs. Eccles stood up, and there must have been a full six feet of her. She put her eye on my guitar, and on my Turkey Hollow costume, head to foot, through the black-rimmed spectacles.

"Barbershop chords, Mr. MacGregor?" she asked, and made up a big smile that I knew was meant to put me in my place. "Barbershop chords? Not for *this* program. This is not hillbilly music, Mr. MacGregor."

She picked up her gloves and purse and put the script in a handsome, light tan, leather grip. With her back to me, Cissie was fixing her lipstick, and Buck was fanning himself with a newspaper, not saying a word. They were all diked out like they might be going to a party, though I could bet it would be just a studio broadcast, with nobody to look at them but the announcer—and me, if they let me in.

Mrs. Eccles corrected me some more.

"Mr. Kennedy's 'Barbara Allen' is a fine Mixolydian tune, very different from the common tunes used for the ballad. I am sure that you, being a musician yourself, would want him to sing it exactly as he remembers it, with all the interesting grace notes and slides and quarter tones. A guitar, as you suggest, would maintain a truer pitch, but then we would lose much of the tone quality of the genuine folk rendering. What we want is the pure ballad."

Echoes bumped back and forth in my head. I rocked on my heels, trying to catch 'em. Maybe Mrs. Eccles had studied it up herself, but to me it was like a big poll-parrot voice repeating Cissie's words.

"I know what you mean, Ma'am," I said—and glanced over at Cissie. She was putting on her hat and wouldn't look at me. Nobody asked me to sit down or to do anything. The black-rimmed spectacles was standing over me, filling the whole room. I made up my mind to talk right into them.

"I was thinkin' about the radio, Mrs. Eccles. They'd drop me mighty quick if I slid off the tune. Besides the guitar helps keep the program lively. Makes it sound like fun, and folks won't turn off the program so quick."

Buck looked like a man that needed a drink, and I guessed maybe he had a pint in his pocket and was looking for a chance to get at it. Cissie had her eyes on him, and I expect she had the same thought I did.

"We better be off," she said. "We better get there a half-hour ahead of time, at least."

Cissie started for the door. Buck come to life and was right after her, squiring her along. I couldn't break in, because Mrs. Eccles was asking me, all of a sudden very polite, if I had my car, and I was saying no, and Mrs. Eccles was offering me a ride. I took the tan-colored grip and held the screen door for her. All the way down the porch steps and the walk Mrs. Eccles was buzzing in my ear about what a wonderful career was opening up for Cissie. "It is a great work that has long needed to be done," she said. And future generations would be thankful to Cissie for preserving Buck Kennedy's songs. They would so soon be destroyed by modern civilization. "And don't you think, Mr. MacGregor," she asked, "that the cheaper forms of commercialized music have a very destructive effect on our folk culture?"

Cissie and Buck Kennedy were waiting at the car, but Mrs. Eccles was running on like a freshet, and I could hardly get her up to the front gate.

"Mr. Kennedy has the most remarkable memory I have encountered in my entire experience with our folksingers," Mrs. Eccles was saying. "We plan to use him for demonstrations during Miss Timberlake's course in ballads at the college. You know, of course, that she is filling in for Dr. Hoodenpyl during the second half-term, and that will be a wonderful bit of academic experience for her. Dr. Hoodenpyl, you see, has his own project and will be away at the Library of Congress and the New York Public Library, and perhaps the Flanders Collection. And we are arranging for a folk festival, a kind of public ballad concert, before the end of the session. I hope you will come, Mr. MacGregor."

"First I've heard of it," I managed to stammer, "but-but-I'll shore be there. If it's Cissie's program, all h—, I mean all creation couldn't keep me away."

"The director of the summer school has been *most* cooperative," she went on, as we walked up to the Buick. "And fortunately we have been able to secure the necessary funds."

Buck was holding open the back door of the car for Cissie, but before he could hop in with her, Mrs. Eccles ordered him up on the front seat with her and started giving him his final instructions. Small chance he would have to sneak a drink. I was on the back seat with Cissie, as far over to Cissie's side as I could get.

As we rolled off, I got her hand and squeezed it. "Mighty big puddin' you've baked since I've been gone!" I told her.

Cissie didn't squeeze back, but she didn't let go either.

"I owe you a lot for takin' me to Buck Kennedy that first time." She was very prim and serious. "His songs will make a big difference."

"And how are your flea bites?"

"It was worth the flea bites—and the rest of the torment I've been through. Mrs. Eccles is wild about Buck Kennedy. Says his ballads are 'vitally important to our regional tradition.' They remind her of Sir Walter Raleigh, she says, and the clear waters of pioneer rivers. Dr. Hoodenpyl says Buck's songs will round out my collection and make it unique. He has been over my transcriptions and thinks I can get it published. Then I will be pretty sure of getting a teaching job."

Mrs. Eccles took the corners fast, while the tires screeched Mixolydian tunes, and the swing of the car flung Cissie and me even closer together, which I didn't mind. I said I hoped all that publishing and teaching wouldn't make any difference in our plans, and Cissie said "What plans?"—as if she didn't know. Somehow in the rummage I lost my grip on Cissie's hand, but she leaned up and whispered, with a little chuckle, "You may not know it, but you must have made a kind of hit with Mrs. Eccles. Else she never would have offered you this ride." And I was saying: "What's she stickin' me for, then? Jest to see if I will bleed?" And Cissie was answering, "She don't mind if you stand up to her. She ain't as rough as she acts."

And I was trying to think of some good way to warn Cissie against Buck. But I couldn't get very far.

"Don't you forget about bewarin' of a fair-spoken man," was the way I started in. And Cissie: "What fair-spoken man?" I pointed my thumb. She laughed: "I don't put *him* down for a fair-spoken man." And I came back—it was all in a whisper, and mighty mixed up: "That might be just fine about puttin' down the notes of his songs, and printin' 'em, too, I reckon, if the Doctor says so. But go slow about showin' Buck off in public."

I was half in a notion to speak to her about what Buck was doing on the side, but that very minute we swished into the parking lot, and Mrs. Eccles shooed us all to the elevator entrance.

"Where are all these people going?" asked Mrs. Eccles as we jammed through the regular Saturday night crowd and waited our chance to ride. She seemed surprised.

"It's Danny's show," said Cissie. "The Turkey Hollow Boys' stage show in Studio B—the big one. They come on after us, but we are in Studio A—all by ourselves."

What Mrs. Eccles said next, I don't know. The crowd pressed in. They spotted me right away. The usual fans, boys, girls, and old folks, looking at my guitar case and asking if we wouldn't sing some favorite number. "Please sing 'White Roses'—please sing 'Tennessee Waltz.' "

When we got out at the 5th floor, there was a noisy crowd moving about the WCC reception room. The Prince Albert show was coming in, from the Grand Ole Opry, over our station, and Cowboy Copas was bearing down strong on his new Capitol record number, and the staff weaving in and out the best they could. I snagged Cissie for a second, while Mrs. Eccles and Buck barged down the hall.

"Is our date all off, then?"

"Take it easy, Danny," she said, over her shoulder, fretting to go, and already walking away. "You see how it is."

I kept right with her for a few steps. "We could eat a late supper somewhere—after we both got through."

Cissie stopped and looked down at the floor. "No, I'm sorry, I have Mrs. Eccles on my hands. It's just somethin' I got into." Then she made her voice sweet. "Please take a rain check, Danny. Call me up tomorrow. I've got to run." And run she did, without a look back, weaving through the fans that were rushing to get good seats for the Turkey Hollow show.

I went back to the desk in the reception room. The front girl gave me her front girl smile and said, "Gosh, Danny we're glad you are back," and handed me a big stack of mail. I slumped into one of the fancy chairs and turned through the letters to see where they came from. Mostly they were fan letters from all parts: Cordele, Georgia; Elijoring, Georgia; Tallahassee, Florida. Some from Atlanta and Macon. Monk's Corner, South Carolina; South Pittsburg, Tennessee. One from Evansville, Indiana; Chicago; Dallas, Texas; Muleshoe, Texas. I opened the one from Muleshoe. It said, "I am a high school sophomore and like your hillbilly songs very much. I always listen to the Kurly Krisps program before the school bus comes. Please sing Tennessee Waltz next Friday morning. Enclosed are some words I made up for the Turkey Hollow boys. Please let me know if you will make up a tune for them and when you will sing it. Also tell me how I can get the music printed and sell some records . . ."

Cowboy Copas and his band were finishing up the P.A. half-hour with the fiddles going hard, the guitar rattling, and the steel guitar pouring molasses over everything. Cowboy Copas was singing fine.

> If you don't want me following after
> Why are you always smiling back?
> I've only got my tears to swap for laughter
> My heart to pledge for everything I lack.

I liked Cowboy Copas and the fiddler, but I couldn't stand the rattle on every beat (it sounded like machines, like coins in slots, and pinballs rolling) and the steel guitars pouring on molasses notes—just a little away from the hot jazz mamas. The lights were making my eyes hurt. I felt tired. The radio was turned up too loud. There were too many people tramping back and forth, running away from something, they didn't know what. The chromium steel chairs with imitation leather cushions were giving me the bellyache and the backache. I slapped the letters together, bundled them up anyhow and smacked them down on the desk. "Here," I said, "put this damn stuff somewhere till I come for it." The girl's eyes got round. I grabbed my guitar and took off. I slipped around to the little soundproof room where we warm up, before the stage shows begin.

Ozro was stretched out on a bench, his big hat over his eyes, fast asleep, and his bull fiddle was stretched out on the floor beside him like both of 'em didn't care. Neither one moved when I tiptoed in. I plugged in the radio they keep there and tuned for Cissie's program, with the volume turned down.

Mrs. Eccles was already holding forth about the program, and what a treat was prepared by Miss Timberlake in having secured the old time folksinger, our well-known friend, Mr. Kennedy of Beaver Valley, to appear on radio for the first time. Cissie took over then and explained the first ballad a little. It was "Gypsy Davy." She struck off the tune, too, on the piano—just the bare melody with a rich chord now and then. It was a surprise to me to hear how good the tune was, played that way. I had never heard her do that. Then Buck's voice come over the radio, in the same ballad I knew—and that was the big surprise. Sure enough, Buck had a good radio voice. A kind of low baritone, though folks that knew him might call it a whiskey bass. Long as you didn't have to look at Buck, you might think he was Lawrence Tibbett. True, he was still slurring the tune around in the old-fashioned way because he didn't know how to sing any different; and he was already changing his style a little—putting in "expression," which is what they do when they are singing for show and not for fun. All the same, Buck was carrying it off better than I would have dreamed he could—though it was something he could never have thought up for himself, and the whole thing might have been flat if Cissie hadn't picked out just the right songs and been there to start him off. She was smart enough to pick the short ballads, too, and have variety. It went right on from "Gypsy Davy" to "The Devil's Nine Questions," then a few verses of "The Miller's Two Daughters," and "Dandoo," and "Butcher Boy." It was a mighty plain sort of singing, for the radio, and I still thought Buck needed a guitar, or at least a dulcimer; and I decided it would really be something like nobody ever heard before if Cissie herself would do the same songs and use that fine piano to back 'em up. Still, almost against my will, Buck's singing got hold of me. I forgot Buck and listened to the songs. And they carried me back.

Evenings in the late summer, when I was a little fellow, we would all be on the porch after supper, enjoying the cool and saying nothing much, but just listening to the crickets and katydids. That would be at the new house Pa built up in Beaver Valley, not at the old MacGregor log cabin where Pa was living when I was born. Automobiles were mighty scarce in Beaver Valley then—and no tractors at all. Wagons would be going down the road after a long day's hauling, wagonbeds rattling, wheels loud on the rocky road, horses' hoofs clopping. Or maybe a single rider going home from the field, trace chains jingling, and the rider singing; like one I can remember that sung every night the same words: "Talk about yo' brick house; You ought to see my frame."

Then, when the first stars came out above the pine tops, and the mountains turned from purple to blue-black, my old Granny would begin to sing, and we would all join in, us younguns, not too loud, but right soft, the way my old Granny sung, and a-quavering and sliding the tune, like her. She was living with us then, after Grandpa died. 'Twouldn't be long before Pa would take a chair, across from Granny—not singing, because he wasn't much of a singer, ever, though Ma was if she had time. But Pa would set quiet till the music worked on him, and then he would hum the tune with us, or maybe take his fiddle and tetch it light and sweet to go with the song. 'Twas so that I learned many a song, them days, without ever knowing I was a-learning 'em.

Sometimes Cissie would come over with her brother Bob, because all the Timberlakes liked to be at our house. In fact they were some kin to us; my Granny used to say we were kissing cousins anyhow, and their farm was next to ours. Cissie and Bob would ride double on an old gray horse, Bob in front and Cissie holding on behind. It would be about first dark, and I would see the old gray horse far up the road before I could see who was riding him. I would call out, "Yonder comes Bob." And my Granny would say, "You don't mean Bob. You mean yonder comes my sweetheart." Pa would say, "Don't be puttin' notions in the boy's head. Let him alone." But Granny would keep on, half teasing, half serious, "Well, he couldn't do better for a sweetheart, and I hope to live to see 'em married and settled. She's done already promised, ain't she, Danny?" I would wiggle my bare toes and say nothing, for being ashamed, but all the same I took it to heart. We would set on the steps, all of the children, with the stars overhead, and there would be Bob on one side, me on the other, with Cissie between us, all singing with my old Granny and Pa's fiddle:

> We'll make a promise, and seal it strong,
> And seven long year we'll make it stand,
> That you won't marry no other woman,
> And I won't marry no other man.

At least we had done that much, for many more than seven years, Cissie and me, and if it hadn't been for the troubles of the times, and the notions and movings-around, maybe my old Granny would have lived to see us married and settled. But my Granny died too soon. And Bob is dead now. Killed at Okinawa. But I can still hear his stout boy's voice singing. And Cissie's voice when she was a little girl—it always was a high treble, and none like it for a sweet tone.

About the old songs, there is something strange that nobody ever explained to me, and it kept coming to my mind while Buck Kennedy was singing. If it is a sorrowful song, and most of the old songs are sorrowful, you still feel good about it when you are singing, even though it's enough to make a body cry. But if it is a jolly song, you feel sad, too, underneath, even while you are merry with the music. Is it the tune that makes 'em like that? Or is it the story? Or is it tune going along with story, the two mixed? I don't know. Maybe it is only that Glad is never so far from Sorry after all, and that's the way the old songs are.

But the more I thought, the more mixed up I felt. In those times we all sung for fun, not for pay, which is surely the way God meant it to be. You wouldn't ever have thought of hiring somebody to eat for you or make love for you. Now it was the other way. I was being hired to sing, and was paid for it, and paid well, by Rufus and the folks that paid him. That was about the only way I could get to sing unless I went off in a corner and sung all by myself, which is a lonesome kind of treat.

Yet what I was hired to sing, the songs they claim everybody wants to hear, was never the good old songs I learnt from my Granny, that had come down to her from her foreparents and the old times, no telling how far back. The hillbilly radio songs are something of the kind, at least a few of them are; and sometimes even the same thing, dressed up and changed. And I'll swear the hillbilly music has its good points, if it's as well done as the Turkey Hollow Boys do it. They are perfect in their kind of music, and I don't know who else would have took the trouble to coach me that they did. Still, if it's flat argument and you take the old songs to judge by, a lot of the hillbilly songs would be like a rag doll compared with a real woman.

Too many programs, too much business, too much money flowing—they almost have to make up rag dolls and try to pass 'em off for the real thing.

It made me terrible uneasy in my mind to think that it took Buck Kennedy on Cissie's radio program to make me be honest with myself and face up to the flat argument. I was fretted with Cissie for getting herself and me into such a tight. Ballad-singing wouldn't change Buck Kennedy; I knew that. But what could I do? Cissie was bound and determined to be a scholar and teacher. Nothing could stop her. She was set on ballads. She would get paid, like I was getting paid, for printing the old songs in a book and teaching 'em. But whatever she got, it wouldn't be a smidgin compared to what I was making and hoped to make. And what about the MacGregor place? And would she always be going off to school somewhere? And traipsing after old scoundrels like Buck Kennedy? And playing ball with Mrs. Eccles and the professors? I was beginning to wonder if she would listen to me any more or even have time to think about me. And even if she got softhearted and married me, wouldn't she be ashamed of me? I wasn't willing to answer that question just yet, but it was bothering me. The only thing I was sure of was that something had to be done about Buck Kennedy for Cissie's sake. If I couldn't think up a way to handle him, Ed Cooley would barge in—

Just as I got to that point, I heard something go plunk-plunk plonk behind my back. It was Ozro and the bull fiddle. He had waked up, just as Buck was singing "The House Carpenter," and was trying to get on the key. Ozro's big hat was pushed on to the back of his head. He was looking pleased and interested. "Sings right good, don't he?" Ozro said, and grinned a mile wide. "He's singin' in G." And he began to follow the tune of that old ballad:

> "Well met, well met, my own true love!"
> "Not very well met," said she.
> "For I'm done married to a house carpenter,
> And a nice young man is he."

It may have been an accident, or it may have been that Buck hit true concert pitch from Cissie starting him on the piano. Anyway, Buck was singing on the radio right in tune with Ozro. I couldn't help grabbing my guitar to come in too. Then all of a sudden, some more of the Turkey Hollow Boys came in, and caught the disease. Pretty soon we were fiddling and strumming away, with Buck leading but not knowing it. By the time he reached the third verse, we had even begun to sing with him, and were having a good time at it.

It was the next verse that got me. The part where the lady says to the devil or ghost or whatever comes after her:

If I forsake my house carpenter
And go along with thee,
What do you have there to entertain me with
To keep me from slavery?

Then the deceiving devil makes some big promises—and he carries her off to perdition and ruin.

I was thinking about Cissie, while the music was going, and it was her voice I seemed to hear instead of Buck Kennedy's: "What have you to entertain me with and keep me from slavery?"

Just that second Rufus come in, fiddle under his arm, hurrying because he was a little late. He stopped short, his eyebrows went up till they nearly met his hairline, and his green eyes snapped.

"What's goin' on here, I'd like to know?"

We broke off in the middle, sheepish-like. Ozro whinnied. But nobody laughed, or even spoke.

I looked Rufus straight in the eye.

"Competition," I told him. "Long-hair stuff."

Rufus listened a little bit. Then he winked at me.

"Too much drag. Needs a hillbilly band to push him along. Who is it?"

I told him it was Buck Kennedy, and I added, "Sponsored by the Chamber of Commerce and the Teachers Association, and presented by Mrs. Eccles, president of the folklore society and Miss Cissie Timberlake, the noted ballad scholar. Long-hair competition, Rufus."

Rufus frowned. "Buck Kennedy? That old reprobate? Turn off that radio."

I clicked it off.

"I ain't afraid of Buck Kennedy's competition. But to have Cissie mixed up in it—that ain't so good, is it? It don't seem right. It ain't like Cissie."

"What's wrong with it?" I asked him. "He's a damned good ballad singer, and Cissie knows what she's doin'."

Rufus put his eyes on me. He looked anxious. "You know what's wrong with it. I don't have to argue about it, and I ain't got time, anyhow. But you better see me and tell me about it. Better tell me what's goin' on around here." He looked at his watch and raised his fiddle bow. "Come on, boys! We've got to warm up, and not many minutes to do it in."

10

DR. HOODENPYL BUBBLES ABOUT BALLADS— AND HILLBILLY MUSIC TOO

"**T**he MacGregors have a family failing, Danny," my Pa used to tell me. "I don't know how they do it, because they are clever folks, but somehow they nearly always manage to git on the losin' side. Hit jest turns out that way. I don't rightly know what it is. Maybe it's a devil in 'em that makes 'em contrary. Maybe it's jest bad luck a-follerin' us. Anyhow it goes a way back. So the old folks used to tell me. They make a fair start and git along right well for a while, the MacGregors do. Then they act the fool somehow and wind up on the losin' side. Your Grandpa, to be sure, he done right well——but then you see he married your Grandma, and that was a streak o' luck. She pulled him outen the hole, more times than one. Now me, I've done acted the fool and dropped back on the losin' side ag'in. And I want you to watch out for that when you grow up. You watch out for the winnin' side, and for God's sake git on it and stay there."

"Why, Pa," I asked him, "what's wrong? Ain't we all mighty happy up here in Beaver Valley? Win or lose, ain't we happy?"

"Call it happy if you want to. Reckon I oughter be glad you feel that way. But I acted a fool to buy this-here farm. Hit ain't payin' off. Hit was the losin' side, and like all the dern MacGregors, I went and got on it. Jest pure cussedness it was, I reckon. Whut I oughter done was to move to Carolina City and git into the autymobile business somehow. We'd have some of that Yankee money, and you boys wouldn't be hirin' out to worm tobacco and pitch hay. So you listen to whut I tell you."

"I'm a-listenin', Pa."

"You look sharp, and git on the winnin' side."

"How am I goin' to know which it is?"

"Well, 'tain't around here noways." Then my Pa would poke me in the chest and take it all back. "But hold on a minute. Remember one thing: *stand up for your rights!* Don't ye never take nothin' from no man! Don't ever lick nobody's boots. I'd ruther see ye lose ever'thing first. Don't ye take nothin' from no man!"

The family failing! I was about ready to say I had it, too, when I begun to have trouble about dating Cissie. The day I thought about what Pa said was one of the days when I had that trouble.

If I called Cissie at home, she was at the college. If I telephoned the college, either her line was busy or the operator would say, "Miss Timberlake is in class." Or some professor would answer her telephone and say, "Miss Timberlake is out at the moment. Will you leave a call?" But if I left a call, nothing happened, no matter how long I waited around.

And maybe when I did finally run her down, later at night, she was full of sweet excuses. It was too bad, but the man didn't give her my call. And "Let me see, Danny . . . No, I can't give up tomorrow night. I have to prepare a lecture." Or maybe she was having a conference with Dr. Hoodenpyl about her transcriptions of Buck Kennedy's songs. And couldn't I call her again in two or three days? It was just so hard to say, definitely . . . Sunday? Well . . . maybe. But I'd better call her again. No, she wasn't giving me the run-around. I mustn't have such thoughts . . .

But I did have such thoughts. And when I tried to put my finger on the main trouble, it always come down to two words: College Education. Right there was where I failed to get on the winning side—College Education. I went and caught the hillbilly music itch when I ought to have listened to the Mr. Fix-it's and gone to college. I could have done it, same as Cissie did.

In fact, we could have married and gone to college together, which I found out too late was the new fashion. Why, they tell me the young married girls have babies and go on and get educated just the same. But I just plain didn't ketch on in time. Now maybe I would lose out because Cissie tore loose and got herself a College Education. And she couldn't bear to have me around because all I had was the hillbilly music itch.

Git on the winnin' side! It was like Pa's words bounced right out of the telephone receiver that day, after Cissie hung up. *But now it was too late.* Then I happened to remember what Ed Cooley told me about his nephew, and I thought, *Maybe it's not too late.* If that Wallace Exum, and him nothing but a ornery disk jockey, could go and study in college, what's to stop MacGregor from doing the same thing? I told myself it was something to think about. *And I believe I'll look into it.* I wondered if I hadn't better sound out Cissie along that line—if I could ever reach her. Then I thought, *But why bother Cissie? Why not just go ahead and do it? Surprise her!*

I put off deciding all that till I could actually get Cissie rounded up for a date. Finally she told me she was just like a business executive, and the best she could do was to meet me for lunch some day. And it would have to be the college cafeteria because she couldn't take the time to drive out anywhere. It was that or nothing.

So, on a hot July day, there we were at last in the college cafeteria, with people clanging dishes and talking all around us. And the whole place smelling like dirty dishrags boiled in the same pot with cabbage and onions! Plastic trays, scoot 'em along the rail, don't hold up the line, grab some grub even if it's only lettuce and Jello, pay the checker, look for a plastic-top table that teeters like a seesaw, lose your paper napkin, pick it up again, wonder if the food ain't plastic too, it all tastes the same—that's the college cafeteria.

But anyway there was the natural-born Cissie with blue earrings to match her eyes, slipping through the tables like a doe in a thicket, and me close after. That made everything ice cream with me.

Right away, she started in on Buck Kennedy, and let out that she was having Buck sing some of his songs over and over, two or three times, because he didn't always sing them twice the same way. And it was taking a lot of time.

"Looks like he could stick to the tune if he really knows it."

"It draws out my thesis work because I have to put down everything. Still, it's interestin'—to catch those melodic variants. I get excited over some of 'em. Scholars are just beginning to realize how important it is to study an individual singer's variants, and not only the variation from singer to singer."

She was taking me into water that was over my head. I wanted to get back to where I had some footing, and away from Buck Kennedy.

"Seems like you want to make me start courtin' you all over again—that's what I'm beginnin' to realize. But I don't mind practicin' a little."

There was so much noise around us, I almost had to shout it in Cissie's ear, which is a mighty poor way to practice courtin'.

Cissie took a sip of iced tea and looked at me over her glass, like she was having a hard time recollecting what I might be talking about.

"Danny, you always were a little slow about some things. But by this time I would have thought you had learned something about my work—and how I feel about it. I thought you might be interested. Excuse me. What's the cattle market like today? Steady, or fallin' off?"

"Maybe I've learned more than you think." I gulped some iced tea myself, and the insult along with it. "I'm willin' to learn more, too. Old as I am, maybe it ain't too late. If them old maid schoolteachers can learn, and these country jakes I see around here, why can't Danny MacGregor?"

"Oh, yes, you can. Sure you can." She said that sort of absent-minded-like and started on her salad. Then Cissie's expression changed. She dropped her fork and frowned at me. "What did you say, Danny? I mean—exactly what are you talkin' about?"

I was about to open up and tell her. But just then I had to dodge and bend over. A line of boys pushed by our table, swinging their heavy-loaded trays too close for comfort. Then Cissie raised up in her chair and waved at somebody behind me. She smiled as if she was seeing angel wings and beckoned somebody to come on.

"There's Dr. Hoodenpyl!" she said.

I thought to myself, "Soon hot, soon cold, and that's the way with a woman."

I looked around, and there was a young-looking fat little man grinning at us, with a tray in his hands and enough grub on it to feed two people.

"I hope I'm not intrudin'," he said. "May I join you?"

"This is Mr. MacGregor, Dr. Hoodenpyl," said Cissie. "Mr. Danny MacGregor."

"Yes-yes," he said, in a bubbling kind of way. "Yes-yes. How perfectly charmin'. Mr. MacGregor of the Turkey Valley Boys. I've heard about you, Mr. MacGregor. Yes-yes. And heard you, too. I make it a point to tune in for the Kurly Krisps program, every week. Turkey Valley Boys, yes-yes."

"Turkey *Hollow* Boys—" I just had to set him straight. Cissie kept her smile going, but it was a frozen smile now. She was bothered.

"Oh, yes. Yes-yes, Mr. MacGregor. Pardon me. Turkey *Hollow* Boys of course. These delightful localisms. I get a little confused at times. I wonder if I might use this opportunity to ask you to explain to me the precise shade of difference between a valley and a hollow. And isn't there still another word? Let me see. A valley and a hollow and—yes-yes—a cove. Perfectly wonderful word—cove. Isn't that it? Cove?"

"There ain't much difference," I said. "It jest depends on where they are and what the folks call 'em."

"I see, I see. Yes-yes." But he didn't seem to pay much real attention, for he was going after his soup in a big way. He had a little blond moustache and a round face. His head was mighty bald for so young a man, and his eyelids drooped so near shut you might have thought he was asleep, except for the way he got rid of the soup and lit into the roast beef and potatoes.

"This is a real privilege, Mr. MacGregor," he said as he changed over from big spoon to knife and fork. "I have long wanted to meet a real hillbilly singer. You get some int'restin' musical effects. Yes-yes, quite extraordinary. I have so much wanted to ask you about various things. The steel guitar, for example."

"I don't go in for that, Dr. Hoodenpyl." But he didn't seem to hear me.

"And the most unusual employment of the bass viol to accent melodic as well as rhythmic patterns. For example in that song—what is it? Yes-yes. 'Ridin' on a Cottonbale.' Enchantin', really enchantin'. Most unorthodox in its progression of fifths. But suitable to the song. Yes-yes, eminently suitable. And that's what one can do in the antique modal scales, isn't it, Miss Timberlake?"

"Cissie ought to know," I broke in—and then stopped quick. I was going to say she was a real hillbilly singer too. But Cissie was red as a beet, and she had fire in her eye. She held the frozen smile, all the same, and said "Yes, Dr. Hoodenpyl" to shut me off. And he went right on eating and talking. I can't rightly tell how he did it, but somehow his eating didn't get in the way of his talking or his talking in the way of his eating. I just set there and sweated like a bird charmed by a rattlesnake, except that Dr. Hoodenpyl was more like a pudding in a sack than any snake you ever saw.

"But perhaps we can explore that subject some other time. It has interested me so much. I have been vastly amused, immensely amused, and, I might add not at all displeased, to see how the hillbilly music has routed the crooners and the other jazzicians of Tin Pan Alley and Hollywood. Yes-yes. Jazzicians, that is my name for them. Jazzicians. Not musicians—jazzicians. The hillbilly performers, whatever else they may be, are certainly musicians. Not quite the genuine folk music, of course, Mr. MacGregor. Not quite. But not so far from it as some people would argue. Not far enough to put my nose out of joint, Mr. MacGregor. After all—yes-yes—after all, no further from folk song than was the broadside ballad. And what a magnificent triumph, Mr. MacGregor, to put the jazzicians to rout. Think of it, Miss Timberlake, to outsell the jazzicians, to crowd them off the best radio spots, Miss Timberlake, and to cut in on the jukebox trade. And to make Grand Ole Opry known throughout our happy land."

Dr. Hoodenpyl had a piece of cornbread under his fork. He was cleaning up the beef gravy and doing a slick job.

"What a victory!" he said, sopping away like a field hand at wheat-threshing time. "What a victory for Grand Ole Opry and the hillbilly musicians! To force them to imitate you or get off the map. Oh, Mr. MacGregor, imitation is the sincerest flatt'ry, you know. I congratulate you, Mr. Mac-Gregor. It has been a magnificent triumph, and no doubt we scholars will some day be writing learned articles about you. About your songs and their origins and so forth. About things like 'Ridin' on a Cottonbale,' ha, ha! You do it awfully well, you know. So much aplomb. Such verve. And the rousing tempo. Ta-ta-um, ta-ta-tum, ta-ta-tum, tum, tum, ridin' down the river on a cotton bale."

And derned if the man didn't h'ist the tune right there, and beat the time with his knife handle on the table. Everybody was looking at us from the tables all round, and the clatter stopped dead for a minute. Cissie's ice cream had melted in her dish, and she was sort of stirring-it-like, with her spoon. She could a-stirred me if she had tried. I was just so much clabber.

Dr. Hoodenpyl popped out of his chair. "Excuse me," he said. "I believe I will get me a piece of pie and another cup of coffee."

My tongue turned to jelly, but I managed to make it work.

"Cissie!" I said. "Why didn't you tell me?"

"Tell you what?" She was looking stubborn.

"Tell me the truth. Why, I didn't know there was a college perfesser in the whole world that listened to hillbilly music."

Cissie was so confused, she forgot to talk pretty.

"He don't teach hillbilly music. I never heard him say nary word about it before."

"Well, he's the funniest man I ever saw, but he talks sense."

"S-s-sh! he's a-comin' back."

Dr. Hoodenpyl had his cup of coffee and pie with ice cream on it. He went right on without missing a lick.

"But, as we were saying in our little discussion of the hillbilly music, the antique modal tunes are the thing. I can't tell you how pleased I am that you keep 'Old Joe Clark' in the Mixolydian. Don't let it get majorized, Mr. MacGregor. Keep it in the Mixolydian. Keep that F-natural. It *is* F-natural, isn't it, Mr. MacGregor? Good old F-natural, not the sharp?"

I thought a minute, and at first I didn't know what he meant. Then I remembered, and sure enough he was right.

"We play it in the key of G," I said, "but in the first part we don't strike F-sharp. It's F-natural, and you are right."

"Yes-yes, of course. F-natural. I was sure that was it. We ballad scholars, you see, have to keep up with these things, Mr. MacGregor. We have our eye on you, don't you know. And that reminds me, Miss Timberlake, have you finished transcribing the Kennedy tunes?"

Cissie began to brighten up.

"Yes, Dr. Hoodenpyl, just about finished."

"And that wonderful Robin Hood tune, what did it turn out to be? Dorian, probably?

"Yes, sir, it was Dorian."

"Dorian hexatonic, no doubt?"

"Well, part of the time Mr. Kennedy sang it hexatonic, then sometimes he would leave out the sixth and make it pentatonic."

"Wonderful! wonderful! Mr. MacGregor, that's the greatest single discovery our bright young ballad scholar has made. I suppose you know that Miss Timberlake is the most gifted and promising ballad scholar I have yet taught. And think of finding a Robin Hood ballad down here in old Carolina. The first American text of this particular ballad. All eyes will be centered on us, Mr. MacGregor. Miss Timberlake's article, containing this text and others, will appear in *JAFL* within the year, I have no doubt. And that reminds me, Miss Timberlake, I have heard from my friends at Harvard, and I think there is no doubt that we can arrange a program there for you and Mr. Kennedy, next winter. Yes-yes, it will be a sensation. But that should be only the beginning. We should be able to arrange a series of engagements after the Harvard program. And that will help with the expense of the thesis, won't it? With a singer like Mr. Kennedy, there should be no trouble about engagements. Or fees either. And with a capable manager and chaperon like Miss Timberlake, it should go very well. Only you will have to ration out his whiskey, Miss Timberlake, yes-yes. But no doubt you know all about that, here in the Carolina mountains."

Dr. Hoodenpyl closed his heavy eyelids and laughed in a funny sort of wheezing way. The coffee slopped out of the cup he was holding, but he didn't notice.

"Here in the coves and valleys of Carolina," he wheezed. "No, the hollows. I beg pardon, Mr. MacGregor, the hollows of course."

I couldn't stand it a minute longer, and I busted out:

"You mean Cissy's a-goin' to take old Buck Kennedy all around the country—her a-takin' him to sing up there, all by herself?"

"Oh, I'm sorry, Mr. MacGregor, it may seem like very sudden news. But it's good news, isn't it? I forgot, when I spoke of it just now, that we had been keeping it a little quiet till that Harvard engagement was fixed. But after all, you're entitled to be one of the first to know, aren't you? I understand that you helped discover Mr. Kennedy, and I tell you, he's a discovery, a great discovery. And don't worry, don't worry the slightest bit. It will be a great success. That I can guarantee. Yes-yes, I can guarantee it. And there might be other results."

Underneath the plastic table Cissie was putting her little foot down *hard* on my big foot. She was shaking her head just the least bit of a shake and looking a *don't* at me across the table. I swallowed my mad and said, "I jest can't take it in," kind of weak.

"Well, yes. I can imagine, Mr. MacGregor, but don't worry, don't be apprehensive. They have never seen his like up there in the North. Never seen or heard his like. And after all, Mr. MacGregor, if John Lomax could go all around the country with Leadbelly—with old Leadbelly, a convicted criminal and jailbird—and present him in concert, think of what our beautiful and capable Cissie—pardon me, Miss Timberlake—can achieve with a real mountain singer like Buck Kennedy, with his wonderful repertory of ancient ballads. We will raise the tone of academic entertainment, won't we Miss Timberlake? I hope I can be with you, but I'm afraid—well, I may be in Washington, or New York, or Helsinki, who knows? But after all, what does that matter? I am only a humble arranger, a plodding scholar, Mr. MacGregor."

Dr. Hoodenpyl chased down the last piece of pie crust and added, like he was talking to himself: "Of course if we could hope to rival the Frank C. Brown Collection at Duke University, or the Flanders Collection at Middlebury College . . . why, then . . . yes-yes . . . but no, I rather think . . . yes, I truly think, just now the metropolitan angle is . . ."

Just then an electric bell rang loud as a fire alarm, and the students begun to rush out of the cafeteria. Dr. Hoodenpyl got up and brushed the crumbs off his coat.

"And now, if you will excuse us, Mr. MacGregor, we will get right at those transcriptions. I would like to check the Dorian pentatonic with your recording, Miss Timberlake. And do let us talk some more, some time, Mr. MacGregor. About that bass viol part. I should like to see that score if you could kindly obtain it for me."

"Score?" I said. And Cissie saw I was bumfuzzled.

"They don't play from any sort of score—the hillbilly bands don't." Cissie was smiling and explaining. "They don't write out the instrumental parts. Most of them can't read notes. They do it by ear—make it up as they play."

Dr. Hoodenpyl's mouth was wide open. He held it there, all surprised. And I just stood.

"I see," he said. "Yes-yes, I see. But if I could just get a notation . . ."

Cissie said, "I'm sorry," and I couldn't tell whether she meant it for me or for Dr. Hoodenpyl.

They left me at the door, and all I got was "So long, Danny," and a little wave of the hand from Cissie. As they walked off down the campus path I could see Cissie opening her big notebook and Dr. Hoodenpyl inching close to look at it with her.

11

A DEAN KNOWS WHEN TO BREAK THE RULES

For the life of me I couldn't tell whether Dr. Hoodenpyl was really on my side or not. Or on Cissie's side. Or anybody's side but his own—and what side was that? All that big talk about the hillbilly music, it sounded like my side—though it was not the Grand Ole Opry line or the regular disk jockey line or any line I'd ever heard before. Maybe Cissie knew what line it was; she'd been to New York. Still, the way Cissie acted—well, I could tell she didn't know *that* was comin'.

Maybe the man was just playing games with all of us. But if he was fixing to put Cissie on the road with Buck Kennedy, Old Scratch himself couldn't have plotted out anything more devilish. And I'd better be making up some games of my own.

Whatever the winning side might look to be, one thing was certain: I was too much on the outside, and I needed to get more on the inside, college education or no education.

I got in my car, turned the key, and started the motor, more out of habit than because I really meant it. Where, I asked myself, am I going from here? Not any place, I answered, where it will do any good to put your foot on the accelerator!

I looked at the new Esso filling station across the street from where I was parked and the Coca-Cola sign next to it that said "The pause that refreshes," and they didn't mean a thing to me. The street was full of cars, all going somewhere in both directions. I said to myself, "Boy, you better be gittin' along into that traffic. You better be gittin' along and bang that old box awhile. Practice for Rufus. That's one thing you shore can do."

A car turned into the filling station and stopped. The sun hit the windshield and came right square-dazzle into my eyes. I had to look away.

There on the campus side the boys and girls walked two and two, some with books, some not, bareheaded in the hot sun, taking it easy and free up the long steps and walks to the white-columned buildings among the trees. Pretty girls in cool summer dresses, bare arms and no stockings, boys in their shirt-sleeves and no worries, laughing and talking like the world would flip to a finger, slick as a cigarette lighter. Some in the shade too, reading their books, or just lying around lazy. But not all of them boys and girls, either. Some of them old as I was, some older, some whiteheaded and solemn.

I wouldn't say I made up my mind then and there, because there wasn't anything working in the place where my mind was supposed to be. My legs and feet just naturally moved me out from under the steering wheel and across the seat and set me straight up on the sidewalk. When I came to, I had flipped the jigger and was just about to shut the car door. "Hold on, boy," I told myself, "don't be a fool and lock yourself out of your own car with the key in the ignition and the motor running." I turned off the motor, put the key in my pocket, locked up, and took the steps.

At the top of the steps I met a man that looked like a professor. He was wearing a straw hat and carrying a leather grip.

"Mister," I said, "where do you go if you want to start in to be a student in this college?"

He opened his mouth, but all he said was, "Er—" Then he shut his mouth and swallowed hard. "Er—well, Sir," he said. "It's pretty late to register. Er—I think you better—er, see the Dean. Up yonder in the Administration Building."

He pointed his finger, and I went where he pointed.

I don't know why, but I had it in my head that a Dean would be an old, long-faced man in a black coat, something like an old-timey preacher. But Dean Bronson wasn't that way at all. He was a peart young blackheaded, black-eyed feller, so agreeable that I almost felt like I'd got into an insurance office by mistake and might walk out with a $50,000 endowment policy and forget all about reading the fine print.

Soon as I named my name to him, he knew right away who I was and said why, yes, of course, his young son and daughter were among my most ardent admirers; they always turned on the Kurly Krisps program, even if they had to run to catch the school bus afterwards. And what could he do for me?

I explained that I wanted to start in college, but all I wanted to study was Miss Timberlake's ballads course, if the college would let me. Of course I'd like to study more than that—in fact, anything the college had to teach if I could learn it—but I knew I was getting started a little late, and maybe I'd better stick to one subject for a beginning.

I had a very strong suspicion that the idea was pretty much of a shock to the Dean. But he didn't fall over. He was just twice as brisk and polite as he had been before.

"Yes, Mr. MacGregor," said the Dean. "That is a *very* popular course . . . we have had an unusual demand . . . And we are so glad to have Miss Timberlake with us this summer, especially in view of Dr. Hoodenpyl's project that calls him away . . . She is doing our students such a great service. I have been greatly interested in that development of our program. But I am afraid Miss Timberlake's course is already full. In fact, I'm fairly sure it is overcrowded."

The Dean pulled a paper out of the desk drawer, and began to run his finger down the page. "Let me see," he said. "One moment. That's not an English course. We put it under Humanities. Yes, here it is, Humanities 401-D."

"I won't make no trouble," I said. "Jest let me slip in the back of the room."

"Oh, no, Mr. MacGregor, I can assure you, State Teachers College would never think of relegating Danny MacGregor to a back seat. Let me see. Humanities 401-D already has 63 students enrolled, and that's an increase of 20 since Miss Timberlake took over."

It never hurts to mention money, I told myself. So I said: "I'll pay cash for the charges and give you my check right now. Just tell me the amount."

The Dean's black eyes bored at me through the spectacles. He put down the paper and took off his spectacles. He looked at me again, without spectacles.

"If you'll just let me have your permit to enter," he said, "I'll see what I can do about your problem."

"That's what I came to you about, Mr. Dean. Permit to enter."

"Oh! And you haven't been to see the Director of Admissions?"

"No, sir."

"Oh, I'm sorry I misunderstood you. I assumed you were registered and this was a request referred to me by the Director of Admissions."

"No, sir. A man told me to come to you. I don't know who he was."

"I see, Mr. MacGregor. But you should have a permit to enter from the Director of Admissions, and various papers, including a transcript of credits."

I picked up my hat and started to go. "Where is his office?" I asked the Dean. "I can settle that credit business in a minute. All he has to do is call the First National Bank. My credit is A-number-one."

Dean Bronson was smiling—or maybe he was trying not to smile. Anyway, I could see his eyebrows arching up above his spectacle rims.

"Just one moment, Mr. MacGregor. I am glad you came to me first, because this is something I would have had to handle anyhow. Now let me be sure I understand the situation. You want to enter as a special student and take only Miss Timberlake's course. Is that right?"

"Yes, sir. That's right. I reckon I am a sort of special kind of student, but I can't help it. That's the way I make my living, with the Turkey Hollow Boys, and I'd hate to think it was held ag'in me. Besides, Cissie's already got Wallace Exum in the class, and he's only a disk jockey."

This time the Dean laughed right out. I was glad he did, for I was beginning to sweat.

"I agree with you perfectly," said the Dean. "It's perfectly true that a distinguished radio singer would be much more highly qualified than a disk jockey. But what you say is news to me. So Miss Timberlake has a disk jockey among her students! How very interesting!"

"Yes, sir, and he's a fine boy, and bound to do well."

"I'm sure he will. But now, coming back to your problem—to that matter of credits—I was not referring to your financial standing but to something else. Not to go into all the complicated details, Mr. MacGregor—but what we need is—well, the rules require that we have a complete record of your courses and grades, in high school and college."

"I never went to college, Mr. Dean. That's what I want to make up for now. But after Pa died, I went to Carolina City High School and finished. And made a living on the side, too. Pickin' and singin'."

"Pickin' and singin'!" The Dean repeated. "How extremely interesting. A catchy phrase, and I want to remember it. Now your not having college credit makes it a difficult case, Mr. MacGregor, but we are not old fogies here at State Teachers College. We are here to serve you—if possible. And as for the rules, that's what the Dean is for, isn't it? A dean may be defined as a man who knows when to break the rules. But maybe we won't have to break them."

The Dean scratched his head. He took off his glasses and looked out of the window. Then he put his glasses back on and looked at me. Then he pressed a button and buzzed his secretary. A middleaged woman with a kind, country face opened the door. "Miss McNamara," said the Dean, "bring me the current Proceedings of the Southern Association." She brought the book. He looked in the book and put it down. Then he got another book out of his desk and looked in it. Then he took off his glasses and looked out of the window again. The telephone rang. He answered it and said yes and no two or three times. He picked up a sheet of paper and began to write on it. The telephone rang again. The Dean said, "Well," and "Yes," and "Tell the president I'll come right over." He began to write faster on the sheet of paper. And I sat sweating, with my clothes sticking to the chair, but chilled to the bone with the idea that I wasn't no more than a lonesome pin-feathered chicken trying to fly up among the happy old hens.

Dean Bronson sat back in his swivel chair and read over the paper. He took off his glasses and looked at me once more.

"What about this arrangement, Mr. MacGregor? Would it suit you to be admitted as a special student in music, with the privilege of auditing Miss Timberlake's ballad course?"

"Sounds fine, Mr. Dean. What is 'auditing'?"

"An auditor, Mr. MacGregor, can attend class and do all the studying and reading he wants to—the regular work of the class. He has the privilege of the library and all other student privileges. But he is not allowed to take the examination, and cannot receive credit for the course, and pays all the regular fees, with no reduction."

"That suits me perfect. I been waiting all my life to study, and not have to take the examination. I'd a-been here before now if I'd knowed you could go to college that way."

The Dean slipped the paper in an envelope and handed it to me. "Take this right down the hall to the Director of Admissions. He'll fix you up and tell you what to do. I'll telephone him you are on the way."

I thanked the Dean and started to go.

"It's a pleasure," the Dean said, "and let me know if I may be of further service to you. It's a pleasure to make your personal acquaintance, too—and do you mind if I ask you a question?"

I didn't mind. But he sounded a little serious. The Dean came around his desk and sat on the edge. He lowered his voice a little.

"Mr. MacGregor, do you happen to know a man named Kennedy? If I am not mistaken, the full name is Buck Kennedy, or something like that."

The question nearly threw me off balance, coming when I was so pleased, and all set to go. I stalled for time.

"There's a lot of Kennedys hereabouts. Which one did you mean?"

"I believe this man is a singer, Mr. MacGregor. Some kind of folksinger."

"Yes, sir," I said—and made out like I was having to think hard. "I do know of a Buck Kennedy that sings ballads, now that you remind me. But I don't see much of him." I wondered how much the Dean knew. I didn't want to lie to him, but I wanted to pass it off somehow.

"He's not one of your hillbilly radio group, then, I suppose."

"Oh, no, Mr. Dean, he's not our kind of singer at all."

"But he's a good singer, you think—a real folksinger."

"That's right. The genuine article when it comes to that kind of singing."
I paused and then added: "At least so I'm told—by them that really knows."

"I'm glad to hear you say that. But what about your hillbilly radio songs?
Aren't they folk songs, too?"

This man's sharp, I told myself. He must be trying to catch me.

"That's why I'm taking Miss Timberlake's course," I said. "I want to
find about that—and a lot of other things." The Dean laughed and said:
"Well, Mr. MacGregor, I'm interested in learning what your objective is,
in entering college. I wanted to ask you, but I hesitated to—to seem too
curious. And maybe after you have had Miss Timberlake's course you'll not
only find out about that folk song matter, but you'll find out more about
this Mr. Kennedy. I know that Dr. Hoodenpyl thinks highly of him. We
discussed Mr. Kennedy, in connection with the allocation of some funds
to pay him for his demonstration of folk songs in Miss Timberlake's class.
I understand Miss Timberlake thinks very highly of him, too. I was just
interested in your opinion. I'm delighted to know you think he's good."

"He's a singer, all right."

"Excellent. Excellent. And I certainly hope you'll drop in to see me. Yes.
I may want to talk with you later."

I felt a little weak in the knees as I walked down the hall, looking for the
Director of Admissions. To be put on the spot about Buck Kennedy, first
thing—that jarred me. That Dean was after something. I was nervous with
wondering whether I'd said too much—or too little. Whether I'd covered
up for Cissie. And about what was really going on in all the fine brick
buildings with high-pillared porches. And the Dean said he might want to
see me later. He made a point of it.

But I soon forgot that trouble and swapped it for a different kind of
thing. They were all polite and nice, at all the offices I went to, but I soon
discovered that getting into college was like being inducted into the Army.
It was paperwork and red tape and filling out blanks and going from one
place to the next. I begun to wonder whether they wouldn't run me into
some big room, strip me naked, and start me down the line for typhoid shots
and physical examination. They didn't do that, but they did try to strip me
naked, you might say, in a bunch of questions, printed on several sheets of
paper, that I was supposed to answer. I glanced at some of the questions,
and they made my hair stand up. Questions I wouldn't be brash enough to
ask my best friend, for fear he'd knock my teeth down my throat. Intimate
personal questions.

"You don't have to fill all that out now, Mr. MacGregor," said one of the
office girls that was helping me. "It's just general information for the college

records, and you can hand it in later. You might want to take it home and think about it."

"I sure would, lady, and I thank you." And I thought to myself—Good God, is this what they put in the college records? And that pretty girl knows all about it.

But one thing I understood, and that was at the business office. They wanted some money, and I had it. And lastly, the bookstore, where they told me what books I had to have for Cissie's course, and sold them to me right over the counter. And jarred my eyeteeth with the price, too, in a polite and pretty way. I staggered out, with books and notebooks under my arm, and walked across the campus to my car, hoping I looked like any other summer student. I was in college, the first MacGregor of all our folks ever to be in college, and praying to God that MacGregor was on the winning side for a change.

12

I SNATCHED OUT MY PENCIL LIKE A REAL SCHOLAR

I didn't slip in at the back, after all. By the time I found Room 200 in the Humanities Building, it was already full ten o'clock, and the only vacant seat in Cissie's classroom, so far as I could tell, was spang in the front row, right among some girls that looked at me real sassy when I took my place. One of them seemed like a familiar face. There was a lot of whispering and giggling around me, and loud talk farther back. It hushed up short when Cissie came in. With her books under her arm, Cissie stepped up to the reading desk as quick and light as if she had her guitar and was stepping up to the mike.

Cissie turned and faced the class from behind the reading desk. She was looking very happy and sweet and not the least bit like a school-teacher until she cut her eyes around that class—and saw me with my notebook open on top of my pile of books, all ready for the lesson and innocent as a lamb.

It seemed like a mean trick, to play on a girl. But then she'd same as dared me to do it. That morning, I was the big surprise package the college had delivered to her. There was nothing Cissie could do but take me in, if the label was right, and the bill of lading.

She checked the label, first thing. Cissie took some cards out of an envelope and flipped through them. She came to a card and frowned. I knew that must be me. Then she got control, and was every bit the school-teacher.

"I will call the roll of the *regular* students," she said. "I will not call the names of the *auditors*." So she passed over my name, and maybe some others. And the class was ready to start, I thought.

But no, instead of teaching us, Cissie walked to the door and stepped out. In a minute she came back, and there was old Buck Kennedy trailing after her, with his head to one side like a bull being led by a ring in his nose. Buck took a chair facing us and crossed his legs as if he was used to the place. He looked almighty satisfied with himself and everything until his eyes roamed around and lit on me. Then he uncrossed his legs, pulled out his handkerchief, and pretended to blow his nose. It was a white handkerchief, and Buck was dressed even better than when I saw him last. He was wearing a sporty tie, and a light summer suit, with trousers well creased. And all this while Cissie was explaining that Mr. Kennedy was with us again and what for. It was so fine to have him there to help her illustrate what she called "native American ballads." Then Buck stood up and started in.

This time, they were all very respectable songs—nothing worse than a few murders and train wrecks, it turned out. I knew them already, and so for a while I put in my time very well by just looking at Cissie as I had done for so much of my life. But I was excited about it in a new way—like a boy at the circus when the band plays, and high up, where they throw the spotlight, the pretty lady starts to walk the tightrope. That high above me, that high and far, was Cissie, and me no more than a roustabout handling rope and stake in the dark below. I was getting a crick in my neck from the strain of looking up. I eased that by glancing around and sizing up the class out of the corner of my eye. There were not near as many old maids and country professors as I had expected. They were mostly young folks, and among them an awful lot of big strapping boys. That puzzled me till I remembered how the government was paying the veterans to go to school. And they could come there and look at Cissie and listen to her, same as I was doing, with all expenses paid—and count it education. I couldn't pick out the Exum boy among them, at first, or anybody I knew, but among the girls—there was a lot of them—I soon recognized Elvira Looney, the Sheriff's daughter. She was right there in the front row, just a couple of seats away from me. Elvira would never take the prize for looks, since she is freckle-faced and tall and stringy like her Pa. That morning, she was writing in her notebook all the time, busy as a fice dog digging out a rabbit.

As for the teaching, when it finally started, that was the big surprise to me. In college, I thought it would all be strict and solemn as church. I was afraid Cissie would be coming down the line and asking hard questions till she would light on me, and I don't even know what the lesson was. But that wasn't the way of it at all.

For a while it was almost like a stage show, with Cissie being the announcer and Buck Kennedy the performer, slick as if they had rehearsed and practiced down to the last gag. First Cissie talked a little about railroad songs. Then she got Buck to sing "The Wreck of the Old 97."

"And did you ever work for the railroad?" Cissie asked, when he sat down.

"No'm," Buck answered, "or for anybody else if I could help it!"

The class laughed, just like the audience in a show. And Cissie picked up her cue and came back at him.

"But how did you learn the song if you didn't work for the railroad?"

"Right up thar in Beaver Valley, whar they never was nary railroad a-tall, that's whar I learnt it. I wouldn't ricollect who I learnt it from. Ever'body knowed it. Like it is about the ships and the ocean. Ain't no ships or ocean in the mountains, but we sings about 'em, jest the same."

Buck was carrying it off right well. But he was putting on the dog and mighty pleased to have the chance. I had to give him credit, but I grudged him the chance, and I was cussing him with every breath. And mighty put out with Cissie even if I didn't cuss her. I still couldn't figure out why she would take the risk of bringing that old rip right into her class there in college, with so much depending on how it turned out. Take that risk, when she might have done just as well or better with some other, and no risk at all. And the Old 97 would go ten times better if you put some fire into it, and had a guitar to back it up—like Cissie and me could do it, and had done it many's the time, for that matter.

And right there before me, Buck was almost getting out of control. Plumb impudent, I thought, the way he was going on.

"Thar's plenty o' folks," he was saying, "that sings the song about rye whiskey, and they don't drink nothin' but the pure corn. Never drunk nothin', their whole lives, but the good ol' mountain dew. Don't even know whut rye whiskey is."

A few of the boys laughed, and some of the girls tittered, but I thought I heard feet shuffling in the back, and maybe a Bronx cheer or two.

But Cissie brushed over that, quick as a wink. Back yonder, she said, the railroad life was a risky, romantic life, full of adventures and accidents. That was how folks happened to make up ballads about it. You had to have a hero. And you couldn't have a hero unless somebody risked his life or even lost it, like in a train wreck, or if some poor old gallant brakeman fell between the freight cars and got cut all to pieces.

And there was Jesse James, for an example to compare, she said. Jesse robbed the Gallatin bank with his brother Frank, he did, but they didn't make up any song about the banker that got robbed, did they? Just to add up dollars and cents and figure out compound interest, that didn't make a hero and never would.

It was the same way about the sailor's life. Nothing about bookkeeping in the sailor songs, but a lot about shipwrecks and sailors getting drowned. Only the songs about train wrecks, just like the songs about shipwrecks and battles, were hardly ever the true stories, exactly, but were mostly made up.

They all follow an "established pattern," Cissie said. A pattern that always made things bigger and better than they really happened. Careless about facts but true to the spirit.

Now I knew Old 97 was wrecked up there at White Oak Mountain, near Danville, the way the song says. Then how could that ballad be careless about facts? I glanced to my right, and there was a pretty brown-haired, blue-eyed coed writing down what Cissie said—and she gave me a side look and a nice little smile. I glanced to my left, and there was a pretty black-eyed girl a-doing the same—and *she* gave me a nice big smile. I glanced all around, and the whole derned class was taking down every word, just like it was gospel. They were all scribbling like an office full of stenographers. So I snatched out my pencil and begun to scribble too.

I couldn't hardly read my writing afterwards, but I could remember and piece out what Cissie said.

"It may be a fact," Cissie said, "that Train No. 97 was wrecked on the Southern Railroad, nearly fifty years ago, in somewhat the way described. But, since the crew was killed and the train destroyed, nobody knows now, and nobody knew then, whether Steve Brooklyn told his black greasy fireman to shovel on a little more coal; or whether he said anything at all to the fireman; or what the speed of the train was; or exactly what happened on the three-mile grade. The ballad is very, very exact about those details, and it seems absolutely convincing. But whoever composed the ballad, and whoever changed the later versions, could not possibly have had first-hand information about the very things that are offered as straight fact."

If a pretty woman can preach, Cissie was preaching. At least it sounded like "Forsake your songs and go to Heaven, or else keep your songs and go to Hell." That serious, I mean. Then she went off into some big talk that I couldn't understand. Something about the "creative imagination of the folk." I don't know whether she was reading it off or just speaking, but I couldn't even spell the words, and so I gave up scribbling for a minute.

I leaned over and whispered to the black-eyed girl, behind my hand, when Cissie was looking the other way.

"She's a-tearin' into it like a whirlwind of woodpeckers, ain't she? Shore is a clever teacher."

The black-eyed girl nodded and looked up through long eyelashes. "But I'd sure like to hear what you think about it, Mr. MacGregor." She smiled again, crossed her legs, and pulled down her skirt—just as Cissie cut her eye around at us. And I straightened up just in time. And got ready to write.

"Furthermore," said Cissie, and stopped, with her eye right square on me. "Furthermore—that warning to the men—no, I mean the ladies, in the last stanza of the ballad—that warning to the ladies doesn't have any facts behind it at all. It sets up purely imaginary motives for the engineer's reckless speed. We are asked to believe there is some connection between the alleged fact that Steve Brooklyn drove Old 97 at excessive speed and some quarrel he had with his wife before he started his run. You remember how it goes."

Cissie came out with the song, and her singing, compared to Buck's, was like a mockingbird compared to a bullfrog.

> So come, young ladies, and all take warning
> From this time now and on.
> Never speak harsh words to your true loving husband;
> He may leave you and never return.

Then Cissie said: "But there is no evidence that Steve Brooklyn's wife spoke harsh words to her true loving husband on the fatal day."

And she begun to explain how it was all part of a "pattern" and the "take warning" was just a "tag" that they stuck on to some ballads whether it belonged or not. Might be some old murdering scoundrel about to be hung, and he would break down just before they led him to the drop, and say yes, he'd done wrong to be robbing and killing, and then would come the tag: "Boys, take warnin' from me." Like Kenny Wagner, she said, or Claud Allen, or Frank Dupree. But Old 97, she claimed, was modeled on "The Ship That Never Returned." Some singers, in fact, called it "The Freight Train that Never Returned." And she set in to singing "The Ship That Never Returned" so we could see for ourselves there was no argument about it.

And good Lord, she was right, there wasn't no argument at all, though the words were not as good, for my taste, as the Old 97. I had never heard the song about the ship or ever so much as thought about what Cissie was telling. And I scribbled hard, all on fire to write it down. But I couldn't keep up. My pencil made a jumble of it. The sweat run down my forehead and dropped on my notebook.

But right there Cissie stopped for a second, like she turned a cartwheel on the high wire and landed right side up. I could almost hear the drum roll when she done it, but there wasn't no sound really but the scratching of pens and the turning of pages and the little quick snap when Cissie slipped a rubber band over some cards she was using. She tapped 'em even at the ends, put 'em down, and picked up another bunch of cards, smiling at the corners of her mouth and looking far away.

I knew that expression of face many a time just before she started a big number. Now comes the next part of the act, I told myself, and I'll bet a pretty that it'll be a honey. And I said to myself, hold on to everything,

MacGregor. She's going out on the highwire again, and what is she going to do? Ride a bicycle maybe, with Buck Kennedy standing on her shoulders.

It was nigh onto that sort of doings.

"We can see the same creative process at work," said Cissie, "in the ballad of Omie Wise." We all started to write that down quick. I peeped over at the black-eyed girl's notebook that was so close to me on the arm of the chair. And I saw she had wrote down: "Same process in O. Wise." O-ho, I thought, so you don't have to write down every word. And so I wrote: "Same proc—OW" It was a good trick to know because Cissie went right along without seeming to care whether we kept up or not.

Cissie was talking about what she called the "love murder" ballad. About how some rounder makes love to a girl, cheats her with a promise to marry her, then tolls her off into some lonesome place and kills her. Sometimes he may stab her right over the grave he's been a-digging all night. Sometimes he drowns her. Then the newspaper slaps a scare headline on the story and slops the public with the gory details. Just sensational "facts," Cissie said. But the ballad maker makes "art" out of it, she explained, because he has his old, tried-out "pattern" for the story. And the pattern nearly always works. All he has to do is to fit the new facts into the good old pattern, even if he has to twist the facts a little or a lot, and then he's got something to remember. Especially if he has a good tune to sing the pattern by. Then, if everything works right, there'll be a tragic ballad—real art, not just a sensational story. And then she told Buck Kennedy to stand up and sing "Little Omie Wise."

After that considerable wait, Buck was r'aring to go. He stood up and sung the ballad right well and about as I remembered it. I put down my pencil and just listened, because I already knew the song. And I could hear the students joining in, soft and a little timid, with the parts they knew.

> He promised to meet her at Adam's springs
> Some money to bring her and other fine things.
> "Come, get up behind me, and we'll go to town,
> And there we'll be married and in union bound."
>
> She got up behind him and away they did go
> To the banks of Deep River where the water did flow.
> "Get down, my dear Omie, I'll tell you my mind
> I intend here to drown you and leave you behind."

Buck heard the students singing, and it whetted him on to sing louder. I had a feeling that he was having too much fun with the ballad; and that it wasn't a sad story to him but just a big joke, and that the students, as he quickened the tempo, were almost making a joke of it too.

On my left, the black-eyed girl was singing. On my right, the blue-eyed girl was not—at least I couldn't hear her. I felt something was sort of pulling me to the right, and slipped a glance that way. The blue-eyed girl had her chin in her hand and was spending the time looking at me.

"Don't you know the song?" I asked her, thinking only to be friendly.

"Oh, yes, I know it," she whispered, not moving.

"Then why don't you sing it?"

The girl lounged back in her chair and gave me the full effect of two big blue eyes. "Why don't you? I don't care for that man's singing. But I'd *love* to listen to you sing it, Mr. MacGregor."

"Well, some time maybe," I said right hasty, and straightened up. Good Lord, I thought, they all know me, and if it's going to be like this all the time I'm a-going to come early and set with the boys. This is dangerous.

Meanwhile, Buck had finished and set down, and Cissie was taking the ball again. "And now," she said, "I am going to call for class discussion instead of lecturing. We have about ten minutes left. The question is: How closely does the ballad of Omie Wise follow the facts? Mr. Kennedy knows the country mighty well, and so I will ask him, first of all, if he can tell us just where the murder of Omie Wise occurred, and when it was. Please talk about it some, Mr. Kennedy."

Buck didn't seem surprised, and so I reckoned Cissie must have coached him. She had put down her cards and papers, and was leaning against the reading desk, tucking in a lock of hair, very innocent-like, more like a calendar girl picture than any idea of a teacher, but she would have scalped me if she knew I was thinking that.

"Well, Miss Timberlake," said Buck, stretching his legs and leaning back lazy in his chair, "there's an Adams Spring right over the ridge from whar I live in Beaver Valley. Hit's about five mile down the creek on that side, in the other valley. I was always told that Omie Wise and her folks lived in them parts."

For once he's telling the truth, I said to myself. That's what my old Granny told me, and Cissie knows it too, so why is she asking? In fact, my Granny, said she knew Omie's folks, and she might have seen Omie when she, that is my Granny, was a little girl, but couldn't remember it.

Cissie's eyes were roaming over the class. My heart jumped when I thought she was looking at me. But no, she was aiming over my head at somebody behind me.

"And what do you say, Mr. Exum?"

Uh-huh, I thought—so they call the students "Mr.," and so forth in college, and not by their first names. A good strong voice answered up, and you could have called it polite, but I would call it a growling between the teeth.

"I say he might as well have said it was in China," said the strong voice. "He don't know what he's talkin' about."

The words bounced out like the Exum boy might be throwing rocks at Buck Kennedy. I screwed around in my seat and saw his red head sticking up, a few rows back of me. His eyes were a double-barreled shotgun pointed at Buck. The class was froze in their seats like woods in winter midnight. And Buck was on the edge of his chair, fists on his knees, taking a gimlet-eye bead on the Exum boy. Cissie had blundered into a ruckus, and why didn't she think first?

But Cissie meant to be the teacher. They would have to do their shooting outside.

"I see, Mr. Exum," she said, smooth as custard pie. "You seem to differ with Mr. Kennedy about this ballad."

"Yes'm," answered the Exum boy, and his voice was softer. "I disagree absolutely. It was more over toward Clay County. I've seen the very stump where Omie Wise mounted the horse behind Lewis. It's a big old white-oak stump right on the main road."

Buck Kennedy was half out of his chair barking back at Wallace Exum. You couldn't tell what he was saying because the whole class had busted out talking. It sounded like Buck said, "I won't stand for no Exum to tell me . . ." But Cissie had turned her back on him and was pointing her finger at Elvira Looney, who was waving her hand around there near me, on the front row.

"Miss Looney," said Cissie, very calm. "Give us your opinion." And Buck sat back, doubling and undoubling his big fists, while Elvira laid down the law.

"I think they are both wrong, Miss Timberlake. I read an article that quoted a newspaper account. And it said that the murder happened at New Salem over in Randolph County, and that Naomi Wise was an orphan girl living with the Adams family. She didn't have any kinfolks. And Lewis, the man who murdered her, was from Guilford County."

"Splendid," said Cissie. "You have been working on this ballad, I can see. But tell me, Miss Looney, when did all this happen?"

"It was in the eighteen-seventies, I think. No, Miss Timberlake, I'm not quite sure, without looking at my notes. But I asked my father about it, and he said it was quite some time after the Confederate War."

"Is that right?" Cissie asked the class, smiling and looking around the room. And the students were all nodding their heads and saying "Yes'm" and I was nodding mine too, and in fact so heated up about the whole idea that I could hardly hold back from waving my hand and snapping my fingers, like we used to do in school, to get teacher to let me put in my two cents worth.

"You are all sure it was after the War?" Cissie was all dimples and mischief, taking a few slow steps back and forth in front of her desk, a school-teacher witch in high heels and sheer-stockinged legs, charming us to follow her off into deep water and doom.

Oh, yes, we were all sure and sartain. Not one to say no. Just charmed to say yes and die. And old Buck Kennedy too, grinning and nodding and watching Cissie's knee action out of the corner of his black eyes.

"I'm so sorry." Cissie turned herself back into a plain school-teacher as soon as she walked behind her desk. "If it happened at all, in the way the ballad claims, it was *before* the Confederate War. Long before. Here is the court record, of the year 1808, of how Benjamin Elliott swore an oath in the August term of court, in Guilford County, about the escape of Jonathan Lewis from jail, where he was locked up on a charge of murder."

She read from the court record. And I sunk down-down-down into the deep water. Down with the whole class and old Buck Kennedy too, and not a bubble to mark the place. Flung off our high horse like little Omie Wise, and trodded down among the crawfishes and water-dogs. It was plain murder but we had to take it. The Omie Wise song couldn't be less than a hundred and fifty years old. The only consolation was that Cissie drownded Buck Kennedy too. He sat limp as a dishrag, twiddling his crooked thumbs, ready for his coffin. And the whole classroom still as a funeral parlor.

"So it's just a story," said Cissie, "like the man says 'Ashes to ashes, dust to dust.' Whatever the original facts on which the ballad was based, 'Omie Wise' is a typical love murder ballad that follows the pattern of 'The Oxford Girl' and many more that I could cite. But our time is nearly up, and I will follow up this discussion later. We will end the class hour by singing 'Omie Wise.' I am sure you'll find that the ballad has lost nothing of its charm because of our study.

"But before we sing, I want to announce that I still have some of the mimeographed sheets that give the assignments and an outline of the course for this half-term. The new members of the class can get them from me here at the desk. And speaking of new members—"

Cissie was not looking at me, but from the tone of her voice I made sure she had decided to take her medicine, even if the medicine was me.

"Speaking of new members, I am sure you have noticed that we have with us today Mr. Danny MacGregor of the Turkey Hollow Boys. You have all heard him sing over the radio or on the stage. He is not just a visitor. He is going to be a member of the class and study ballads with us."

There was a little handclapping. I could feel that everybody was looking at me and whispering. And to be between two pretty coeds, like I was, was like sitting between two high-frequency radio sets. They were both broadcasting and I was caught in the vibration, while red blushes and wild getaway feelings ran up the back of my neck.

"And now let's sing," Cissie was saying. And by the time the electric bell set off a big fuss, we were all going strong, as the class broke up, on

> She got up behind him and away they did go
> To the banks of Deep River where the water did flow.

Then I was caught in the squeeze of the crowd, as the next class tried to get in the room, and the ballads class rushed to the front and jammed around Cissie and Buck Kennedy. On one side of me the black-eyed coed who grabbed me by the hand was just out-and-out: "It's *simply thrilling* to have you in our class, Mr. MacGregor." But on the other side the blue-eyed girl was more clever. She managed to drop all her books right in front of me, and I had to pick them up for her, and while she took them one by one she was exclaiming, "Oh, thank *you*, Mr. MacGregor. You are *so* nice. *See* you at class—tomorrow." I was trying to step up politely to Cissie's desk and get my mimeographed sheets, but the rush of coeds and boys cut me off. Finally Cissie saw me and shoved the papers at me over somebody's shoulder.

"There is your syllabus, *Mr.* MacGregor," said Cissie—and came down hard on the *mister*.

I felt a hand on my elbow. It was Wallace Exum.

"Can I speak to you outside?" he asked. "I've got something to tell you."

13

A LITTLE WALK ACROSS THE CAMPUS

I folded the mimeographed sheets into my notebook and followed Wallace Exum through the crowd. It took some time to buck our way against the stream of boys in sport shirts that were sweating hard, and the pretty coeds that somehow managed not to sweat at all. As we pushed through the hall and down the stair-steps to the main door, I was thinking it was a good thing there was one person in the class I knew. Maybe Wallace Exum could give me some pointers. Yet though he was Ed Cooley's nephew, I didn't know him too well after all. Only the way you get to know any other disk jockey around a radio station. Pass the time of day now and then; see him hanging around and swap a few words; make sure to keep on his good side. Not much more. And I didn't have the least idea how he happened to be a disk jockey in the first place or what brought him into Cissie's class. And now I'll find out, I said to myself. He favors Ed a little, in his round face and strong chunky build; but he's redheaded as I am and maybe not as good-humored as Ed. He has dark eyes and his hands are delicate as a woman's. I reckon he never did much farm work. I reckon the Exums didn't lose much time moving to Carolina City when farming begun to play out. Still, Wallace must have had a country raising.

We came through the tall white pillars and down the steps to the wide concrete walk where there was more room for foot traffic.

"Do you have to go anywhere—right away?" Wallace's voice had an edge to it.

"One o'clock is my next broadcast. I'd like to pick up my mail and get a sandwich. Have one with me?"

"No, thank you." He was flipping his cigarette lighter and having no luck with it. I thumb-nailed a match for him, and we both lit up. Wallace spat into the grass. "It takes my appetite—to have to sit and look at Buck Kennedy a whole hour."

Wallace seemed nervous and upset. His dark eyes seemed to be trying to read my thoughts. "Well, I just look at Cissie and try to forget Buck," I said.

"Yes, that helps. But he draws me like a snake. And did you hear him advertisin' his stuff?"

"You mean his singin'?"

"No, I mean that about rye whiskey and corn liquor?"

"That was just his big talk. He can't help actin' a fool."

"It was a pretty big hint to them that knows. I don't see why Miss Cissie don't ketch on. He'll ruin everything for her."

"Don't you think she can handle him?"

"How can she handle him if he's sellin' corn liquor right here on the campus? And no tellin' what other meanness."

"What! You don't mean in broad daylight?"

"He might be. You take a little walk with me. I'll show you."

I hesitated, for Wallace seemed too excited and eager. He had thrown down his cigarette and was shaking another one out of the pack. I wondered what I was getting into.

"I know you don't believe me," he said. "I don't blame you. But I've found out where he parks. You can see for yourself."

"Will we have time?" I asked. "Won't he be there already?"

"Oh, no, there are always some coeds hanging around him after class. They'll keep him awhile. Besides, he'll take his time and sneak around the back way. Around noon—that's when he likes to meet his customers."

"Let's go, then. 'Twon't hurt to take a look."

Wallace seemed very much relieved, and we struck out up the walk. The sun was right overhead and bearing down hot. We were moving up the main slope of the college grounds, where the big buildings all face to the inside of the long square, and the wide concrete walks line up perfectly straight from the front of one building to the next, with steps at the different levels.

"No need to walk fast," said Wallace, when I begun to stretch my legs. "Take your time and see where the taxpayers' money goes." He gave a little sarcastic laugh. He seemed right gay, now that we had started.

I never had paid much attention to the place before, just running in and out. But it was a place to see, all right.

Whoever laid off the grounds had left all the middle part open, and had cut out all the old forest trees that must have been there. So all the brick-and-stone fronts and the rows of windows glared at you, no matter which way you looked. And there was no shade. Only bushes and flower beds spotted around, and a few weasly nursery saplings, all of 'em already turning sick in the July heat. And the noise of all kinds of machinery made a big rackety-rack in every direction. Men were chasing motorized lawnmowers back and forth over the thin grass that ought not be mowed at all. In one place a truck was dumping raw clay from some new digging, and men were spreading it over the discouraged grass. When we came up the next level I saw where the digging was. In a gap between the buildings a power drill was chattering something terrible, a bulldozer was shoving rocks and earth, and dumptrucks were snorting and backing up. Next to the diggings, a brand-new building was just being finished. Workmen were hammering along the edge of the roof and on the peak. Large crates were being unloaded from a big trailer truck at the side of the building, and from the inside I could hear floor-finishing machines squealing like stuck pigs. The noise seemed to make the heat worse. The glare from the buildings and walks hurt my eyes.

"I thought college'd be a quiet sort of place," I said. "I don't see how they study, or even hear the teachers in all this noise."

Wallace gave another little sarcastic laugh. All of a sudden he seemed very cheerful, and began to talk a blue streak, like a disk jockey running off his stuff between the records and the commercials.

"Well, I'll tell you. You don't want to forget our good friend, the Hon'able Carlos B. Reddy, on a fine July day like this, because he's the man that pulls the wires and gets the money. And he's the real sugardaddy of Teachers College, the one I mean that got a college put here in the first place, even if it was the place that nobody but Carlos B. Reddy and the Carolina City Chamber of Commerce would have thought about for a teachers college. Don't you remember? He wants to provide educational opportunities for poor mountain boys like MacGregor and Exum, and fight illiteracy, and correct our speech defects. Course he's in Washington, most of the time. He can feel the pulse of the NEA and the PTA and all the other A's better in Washington. When the pulse throbs a little faster, he telephones another half-million dollar prescription, and all we have to do is pick the medicine off the counter and take the dose. It's easy. Just listen to it fizz and swallow it right down.

"Now—don't you feel better already? If you don't I'll play the other side of this record. That big hole where they are digging—that'll be our new psychology lab, pretty soon. Where we'll bring in some Yankee profs to teach the coeds the psychology of sex and not be all repressed and inhibited. And the building just finished—that's for Audio-Visual Education. Right down your line, brother. And they're unloading television equipment right now. The other buildings are old stuff. Must be ten years old or more. That's the old chapel—they tore out the benches and equipped it with posture chairs and a sort of stage! The women's dormitories are over to the left, on that side of the ridge; and the men's dormitories to our right on the other side. And that big building in the middle is the library—"

"Where is the cafeteria?" I interrupted him. "I was in one with Cissie. But I'm all turned around—"

"Oh, that's down the hill, at the other end, in the Student Union Building. Has a long porch on the side toward the boulevard, and a parking circle. Doesn't have any jukeboxes in it yet, but the Student Senate is petitioning for some, so they can have music with their meals and dance every night. They want one in the snackbar, and one in the main dining room too. Let's cut across here."

We cut across the level stretch in front of the library and angled across the grass toward the men's dormitories. The buildings along the ridge had big trees around them, and there were trees along the walk, and a little breeze was moving in the shade.

"This is the old part of the campus," Wallace said. "And back of the men's dormitories is the Shelby House. It's really old. Belonged to Colonel Shelby, you know—the old mansion. They'll tear it down as soon as they get money for a new dormitory. But right now they are using it for the overflow of G.I. students. And that makes it mighty convenient for Buck Kennedy."

"How is that, Wallace?"

"I'll show you. We'll be there in a few minutes. Right this way."

We cut around the back of a big three-story building and came into a path that wandered through overgrown bushes and across good sod where the grass grew thick and healthy in the half shade. Through the trees ahead I could see the Shelby House—an old-fashioned red brick house, two stories, with a pillared porch that looked square into the back windows of the dormitory that had been built almost jam up against it. Between us and the house were some panels of an old wooden fence, half falling down, the white paint mostly gone.

"You keep right up with everything?" I said. "I don't see how you do it."

Wallace turned quiet again. "Oh, I just start talking. With this disk jockey job I get plenty of practice. It begins to come natural. I just start talking— about anything, it doesn't matter. Then other people start talking too. Same as canary-birds begin singing if you make a steady noise. People seem to want to spill everything they know. And dying for the chance. So I pick up information. You'd be surprised at what goes on around this campus."

I didn't say anything. Wallace went on like he was thinking out loud. "But that isn't why I'm taking the ballads course. I'm majoring in music, and I thought I'd build up on the folk song side. Of course, with the DJ work I have to keep right up with everything in the hillbilly music field.

And I'm crazy about it—especially the kind of thing you and Miss Cissie do. I thought maybe I'd start me a little band of my own some time. But I'm not good enough with a guitar. I've got too much piano in me, and I like symphony and opera too well. I got the idea of spinning a real ballad record now and then on that Night Watchman hour, 12 to 1 A.M. I didn't get any complaints, and so I had the notion that might be a new line to take some day. Folk song at a higher level than hillbilly radio takes it. Soon as I heard Miss Cissie was working with ballads, I thought she might have that idea too. And so I registered for the course. And I wondered, soon as I saw you, if you were thinking the same way."

"Well," I said. "Not exactly. But I might be."

"Anyway, I'm glad you're in the class. That'll make a big difference to me."

Wallace stopped and pointed. "There's his jeep. Right yonder."

We were back of the Shelby House, in a spot where the hedge plants hadn't been trimmed in a long time, and had grown up high and bushy with seedling sprouts all around them. It was a regular thicket, with an old brick walk leading into it from the back of the house, up to an old incinerator piled full of cans and trash. Looking through the thicket, I could see back of the incinerator, an open space, and back of the space was what looked like a row of old brick stables, with sagging wooden doors closed except where somebody had parked a nice new automobile.

The jeep was in the hedge-plant thicket, just far enough out of the open space so as not to be noticed. You wouldn't see it if you didn't know it was there.

"We can stay in these bushes and watch him," Wallace whispered. "He'll be coming along soon."

The idea didn't appeal to me. We both had on light-colored clothes.

"No," I said. "He's a mountain man. He'll spot us. What's in them old stables."

"Nothing, I reckon. The boys don't use 'em much. I don't know what that car is doing there."

"If we can git into a stable, we'll be safer, and we can watch through the cracks. Let's try it."

We walked across the dusty ground. Back of the stables, I could see, was an alley or lane. Maybe Colonel Shelby used to keep his carriage and horses here, and his black driver would bring the carriage around to the front through that alley. The double doors dragged hard, but we opened one and closed it carefully behind us. Inside, there was still a smell of horses—and of gasoline and oil mixed with it. The old door had plenty of cracks, just the right size. We stood side by side, peeping through, waiting for Buck

Kennedy. I could see the back end of the jeep through the bushes. Wallace was nervous again. I had to stop him from lighting a cigarette. The smoke might curl through the cracks. We waited, restless.

"Looks like Buck is takin' a big chance," I whispered, "to operate in broad daylight."

Wallace shook his head. "Oh, no. Not much. Nobody ever comes here except the trash truck—and Buck's customers. And maybe the watchman, late at night. Besides, Buck ain't much scared. He don't act scared. I think he must have protection from the city police. Must be tied up with some joint in the city. But he wouldn't have protection from the county officers. I could swear to that. Sheriff Looney don't go for it."

"You think he's got whiskey in that jeep now?"

"I haven't seen it for myself. Fellows tell me he sells it, right out of the jeep."

It was hot in the smelly old stable. I looked at my watch. Eleven-forty.

"Don't the campus have no police?"

"Just one old man, in daytime. Buck wouldn't be scared of him." There were quick footsteps on the walk. "S-s-h, here are his customers," said Wallace.

Three or four boys had come together. They were waiting near the jeep, and the only one I could see was a fat young feller in a flashy shirt that was standing at the edge of the thicket. They kept their voices so low at first that you couldn't tell what they were saying. Then a fourth feller came up. He spoke right out.

"You-all been waitin' long?"

"Long enough to git up a thirst," said Chubby.

"My G.I. money's burnin' a hole in my pocket," said another.

"How d'you git a-hold of any G.I. cash?" asked a third. "I never see any."

"It's a manner of speakin'," said the other. "My old man don't understand the G.I. bill and sends me tuition money."

"What d'you reckon is keepin' him so long?"

"It's that ballads class, ain't it? I think he hangs around with the girls afterwards."

"Maybe we ought to bring some girls—he'd git here faster."

"Well, I want to git two pints and shove off," said Chubby. "My date is so nice she won't drink out o' the same bottle with me. Has to have her own."

"Who could blame her, Chubby," one said, and they all laughed. The same voice asked, "Chubby, why you got your car parked there in that old stable?"

"Well," said Chubby, "if I park over on the campus, I'll git a parkin' ticket. I ain't got no parkin' permit."

"Why don't you go on and git a permit?"

"Well," said Chubby, "if I apply for a permit, they'll find out I ain't got no driver's license. It was took up after my last accident. So I park off campus mostly."

"Where you takin' your date, Chubby?"

"Oh, out to the bathin' beach, I reckon."

"I'll bet!"

"I'll bet she won't hang her clothes on no hickory limb."

They began to laugh, and stopped quick. It was Buck, stepping fast on the walk.

"Gentlemen," he said. "Don't make so damn much noise. I ought not to do this, anyway. It ain't really safe, and I wouldn't do it, except to accommodate you. And I ain't got but a few pints left, today, anyhow."

I was trying to get an angle through the crack where I could actually see a bottle and some money pass, but all I could get was a view of Buck's back and shoulders. But Chubby gave me a chance when he spoke up and Buck turned to him.

"I want two pints," said Chubby.

Buck was fumbling in the jeep. He came out with a tow-sack, grabbled deep in the bottom of it, and handed the boy a bottle.

"A pint's all I can sell you, and accommodate these other gentlemen. And that'll be $3.00, please."

"Oh, hell," said Chubby, and took his pint.

"Ain't that a little high?" asked a voice, complainingly.

"A man has got to live," said Buck. "I take the risk. And I don't get nothin' hardly out of this ballad singin'. But it gives me a chance to accommodate you gentlemen on the side and make a little something."

"How old is this damned red-eye of yours?" asked another.

"It ain't red-eye, and it ain't white mule," said Buck. "It's the genuine mountain dew, none of it less than a year old, and aged in white-oak kags."

"He's a damned liar," Wallace Exum was hissing at me. "If there ever was a white-oak keg on the place I'll eat a sugar barrel."

I thought Buck was lying, all right, but I had to poke Wallace and shush him. The chubby boy was getting into his car, right on the other side of the partition.

"Now, gentlemen, that's all," Buck was saying. "If you need any more, you'll have to see me tonight, out at Art's Grill. I'll be there, after nine o'clock, in the parking lot. But if I get a chance, I'll leave some at the Shelby House, with you-know-who. And I thank you."

"That's his police protection," Wallace was whispering. "Art's Grill." I nodded. I knew about Art's Grill.

The boys in Chubby's car were getting out fast, and we were waiting for Buck to get out. Or I was. Wallace was r'arin' to go.

"Let's step out and teach him a lesson," he was mumbling. "There's two of us, and we can knock the hell out of him."

I held him down. "No, you won't. We got to handle it some other way. I've been workin' on it with your Uncle Ed. You got to keep Cissie in mind." He subsided then, but I kept my hand on his arm. I didn't know but what the boy had a knife in his pocket and might rush out at Buck.

Buck, meanwhile, was taking his time. He looked up at the sun. Then he looked at his watch and yawned. He folded up the tow-sack carefully and laid it on the front seat. Then he slowly got into the front seat, started the jeep, and began to back out of the little thicket. Just then I heard slow steps in the alley, coming around the corner of the stables and into the open space. A voice said, "Hold on there a minute, Mister."

It was a policeman.

"That's him," whispered Wallace. "That's Cap'n Bills, the campus policeman. Golly, d'you suppose he'll take Buck in."

Buck stopped in the act of backing around, and was looking over his shoulder.

"Who are you and what are you doin' here?" said the officer. His voice was rough and meant business. "Git out o' that jeep and let me look at you."

Buck was out of the jeep, and just as polite as he knew how to be. "Yes sir, Cap'n," he said. "I'm jest a visitor, but in a way I belong here. In fact, I'm workin' for the college, you might say. My name is Kennedy. And I have been singin' for Miss Timberlake's ballads class this mornin'. Dr. Hoodenpyl arranged it. And you can ask Dean Bronson about me."

I couldn't see the officer's face. I didn't know how impressed he was. But I was afraid he would arrest Buck, right off, and I sure didn't want that to happen, though Wallace was fairly shaking with joy.

"You stand right there," said the officer. "I'll look over your car."

I spoke into Wallace's ear. "We got to walk out there and certify Buck. Won't do to let him git arrested. That officer might arrest him."

Wallace turned up a red face and glaring dark eyes. He was shaking his head stubbornly and trying to push me away. He said he'd be damned if he'd certify that old bloodsuckin' weasel. "Come on," I said, taking him by the shoulder. "It won't look right if we open this door. I'm goin' over the partition into that next stable where the auto was parked, and out that open door. You follow me and back up my story."

I started to scramble over, soft and easy, but it wasn't easy with books under my arm. I heard the officer asking Buck about his parking permit, and then, "What are you doin' parked over here in the bushes if you was singin' for Miss Timberlake?"

And Buck was saying: "Cap'n, I was jist goin' to meet some o' the mountain students and ride 'em out to my place for a picnic. They said they wanted to git back out in the cool mountains . . ."

Right then I walked out. "That's right, Cap'n," I said. "We are the ones. Hello, Mr. Kennedy. Wallace and me was studyin' our lessons, back there out o' the heat, and jest gittin' through."

The officer blinked and looked at me. I could hear Wallace coming up behind me. He looked at Wallace. He looked at the books under our arms. He was an old man, sort of bulgy around the stomach. But his pistol was in plain view at the belt, and his face was about as hard-looking as the pistol.

"All right," he said. "I reckon it's all right. But that old stable is a damned funny place to be a-studyin' lessons, and this is a damned funny place to meet anybody."

He took out his pencil and began to write down Buck's license number. "I reckon it's all right. You don't seem to have nothin' but a tow-sack in that jeep. I've got my orders from the Dean to watch out for strange cars. You better go to the traffic committee and get a visitor's sticker." He rocked on his heels, studying us.

"Come on, Mr. Kennedy," I said loud and cheery, "let's get started for the mountains."

The policeman turned away.

I gripped Wallace by the arm and more or less shoved him into the back seat of the jeep. I got right in with him and put one hand over his mouth. I dropped my books and held him down on the seat with the other hand. It was a ride he'd never choose of his own free will, and he was already spluttering and struggling.

Out loud, in case the policeman was hanging around, I said: "Sorry to keep you waitin', but Wallace and me was right in the middle of a ballad." And in a low voice: "Buck, you fool, git started."

Buck had his hand on the door. His mouth was working, but he couldn't make the words come. Then he jumped behind the wheel, slammed the door, pressed the starter, backed the jeep into the alley at high speed, jammed the brakes hard, shot down the alley a few yards, then stopped with a jerk that threw Wallace and me off the seat. He glared down at us from the front seat.

"I don't keer about haulin' no Exums in my car, and I don't mean to start now. Git out."

It was taking all my strength to get Wallace back on the seat and hold him there. By this time Wallace was cussing Buck and me both. Wallace had no weapons but books. He was doing his best to brain Buck with his copy of Child's ballads.

"You've done took too many chances already today, Buck," I said. "You've got jest one chance to git out o' this. That is to drive us around by the boulevard and drop us on Shelby Avenue where my car is parked. And keep your mouth shut afterwards."

Buck grunted, and put the jeep into another hot spurt. When he came to the boulevard, and had to stop for the traffic and pedestrians, he looked over his shoulder as fierce as ever.

"Git out," he said again. "I won't haul ye a foot more."

"We'll git out when we are ready," I told him quietly. "Besides I've got something confidential to tell you. I don't want to yell it out here in front of these nice people."

A truck had come up behind us in the alley and was honking. Buck had to move. "Turn right," I said. And he turned. We were in traffic. Wallace had decided that a jeep on the public street was a poor place to ambush a Kennedy. He was sitting back, limp but still mad.

I leaned up close to Buck's right ear.

"Keep your eyes straight ahead and watch the traffic. And listen to what I'm tellin' you." I made the words hard as flint rocks, and with the steel of truth I struck the sparks off into his hairy ear. "I know all about your doin's, and if it wa'n't for Cissie I'd stop your doin's right now. I'm a-goin' to protect Cissie first of all. I don't give a damn how much bootleggin' you do so long as Cissie is protected. But if you mean to stay out of trouble, you keep your doin's off the campus."

"You better not try to lay a finger on me," Buck said, growling and looking through the windshield. "You cain't tetch me, you ner nobody."

"Try it and see," I sparked into his big ear. "There's more than one kind of police. And police ain't all, either. Jest keep your stuff off the campus and behave, and you'll be all right."

"You cain't tetch me," he said. "But don't you tell Cissie."

"Jest keep your liquor in them white-oak kags," I said. "Anyway, don't bring it on the campus." Buck groaned. He knew then how much I knew. "My car is in the next block."

He stopped and let us out without another word. Wallace stood on the pavement, dazed and rumpled. "Come on, boy," I told him. "I'll ride you now. Don't you worry. He won't be selling it on the campus for a while. He'll lay off for a few days anyhow—jest to play safe."

"I don't care, one way or the other," said Wallace. "I mean—he's just as low-down, no matter what he docs. But a polecat will always come back to your yard, won't he? He'll be comin' back with it—"

"Yes, Wallace," I said. "He'll be comin' back with it sooner or later. But maybe that'll give us time to make a trap."

We got into the car.

"Right now," I told Wallace, "I got to study some. Hit's been a powerful long time since I studied a book."

14

A POWERFUL LOT OF STUDYING

Soon as I got home and looked at Cissie's mimeographed sheets, I saw I'd have to do a powerful lot of studying if I ever hoped to get up on that ballad tightrope and walk it with Cissie. Them papers—why, they were like a set of ladders. You climbed up one ladder—that was the first week's lessons; then there was an extension ladder from the first week through the second. And so on for ten weeks—all of it locked tight together. The class was already halfway up Ladder No. 5—and if I meant really to ketch up, I would have to go back to Ladder No. 1, and begin with the oldest ballads. I would have to climb all ten ladders in the time the class was taking to climb the last four-and-a-half. And at the end of the ladder schedule Cissie had stacked up a long list of books. More books than I had ever read or even seen. Many times the books I'd studied in school, all put together. And the ten ladders were propped square against that tall stack of books. That's the way I figured it out.

Likewise I figured that if I was to take Cissie for my teacher and come out even with her class at the end, I would have to watch my step while I was climbing, and not get knocked off. I couldn't risk goggling around at the scenery.

I tore a leaf out of my notebook and made me out a program. This is what I wrote:

SCRIPT FOR D. MACGREGOR'S BALLAD ACT

Number One	Is do Ten Weeks in 4 1/2 = 2 days work in 1, every Day and Some Extry
Number Two	Is Set in Back of Room and KEEP AWAY from coed girls. Remember ARRIVE early & don't get roped.
Number Three	Is Lay off courting Cissie awhile, you fool, she is the TEACHER

Number Four	Keep your big mouth SHUT & speak when spoken to
Number Five	Is Study
Number Six	Keep Studying
Number Seven, etc.	Study some more

I took that sheet of paper and glued it on my bathroom mirror with some Scotch tape. That way, I would have to think about my resolutions every time I shaved. And if I got excited thinking about 'em, and cut myself, why, I could sign 'em again, in my own blood, to show I meant business. Then I happened to remember that I was working for Rufus, too. I got Rufus' timetable, far as it was up to date, and stuck it on the other side of that mirror, for another reminder. And there was my own face looking back at me between the two papers—ballads to the right, hillbilly songs to the left. That big head of reddish hair, with the cowlick always lopping down over one eye, and nothing I could do about it unless I got me a crew haircut, but Cissie had always yelled murder if I so much as mentioned it; she said she liked the cowlick and with my kind of face I needed a lot of hair falling over it. A gaunt, hungry-looking face it was, underneath the red shock—plenty of nose and chin, and high cheekbones, and a wide mouth that I never could stop from grinning. The eyes, call 'em gray-green, or green-gray, looking off yonder, like for bear on the mountain or cattle in the valley, and back of the eyes somewhere was me, the man I couldn't figure out. I made the eyes roll to the right and there was ballads and Cissie and Buck Kennedy, and I said to myself, "Oh, Lordy." I rolled 'em to the left, and there was hillbilly songs and Rufus and the mortgage on the MacGregor place, and I said, "Jesus, help a pore sinner." I shut my eyes, and shook my head, and heard my brains rattling like peas, and came to life again. But if I had been a drinking man, I would have poured myself a double shot of whiskey right then, even though I'd a-knowed it wouldn't do no good.

Nothing will do any good when a man's in that fix—unless it's work. I lit in and worked.

For the next week or two, it turned out well enough to follow my script. The first morning I came back to class, true enough, I felt like I was walking on ice when I arrived early, as I planned, found Miss Black Eyes and Miss Blue Eyes there already, in the same seats in the front row, with the same seat vacant between them, like an ambush of angels on the banks of Jordan. I couldn't deny I took some wounds, but I managed to skate along, and steered for the middle aisle and the back of the room, where I landed safely, in one piece more or less. Wallace Exum soon spotted me, and from then on Wallace sat with me pretty often, in what must have been Football Players Row, for back there they were mostly big rangy fellows who couldn't pronounce and spell, it turned out, much better than I could.

Wallace elected himself, right away, to be my private information service. Before class and after, if nobody butted in, Wallace slipped me the campus news, or sometimes whispered in my ear or wrote me little notes while the class was going on. Buck Kennedy, he said, was making himself scarce around the campus, and so maybe my guess was right about him—maybe he was scared. But maybe it just wasn't convenient to sell right out of the jeep, except on the days when Cissie brought him in to sing; and she wasn't using him for that very much any more. She was singing the ballads herself, or using a record player, or just lecturing straight. But Wallace thought Buck had a student salesman in the Shelby House, because the stuff was coming on campus just the same. The boy picked it up at Art's Grill and brought it in his own car. Wallace thought he had spotted the very one. And how did he spot him? Well, Wallace hid out in his own car in the parking lot at Art's Grill; he got a look, even if it wasn't a good look, there in the dark.

"It ain't safe, Wallace," I told him. "Don't you go messin' around a bootlegger's place at night."

"Oh, it's safe," said Wallace. "Uncle Ed comes with me. We can look out for ourselves."

"That makes it twicet as dangerous—two fools instid of one."

"Oh, no. We got to be ready, you see. When you need to set that trap— and bait it. Got to know where a varmint is if you're going lay a trap. And we'll have to, sooner or later. Because the Dean—"

"What about the Dean?"

"I'll tell you another time," he said—and broke off as somebody came up.

Wallace told me, as soon as he had another chance, that the Dean was suspicious. The campus policeman had traced down Buck's license number, and checked him up, and turned in his name and license number to the Dean. He didn't have any evidence, of course, but the Dean was suspicious all the same.

"And how in the world did you find that out? Have you got a pipeline into the Dean's office?"

"Yes," said Wallace, looking embarrassed. "Elvira tells me. She types for the Dean—parttime."

I had noticed that Wallace sat with Elvira Looney, quite often, and sometimes walked off with her after class. She was studying to be an English teacher, he said, and they were reading T. S. Eliot together. I didn't know who T. S. Eliot was, but I liked to hear Wallace spin his yarns about the people in the class, and what they were all doing. I tried to keep him on that subject, and away from the Buck Kennedy theme song. Who was the blue-eyed coed, I asked him. Oh, said Wallace, that little trick, she was Vera Pickens, and was majoring in music, like Wallace; and she wanted to be an opera singer. And so did the black-eyed girl—she was Joyce Tolliver. There were a lot of music majors in Cissie's class. They were all wild about Cissie—and besides, folk song was the newest rage in the music department. But the English and Education majors in the class—they were the same. It just took 'em by storm when she turned up on campus—to have a real mountain girl who'd gone through the mill at hillbilly singing, and then come back to the true music. They hadn't thought much of Dr. Hoodenpyl and his course till Cissie burst into sight. And that made all the difference. Didn't I think so too?

I did. I was happy about it as a squirrel up a hickory-nut tree. Running all up and down ten ladders of mimeographed paper, bending the wild nuts over to my mouth, spitting out hulls, and going after the meat.

Only, that studying. It gave me some hard nuts to crack. Hard as thick-shell, creek-bottom hickory nuts.

Sometimes I could barely even spell out the words printed in the books, much less pronouce them. Words like *etymological* and *contamination* and *Scandinavian* and *incremental* and *hypothesis*. It was easy enough, and sometimes like a picnic for me, to go along with what the class was studying from day to day—those "native American ballads," the cowboy songs, and lumberjack and sailor songs, and all the rest; and if you doubted anywhere, or dropped into a bog, there was Cissie, waving a white hand, and you came up out of the mud like magic. But the first part, where I had to study up the history and the whole big tale of ballads all by myself, with no Cissie to whip me through the mudholes—that was a teasy business. It just about fried me in my own grease.

All the same, I followed the directions on Cissie's mimeographed lesson sheets, read the ballads, and tried to read the books about the ballads. When Cissie said learn, I learned. If I couldn't understand it by reading it over, I set in and memorized it word for word, as much as I had time for.

At first I thought what a big old ignorant fool I must be, with it all printed plain before my eyes, and me still not knowing what it said. Came to find out, though, I wasn't the only one in that fix. There was boys and girls sharp as a tack, and been going to college, and there was teachers that had been teaching, and they were doing exactly the same thing—just memorizing the book, and didn't know what it meant.

As for Cissie, there was no doubt she was a couple of hundred miles ahead of all of us. One way or another, she had it all worked out, and had an answer for nearly any question. Besides, she was the teacher, and if there was something she didn't remember offhand, all she had to do was to glance at the notes on her cards.

But the plain way of saying it doesn't tell it. The classroom, so square and ugly, as if it was made ugly on purpose, to try and see how ugly a room can be; the gray walls that needed paint; the smudgy ceiling with one or two fly-specked overhead lights; the reading desk that was no color at all; the blackboards that weren't black; the windows that let in the sun glare, and the heat with it—all that vanished away when Cissie's heels came clicking fast on the plastic floor, and she stood framed by the blackboard, tossing back her yellow hair, drooping long eyelashes to look at her first notecard, then lifting that card with slender fingers and opening her eyes wide and friendly to let us into Kingdom Come. That was the minute when the rows of backs in front of me all straightened, and all caught their breaths in one big sigh all together, like when the house lights go off, and the curtains open, and the show is on. The buzz and roar of the trucks and bulldozers backed off and away into Hell, where they came from, and we were in the heavenly mountain valley of some old ballad song. It might be "Drowsy Sleeper":

> Awake, awake, you drowsy sleeper!
> Awake, awake, it's almost day.
> Why do you lie, and sleep and slumber,
> And your true-love going far away.

> "Who is it at my bower-window,
> A-calling of my name so sweet?"
> "It is a young man you were loving.
> One word with thee I wish to speak."

> "Oh, true-love go from 'neath my window!
> My father's on his bed of rest,
> And in his hand he holds a dagger
> To kill the one that I love best."

What happened after that was like something in a deep valley fog where you hear voices crying out, yet won't know what is going on till the sun comes up. And whether it was the girl that plunged the dagger into her own snow-white breast, or the father that killed the lover, or the lover that went off in some lonesome place and perished, we couldn't decide, frowning and questioning back and forth, like we were in that old house the same night, and afraid the old man would wake up. But if Cissie listened to us awhile, gasping out our wonders and doubts, and then sung, low and soft—

She wandered down by the flowing river,
And then prepared herself for death.
She took from her bosom a silver dagger
And pierced it through her snow-white breast.

Why, of course, all we had to do was to roll our eyes up at Cissie and say, "Yes, Lord, I believe"—no matter whether we thought the ending fitted or not.

What the rest did, after such a time as that, I don't know. I would drift away with the song on my mind, and if I was free to go home, I would be strumming it on my guitar and singing. And then have to pinch myself and begin studying if I wasn't going to turn into a mooncalf.

The studying was entirely a different sort of doings, because if I studied I would have to think, which was always a lot of work for me.

After I got used to reading about ballads in the books, I finally decided that the big tale about the old ballads took a lot of believing. The songs were there in the books, all right, and I plain admired to see how folks had been gathering 'em up, writing 'em down, and printing 'em, sometimes with tunes, sometimes not, ever since Shakespeare started growing whiskers, and maybe before. That was like a big barbecue for me. But the big tale about 'em—how they first begun—it was like cowpaths in the brushy pasture, going every which-away and leading no-way, and if you followed the paths, you'd never bring the cows home to milk.

Some of what they said, I couldn't swallow—like claiming that ballads just kind o' made themselves up when folks got together and started in drinking and dancing. Didn't I know that Rufus could make up a ballad any time he wanted to, if he felt like it and set his hand to it, and done some sweating? And Ozro could, too.

And maybe I could. That was an idea! It was our business, you might say—and my business—to practice that kind of thing. Not ballads exactly. Yet something like ballads. But only if we had a good idea and sweated over it. Just passing 'round the jug and patting your foot and swinging the gals to a fiddle tune wouldn't ever make anything but a good time.

I like best of all the books that just printed the old songs without too much fancy talk. And it was the biggest wonder of the world to see what that man Child had got together in that big book of his. I say *book*. That's what the library called it. But it took ten books, all bound up separate, to hold what that man Child would hold fit to be called *his* ballad book. Started out to print all the ballads in the whole country, but he died before he got through, and no wonder.

I got so fond of Child I used to call him Frank when I was studying him. Or even Frankie. His name was Francis J. I didn't say Frank out loud, only to myself. It was something between me and him. And I took the notion that if he could be around, he would look over his glasses and say, "Now Danny, look at this one. Ain't it a humdinger?"

At the library I would have to put down my name and wait my turn to use the Child books—and sit right there in the library to read it. They wouldn't let you take it out of the library at all, and when I asked why, the woman at the desk said well, the set cost a couple of hundred dollars, and they had to guard it.

When I got the Child book at last, I would find me a table in a corner, away from the boys and girls that were working harder at courting than studying—a corner where a little breeze would come through, and outside, I could see the high-pillared porch of the old Shelby House. There I would read. I would leaf over pages and pages of "Lord Randal's" and "Barbara Allen's," all alike yet all a little different, and I would say to myself, "This man Child has done cut and shocked all our wheat and there ain't nothin' left to do but thrash it."

But I found some wheat to cut and shock, after all. There were some books that the library would let me take home, for overnight at least. And evening, out at the house, I would sing out of them—sing the ballads to some tune or other, whether the book printed the music or not. I could read the music better, it might happen, than the old-timey words of some ballads; and I was glad Cissie had made me learn my notes, years before. She said she wasn't going to stand for me slopping around and playing only by ear. She was always promising to teach me harmony, too, but never got far into that.

I said I took the books out to the *house*. Well, I meant *apartment*, but I never could get used to saying it. It's nothing but what used to be one big room cut up into two little ones, with a bathroom squeezed into the old clothes closet, and a little refrigerator and grill tucked into what closet space was left. What they call a bachelor apartment. I'd a thousand times ruther been living at the MacGregor Place, and drive in every day. But the apartment was all right for a place to sleep when I was in town, and I could fix myself a snack if I was hungry. Nobody in that apartment house cared whether I was coming or going, and since I was upstairs on the third floor, 'way in the back, my practicing never bothered anybody much. I practiced in the bedroom where there was an overhead light and space to walk a few steps back and forth. The best studying I did was there. It would generally be after I got through some program at WCC, or a practice for Rufus. Part of the practice would always be on the new singing commercials that somebody in an advertising agency kept thinking up and handing over for us to learn.

It made me feel like a fool to be singing some of them, especially when they took some good old-fashioned song or fiddle tune and spoiled it. And the bad part was that the banks and investment houses decided to use the same kind of thing as the cigarette people and the drug stores. I remember the day when Rufus came in and sung off one for us.

It went to the tune of "Pop Goes the Weasel," and it was like this:

> If you would win success in life
> And keep up with your neighbors,
> Come and start a savings account
> And cash in on your labors.
>
> Draw interest with security
> And make your dreams come true, all
> Join the crowd and come today,
> Bank at Farmers National!
> Bank at Farmers National!

We busted out laughing when Rufus sung us that one. "What's the matter?" asked Rufus. "Don't you know it must be mighty good music if the bank hires it?" We kept on laughing. Rufus shot his eye at me, and said, "What do *you* think, Danny?" I said, "Rufus, I think it's the limit. Makes me want to take my account out of that bank, and derned if I don't believe I will." Rufus grinned. "Well, of course, hit does make you wonder if they got good sense. But hit's their program, and money in our pockets, and let's git it over with and learn it. And don't you start no run on that bank because I got some money in it too."

But it left a bad taste in my mouth, more and more, and I understood, more and more, why Cissie was so bound and determined to try and turn some furrows in another kind of field. And for me to get away from the commercials and the crowd at WCC, and push "Golden Cowboy Moon" and "Tennessee Waltz" out of my head and get back to ballads, was ever more like the shade of a great rock in a weary land and the pouring down of God's mercy.

If I had a book out of the library with the tunes in it, I would open it to one I liked, in what we call a minor key, but maybe without a sharp or flat where you would look for one to be; and I would fasten that book on to my music rack with rubber bands. (The music rack was left over from the days when I fooled around some with a saxophone and cornet; I never used it, ordinarily, for guitar picking.) I would stand up to that ballad tune, and sing it off the page, and see if I could get the right chords on my guitar, just by ear, and that sometimes took a lot of figuring, because often it seemed no kind of chord whatever would exactly suit the tune. Trouble was, when I got worked up with the ballad tunes, I would soon be going from one tune to another till, first thing I knowed, it would be one o'clock in the morning and I hadn't studied. However, I would still keep thinkin': "Now wouldn't this one be a honey on the radio, and I wish Rufus would let me try it once." Or else, "If I could jest git Cissie to sing this one, and me handling the guitar."

It was late one night, like that, when I first floated up against the idea that maybe Danny MacGregor, by a turn of luck, might hit off some ballad of his own. A brand-new one, and why not? I was picking away at some chords for a tune in the back of a Virginia ballad book, and wandered off into a piece of another tune that wasn't the same at all, nor like anything I had been playing or knew about. It was just a piece of a tune at first. I played it over and over, and it seemed to be telling me something. Something about Beech Hollow, and me coming down there with Ed Cooley, and no words to say what was gnawing at me. That night, I couldn't take the tune any farther, or think of any words to go with it, but it stayed with me, pestered me out of all studying, went to bed with me, and pounded in my ear on the pillow, along with the beating of my heart, and from that time on never stopped being a trouble to me.

It was soon afterwards that I found out the ballad study was beginning to spoil me for the radio and the hillbilly music. It came up on a Friday, when we had just finished a noon program at WCC. I was glad when it was over, and tore out of Studio A with my head down, saying nothing to nobody, and aiming to grab a bite and get right over to the library for a spell.

Ozro came running down the hall after me. "Hold on, Danny. Didn't you hear Rufus?"

"No, I didn't hear him. What's *he* want?"

"He was yellin' his head off for you to wait. You must be gittin' hard o' hearin'."

Ozro twisted his head to one side and looked down at me like a old shikepoke making ready to dab for a fish.

"'Course I know," he said, "if it had been a sartain *other* pussen callin', you'd a-heerd her through them soundproof walls." He grinned and dug his long finger into my ribs. "But it's a good proposition Rufus has. If you don't want it, some of the rest of us could take it on. We ain't near as busy as you, these days."

He laughed his big heehaw laugh and went on. I turned back and met Rufus in the hall. He had his fiddle under his arm and a letter in his hand. His eyebrows were twitching.

"What's the matter with you, Danny?"

"Nothin' the matter. I'm fine. Did I flub anything?"

"Naw, you played all the chords. And you sung the music."

"What's wrong then?"

"You are the one I'm askin'. All I know is you jest haven't got that old oomph. You are singin' like you don't care."

"I'm singin' the same as ever."

"No, you ain't. And the radio audience knows it. How's your mail holdin' up?"

"Aw, Rufus, I haven't paid much attention. Maybe not so many letters as common. But it's summertime, and too hot to write letters."

"Well, the rest are gittin' plenty of mail. But I'm not gittin' so many requests for your songs. You look a little peaked, to me. Are you sick?"

"I'm all right." I didn't want to tell Rufus how late I'd been studying, the night before, and every night.

"You better take some vitamins, then. I can tell you ain't quite up to snuff. But look here, this is what I wanted to see you about. Bob Greenhow passed me this letter, and I thought I'd throw you the proposition if you are interested."

I read over the letter, feeling Rufus' eyes on me, all the time. It was a new doughnut bakery, just starting up, and they wanted somebody for a singin' and talkin' program, fifteen minutes, six afternoons a week. It would be good money, and would give me a special spot of my own. But it would break right into the middle of every afternoon and spoil my plans.

"It's a good proposition, Rufus," I said. "And I sure do thank you. But I can't take it right now. I won't have the time. Not for the next few weeks."

Rufus frowned. "That's too bad, Danny. I'd shore like for you to—"

"Ozro or some of the others can have it. They could do it better'n me, anyhow."

Rufus was frowning hard. "Danny, I don't like to hear you talk like that." He hesitated, then came at me straight. "How long," he asked, "are you goin' to keep up this danged foolishness?"

"What foolishness? What are you talkin' about?" I knew what Rufus was talking about. I was trying not to get mad.

"Over at the college, I mean. You know what I'm talkin' about. You didn't take me into your confidence, but I know about your carryin-on's,

Danny. We all do. You can hear plenty about it. And we can all tell you ain't the same man. It must be gittin' on your nerves."

I felt stiff all over, and didn't know what to say. I didn't want a fuss with Rufus. I had enough trouble already.

"Is there anything wrong about my carryin-on's? You don't hold 'em ag'in me, do ye, Rufus?"

"Naw, I don't hold nothing ag'in you, Danny. I don't blame you for stickin' close to Cissie, and don't think we ain't on your side—and hers. But I've a stake in you. In both of you, I hope. And I was jest askin'—how long? How long and all that?"

"Don't worry, Rufus. The worst will soon be over. Jest put up the axe for about another three weeks. That's all I ask."

Rufus' face cleared up. "Oh, is that all? I reckon we can stand it for three weeks, and I wish you good luck. But I'm sorry you can't take the doughnut program."

I thanked Rufus again and turned away. But Rufus grabbed my arm, and walked with me down the hall. He was very friendly again.

"I don't blame you for stickin' close to Cissie," he said once more. "But there's two people she's got to watch. And if she don't watch 'em, you got to do it for her. One of 'em is Buck Kennedy."

"What do you know about Buck Kennedy?"

"Plenty. And it's a big risk Cissie is takin' with him."

"And who is the other?"

"The other is a faculty member. I think his name is Hoodenpyl."

I was surprised. I thought Rufus was going to say the Dean.

"Why he's just a college perfessor," I said. "Cissie thinks he hung the moon. He's her teacher."

"That may be," said Rufus. "You watch him, all the same. I've got a line on him."

"Tell me, Rufus—watch him for what?"

We were at the elevator. The girl at the desk waved at me and said, "Telephone call for Mr. MacGregor."

Rufus said, "You jest watch. I'll tell you some time. I bet that's Cissie calling you, right now."

He stepped into the elevator. I looked at the call slip. It was the college number, and a station number after it. I went to a booth and dialed.

It was Cissie, and she was talking to me same as if she never had been my teacher at all.

"Danny," she said, "I need some help, and it's worse than gittin' over the branch."

"Then I'll borrow a Model-T Ford and bring my fishin' boots too."

"No, it's all on dry land. Very dry land. Are you free after class tomorrow?"

Naturally, I was.

"I have a lunch meeting at the college cafeteria, but we'll be in a private dining room. Dr. Hoodenpyl is in town and will be there. Maybe some others. I want to see you alone first. Do you mind?"

I didn't mind. And Cissie said I was to speak to her right after class. That wouldn't be alone, I objected. "You leave that part to me," Cissie said. And her "Goodbye" sounded almost like "Come on."

15

CAUGHT IN A CONFIGURATION

Next morning when I climbed the steps of the Humanities Building, Cissie popped out from behind a pillar. She had a big load of books and papers.

"I'm glad I caught you before class," she said, hugging the load tight with both arms. It almost reached her chin. "Where is your car parked?"

"On Shelby Avenue. Near the steps where you come on the campus. Not far from the traffic light." I was trying to help her with the load, but she kept backing off.

"Good," she said, but she seemed fretted. "Danny, don't try to see me in the classroom. Go to the car and wait for me. I'll come, the minute I'm free."

Cissie backed off again and turned away, tucking the load against her chin. But first a little book slipped, then a big book skidded loose, and then papers began to flop. Before I could catch the pile, everything was tumbling—books, student papers, and a big stack of mimeographed sheets. I plopped my own books on the floor and scrambled to pick up.

Cissie was scrambling with me, all red and flustered. "Oh, Lord," she panted in my ear. "I got over here at seven o'clock to run off Dr. Hoodenpyl's stencils. And sat up late last night cuttin' 'em. I wish to God—"

She didn't say what she wished, but it couldn't a-been a blessing. I had the stack in hand. "I'll tote 'em for you," I offered, and reached for my own books with my free hand.

"No, you won't. Just load me up."

I loaded her up. Cissie was biting her lip and looking down, not smiling. She hugged the stack tight again and ran for the big front doors. But there, where the students were streaming in, I noticed that she slowed down and let a couple of boys take over her load. So! I didn't rate *all* the student privileges even though I was a registered student. I chewed on that thought and took my time climbing the stairsteps.

In the classroom Cissie was handing out mimeographed sheets, with a boy helping her. And there was Dr. Hoodenpyl with his back to the class, mopping the sweat on his bald head and showing a couple of boys where to stick up a lot of charts and maps on the blackboard. They had just about covered the blackboard, wall to wall, in front of the class. There were stacks of papers on the teacher's desk.

I took my usual seat next to Wallace Exum. On the arm of the chair was my copy of the mimeographed stuff. At the top of the first sheet it said: "Please answer all questions and return to Professor J. Chauncey Hoodenpyl, Humanities Division, State Teachers College."

Above the noise of talking Dr. Hoodenpyl was saying, "If you please— attention, if you please—just a moment and I will explain our little project. Do not write in the blank spaces yet. I wish to explain."

The noise let up, then went on louder than ever. I looked at the sheet again. There were a lot of big words. I thought to myself: *Now this must be the real College Education, and I better start copying it in my notebook to be sure and remember. That man is a Ph.D.*

Though the words didn't make any sense to me, I started copying just the same. He promised he would explain. The paper said:

SOME HUMANISTIC ASPECTS OF FOLKLORE STUDY
A Survey of Urban-Rural Configuration of Ballad
Culture Areas

"A culture area is characterized by a catalogue of traits or features material, artistic, religious, ceremonial, social . . . but also by the way in which such features are associated, interrelated, colored by one another . . . Such culture *complexes* show a remarkable tenacity and chronological persistence."—Goldenweiser.

Then the questions started. There were three solid pages of questions, with blanks to fill in. I didn't have time to copy them all, right there, but later on I snitched the sheets from Cissie and put them in my notebook. This is the way they led off:

1. Do you own a radio? _____
2. If not, does your family own a radio? _____
3. Which of the following radio programs do you *habitually* listen to? (Check in blank space and add any other favorites not mentioned.) Metropolitan Opera_____ NBC Symphony_____ Telephone Hour_____ Boston Pops _____ Fred Waring _____ Guy Lombardo _____ Frank Sinatra _____ Bing Crosby _____ Burl Ives _____ Grand Ole Opry _____ _____ _____ _____ _____ _____

4. Which of the above-mentioned programs do you *occasionally* listen to? ____ ____ ____ ____ ____ ____
5. Do you read music? ____
6. If so, what is the extent of your musical education? (Check in blank space.) One year ____ More than one year ____ High school level ____ College ____ Private lessons ____
7. Do you yourself sing? ____ If so, check as indicated in space below.
   a. For pleasure (1) Only when alone ____
                 (2) While working ____
                 (3) When with a social group ____
                 (4) In choir or other organized group ____
   b. For profit (1) Professionally ____
              (2) Semi-professionally ____
8. Name the ten songs that you best like to sing or hear sung:
   ____ ____ ____ ____ ____ ____ ____ ____ ____
   ____
9. What musical instrument do you play, if any? ____
10. If you play a musical instrument, do you play it for
   (a) Your own pleasure only ____
   (b) In company with others, for pleasure only ____
   (c) Professionally or semi-professionally ____
11. If you do not have a musical education, from which of the following sources did you learn the songs you like best?
   (a) Parents or other relatives (specify) ____
   (b) Friends ____
   (c) Public concerts ____
   (d) Radio ____
   (e) Phonograph ____
12. If you do not have a musical education but nevertheless can play a musical instrument, indicate below how you learned to play.
   (a) Self-taught ____
   (b) Taught by relative or friend ____
   (c) Other influences ____
13. Where were you born? ____
14. Where were your parents born? Father: ____ Mother: ____
15. What is your father's business or profession? ____
16. Does your mother have a job? ____
17. Within the past ten years, has your family moved from country to city (or town)? ____ From city (or town) to country? ____
18. Do you attend church?
   (a) Regularly ____

168

(b) Occasionally _____
(c) Not at all _____
19. Of what church are you a member? _____ (If not a member, so specify.) _____
20. Do you go to the movies? _____ How often? _____

That wasn't all. On the next page there was a list of twenty-five ballads. Dr. Hoodenpyl wanted us to check any we knew by heart and to say whether we learned 'em from father, mother, or some relative or friend, or off a phonograph record or from the radio.

The next sheet was a rating sheet. He wanted us to rate—1, 2, 3, 4, and so on—a long list of singers: Frank Sinatra, Bing Crosby, Roy Acuff, and a lot more, including some people with foreign names.

Then we had to sign our names, give school or college, class, residence address, and tell what profession or business we aimed to be in.

By the time I got through glancing over the sheets, I was nearly seasick trying to guess what my owning a radio had to do with a culture area and twenty-five old ballads. If that was college education—well, it looked more like a Hooper Rating Survey—but I had to know the answers, and Dr. Hoodenpyl was up front explaining.

"First, may I apologize—yes-yes, humbly apologize for intruding my little project—for shamelessly interrupting your organized program with side issues. I do apologize—humbly—yes, humbly apologize."

He bobbed his head at us several times from behind the reading desk, almost like bowing to all of us from right to left. Then he stepped over towards Cissie. By stretching my neck, I could see where she was sitting in front and half-facing us. Dr. Hoodenpyl bobbed his head at Cissie.

"Humbly apologize, Miss Timberlake!" he said, and kept bobbing his head until she nodded back at him with a sort of weary smile.

It was catching. I could hardly keep from bobbing my head too. If he had gone on another second, we would all have been bobbing heads at one another like ducks on a pond.

"But after all, I am not an utter stranger to you." He showed all his teeth in a large oily grin and looked around as if he expected the class to stand up and cheer. Nobody moved or said a word. He pushed his lips into an O and put on a scared expression. "Surely—not—an—utter—stranger!" He was grieving like maybe some awful mistake had been made and he had somehow got into the wrong room. Some of the girls giggled. Dr. Hoodenpyl brightened up. He seemed relieved, shuffled the stack of papers on the desk, pulled out one of them, and began tracing out something with his finger. With his other hand he was smoothing his little moustache.

I had my mechanical pencil out, ready to take a flock of notes, but it was frozen in my hand. I didn't know a Ph.D. would act like that. And Dr. Hoodenpyl didn't *look* like a Ph.D. He had on a sports shirt with large pictures splashed on it, and no tie, and a summer coat and pants of a sickly greenish-blue color not suitable to his type. The only Ph.D. thing about him was his peculiar eyeglasses—just half-moons of glass without rims that he kept pushing back and forth on his nose, and taking off and putting back on. His pale blue eyes darted at us over the half-moons of glass, and disappeared entirely when he dropped his heavy lids and seemed like a blind man standing before us.

As soon as Dr. Hoodenpyl had traced out whatever it was on his paper, he began to talk pretty fast. I took notes the best I could though they meant practically nothing to me. But I could tell what was important because Dr. Hoodenpyl seemed to bounce up and down when he came to the important parts. If he rolled out a big word that I couldn't spell, I just glanced over at Wallace Exum, next to me, and out-and-out copied it.

"A ballad culture area," said Dr. Hoodenpyl, "is not necessarily a geographic area, even though it can be mapped—as you see." He turned and pointed a ruler at several maps, one after another. "Because a culture area involves a *psychological adjustment* . . ." He bounced on the two big words, and I copied the spelling from Wallace. "A *psychological adjustment* that may be independent of purely geographic factors. Really it involves a process of acculturation as my Frank Sinatra chart clearly reveals."

Dr. Hoodenpyl grabbed his ruler and rushed to the chart display. He stabbed a chart with his ruler, like a man gigging for a bullfrog on the bank. With one hand reaching out, he held the ruler firm on the chart, like Frank Sinatra might be trying to hop off. At the same time he turned towards us and held up one finger.

"I am but a modest scholar," he said. "Yes-yes, only a modest scholar. But I am *proud* of my Frank Sinatra chart. I can assure you it is unique."

I was running 'way behind on note-taking, but I wanted to know about a word. "What is 'acculturation'?" I whispered to Wallace, and pointed with my pencil to his notebook.

"Oh, a whole lot of stuff! Sociology! Gettin' used to city life mainly."

With his ruler Dr. Hoodenpyl was following out wiggly lines on the Frank Sinatra chart.

"Now this line shows the incidence of radio preference for Frank Sinatra among 157 students in a suburban high school of New York City. You can see from the curve that Sinatra preference runs very high in that group. And just beneath it, you see, I have plotted for that same group their incidence of knowledge of traditional ballads. Alas—alas—you see—it is—very-very-low!"

Bending over, he dropped his voice to a whisper on the word *low*. He screwed up his face in a pained expression.

"In fact, it approaches—"

He paused, opened his mouth wide, rolled his pale-blue eyes, and breathed the barest whisper of a word:

"—zero."

Dr. Hoodenpyl hung his head, dropped his arms to his side, and seemed to be burying the 157 students. "Zero," he repeated very mournfully, and wagged his head slow and weak.

Then he came to life, jumped at the wall, and stabbed another chart.

"But LOOK!" He shouted like he had discovered a gold mine. "Look-look-look-look-LOOK!" He rapped the chart with his ruler. "Look at Laurel Gap, North Carolina. I know you will be proud of Laurel Gap, North Carolina."

He stuck out his chest, waved the ruler like a flag, and made a big, loud oration.

"I am PROUD of Laurel Gap, North Carolina, where, among 43 students of high school age, the incidence of knowledge of traditional ballads is very HIGH." He was standing on tiptoe, reaching up. "In fact, almost ONE—HUNDRED—PERCENT. See-see-see-see-see! And the incidence of radio preference for Frank Sinatra is—ha, ha!—very *low*! Isn't that glorious? GLORIOUS!

"There is just a wee bit of a Sinatra influence. A trace only. Just a slight contamination.

"And now one more thing—this is *very* interesting. I have also coordinated and plotted radio preference of Grand Ole Opry, and you see—you see!" He was busy with the ruler again. "The Laurel Gap students have a good strong Grand Ole Opry curve—stronger than the ballad curve in fact. But their ballad knowledge curve is strong too. Very int'resting. There is evidently a close correlation. A positive—yes—a positive correlation between a strong ballad knowledge curve and a Grand Ole Opry curve. And where those two curves are strong, the correlation with the Frank Sinatra curve is weak—in fact, largely negative.

"And now about access to radio—let us correlate that too."

He rushed to the other end of the blackboard and tapped a big colored map with his ruler.

"This is very important," said Dr. Hoodenpyl. "This overall coordination of knowledge curves and incidence of radio preference with degree of radio access. I might almost say *radio-activity*! Ha, ha!"

He laughed, but the class took it solemn.

"You cannot read the map from where you sit, but you can examine it later. The most heavily shaded areas indicate the heaviest degree of radio access. *Radio-activity*, as I was saying, though perhaps—ha, ha!—*radio-passivity* would be an even better term. The lighter-shaded areas are those where radio-activity (or passivity) is least. And on all shaded areas I have placed quotient numerals which represent the combined factors that we have today been sampling and studying. And now I will interpret for you.

"This will be a tentative generalization. Just a working hypothesis as yet. Very tentative. We *must* be scientific. We cannot be sure until we procure many more samples and plot the graphs of those samples. But it seems likely that the heaviest degree of radio access, which means also, as you have observed, a heavy degree of radio-activity-passivity, correlates negatively with ballad knowledge, as also with habitual activity in singing and in playing an instrument. But on the other hand, *some* degree of radio access is by no means unfavorable to ballad knowledge, and, furthermore, Grand Ole Opry—and for that matter other hillbilly or country music groups—may give us a very nice correlation with ballad knowledge. Very nice. Not bad at all.

"And now you see what my little project is. Will you submit to the sampling process? Do you mind being guinea pigs? I will truly appreciate your being my little guinea pigs for a very few moments. For just the time it will take to fill out the questionnaire. You understand, don't you? Not in your valuable class time. At your convenience of course—and bring the questionnaire back to Miss Timberlake tomorrow or the next day, if you please."

Dr. Hoodenpyl seemed about ready to quit. He was gathering up papers and shuffling them around. The class was wiggling in their seats, yawning and talking. I was half-asleep myself, or maybe just stunned. I waked up long enough to ask Wallace a question.

"What is *correlation*, Wallace? I know I got a lot of relations, but I don't know nothing about my correlations."

"Aw, it's nothin' much." Wallace yawned and stretched. "He just means that if you listen to radio all the time, you'll forget all about ballads. That's correlation. Negative correlation."

"Does he have to draw all them charts to find that out? If he'd just asked me, I could a-told him that."

"He gets paid for it," Wallace said. "He has a Guggenheim Fellowship—or somethin'. He gets paid for making charts of what everybody already knows."

Cissie had come up to the desk and was helping Dr. Hoodenpyl shuffle papers. She dug some papers out of the bottom of the stack, handed them to him, and went back to her chair.

"Just one moment before I go," said Dr. Hoodenpyl. "You have been most patient, and I want to give each one of you a little keepsake. Will you pass these out, please?"

Some students in the front rows took the papers and started passing them out. I could see those two pretty coeds, Miss Blue-eyes and Miss Black-eyes, with papers in their hands, and both headed for the back of the room. Elvira Looney was helping too.

"Please accept from me," said Dr. Hoodenpyl, "this copy of a recent issue of *Turntable Notes*. It is a little periodical published for the benefit of disk jockeys in particular and for the great new world of radio in general. A kind of trade journal—not a scholarly periodical exactly. But you will find there an illustration of the useful, or I might say the commercial—yes-yes—aspects of the project I have outlined to you. *Turntable Notes* was kind enough to carry a little story about my project, and also the little column that I am syndicating. A byproduct of research, you might say. Yes-yes, a side result. But I hope not too unworthy. The Hoodenpyl Rating System, I am tentatively calling it."

He coughed and pulled out his handkerchief.

Wallace was sitting up on the edge of his seat, ready to grab. His eyes were big and round. "He's got a racket then, the damned old stinker!" said Wallace.

"Do you know about it?"

"Never heard about it before."

But there were Miss Blue-eyes and Miss Black-eyes, each one smiling sweet, and each one trying to hand me a copy of *Turntable Notes*. I smiled right back and took both copies. They passed on slowly, not seeming to notice Wallace. I started to give him one of the papers. But just then Elvira Looney turned up all of a sudden. She leaned over and whispered to Wallace. He nodded his head. She gave him a paper and went on.

Dr. Hoodenpyl's picture and the story, with big headlines, were smack on the front page. COLLEGE PROF DEVELOPS SCIENTIFIC RATING SYSTEM, the two-column headline said, and right next to the story was that syndicated column: HOODENPYL RATING SYSTEM OF POPULAR HITS AND STAR SINGERS.

"Look here, Wallace. That man must be cashin' in. I didn't know a Ph.D. would do this."

Wallace didn't seem too interested. "Um-hunh," he said. "Funny doin's, ain't it?" Then he leaned closer to me and whispered. "Elvira wants to see me after class. It's about Buck Kennedy."

Dr. Hoodenpyl was bobbing his head again. "Sorry to intrude. Sorry to take your time. But I thought you might . . ." He trotted to the door with little patting steps and turned. "By-by!" he called, and waved his hand. "Carry on!"

Wallace was squirming in his seat. The ballads class was coming alive again. At her desk, Cissie, looking a little pale and puzzled, was putting a phonograph record on the college machine.

"I hardly think it wise to start on historical ballads today," she said. "We'll play records and sing for ten minutes."

When the bell rang, we were right in the middle of a lively old song. Miss Blue-eyes and Miss Black-eyes were right in my way, singing it into my ear while I scrambled with the rest:

> I wish I wuz a apple on a tree!
> I wish I wuz a apple on a tree!
> If I wuz a apple on a tree
> My boy'd come by and take a bite out o' me.
> I wish I wuz a apple on a tree!

16

NOT A CASE OF A NEGLIGENT NYMPH

When I finally squeezed through the door and made for my car, I saw Wallace and Elvira off to one side, heads close together. I highballed past them without speaking. For I hated to meet Cissie with bad news for company.

But Wallace rode his bad news like it was a jet plane. He swished up behind me on the concrete walk.

"That ol' devil—he's workin' the campus again." He touched my elbow. "The Dean is turnin' the heat on the Sheriff."

I quickened my step, but Wallace caught up and began to put out his news in broken doses. Buck was back. The college boys were getting too careless. They threw empty bottles out of dormitory windows and into parking lots. They even piled whiskey bottles in the washbasins of classroom buildings. The night before, a whole carload of students had got arrested down town for disorderly conduct. The Dean had to bail them out and hush the thing up at 2 o'clock in the morning. He didn't enjoy that. Neither did he like to punish all those G.I.'s that might have been parachute troopers or Navy gunners. So he was after the Sheriff to nab the bootlegger.

"Does he know it's Buck Kennedy?" I asked Wallace.

"I can't be sure. But he'll find out sooner or later. Somebody will squeal."

"Does Cissie know?"

"I would doubt that. A good many in the ballads class know, but you can bet they won't tell her."

If Cissie still didn't know, and if the Dean hadn't found out, there might be a chance for our side to play some tricks.

"Wallace," I said, and rested my hand heavy on his shoulder, "we'll get together on this—you and me and Ed. I'll let you know. But I've got a date with Cissie now."

I had parked my car in the shade of a big maple tree, but the sun had moved, and the car was like a hot stove when I got into it. I rolled down the windows, lit a cigarette, and waited. It wasn't long till I heard Cissie's heels tapping quick on the concrete. When I started to jump out and open the door for her, she snapped, "Don't be so darned polite," and piled in. "Get started. Drive on."

"Drive where?"

"Anywhere. Just drive—no, let's go to a drugstore and get a cold drink. Some place where the students don't hang out. I'm perishin', and I can't take but a few minutes to talk."

Cissie was sitting up stiff as a board and glaring ahead through the windshield. She got out her handkerchief and dabbed at sweat on her forehead, but didn't get out her compact to powder her nose or fix her lipstick. She was downright fightin' mad.

"You must be caught in a configuration, Cissie," I said as I pulled into traffic.

"No-no—NO!" Cissie shrieked. "I'm *not* psychologically adjusted, and I don't aim to be, ever, if I live to be a hundred years old, and a toothless ol' granny dippin' snuff."

She bit her lip and said no more, but after two or three traffic lights she opened up again.

"It's the folk festival," she said. "They just keep pilin' things on. If they would just let me alone—"

"Tell me about it, Cissie darlin'. What's a folk festival?"

I found the right drugstore, not many blocks away. We were well ahead of the noon rush and had our big Coca-Colas in a booth at the back. There was a rackful of 25-cent paper books with cheesecake pictures on them to screen us from the public view. *I, the Jury* was staring me right in the face. I turned the rack a little to get it off my mind. But the cover picture of *The Case of the Negligent Nymph* came up next. It wasn't any nicer, since the woman in the water had on no clothes at all, but naturally it sort of caught my eye.

"Well, anyway," I said, "you ain't no negligent nymph. That's not your trouble."

"What are you doin'—lookin' at those dirty pictures? You put your mind on this. It's all Mrs. Eccles' idea."

Cissie's voice was fretful. She looked hollow-eyed and unhappy.

"I can't get out of it," Cissie said. "I have to go along with Mrs. Eccles. And with Dr. Hoodenpyl. This is the plan for the folk festival. I mean it's a kind of program. Look at it."

She took some papers out of a folder and laid them in front of me. The first one had F O L K   F E S T I V A L lettered at the top, and under it S I N G E R S   A N D   T H E I R   S O N G S—all as pretty as could be. Below that was a list in Cissie's handwriting. I looked down the list and saw Aunt Lou Watkins and others that Cissie and me had tape-recorded, and one or two, like Ike Rountree, that Cissie must have rounded up by herself.

And Buck Kennedy was there with the rest. I decided to beat the devil around the stump a little before mentioning him to Cissie.

"So it's a stage show, is it?—this folk festival? Or a radio show?"

Cissie took a long sup of Coca-Cola, then a long drag at her cigarette.

"Yes, a kind of stage show. In the old chapel—where there's no good stage arrangements." She leaned her head against the back of the seat and closed her eyes. I had never seen her so wore-out. And the little throbbing blood vessel in her temple where she kept trying to push back her hair. She went on talking as if she despised to think about it.

"I hate to have to explain it. I'm tired of explainin' and explainin'. But I'm the one that's elected to get all these old folks to come and sing ballads. Tell them what to sing, and make 'em promise to come, and—git 'em here, some ways. Drive all over the hills and hollows and be nice and sweet to 'em. Listen to 'em talk about their rheumatism and stomach trouble. Worry about 'em gittin' here on time and rememberin' whut they told me true and promised to sing. Look after their kinfolks and grandchildren. Feed 'em supper. Find 'em if they git lost. All of that and a 'tarnation lot besides. Oh-h-h-h!"

It was a groaning, not a weeping. It must a-been the first time I ever heard Cissie groan. But I could tell there wasn't anything mournful and meek in it. I knowed for sure she was gritting her teeth and really like a wildcat up a tree, arching her back to jump and claw the life out of anything she happened to hit. So I drawed off to what I thought was the safety zone.

"Well, I'll be glad to help. I'm used to that kind of a jamboree, and so you just tell me what—"

"*Don't* you call it a jamboree!" She came to life and slapped her fist down on the paper. "*Don't* you let Mrs. Eccles hear you speak that awful *word*. Even if it is a kind of jamboree . . . of course it is . . . just a big . . . ballad . . . jamboree."

Cissie shut her eyes again and wagged her head. "Just a big ballad jamboree."

Then she showed all her pretty teeth and red mouth in a long yawn and stretched her whole length, pulling back her shoulders and curving out her breast till I was plumb captivated. And then she went into reverse. Out came the compact, and she started in on lipstick and powder, chattering bright and so lively that I could hardly keep up with what she was saying.

It was all Mrs. Eccles' idea, Cissie said again, and it happened because Mrs. Eccles had been off to a big folk festival at White Top Mountain in Virginia, and another one in West Virginia. She came back all on fire about folk festivals, and nothing would suit her but to have one in Carolina City too. But the folklore society didn't have any money, and so she decided to get State Teachers College to sponsor it. Dean Bronson said all right, that was just fine, and he thought it was a good project to try out on a small scale because maybe it would help public relations, but the college couldn't finance it unless it was definitely educational. It would have to connect up with the ballads class somehow or other, and Dr. Hoodenpyl or Cissie would have to be responsible for arrangements. That was how Cissie got elected, because Dr. Hoodenpyl was flying off to Washington and God knows where else . . . "And here's where you can help, Danny, if you will—and you won't have to carry any recordin' machines up the mountain ridges. I'll type a copy of this list for you. You help me to see the singers and get them promised. Explain everything. Be sure to make it sound big. We'll pay 'em a little somethin' for singin'—that is, the college will. Then you help me get them all here in plenty of time. Do the haulin' and runnin' around. That will really save my life. There might be a few other little things—but that's the big thing."

I ran my eye down that list again. "Sure I will, Cissie. I can help you, and I will."

She was looking up at me sideways, most fetchin', and what more natural than for me to ease one arm up around her shoulders. I could feel Cissie edgin' closer, and Lord, how I did hate to say the next thing. But I had to.

"I'll sure help you with the singers, and anything else. Except for one thing." I put my finger on one name. "Just so you don't ask me to haul Buck Kennedy or have anything to do with his doin's."

Cissie frowned and drew back. "Oh, that! That's already arranged. Just forget about Buck Kennedy."

I frowned on my side. "I'm sorry it's already arranged. I wish you could leave him out entirely. You can't depend on old Buck Kennedy. You never know what a man like him will do."

Cissie was flustered. I wondered if maybe I hadn't better bust out and tell her more. But while I hesitated, she glanced at her wristwatch and said: "I've got to run in a few minutes. You just better keep off that Buck Kennedy angle. You don't realize Danny—well, it's all mixed up, and I've done told you and told you I don't want to have to explain. Not now."

She wasn't meeting my eyes. She was looking down at the plastic-top table and moving the papers around. The picture cover of the *The Case of the Negligent Nymph* was still staring me in the face. Just for luck I gave that bookrack a whirl. It creaked around, and this time it stopped at the westerns: *Six-Gun Man, Trouble on Cimarron*—and *Betty Crocker's Cookbook*. I took it for a good sign and thought I'd try to toll Cissie along.

"Tell me a little right now. Maybe I could help you better, if you would."

"Don't ask *me*. Ask Dr. Hoodenpyl."

"Is *he* in it, then?"

"Figure it out for yourself. He's a-goin' out with Buck Kennedy this afternoon. Carryin' a photographer along to take pictures up in Beaver Valley, at the Kennedy place and all around. I think he's goin' to write a magazine article about Buck Kennedy."

"You don't say so!"

"Yes, Buck Kennedy is Dr. Hoodenpyl's idea of a real ballad singer. Local color and all that. And he's a-takin' Buck back to Washington with him, I think—to have the Library of Congress people record him. Put his ballads in the Archives of American Folksong."

Cissie had both fists clenched on top of her papers, and was looking venomous and ready to cry, all at the same time.

I was trying to figure it out for myself, like she told me, and it didn't add up right.

"But I thought—I was figurin' you'd have Buck's songs in your thesis?"

She just nodded, and it was a mighty glum sort of nod.

"And didn't that fool man say *you'd* write some sort of piece for a magazine about Buck's songs? What was it?"

Another glum nod, and she just barely spilled some words out between her teeth: "In the *Journal of American Folklore*."

I was getting mad. "Why, Cissie, damn it—that's stealin', ain't it? Jest plain stealin'."

"Yes— and no, Danny." Her voice was dry and stiff, like it hurt to talk. "Up in Beaver Valley, we'd call it stealin'. But in graduate school it's scholarship— and promotion. I've heard a lot about it. People have warned me how some professors treat their students like that. But not all of them do."

"Well, I'm goin' to call it stealin', for that's what it is."

"It's goin' to hurt me some, but it won't hold up my thesis."

"Dr. Hoodenpyl comin' back soon?"

"I don't see what difference that makes—and why do you want to know, anyhow? He'll be back for the ballad festival, I think. And he'll bring Buck back if he doesn't come sooner. But why talk about it? There's nothin' I can do. And nothin' you can do about it, either."

I was beginning to see a light—just a little bit of a light. "Maybe there's somethin' I can do," I said, more to myself than to Cissie.

"No, you forget about Buck Kennedy. I'll handle that." Cissie put the papers back in her folder. She was looking at me straight, trying to figure me out. I was trying to figure her out—and figure out myself too. Before us were the Coca-Cola glasses with the ice melting down in them, the wet tabletop, the paper napkins sticking to the table, the ashtray with the mashed cigarette stubbs spilling over. It was cool in the drugstore, and I had Cissie there in the booth with me, yet I still hadn't said what I really wanted to.

"You drive me to the Student Union Building." Cissie picked up her purse and papers. "I have to go to this lunch meeting with Mrs. Eccles and Dr. Hoodenpyl and the Dean. They all want different things. Mrs. Eccles wants a whole day and then an evening of folk festival, with thirty or forty singers and some fiddle players. And Dr. Hoodenpyl wants to bring Rufus and the Turkey Hollow Boys into the program somewhere."

"What?"

"Yes, he's tryin' to bring you-all into it, and a lot more. And the Dean wants to keep expenses down and public relations up!"

"What about you—what do you want?"

She smiled—and it was the first good smile that morning.

"I want to get through it with the least possible work for Cissie. I want to finish my thesis, and how can I do it if they keep pilin' on? I've got to whittle them down somehow. Mrs. Eccles will have to settle for a short program. And I want to have the ballads class take some part in it. It ought to be for them, really. After all, they're the ones that are studyin' ballads."

Cissie let out a long sigh. "You don't know how lucky you are, Danny. Nothing to do but put on a few radio programs that you've already got memorized. Just a little pickin' and singin', and none of the managin'. Rufus and Bob Greenhow lookin' after all the problems."

"Hold on, Cissie, you forget. I've got my lessons to learn. I'm still about two weeks behind the class, but I'm gainin' ground all the time. I'm workin' on the second volume of Cecil Sharp right now, and I ought to be studyin' this minute."

Cissie's eyes were round. It was the first I had ever told her about my studying. She didn't know what to say. She was making motions to get up and go, but she couldn't, because I was still on the outside, and had her penned in.

"You think I come into your class just to be a-courtin' and a-pesterin' you. Well, think again. I'm a registered student at State Teachers College, a *special* student in music, by Gad, and I mean to git my money's worth. I might even write a term paper for you like you said for the class to do."

180

"Oh, for God's sake, Danny—don't do that. I've got enough papers to read already."

"I know I'm jest an auditor," I went on, "and you don't *have* to read my paper. But I might write one and hand it in anyhow. Maybe you'd look at it—and mark it—as a special favor?"

If I'd jumped out of the bushes and stuck a pistol in her face, Cissie couldn't have looked more panicky and distracted.

"Danny—Danny," was all she could say at first. And she was staring at me like there must be some mistake and I couldn't be the Danny she had always known. "Let's talk about it later," she said nervously. "I've got to run now, I really must. But you're doin' so well with Rufus, I don't see why you bother with ballads—and studyin'."

"You wanted me to, didn't you? I thought at first you must be crazy. But I'm havin' the time of my life. You're on the right track; I'm not the only one that thinks that. They all think you are the best teacher in the college, and if Hoodenpyl butts in again, they'll purty nigh lynch him."

Cissie kept struggling to get up, and I finally made way for her. "Aren't they wonderful?" she said. "Those students! But I'd hate to see you get into my fix. I hate to make trouble for you, but—" She leaned over and surprised me with a quick little kiss.

"No trouble at all," I said, and walked with her to the car.

But that was just talk. Trouble was boiling up all around us. Soon as I had hauled Cissie back to campus, I found a telephone booth and arranged everything with Wallace and Ed. I told them to drive out to the MacGregor Place for supper. We would make our plans out there.

Time I got through telephoning, it had begun to rain. It was just a good shower. By four o'clock the weather had cleared and turned cooler. Soon afterwards I was steaming up the avenue to the house and praising God Almighty for having one quiet place to come to.

17

SWEET WATER IN THE CREEK AND THE POWER OF GOD IN IT

Time we got through supper, first dark was coming on. A little piece of new moon was out in the west, and sinking towards the roof of the cabin with a big star traveling close by and many another star brightening in the clear above the black mountain ridges and sailing between the slow clouds. Fog was lying along the creek, and wherever there was running water among the trees, the fog marked that line. There were spots where it reached up in streamers towards the clouds.

Running water all around us, after the rain—that was the main sound of the night, and no human sound anywhere to walk the air except one deep voice that belonged to the place. It was Old Man Parsons singing to himself in the cool of the evening where he would be sitting below us in the dog-run of the cabin and watching that same piece of new moon. The night, so still it was, carried the song to us. To Ed and Wallace and me on the steps of the big house after supper, the song floated up, every word clear, and the slow, old-timey tune that marked out the sacred words like bell chimes ringing long quavers to the stars and moon.

> A charge—to-o-o kee-ee-p I-I ha-a-ave,
> A-a God—to-o—glo-ri-i-fy-y-y.
> A-a nev—er dy-i-i-ing soul to-o sa-a-ve,
> A-and fit i-it for—the-e-e sky-y-y.

In all the valley there was no light showing but the lit window of the kitchen below, where Mrs. Parsons crossed now and then as she washed and put up the dishes. And not a man of us opened his mouth to say a word, though we came there to talk. Even to whisper would be like making a noise in church, with the song and the new moon holding us worshipful in front and the old house at our backs, pitch dark, quiet as a congregation waiting for the blessing.

I wished it would always be like that—a place where nobody could ever bring a noise, but it would have only the sounds that belonged to it, and I swore I'd never buy a tractor if I could help it, or a powersaw, or any such thing to keep on that farm if it made a machine racket. Maybe I couldn't live up to that idea, but it was what I wanted. I like a farm bell. It makes a sound, a sweet sound, but not a noise. And a voice calling "Whoo-ee-ee" far off on the hill—that's a sound. An axe, it makes a sound, and a handsaw does, and a horse's hoofs on the road, but all a machine can do is make a noise, a racket. The more machines you have, the more racket, and all the different rackets fight one another. But in a country place it's all sweet sounds running into one another like they might have been tuned to play together. Underneath "A charge to keep" I could hear the creek flowing; and the cattle cropping grass near the fence and blowing out their breath; and Old Man Parsons' shepherd dog on the ridge, hunting on his own; and the crickets in the grass by the porch steps; and there were some fog voices, too, big and little. They all bore up the song, and helped it.

A charge to keep I have. That I knowed well. The place was perfect except for the one thing. It needed a woman. And so did I need Cissie.

The cold mountain air was coming in more and more. Wallace reached for his coat. The moon was sliding down to the mountain ridge. I felt my way into Grandma's room and lit the lamp. It was colder in the room than outside. I lit the fire and soon heard Ed and Wallace clumping in. They pulled up chairs to the fire, but still we said nothing.

With no rugs or carpet on the floor, and no curtains, that old room looked mighty bare. All I had in it was the furniture Ellie May let me have—the bedstead, a few old split-bottom chairs, a washstand with a bowl and pitcher, and one lamp on the mantel. I had a good table in the room across the hall, and some more chairs—and that was about all the furniture. I'd had it in my mind to look for some good, solid old furniture that would suit the place, and had even priced some, here and there, but I got discouraged when Cissie broke up with me and went off to New York. It was just a place to camp out—good enough for men folks to sit and smoke in after a big fried ham and new corn supper like we'd just had, or a day in the woods like I managed now and then. The fire made it more cheerful. It was good hickory and oak, with some ash, all cut and split on the place, and the yellow light went up to the high ceiling and far out into the corners. You could sit there and think there all you wanted, and nobody could bother you. It made me easy in my mind just to sit there and watch the fire. You could walk around the room, too, without having to dodge the furniture. But somebody had to start the talking, some time.

"Old Man Parsons," I said, "he'll sing like that till the moon goes down. He'll sing the moon down, then read a chapter in his Bible and go to bed. But if he's restless and can't sleep, he'll git up and walk the earth. He'll pull on his trousers over his nightshirt, tuck it in, call his dog, and walk the place with his stick in his hand and look at the stars."

"The movie folks," said Wallace, "they take sleepin' pills. And so do some of these radio people."

"You couldn't git Old Man Parsons to take a sleepin' pill. He jest tucks his nightshirt into his trousers and walks the earth. Sometimes don't even bother to put on shoes. Old Shep comes to him, and they walk amongst the cattle. They listen to the fox barkin' on the ridge and the screech-owls hollerin'."

I paused and heard the sound, like I had called it up by mentioning it. "And there's one now. Must be right out on the porch."

It was loud enough to be right in the room—that long trembling cry, the kind that puts a shiver in your blood.

"Don't you go callin' up screech-owls," complained Ed Cooley. "Hit ain't a lucky sign."

The sound came again, like it might be at the window. "I can't stand that," grumbled Ed. He got up and turned the shovel and poker upside down. He took off both shoes, turned them around, and set them with the toes pointed towards his feet. "That'll fix him."

He sat listening, with his face turned to the window. The screech-owl called once more, then broke off. We waited and heard it again, farther away and faint. Then it stopped.

"It never fails," said Ed Cooley. "But don't you go callin' up ghosts. I don't know no way of runnin' off ghosts. And now don't you tell me this-here house o' yourn is ha'nted."

"It's old enough to be ha'nted. I wouldn't swear it ain't ha'nted, either, but I'd ruther meet my own Grandpa's ghost, right now, than some people I know in the flesh. But I been sleepin' out here a good deal, off and on, and my Grandpa ain't walked in on me yet, the way he used to walk in on folks when he was still livin'. He used to make the rounds at night. Scared of somebody settin' the house afire, Grandma said. He'd scratch on the door, or maybe knock, and if they didn't answer right up, he'd walk in on 'em, even if they was in bed. Look at the fireplace, then walk out ag'in."

A little breeze must have blown into the hall just then. A door creaked somewhere, and the fire popped loud as a gun. Ed and Wallace jumped and looked over their shoulders. I didn't feel too easy myself.

"I b'lieve I'll jest—" Ed Cooley walked to the door in his sock feet. "I'll jest shet this door." He shut it. "Keep out the night air."

184

"But I'd rather *see* a ghost," I went on, "than to hear one scratchin' on the other side of the door."

"Man, don't be a-talkin' about no ghost," Ed complained. "That ain't whut we drove out here to talk about." He slipped his shoes back on and looked solemn.

"All right, then," I said. "There's Buck Kennedy. He ain't no ghost, and you can't run him off by turnin' the poker and shevel upside-down. We've got to put a hobble on him. It'll take more doin' than we first thought. We'll need help."

Ed Cooley had taken a pack of cards out of his pocket. He began to shuffle them, on his knee, over and over, and look at me sideways. Wallace had the poker and was making fierce little punches at the biggest log.

Ed stopped shuffling cards and gave me a hard look. "If you know how to do all that, what are we waitin' on? Don't hold out on us." He spit into the ashes, slipped a card from the deck, looked at it, slipped it back. "You're a lucky devil!" he said, and poured the cards back and forth easy as I could pick a guitar.

"I'm not goin' to hold out," I said. "I'll bring you up to date. But you know a good deal of it already."

Just to remind them, I went over the whole situation. We didn't want any public trouble, especially on Cissie's account. If anything got into the newspapers, the college might hold it against Cissie for bringing Buck Kennedy onto the campus. But if we didn't stop his bootlegging, the trouble would soon be in the open, and Cissie would lose out anyway. And Buck thought he was riding high.

"He brags about how the law can't touch him," Wallace broke in, "because he's got 'political influence.' Still, he wouldn't want his ballad singin' cut off. The Dean suspects who the bootlegger is, but don't know for sure. The Sheriff knows, but won't tell the Dean."

"Maybe the Sheriff jest can't git the evidence?" I asked Wallace—and tried to keep a straight face.

"Oh, you know—he could—if he really wanted to." Wallace was red in the face.

"I see. Elvira must have spoke to her Pa—sorter hinted to hold off a while?"

Wallace grinned. I went on thinking out loud. For a while I had hoped (I told 'em) that if we could just rock along for another ten days or so, school would be over and we wouldn't need to worry—especially if Cissie didn't know about it.

"Everybody's keepin' it hid from her," Wallace interrupted. "They don't want her bothered and—"

But the Dean might call in a detective or the officers any time (I said), or something might happen. Above all, we had to protect Cissie. We had to take action right soon, but keep her out of it entirely. There were only two ways to do it: either we had to bear down on Buck ourselves, without the law; or we had to get the law to bear down on him, but not in the open.

"Why not do it ourselves?" Wallace proposed. "Let's don't be foolin' around. Give him a good whuppin'. Git a bunch together and lay for him. 'Twon't do no good to try the law on him. He'll run rings around you."

Wallace stood up, poker in his hand, his hair falling over his eyes. In the firelight the dark eyesockets looked hollow, but his teeth showed white.

"It could be done," Ed Cooley said. "He's got it comin' to him."

"You mean you would Ku Klux him?" I asked. "Folks go to jail for that. It would jest make things worse."

"Aw, shucks!" said Wallace angrily. "We ain't goin' to dress up in sheets and all that rot. It's out of date. But it's never out of date to let a dirty bastard like Buck Kennedy know how you feel about his doin's. Some of the boys in our class have already been talkin' about it. They would a-whupped him long before now if Cissie hadn't been sponsorin' him. It's not only the advantage he takes of her with his bootleggin' and meanness. But he's too free with the girls—he's a regular devil with 'em."

"What chance does Buck have with those young coeds?"

"Oh, they hover around him after class and beg him to sing some more. So he does. Off-color songs, too—and thinks that gives him a right to make passes. Tries for dates and may be gettin' 'em. He is always lookin' for some excuse to take a girl ridin' in that jeep."

Ed broke in. "Buck has always been like that amongst the women. They know he's mean but go to him jest the same. Back yonder when Buck left Beaver Valley, it wa'n't jest that he got a chancet to run off with the circus. It was a angry Pa after him about his gal—now let me see, wa'n't it Old Man McCla—?"

"Hold on right there," I told Ed. "No use goin' into all that. Don't you know I would a-knocked Buck Kennedy into the middle of next week long before now, if only—and I come mighty near to it, one time."

I could see Buck's old run-down front porch, and Buck's nasty grin as he watched Cissie reading his ballad sheets—him sorter bending over too near her. The mad begun to rouse up in me.

"I won't say it might not come to fightin' in the end!" They both sat up quick—mighty stiff and sober. Then I got back control and put down my mad.

"But right now, it would spoil everything. We've got to inch Buck into a tight corner where *we* will have the say about how he gits out. And we've got to bring some other people into this. Now can we git Sheriff Looney to help us?"

Wallace looked pleased at last. "I think he's hopin' some good idea will walk in his front door."

Ed Cooley said: "If we could jest git him to lay out on Beaver Creek Pike and ketch Buck for speedin'! Buck would sure think it was for bootleggin'. The Sheriff could jest warn him and let him go—give him a good skeer, though. Maybe Buck would git the point."

"Right idea—wrong method," I said. "But anyhow, we can't do anything but plan until Buck gits back from Washington."

Ed almost fell out of his chair. Wallace dropped the poker.

"Cissie just told me," I said. "Buck is goin' to Washington to have his ballad songs recorded at the Library of Congress, the same ones Cissie herself has already recorded. Hoodenpyl is mixed up in it, and it's a dirty shame, but it gives us time to git ready for Buck. He'll be back, soon enough, because he will be one of the main singers on this big program Cissie has to get up. They call it a folk festival. It'll be at the College about the end of next week. It strikes me that's the one place and the one time for us to give Buck Kennedy the right sort of scare, and get him out of Cissie's way, and our way."

"MacGregor, I believe you've hit it," said Ed.

"Fix it so I can get one lick at him," said Wallace.

"It's goin' to be ticklish because Buck is one of the stars on Cissie's program. We can't go into action till he's through, or just about. We don't want him to ball up Cissie's big show—though it would almost serve her right if he did, for she's been so derned stubborn about him. But we'll have to take some chances; and after all, you know, Cissie is right masterful. There's two things, though, we've got to be sure about: we've got to have the Sheriff on our side and somehow git him to act at exactly the right minute; and we've got to keep the Dean out of it. That means we've got to see the Sheriff right away. And somebody's got to fix the Dean."

For a moment nobody said a word. Then Wallace had an idea.

"I'd better line up some football players—in case!"

"That might be a wise thing," I told him.

"Buck will have liquor in his jeep," said Ed. "He wouldn't miss the chance. When he sees the Sheriff, he'll run."

"That's the part we need to work out," I said.

The fire had died down. The coal oil was giving out in our lamp. We were almost in the dark.

"Looks like we could skeer him good," said Ed. "Freeze his marrow when he sees old Sheriff Looney in a dark corner."

He rubbed his hands and chuckled to himself.

At the closed door there was a little scratching sound. Then something like a whimper or a moan. A chill was running up my back. We were frozen to our chairs, looking over our shoulders. I wanted to guess what it was at the door, but was afeard it might be something else.

There was a long kind of sigh back of the door and another scratch, then a soft thump. Then the knocking started.

"God-a-mighty," whispered Ed. "Don't you open that door. Turn the key in it. I'm a-gittin'." He started for a window. Wallace grabbed the poker. I made myself take a step toward the door. My throat was dry, but I forced the words out: "Come right in, Grandpa!"

"Don't!" Ed groaned. The window was stuck.

But the door slowly opened. Something dark shot in, along the floor. In the black of the door frame was a white shape, with no eyes in the middle of whiskers and hair. But it was Old Shep at my feet. I busted out laughing and hollered, "Come right in, Mr. Parsons!"

He hadn't bothered to pull on his pants, but was standing there in his nightshirt and bare feet. "It's that-air telephone," he was saying. "It's Cissie— wants you to call back right now."

"Hello, there," said Ed. "It was gittin' too close in here. I was jest goin' to let in some air." He had finally lifted the sash and pushed it all the way up. Wallace was jabbing at the dead logs.

"Man knoweth not the day nor the hour," said Old Man Parsons. "I was awake, and thinkin' on the day and the hour. And I jest had shet my Bible when that telephone bell run. She shore does want you bad. I told her I'd come right over."

The clouds had gone. I ran in starlight under thousands of stars towards the one low star that was the cabin window, and soon was panting Cissie's number into the telephone. Her voice sounded wide awake and cheerful as a cricket.

"What are you doin' out there, Danny? Did I get you out of bed?"

"Oh, no, Cissie, I'm out here studyin'. It's a good place to study. What's up?"

"I called and called at WCC and your apartment. Then I happened to remember you might be out there listenin' to the owls holler."

"They're hollerin' right peart tonight. They're a big help."

"Woo-oo-oo-oo!" said Cissie. "I'd love to hear 'em. Wish I had nothin' to do but lie around out there and listen to the owls."

She must have knocked a home run, I thought to myself. She sure is feeling good. She hadn't talked like that in a coon's age.

"At the lunch meeting," she began. "I want to tell you about that, but I'll go into it later. We had a big fight—Mrs. Eccles and the Dean and Dr. Hoodenpyl and me. Me in the middle. But I won. The Dean backed me up."

"That's good," I said. "He's got the aces, ain't he?"

"Yes, I had to lead with my pore little Jack. Mrs. Eccles thought her Queen was good, and Dr. Hoodenpyl had a King. But Dean Bronson laid down his Ace and saved my Jack. That's you, by the way. You're the Jack."

"Go right on, Cissie. I'm the Jack."

"Yes, and if I hadn't had you in my hand, Danny darlin', I never could've drawn out that King and Queen just at the right time for the Dean to put down his Ace. He wants to see you right away, Danny. You telephone him tomorrow morning. You've got to see him *tomorrow*. That's the message he said for me to give you."

"My God, Cissie! Can I see you first? You got to coach me."

"All right, Danny, all right. You call me as soon as you get the appointment with the Dean, and we'll see. I want to go over the program with you. Yes, I do want to see you tomorrow, sure. We've got to work fast. There's not much time left."

"It'll be a big day. But I'll be there. Tell me some more."

"I'll tell you more tomorrow. Now I'm going to have the whole ballads class sing together on our program. That's where I won out. Buck Kennedy is goin' to lead the class—and the audience—in singing the last number on the program. It'll be . . ."

"Cissie!" I fairly shouted. "You mean old Buck Kennedy—leading the last number?"

"Yes, Danny. Don't you see, I had to take Buck Kennedy with the package. That's how I sold the idea to Mrs. Eccles and Dr. Hoodenpyl. They agreed to the class singin' if Buck Kennedy would lead. They like that idea. D'ye see?"

"I see. I see a great light."

"Well, were you in the dark? How are you anyway? Are you feelin' all right?"

"I'm walkin' on air."

"Well, don't stump your toe on any weather balloons. See you tomorrow."

"I'll see you."

"Don't let the owls keep you awake. Good night, Danny."

"Goodnight, sweetheart," I said. And walked out under the stars saying

"Goodnight, goodnight, sweetheart," over and over to myself. It was like I had reached up and pulled an early-ripe apple off a low branch, a rare old Winesap on my own place, rolling it over in my hand till there in the dark the smell of apple put full summer in my mind, but I wouldn't eat it because then I wouldn't have it no more. It was like I could smell apples in the dark that night, walking up across the wet grass and crossing the stile.

Old Man Parsons was standing by the cars, with Ed and Wallace. I could see the nightshirt and headed right for him like he was the Holy Ghost sure enough. When I got near, Ed Cooley called out, "What'd she want? Is it all right?"

"It's still all right, but it's some different. We got problems. I'll tell you more about 'em when I find out more. Cissie says the Dean wants to see me tomorrow."

"That's perfect. You can fix him, right then. Hit'll be yore chance. Make him understand we'll handle the bootlegger."

"Yes," I said. "I know that's the idea. If I can jest figger out how to handle the Dean! I don't know what he wants. But I know one thing. We got to talk to that Sheriff tomorrow. Ed, I want you to call Sheriff Looney and find out when we can see him. I'll call you in the morning, soon as I know my schedule. Then you may have to call me back. I ain't sure where I'll be, but I'll give you some idea, and you jest keep callin' till you reach me."

"O.K.," said Ed Cooley. "I'll do it."

Our voices echoed against the front of the MacGregor House, even though we were not talking loud. It was a quiet night, a night deep and quiet. And Old Man Parsons was standing solemn, barefooted in the grass, just listening and not minding the cool of the night one bit. He wasn't listening to us. Only to whatever went on in the night and in his head. I watched the headlights of their cars stab down the avenue of trees. I heard the chains jingle on the gate when they opened it and when they shut it again. Their headlights were a little thing on the road, against the dark ridge beyond Beaver Creek, till even that little thing was gone. All you could hear was water running in the creek, way off, but softer now.

"And the light shineth in darkness," said Old Man Parsons, "and the darkness comprehended it not."

I didn't answer him. I knew he was talking to himself, and I was studying up something on my side.

"Thou art the man," he went on. "A man like you that's got the grace of God in his heart, he ought to be makin' up his own sweet songs out of that power, not always singin' other folks' songs. You have the power."

"Why, Mr. Alex," I said, "I thought you didn't like the worldly songs."

"The power of God, hit's in a lover too, if he's got the grace of God in his heart and is a true lover."

Somehow it seemed all right to be talking about that, there in the night, with our feet in the wet grass, underneath a million stars.

"You mean, if I'd make up a song about my own sweetheart, and believed in it, it might have the power of God in it?"

I'd never talked to anybody about such a thing before in my life, but it seemed right to do it. The words came out as if I didn't have to think about it.

"It would be runnin' in your heart like sweet water in the banks of the creek, and the power of God in it."

He moved away, his nightshirt whipping against his strong legs, and Old Shep came to him. "You tell Miss Cissie," he said, "that I'll be glad to sing to her machine if she wants what I can remember. You tell her."

I followed him to the stile, hardly knowing what to say, except "I'll tell her. She'll be glad." Then I thought of one of the things I'd been studying up. "If we could have a barbecue out here, some time—a good old-fashioned barbecue some night like this—and some of Cissie's friends and mine. That's what I been intendin' to ask you about, Mr. Alex."

Old Man Parsons was high on the top step of the stile, with his stick in his hand and the shepherd dog beside him, framed in the starry sky.

"A barbecue? It's been many a year since I barbecued meat, but I ain't forgot how. You furnish the meat, and tell me when, and how many folks there'll be."

"It'll be pretty soon. I'll let you know."

He was walking towards the cabin light, and still talking the Bible. "They go up by the mountains," he said to the night. "They go down by the valleys unto the place which thou hast founded for them."

Behind my back a mockingbird stirred up in a bush and fussed at me once or twice. Then he thought he might try a late summer song, and he tuned up. When I went to bed, he was going strong, making his voice a light in the darkness.

18

RAINY DAY IN AUGUST

Next morning I was up early, and drove into Carolina City in the rain. Showers boiling up, one after another like spring rains, not a speck of blue in the sky, and everything steaming, the air already hot and sticky. I got right at the telephone, and managed to catch Cissie at her office before class. Come to her office, she said, after class was over. Better give her about fifteen minutes leeway, though. And the appointment with the Dean, she said, was for one o'clock sharp. Ed hadn't got hold of the Sheriff—he was out on some business—but I passed the news to Ed about where I'd be, and he said he'd keep bearing down on the telphone. With all that, and one thing and another, I got into ballads class a little bit late. Cissie was already explaining about the folk festival and how she wanted the class to sing a number on the program.

"The House Carpenter" was the song the class sung best out of a lot that we had tried. We practiced singing a good deal, off and on, and that was the part the class always enjoyed the most. Cissie was never satisfied, any time, just to read songs out of a book and talk about them. She would sing them, and explain how that was the way they had always been known and remembered. It was a sin and foolishness to read them in books and do nothing more.

"On the printed page," Cissie would say, "a ballad is dead. Dead as a stuffed coon or a pickled fish. No better than a skeleton of the real thing. And the words in print, compared to Shakespeare's poetry, may look like trash. But with the tune it comes alive—it's entirely different. It's as good as Shakespeare then. And you can't help rememberin' it."

Then Cissie would step out from behind the reading stand and teach us the tune, beating time with her hand and walking back and forth, every step a picture and almost a dance, bending and turning and singing with her blue eyes on us, and her golden hair on her white neck, and her voice flowing in time with her steps and the story, till we were like sinners caught up in a chariot and carried over Jordan to the Promised Land. The boys would follow her, all in love with her, as who could blame them, and forgetting to be ashamed to sing, and the girls would do their best to imitate her when they saw what the singing did to the boys.

So it was whenever we practiced the songs. And it so happened, since I was a registered student and Cissie couldn't prevent it, that I had more and more lifted up my voice in songs, even though I was only a hillbilly radio singer. Finally Cissie had come to count on me to help out some with the hardest tunes when the class hesitated. We could come to one of them flat notes at the place where you might not expect it—or maybe it would be a sharp—and I would see Cissie looking at me out of the corner of her eye, or at least I thought she was looking at me. When I held them true to the tune, she would nod her head and look pleased.

But the reason why she picked out "The House Carpenter" for the program, I knowed very well, was that it didn't have any queer notes in it. It's just a sweet, easy tune with a good deal of swing to it, and we could have put in alto and tenor and bass if Cissie had let us, but she wouldn't stand for that. She stopped the singing right now if any of the girls slipped into alto as they were always wanting to do.

Cissie explained how she wanted "The House Carpenter" to be the last number on the program, with Buck Kennedy leading on the stage. She would try to get the words mimeographed, so they'd all be singing the same version, she said, and she hoped some way or other the audience could join in before the song was over. And maybe they would use a piano to help.

After that explanation, there was a little buzz of excitement. Then we went right on with the lesson. Wallace was not in his seat. I judged he must be cutting class to do some planning with Ed, or on his own. Rain was coming down hard, outside. Cissie was giving us a lot of talk about cowboy songs and sailor songs, but somehow I couldn't put my mind on taking notes. Everything seemed to drag.

After class, I didn't rush. I gave Cissie time to get away from the students and get settled. I smoked a couple of cigarettes on the big porch, between the high columns, and watched the crowd thin out. Then I set out, walking slow. It was a dark day, with the rain passing into a drizzle and a muggy feeling in the air, and the lights were in the buildings. There was nobody on the big lawn, and nobody on the walks except a few late students hustling along in raincoats. Wet bushes hung over the steps by the Home Economics Building, where I turned. The flat in behind the Humanities Building, where the cars were parked, was covered with water, and I went around the edge of it to the basement door. Inside, the hall was so dark that I couldn't read the room numbers. But there was a light shining through a glass door, and that was it. I knocked, and Cissie's voice said "Come in."

I let the door close behind me.

"Leave it open," Cissie said. "You have to prop it with that jigger at the bottom."

I let down the jigger and propped it. I always did mind my teacher.

"Have a chair, Danny," she said, not looking at me, hardly.

Her desk lamp was lit, and her papers were spread out under it. It threw shadows on her face where she sat behind the big desk. The only other chair I could see was in front of the desk, opposite Cissie. I took that only chair.

She got right down to business.

"Danny, I don't like to have to mimeograph 'The House Carpenter' and pass out sheets with the programs. And it will run up expense to print the words on the program. But what else can I do?"

"Well, I can borrow a projector somewhere and a movable screen. It wouldn't take but a minute to set up the screen. We could throw the words on the screen easy enough."

"Danny, you've already been such a help. I don't want to put too much on you. But could you do that for me, too?"

For the first time she lifted her eyelids and looked right at me across the desk—like the room and the desk was all one big trap, with the papers and books for bait. And her feet were caught in that big trap.

"Sure I can do it, Cissie. And I will."

"I just don't know how I can get all these things done, on top of everything else—with my papers to grade, and the examination to make out, and—"

"Don't you worry. I'll get that projector and screen, and get somebody to make the slides for you. And I'll rig the stage—all of that stuff. Wallace Exum and some of the boys can help. And I'll start on linin' up the singers. I'll see Aunt Lou Watkins tomorrow, and anybody else in the neighborhood."

"If you could turn off at Pegram's Cross Roads and see Whit Marler, I'll go out and talk to Ike Rountree—"

"What did you decide about payin' 'em?"

"Mrs. Eccles didn't like that idea. She claims it violates the amateur principle. But finally she broke down and agreed. Do you think five dollars apiece will be enough? Ought we to make it ten?"

"Ten would be a waste. Make it five, and throw in a good supper."

Cissie got busy with her pencil for a minute. She seemed more pleased—then she began to frown and dab at her hair.

"Mrs. Eccles wants a regular 'dinner' with the President and the Dean and me sitting with the singers. That means more trouble for Cissie."

"Oh, Lord!"

"It means I have to get them all together in the lounge of the women's dormitory beforehand—after we've broken our necks to get them on the campus in the first place. That's where we'll have dinner—in the women's dormitory—Highgate Hall—the newest one. Danny, you know I'll have to watch those singers practically every minute. No tellin' what they'll take a notion to do."

I could hear the thunder coming on. It was getting darker outside. All of a sudden Cissie didn't seem like my teacher. She was just Cissie, the one I'd always known. I didn't say a word. I just got up and came around to her side of the desk.

"If I hadn't promised Mrs. Eccles—if she hadn't done so much for me—"

Still I didn't say a word, but I bent over, close.

"It's all just for her glory. She's usin' me and she's usin' those old folks. That's all she cares about it. Just to be up there on the stage, talkin' about folklore—as if she knew. But those old singers are really just another kind of hillbilly to her. And so am I. She don't really care anything about ballads."

"But Cissie, you care. And I care." I said it low, close to her ear, and I put my meaning into it. But she didn't seem to hear me. The thunder was rolling, and the rain was hitting the window. Cissie wasn't so much as looking up at me, or leaning towards me. She was just thinking out loud, and looking straight ahead.

"You kept tellin' me," Cissie said. "Maybe I ought to a-listened to you. Maybe I ought to a-gone on and been a hillbilly radio singer in the first place—if these Eccles sort of women are goin' to make me one anyhow."

"Oh, no, Cissie. It was you tellin' me. You was right, and I was wrong. I can see it all."

"I'm sick of it. It's wearied me to a frazzle."

"No, Cissie. I won't have it. Don't let 'em weary you out. Don't think about goin' back to hillbilly music. It's no life for a girl like you. You keep right on with ballads. It's the road for you to travel."

"I'm sick of it, I tell you. I'm burnt out with books and footnotes—and publicity—and silly women."

There came a big thunderclap. The rain dashed the window till you couldn't see out. The lightning hit somewhere close, and the thunder cracked hard, again. Cissie jumped up. The lights went out. I could hardly see her, there in the dark basement office, but I thought she might be crying. Another minute, and I would've had my arm around her, teacher or no teacher. But just then a class let out, the lights came back on, and people begun to pass the door. Cissie turned her back to me and walked towards the window. The hard rain let up. She was watching something outside.

"I wonder what *he* wants," she said in a choked way. "I thought they had gone!"

Through the rain-streaked windowpane I could see the yellow and black of a taxicab, there in the parking place. A man in a raincoat was telling the driver something. The man was Buck Kennedy. He sloshed away with big steps across the puddles and toward the building, while we looked on. The cab driver backed his car into a parking slot and stopped.

"He's comin' in here," Cissie snapped, and she rushed back to the desk and began to grab at little things. "You sit down in that chair. No, move it around on my side." She was dabbing at her eyes and face with a paper handkerchief and pushing at her hair. "Make it look like we were working at some papers together. Here, take this." She shoved something into my hand. "And keep your big mouth shut, Danny. If you can't be polite, you can at least stay quiet. I'll handle this."

"Barkin' saves bitin'," said I, "but I can be dumb as a adder." And I looked at what was in my hand. It was the music to "Ridin' on a Cottonbale," all written out in ink on music paper, with "Arranged by Cecily Timberlake" under the title, and "Voice," "Fiddlers," "Guitar," and "Bass" marked at the side for the parts, and the words there too.

But before I could quite take that in, here came Buck, busting through the door like he owned the place, and his hat and raincoat dripping. He stopped like a shot when he saw me, and his eyes went wide. Then Cissie took hold.

"Come right in, Mr. Kennedy. I thought you'd be in Washington by this time, but it isn't good flying weather, after all. That's too bad."

"Well, no'm—yes'm." He was uncertain what to say, but too swelled up with pride to keep anything back. "Hit ain't so very bad. The Doctor, he was out to my place last night, and we jest decided not to take that airly mornin' plane."

"Won't you sit down?" Cissie's voice was sweet as pie. "Pull up one of those chairs over in the corner." I looked, and there were a couple of chairs that I hadn't noticed before. "Danny and I were just workin' over a little stuff here—for the festival."

Buck looked into the corner, but didn't seem to be interested in a chair. He took off his drippy hat—at last—watched the water dribbling from the brim to the floor, and stepped right on up to the desk. He had been to the barber, I saw. His handsome black hair was neatly clipped and smoothed. Underneath his rain coat, a fine-looking dark gray suit was showing, and he had on a white shirt with a blue figured tie. His black eyes were snapping, and his white teeth showed in a triumphant grin.

"No, thank you, Miss Cissie. I won't hardly have time to set. And I see ye've got company." His grin turned into a leer, and he gave his head a wicked little twist towards me. Then the words came tumbling. "We're ketchin' that twelve-thirty plane. The Doctor, he got a little damp comin' in from my place and had to change his clothes. He said please excuse him for not comin' over himself, and he sont me over to fetch them things he wants to take to Washington. Said he fergot to mention 'em yistiddy, but you'll know—"

"No, I don't know," Cissie said, still trying to be sweet. "What things does he mean? I went through the file with him. Let's see if he left something on the desk." She began to lift up stacks of papers and ruffle through them. Her fingers were fluttering nervously.

"'Tain't nothin' of his'n," Buck went on, and his voice was getting rough and loud. "Hit's *mine*! Hit's *my songs*—the words to 'em that you wrote out, and the music too. He said we'd better take 'em along to Washington. And that other music you was workin' on for him—Cottonbale song or somethin'. He said you'd know. Said he wanted that, too. Said he'd telephone you ef he got time. Didn't he telephone you?"

Cissie shook her head. She was biting her lips, and turning first white, then red. "But that isn't what I . . . he didn't say . . . I think I'd better . . ."

"You better telephone the Doctor," I said. "It might be a mistake. I'll git his number." I reached for the telephone book, but Cissie put her hand on my arm.

Buck was strutting and ruffling his feathers like a black Langshang rooster safe on the other side of the fence from me and my Cissie.

"Ain't no mistake a-tall." He made a big brash peck. "Them's the orders he give me." That was another peck. Then he begun to scratch dirt. "Course I don't r'aly need no words wrote out. When I sing I don't have no words pasted on *my* git-tar where the folks can't see 'em, like some o' these-yer—these-yer so-called radio folksingers. I knows my words, by heart, and no foolin'. But the Doctor said, better take 'em along, so them Washington fellers can foller the writin'. And git the words right when they print 'em. They don't understand Carolina talk too well. And check the tunes too and git them right, and see if . . ."

He cut off his bragging. He was slamming me, but he didn't quite have the nerve to finish up and say the Washington folks were going to see if

Cissie had his tunes down right. I couldn't help rising up in my chair. I stood right up, and dropped the Cottonbale music on the desk.

"You wouldn't be meanin' *me*, by any chance, Buck," I said, right cool and calm, "when you made that crack about pastin' words on a guitar?"

"If the shoe fits you, wear it!" he came back, sassy as a billygoat. Then his eyes lit on the music. "That's it right thar. That Cottonbale song. I'll take hit right now."

He grabbed for the music. I put my hand over it. Then Cissie's soft hand came down and took it gently away.

"I'll call Dr. Hoodenpyl," she said firmly. "I understand what you want, Mr. Kennedy, and of course you can take along your words. I'll lend you the carbon copy, and make you a real good one some time later. But Dr. Hoodenpyl and I must have our signals crossed somehow. I better call him."

She dialed the number swiftly. I sat back in my chair, with my eye on Buck. Buck was leaning over, his hands on the edge of the desk, his eyes watching Cissie's fingers. In another two seconds we could hear Dr. Hoodenpyl bubbling away. I couldn't quite make out his words. He must be humbly apologizing. And Cissie was politely laying it on the line.

"No, I just don't recall it, Dr. Hoodenpyl . . . You must have forgotten to tell me . . . Yes, he's right here now . . . Why, certainly he can take the words along . . . They are his songs . . . Naturally . . . But about the transcripts of the tunes . . . Well, I just have rough copies, mostly, and my notes in the margins of some . . . I just haven't had time to make . . . No, but I will, of course I will . . . I want you to have copies, of course . . . But about that Cottonbale score, I just haven't quite . . . No, I haven't scored the chorus yet, not all of it. And there are some variations in their instrumentation for the different stanzas . . ."

"That's Rufus' song," I whispered. "Don't you let that man . . ."

Cissie frowned at me impatiently and waved me down with her free hand.

"Very good, then, Dr. Hoodenpyl . . . Oh, I know you'll have a wonderful trip with Mr. Kennedy. I wish you both good luck . . . Yes . . . You want to speak to him? . . . Just a minute."

She put her hand over the receiver and said softly, "Dr. Hoodenpyl thought I was farther along than . . . he just misunderstood my situation . . . He's very nice about it . . . And he wants to speak to you, Mr. Kennedy."

Buck took the receiver and began to say "Hello" and "Yes, sir," "Yes, Doctor . . . Whatever you say . . . The taxi's waitin' . . . I'll be right over."

Cissie went to a big metal file and took out a folder. "Here are your words, Mr. Kennedy. That's a pretty good carbon. And later on I'll bind up a real nice copy for you . . . The whole thing."

"Yes'm, thank ye," said Buck. He took the folder, grabbed his wet hat from the desk, and started for the door. Cissie went right along with him, buttering him up the best she could.

"I hope you'll have a fine trip and a fine experience. And drop me a postal card from Washington, won't you? And don't forget to be back in time for the festival. We'll be counting on you."

"I'll be back," Buck said grimly. "I'll be back here in two or three days, mebbe." He glared at me once, and was gone.

Silence—for a spell. Silence as thick with trouble as a honey locust is with thorns. Cissie standing, with her head bowed over and her hands pressed against her cheeks. But bristling too. All prickles and stickers. Not a soft spot in her.

"The dirty dog!" She stamped her foot and came back to her desk, chin in air, spike heels tapping like rifle shots.

"A couple o' dirty dogs!" I added, for the principle of the thing.

"But I *have* to get along with 'em. Pretend to be nice." She was moving papers around, making stacks of them, slapping 'em down any old way. "The impudence of it. Sending Buck Kennedy over here to get my transcripts. Why did he do that? I can't make out what's goin' on. Takin' the best part of my thesis off to Washington, right when I'm tryin' to finish. What for? He's been over 'em all. He never said a word to me about takin' 'em with him. Didn't have the nerve to ask me to my face."

"Stealin'," I said. "Just plain stealin' like I told you. That man's got some sort of racket."

Cissie rested her chin in her hand and thought a minute.

"Umm-hunh, yes, that's what *you* call it. But you don't see the clever part of it. And I didn't either, at first. But now. My God, it really *is* clever. Danny, they are Buck's songs, you see—*his* versions and tunes in a way, even if he did learn 'em from somebody else back yonder. He has some sort of rights in 'em, even though the actual transcriptions are *my* work. Well, it's just too complicated to talk about—but maybe he thought I'd have a hard time refusin' to loan Buck his own songs . . . And that's why he sent Buck. And Buck didn't take it any too well, either, did he? He was pretty bold about it. But anyhow, what would Dr. Hoodenpyl want to *do* with 'em, there at Washington? That's what I don't get."

"Steal 'em," I insisted. "What else? Some sort of stealin' you never heard about. Well—I had an idea college professors were all sort o' dreamy. Respectable, but dreamy. But nobody ever told me they'd dream up crooked shenanigans. I didn't know they were like that."

"Oh, they are *not* like that—not at all. They're fine men, these ballad scholars. I could name a lot of 'em, only you wouldn't know them. Like

Dr. Goodenow, up there in New York—he was wonderful to me . . . And if I could have gone up to Chapel Hill—to the university there—or the University of Virginia or some place like that. But I thought Dr. Hoodenpyl was all right until—"

"Well, why didn't you go to Chapel Hill or some place like that?"

Cissie blushed. In fact she pouted and blushed at the same time.

"I've done enough explainin'. You explain some. Maybe it was just because I'm queer—queer as a chicken hatched in a thunderstorm."

"Me—I can't explain anything. What I'd like to see explained is this." I picked up the Cottonbale music. "What did he want with Rufus' song? It's Rufus' song—and he shore don't like to have folks messin' around his property."

I could see Cissie was anxious. "That's another matter," she said, "and the strangest thing of all. Dr. Hoodenpyl has the Decca record, and he kept after me to write out the instrumental parts. I couldn't refuse, the way he put it, because he said he wanted to make a study of it and maybe write a paper. And I was to go over it with him while he played the record. But why he wanted to take it to Washington, I can't imagine."

"You better put your foot down. You better tell him where to get off."

"I can't do anything of the kind. You don't understand. He's got me—until I get through my thesis, stand my final examination, and get my degree. Why, Danny, Dr. Hoodenpyl could ruin me. He could reject my thesis. He could make it hard for me on the examination—even fail me. Even after I get my degree, I'll still need his recommendation if I am to get a teaching job. And—and—well, he might make it hard for me to get anything published. I can't afford to get on the wrong side of the professor that's directing my thesis. He can make me, or he can break me."

That stopped me. At least it stopped me from saying much more. "Blackmail—it's mighty like blackmail." I managed to get that much out.

Cissie sighed, and began to pull out one desk drawer after another.

"Anyway, you better hang on to ballads, like I told you, Cissie."

"I'm hangin' on right now. I'm lookin' for that program. Here it is. Don't you think it's nice?"

There it was, the program, with "An Evening of Carolina Folk Song" lettered across the top, and a picture of a fiddler on one side and a singer on the other, with folks dancin' in between.

"Mighty pretty," I said. "Who did this? Did you?"

"No, Elvira Looney drew it—and maybe I'll need you to help me with the printer."

Just then the telephone rang. Cissie picked it up and answered. She glanced at me suspiciously and handed me the receiver. "It's for you. It's Ed Cooley—and how did he know—?"

Ed's voice said: "It's all fixed. Be at the Sheriff's office in fifteen minutes. We got to do some talkin'."

"I'll be right along."

"Wallace and me—we'll meet you at the elevator."

"Good."

I put down the telephone and looked hard at Cissie.

"You hang on to ballads. And I'll hang on, too, right with you. And I'll help you with the printer. You better loan me that program design. Does it have the singers and their numbers with it?"

"No, but I've got that all worked out. Here it is."

Cissie looked up at me in a dazed and weary way and handed me the program design and some typed sheets. I tucked them into my big notebook and picked up my hat and raincoat.

"Danny, what are you and Ed Cooley up to?"

"Cissie, when the bugs give a party, they never ask the chickens. Furthermore, a limber neck outlasts a stiff one, an ounce of prevention is worth a pound of cure, and above all it's a sin and a shame to give a blackmailer an inch, for then he'll take an ell. That's one mistake Ed and me don't have to make."

I put my hand gently on her shoulder. She was trembly as a dove, but her eyes told me she had the grit to see it through. She knew she better not ask questions. "So long, Cissie," I said. "See you later," and I ran through the rain to my car.

19

FEELIN' OUT THE LAW

Sheriff Looney ain't one whit like the sheriffs you see in the western movies, though he is a real tall man and skinny as a beanpole. Elvira takes after him. Sheriff Looney has a long hatchet face, with a long nose, and a head of black hair with patches of white in it, and he wears black-rim spectacles like Mrs. Eccles. He looks more like a professor than most professors do, except that he grins mighty easy. When he grins, the corners of his mouth go back nearly to his ears. See him in a crowd and you couldn't miss him if you knew him. You can see that spotted head of hair a mile off, and it always sticks up above everybody else's.

His office ain't like a sheriff's office, either. It's more like a business office. So they all are, in our new court house. We got to the office door—Ed Cooley and Wallace and me—not more than a minute or two late. We all sat down in chromium steel chairs with leather cushions and looked at the Sheriff. And he looked back at us across a metal-top desk that was as clean as any businessman's desk. I offered him a cigarette, which he refused as I knowed he would, because he don't neither smoke nor drink, and when we had passed the time of day, Ed lit in and asked him whether he had a warrant out for Buck Kennedy.

I saw his grin starting. The Sheriff took off his glasses and rubbed his eyes and mouth, but the grin was still there.

"I might have a warrant," he said, "and then ag'in I might not."

Ed looked a little bothered, but maybe he was just putting on.

"Ain't Dean Bronson been around to swear out a warrant?"

"The Dean is quite a hand at writin' letters and telephonin'. Maybe he don't understand about swearin' out a warrant. He ain't been around, if that's what you want to know."

"If a warrant is what you need, I might have somebody that would swear to it." Ed looked over at Wallace. Wallace eased the back of his neck up off the chair where he was slumped, took his hands out of his pockets, and spoke his lines like he'd memorized 'em.

"That's right. I could do it. There's a dozen more that could. We can git the evidence, and that's one thing the Dean couldn't possibly do, and the campus policeman's too slow on his feet. We've got that old college spirit, us boys have, and we want to clean up the mess right away if you—"

The Sheriff interrupted him. "If I had a warrant, I reckon I'd have to serve it. But you know the old sayin', 'as welcome as the sheriff.' It might be inconvenient for somebody. Wouldn't it, Danny?"

The Sheriff grinned again and winked at me.

"'Twouldn't inconvenience me none," I answered. "But there's another old sayin', you know, and that is 'Every man is a sheriff in his own house.' If the law don't take hold, you see where that puts me."

The Sheriff went on talking as if he was thinking out loud.

"Of course it really is a Federal case if Buck is makin' the stuff out there. All I could get him for would be under the State law. And if I got him, and then turned him over to the revenue officers, it sure wouldn't get any votes for Sheriff Looney, this election, up in Beaver Valley and all around there."

"Naw," Ed agreed, "it shore wouldn't. When that Beaver Valley box come in, there wouldn't even be a preacher vote in it for Looney."

"But on the other hand, if I don't do something to satisfy the Dean, next thing I know, the teachers assocation will be a-meetin' and a-passin' resolutions, or this League of Women Voters here in Carolina City will go crusadin'. And that won't exactly do me good either, will it?"

"That's right, Sheriff," I said. "Ever'body knows the college is in politics, and I reckon the Dean must know the ropes." I didn't really know anything of the kind, but I wanted to make the way easy for what I thought had to come.

"And furthermore," said the Sheriff, leaning back in his chair and hoisting his feet right up on that clean metal-top desk. "Furthermore, I've been gittin' a kind of inside view of this thing. In the bosom of the family, you might say. I'm bound to think some about the young ladies. Elvira's been tellin' me. She sets a lot o' store by Cissie, and I do too. And she's crazy about ballads. And I understand Cissie depends pretty heavy on Buck Kennedy— though I don't quite git her idea about that. And I hear the girls like him a lot—which is plumb foolishness, if you ask me. But Cissie is a fine girl. I don't want to upset her—and break these young ladies' hearts—and if I set in and arrest Buck Kennedy for bootleggin' on the college campus—well, a cat that swims in the ocean is shore to drown!"

"Sheriff," I said. "You're a-takin' the words right out o' our mouths. We got a proposition."

He didn't seem to notice. "I was a-hopin'," he continued, "that, bein' as it's so near the end of summer school, I could wait a few days and then do this thing quiet, somehow or other. I don't want a big scandal breakin' out in the newspapers while the school is still goin' on. That's what I was thinkin'. Maybe you have a better thought."

"Don't look at me, Sheriff," I told him. "I can't think about nothin' but ballads till school is over. You ask Ed. He's a real thinker. He can think and talk at the same time."

Ed cleared his throat and started to speak his piece, but Sheriff Looney stopped him. "Hold on a minute, Ed. I want to tell Danny somethin'. I'm in the same fix you are, Danny, about this ballad thing. Why, that gal o' mine, she can't do nothing but talk about ballads, or sing 'em, day and night. Or listen to records. It's terrible at my house. Her Ma and me—well, we can't tune in any of our favorite radio programs if Elvira is around the house. She won't have it—neither Rufus and you boys, or Grand Ole Opry, or Amos and Andy, or the Telephone Hour, or Firestone. She puts her foot down. Claims it interrupts her studyin', or maybe she wants to play over some ballad records, or maybe she jest up and says it's plain tacky—that music we thought was so sweet.

"And demned if she ain't gittin' me sorter interested, too. That's the funny part. I'm ketchin' the disease. She started in to cornerin' me, every chance she got, and askin' me if I don't remember some ballads. Read me off a list. And sure enough I did—though I reckon I hadn't thought about 'em in forty years, her Ma and me. Had us both a-singin' 'em and tryin' to remember.

"And the next thing was, she had me prowlin' all around this court house and lookin' up old court records. We even got up in the attic and found some stuff the court clerks didn't know about.

"Let's see—they were all bloody murders and some of 'em rapes. The sort o' thing no young gal ought to be pryin' into, but Elvira claimed it was studyin' and that Cissie said it was all right, and so I humored her. 'Omie Wise'—we tried that, and didn't get anywhere. And 'Frankie Silver,' 'Tom Dula,' and a lot more. But of course she couldn't find a trace in this county. But up there in the attic, amongst some old papers, she did find 'The Blockader's Trail,' printed on a little old sheet of paper, like the fiddlers and singers used to sell on the square, on court days, you remember."

He paused, rubbed the back of his head, and looked over at Wallace.

"If you want to set Elvira up, that's the way to do it, Wallace. Don't fool around with candy or auto rides. Jest find her one of them ballad sheets.

She thought she had found a treasure when she found that old copy of 'The Blockader's Trail.' I looked at it, and demned if I didn't remember it, though not quite the same words. You remember how it goes, don't you—"

> On the way to the mountains to get their junk
> They hid their jug in an old hollow stump.
> When we got to the place where the liquor was at,
> There stood Bob Dula, as watchful as a cat.

> He was standing on a log on a side of the hill
> His Colt on his hip and his eye on the still.
> He was pleased with his job and so proud of his gun
> He wouldn't punch the fire, nor the liquor wouldn't run.

"Elvira loved her Pa about twice as much, after that, and we've been goin' strong ever since."

Sheriff Looney rubbed his head again, and Ed thought it was time for him to start, but the Sheriff held him off.

"Wait another minute, Ed. I'll tell you some more. This thing is really complicated.

"That Elvira of mine—she's turned out to be a regular bloodhound after the facts. Now Ed, you may not like this too well. But somewhere along the line Elvira picked up that old story about the trouble between the Kennedys and the Cooleys. So she went clear back to the Confederate War and the Carpetbagger times and dug out the whole thing as far as she coud find it in the court records and the tax records and the land sales."

Ed and Wallace were sitting on the edges of their chairs, and Ed was red in the face. "Well, what of it, Mr. Sheriff?" he said, a little testy. "That ain't no news around here. Ever'body knows the Kennedys are a bad lot—and how the trouble started."

"Elvira didn't know about it. Somebody must have put her on to it."

Wallace was squirming, but he knew it wasn't time for monkey business. So he came out with it.

"I told her about it, Mr. Looney. Elvira was gone on Buck Kennedy like all the rest of 'em, and I had to put her wise. She wouldn't believe me at first. Said I was prejudiced. And that's why she looked up the records."

I decided it was time to get back on the track. "Sheriff," I said, "that don't have a thing in the world to do with ballads or this trouble on the campus."

Sheriff Looney stopped grinning. He pointed a long bony finger at me and pulled his lips tight together. Then he said: "Yes, it does, my friend. That's the very point. It does. And the point is—well, I don't know what your proposition is, but let's have one thing clear. You are not goin' to get the Sheriff or the Sheriff's office into any sort of grudge fight. No feudin'. No sort of shootin' scrape. I'd forgot all about the Kennedy and Cooley feud till Elvira dug up the facts—then of course I remembered the story quick enough. And if any of you think you can get the Sheriff's office to help you pay off any old scores, you better think again. I won't touch it."

We were all three stiff and quiet. I was remembering what Ed Cooley told me in the barbershop, that day. It looked like Sheriff Looney was going to be a tough customer for us to handle.

Then the Sheriff took his feet off the desk, rocked in his swivel chair a little, and put on his grin once more.

"But if you have a different sort of proposition, I'll be glad to hear it. I do want to put a quietus on Buck Kennedy and take the heat off this office."

So that was my cue, and I took it. "I've done talked all that over with these boys, Sheriff, and that part's all settled and well understood. We think we've got a little scheme—a nice, peaceable, quiet little scheme. And we think it'll work fine if we can jest git you to help us some."

"All we mean to do," said Ed, "is give Buck Kennedy a good scare—at the right time and place."

"How are you goin' to scare a man like him? Buck Kennedy don't scare easy. Besides, he probably packs a pistol, and you'll run into shootin'."

Wallace eagerly put in his word. "He don't carry a gun when he's on campus. Only at night, when he's hangin' around Art's Grill."

The Sheriff looked at Wallace sternly. "You're a mighty well-informed young man. You are takin' a mighty big chance if you've been hangin' around Art's Grill yourself."

The Sheriff had Ed and Wallace bluffed. I could see that, and I could see they weren't going to get very far with him, the way they were feeling. But, I told myself, he's really with us. He's as much as told us that. With us—if we work this thing right.

"Sheriff, Ed had the principle of the thing right—we aim to give him a scare. That's all. And I'll bet he'll scare a good deal easier than you think. Buck Kennedy's developin' some new interests in life. My idea is, he's about ready to get out of the bootleggin' business anyway. It's tided him over. But he might be glad to have an excuse to quit, and he don't want to git into court, by no means. Now look at this."

I took Cissie's program for the folk festival out of my notebook and spread it on the desk. And we all stood up and gathered around the Sheriff while I laid our war plans before him. As I talked, the Sheriff's grin spread back to his ears, and I felt sure we would win him over, but of course, being the Sheriff, he had to think up all the objections.

"This plan calls for the use of our cars," he said. "And Danny, there's been some criticism of the Sheriff's office for lettin' the county cars be used for private purposes."

I talked my way out of that one, easy enough. "Anything we can't fix, Rufus can. You know that, Sheriff."

"So Rufus is in on this too?"

"Well," I said. "Rufus and the Turkey Hollow Boys are comin', that night. Cissie told me they'll be on the program somewhere. At the dance afterwards, if not in the chapel. I think you can count on that. And Rufus will help us—there at the end—if we need him."

Ed put in a thought. "We could use Rufus' Cadillac, if we have to. He don't like this bootleggin' and cavortin' around no better than the Dean. Ain't that right?"

That was right, and I backed Ed up. Rufus is mighty strict about such matters. He don't like for his singers or any of the folk singers to get a bad name.

"Anyway," I told the Sheriff, "you will be actin' bony-fidy if you use the county cars. We'll see that you have information—better than any the Dean can give. And you can bring along a search warrant. There's no harm a-tall in a search warrant, is there?"

"Under the circumstances, I should say not." He paused and began to laugh a little, and I figured we were winning him over. "I could even use an old search warrant, maybe," the Sheriff continued. "Stick Buck's name in it, the way Triplet stuck in Holzclaw's name in 'The Blockader's Trail' ballet. Pore old Holzclaw, he was innocent, and had to serve two years all the same." The Sheriff laughed some more. And we all laughed.

"Look-a-here, Danny." His eyes bored at me like steel. "You are timin' this thing mighty close, ain't you? If Buck makes a break *before* we are all set and ready, what then?"

I went right on with the war plan.

"Buck's got to lead that last song, with the class and ever'body joinin'. All that's needed is for him to spot the Sheriff when he starts to sing, or even while he is singin'. He'll be there on the stage with the others, and no easy way for him to make a break till it's all over. We'll have a boy run and whisper in his ear and pretend to warn him, as soon as he steps off the stage. That's when he'll make his break."

"And then what?" insisted the Sheriff.

"We want him to make his break then get away to his jeep so that he'll be clear away from the crowd. Nobody will know anything about it except us that are in on it. You can have a deputy posted at his jeep, to hold Buck long enough for you and us to reach our cars. The rest of it can be finished up while the crowd is moving over to the gymnasium for the dance and all. Not even Cissie will ketch on—and that's a mighty important thing. You can ride out to Buck's place and do what we've figured out and be back at the gymnasium before the dancing gets started good."

"Let's see now," the Sheriff said, rubbing his chin thoughtfully and keeping his eyes on the program. "You don't want me to make an arrest. And I don't want to either. The idea is to scare him and get him out of Cissie's way and your way and my way. Then we can all have some peace till school ends, anyhow."

He looked from one to the other of us with them steel-boring eyes and did some figuring out loud.

"I think it might be better not only to have a deputy to hold him at his jeep, but another one near the door when Buck makes his break. Near enough for Buck to see him and me too, not near enough to ketch him right away. I want him to have a good long lead, so he'll have time to git his stuff out of the way. I'd hate to have to chase him. That wouldn't be fun, and I want to git some fun out of this. I have more'n enough of chasin' as it stands."

"All right, Sheriff," I agreed, "we'll do it yore way."

"Well boys, by Jerusalem, we'll give the old scoundrel a good run. But this plan is a little tricky. And Buck is a clever old coot. There might be some angle you haven't figured. I think I can do it, but I better study it some. You call me about this time tomorrow."

Sheriff Looney got up. He walked around the desk and stood amongst us, taller than any of us. He draped one arm around me and the other around Wallace.

"Glad to see you boys. And Wallace, I'm glad to see you here at the office for a change—instid of around my house!"

Wallace's face was red. Ed had the dry grins.

"I was plannin' on comin' to the singin' anyhow," the Sheriff said. "On Elvira's account. I couldn't miss it. Anyway, didn't Carlos B. Reddy tell us all to git right behind this ballad collectin'. I'm kind o' ridin' that bandwagon, boys."

Soon as we were in the hall, Ed and Wallace were as merry as mice when the cat's away. "It's as good as settled," said Wallace. "He was just stallin'—to put up a front."

"We'll give Buck a short haircut," Ed added. "Curry his hide."

But I still had to fix the Dean.

20

IT WAS A THURSDAY

If only everything else had been as easy as fixing the Dean!

When I walked in that office door, it looked to me like a steep, slippery, double-S curve on a foggy night. Time I walked out, I was zooming along a straight, level road with no traffic in sight and sunshine ahead.

Before I could hardly sit down, the Dean was offering me a job. At least it sounded like an offer.

My name had come up in their conference, he said, in connection with expanding their program in audio-visual education.

"We need someone," he said, "to help us bridge the gap between the commercial and the educational exploitation of folk song. Someone with actual radio experience in the—ah—hillbilly music."

"Country music, some calls it," I said, to be polite, but didn't see what he was driving at.

"Thank you, the country music. We cannot extend the influence of folk music unless—well, in our Music Department as it now stands we have no one with experience in the hillbilly—that is, the country—music and who also knows folk songs thoroughly. But if we could secure a grant from one of the foundations for an experimental program . . . We could not offer a professorship, you understand. It would have to be lecturer or technical consultant. Something of that kind . . ."

"But you've already got Cissie—I mean Miss Timberlake. She knows radio, and ballad songs, and more about books than I would in a hundred years."

"Certainly," said the Dean. "We have Miss Timberlake. A most remarkable young woman. We are greatly interested in her work. How-ever—"

He turned his swivel chair and looked out of the window like he was reading words in the sky.

"However, the College must consider all the angles, including the financial. Of course if Miss Timberlake could secure a grant, that would . . . Yet situations might arise. Situations that a woman might have difficulty in handling, especially a young, attractive woman."

I saw my chance. "Yes, sir," I said. "I know about them situations. You jest leave it to us boys, and we'll guarantee to handle a little situation that's been a-botherin' you. Ain't no sense in the Dean of a college having to root out a bootlegger."

The Dean got up and came around on my side of the desk. He sat on the edge of the desk and lowered his voice. "I am greatly interested," he said. "Could you by any chance be referring to—?"

"Better not name no names, Mr. Dean. What you don't know won't hurt you. But some of us have known this campus bootlegger from 'way back. And we're hurtin'."

"Is there something you want me to do?"

"Nothin'! Nothin' but jest have faith in us. And don't go swearin' out warrants for somebody's arrest."

The Dean busted out laughing. "What a picture for the *Carolina City News*! Just imagine!" A buzzer sounded. He lifted his desk telephone. "Yes. Yes, Dr. McCollum. I'll be right over." He stood up and held out his hand. "I have to step over to the President's office—if you'll excuse me—but I think we understand one another perfectly. I have faith in Danny MacGregor and the 'boys.' I promise to—well, turn my back . . . not look . . . not swear out any warrants, for the time being. And meanwhile, Mr. MacGregor—" he gripped my hand firmly. "No publicity."

"That's right, Mr. Dean. No publicity."

The whole thing did not take five minutes. I felt sort of dazed, and must have looked like a dying duck in a hailstorm, but that didn't keep me from stepping out on the road the Dean had opened.

But there were some rough spots in it that I didn't see right off—and a blind turn.

It was a Thursday when I came to that turn.

A Thursday—and I was already having to stretch out if I was to keep up in the race and get everything done that Cissie wanted done, on top of what Rufus had booked for the Turkey Hollow Boys and all the things that Ed Cooley and Wallace Exum could dream up to worry me about. Cissie had me on the telephone a dozen times, and if it wasn't Cissie it was Ed or Wallace.

Friday—I knew Friday would be the same thing, only more of it.

And Saturday—that was the big day. Then I was going to have to *level out*—or quit. And I wasn't going to quit. I felt pretty much like a boiled rag, but I starched up my spirits with all the grit I could muster till I must have looked like I swallowed a yardstick. *A wedge of the same wood will split any oak*, I told myself, and gave them back all they were giving me, and so we had it, up and down, all that Thursday morning.

But, come twelve o'clock noon, we were just finishing a housewives' program at WCC, and Rufus was shooting up his eyebrows at me and wiggling his scalp.

"You all set for Saturday night, Danny?"

"A wheel that can't turn can't spin," I told him. "I'm already turnin' like a circular saw, and I mean to spin. So look out. Give me gangway."

"All right, Danny, but jest don't let anybody put a spider in yore biscuit. Or my biscuit either. Look at this."

Rufus whipped a letter out of his coat pocket and shoved it at my face. Ozro was heehawing, and Wallace Exum was crowding in, ready to grab at me.

The letter was on WSM—Grand Ole Opry—stationery, from somebody I didn't know—the name was J. Theo Brewbaker—and it said he was coming to the folk festival Saturday night and wanted Rufus to fix it for him to see Cissie and me.

"I don't know him," I said. "What does he want to see us for?"

"Sure, you know him," Rufus said. "Don't you remember? At the Future Farmers shindig. Came in late and sat in the front row. You met him on the stage afterwards."

I begun to remember. I remembered picking my guitar while Cissie sung, and I was climbing up a ladder of guitar strings into the white roses . . . A lot of faces—mostly a blur. And a man in a front seat beating a notebook with his hands . . .

"I reckon I do remember. I reckon you mean . . . you mean Mr. Polka Dot Tie."

Rufus was grinning now. The others were laughing.

"That ain't his name, but you've got him right," said Rufus.

"That's him," bawled Ozro. "Polka dots big as a mule's eyes." And he nickered.

"But you ain't read all the letter." Rufus tapped the paper. "Look ag'in. Read some more."

I was still holding the letter—like a dummy. I looked at it again, and further down it said the man would talk to Rufus about the Grand Ole Opry engagement and maybe a swing around through Tennessee and Kentucky and some more places, all the way to Texas.

The Turkey Hollow Boys were crowding up close around me. Wallace was stretching his neck to peek over their shoulders. Rufus was wrinkling his forehead and saying nothing with his mouth, but his eyes were saying plenty.

That letter—seemed like it was beginning to burn my fingers. I shoved it back at Rufus.

"Looks like that's it, don't it?" I let my eyes roam around, and every man was staring at me as if I was holding a gun on 'em. "Congratulations! You're a-goin' right to the top."

"What do you mean, saying *you* like that?" Rufus was red in the face. "Don't you be thinkin' about runnin' out on us. Got to have you. Got to have Cissie. Come here now, I want to talk to you."

He yanked at my shirt, then took my arm and steered me to the hall. I went along like a man sleepwalking. When I passed Wallace, he gave the signal that he wanted to see me. I couldn't even nod back.

Next thing, Rufus had me backed up in a corner in one of the little recording rooms, with the door shut. His face was close up to my face. He had his hands in his pockets, and was wiggling both elbows. He was talking fast, and he meant it.

"Danny, I'll give it to you straight. I ain't sayin' that what you are doin'— you and Cissie—ain't a good thing. But there's a hell of a lot of difference between a *good* thing and a *sure* thing. This Grand Ole Opry engagement, it's the difference between selling records in the thousands and selling in the millions. We can't afford to miss it, and you can't either. You've got a good farm place—with a mortgage on it. You aim to git married, and I think you will. You've got big expenses—and you'll have more. This is your chance. You know you can't lay out on us. You may be in love, and crazy as Tom Tyler's old bitch, but that ain't no punkin-head under that red hair of yours."

"I never said I was goin' to lay out. Hit's the big chance, all right. And I don't blame you for latchin' on to it."

"Then what are ye lookin' so sick about? You act like the bottom had dropped out of the kittle and you had nothin' left but the rim."

There was no way to explain my fix. This was what we'd all been hoping and working for, but now that it was in sight, I was half-hearted as a stableboy on a cold morning, sent to curry a muddy horse before breakfast. Lead in my feet, fur on my tongue, no sap, no spunk.

"I ain't had no notion o' lettin' you down. But I'm troubled in my mind. I'm mixed up in my feelin's. I'm afeard I won't be much good to you and the boys."

212

"Aw, shucks, hellfire and damnation. Is that all that's worryin' you? Danny, you won't git nowheres by sullin' around and bein' mixed up in your feelin's. Now I ain't no man to mess in somebody else's business, especially in his love affairs. And you'll have to admit I've humored you a lot. I've made it easy for you. Here you run off, a-studyin' ballads at the college, and I didn't raise no howl, did I? Long as you kept up with our regular stuff—and you *have* kept up—I didn't crowd you, did I? Besides, I thought it might be a good line for you to try out. There's no tellin' what's ahead of us in country music. Television's comin' on soon—sooner than anybody around here figures, and that'll be a big change for the radio business. We got to look sharp. But there's no money—there's not even a pore livin' in what Cissie's tryin' to do—all that college stuff. You both better stay hitched with us till we know what's what. And of course there's no tellin'—things can change fast—there might be somethin' in the ballad line that we could . . . Well, anyhow, here I am a-helpin' you, ain't I? And we all are with you in this Buck Kennedy thing and this-here folk festival. Do you think I'd do that if I didn't believe in you? I'm on your side, Danny MacGregor."

It was the longest speech I ever heard Rufus make. I didn't have any speech. I had a question.

"You understand about where to park your car, don't you? On Saturday night? Wallace told you?"

Rufus took his hands out of his pockets and walked around the little room. He stopped by one of the machines, turned, and pointed his finger at me.

"I understand. And the Cadillac will be right there. And let me tell you one thing." Rufus jabbed his finger at me. "There'll be a gun in the sidepocket of that Cadillac. Maybe in both sidepockets. I ain't takin' no chances."

"Rufus, all we aim to do is scare Buck Kennedy. No rough stuff."

"Danny, I don't know what makes you so innocent. Where was you raised? How long does it take you to ketch on? These-here devils are out to ruin us all, if they can. That's what makes it serious."

"I know about Buck's tie-up with Art's Grill if that's what you mean."

"Oh, that—that's jest common ordinary whiskey-runnin' and hi-jackin' with police protection. That's bad enough—especially on Cissie's account, and her dependin' on that fool Buck Kennedy. But what sticks in my craw is this Hoodenpyl man. I've picked up some news about him. We've got to watch him. Somebody's tryin' to muscle into the country music business in these parts, and I figure the Hoodenpyl man might have a finger in it somehow. I don't see how Cissie ever got mixed up with him. If college professors are like that, I'm ag'in college education." It was no more than

I'd been suspecting, but I didn't tell Rufus that. I tried to put a good face on it.

"You don't need to worry about Cissie. She's gittin' worn out with Hoodenpyl, I think. If we can settle Buck Kennedy's hash, Cissie will handle this Hoodenpyl—I would bet on that."

"Well, maybe—that ain't exactly what I meant. But all right, never mind. Let's come back to what we was talkin' about before you mentioned the car. There's one thing more I want you to be thinkin' about."

Rufus stuck his thumbs in his pants pockets and looked very solemn.

"I'm thinkin'—I've been thinkin' already. About somethin' new, if that's what you mean."

"That's it, Danny. Somethin' new. We need some new songs—our own kind of stuff. It's about time for you to come forward with one. What d'ye say, Danny? Make us a song. Make a bunch of 'em."

"You think I could?"

"You've got it in you if a man ever had. I don't know what you're waitin' for."

"There's many that could do ten while I'm worryin' out one. And they're bringin' 'em out new, every day."

"Hell, yes, Danny, but ninety-nine out of a hundred are jest imitation. Warmed-over stuff. No feelin'. Not much music. You've got the feelin'. You've got the music. You're young, but you think deep and you remember far back. And you love singin'. You believe in it. If you make a song, you'll mean it. That's what country music needs. We are all gittin' tired of howlin' and screechin' about nothin'. Same old thing all the time. Now that's all I got to say."

Rufus made for the door. He turned his head, with his hand on the knob. "I ain't askin' you to promise. I know how you feel, but I know, too, that you play the game straight. Now you talk to that J. Theo Brewbaker, that Polka Dot Tie feller, you and Cissie. Talk all you want to, but don't you forgit that old Rufus and the Turkey Hollow Boys take in a lot o' territory. What anybody else kin do, we kin do. I'm goin' to tell the boys it's O.K."

He didn't make it a question. So I didn't make an answer. We walked down the hall, Rufus grinning, with his arm on my shoulder, and waving his hand as if nothing at all had happened.

Wallace tagged me at the elevator.

"Where you goin' now?" he whispered.

"Out to the MacGregor Place when I git through with ever'thing. I've got to be alone. I've had enough talk for one day."

"What time you goin'?"

"It'll be dark, I reckon, before I'm through, or near to it."

"You watch out. Buck Kennedy's back in town."

"He damn well better be. He's supposed to be."

"I don't mean that. It's the crowd at Art's Grill. They somehow found out about our going to see the Sheriff. They must have some stooges in the court house."

Wallace seemed anxious, more than common. He kept looking over my shoulder.

"Turn around slow," he said in a whisper, "and look at that fellow with the picture shirt, the one that's talking to the receptionist."

I turned around slow. There was a skinny little half-bald man at the desk, and he was wearing a loud sport shirt, a picture shirt.

"What of it?" I said. "He's just buying some tickets, ain't he?"

"Yes. But I think he's one of 'em. He hangs around Art's Grill. He might be tailin' you. You better watch out."

"If Old Man Parsons and me can't handle that little squirt, I'll quit."

"There might be a gang, and you better watch out. I'll watch out too—and see what my pipeline says."

I stepped on the elevator. Wallace must have been reading detective stories, I told myself. Excitable boy, always imagining things, but he meant well. I decided to put it all out of my mind and finish up what was on my list. There was still a lot to check off. Just as the elevator girl started to close the door, a voice said "Down," and a man stepped on. It was Mr. Picture Shirt—with some tickets in his hand.

21

MACGREGOR'S SONG—AND TWO WARNINGS

Come good dark, I was butting through the late traffic and heading west for the MacGregor Place, glad to be shed of Thursday, and all too sure I was leaving it behind among the electric clocks and neon signs. It wasn't cheerful to be told somebody was following you; and if he is (I said to myself) he must have the wrong man. For what did I ever do to Mr. Picture Shirt? I put him out of my mind. Yet things kept catching up with me, all the same. Catching up, and wanting to ride. Rufus and the big chance, for example, but not the fun and glory of it, or the money. It was what you had to take with it—what came to boot. That awful commercial we had to sing for the housewives' program—every beginning and end—it was right in the car with me, turned up full volume, and I couldn't get it out of my head. That "Chick-Chick-Chicka-Pick-a-Chick" thing and all the rest of the clatter. Big grown men acting like dummies and making funny noises just to advertise dressed chicken, wasn't it crazy? Grand Ole Opry carried that kind of clap-trap, too, and you had to sing it as if you liked it. It was enough to make a hog blush.

I couldn't get Pick-a-Chick out of my mind till I turned at the Texaco filling station and breezed along that stretch of ridge road where you can look down and see Carolina City spread out on both sides. The cool night air hit my face, and I saw the WCC radio tower away off, with its string of lights up and down, and the level strings of street lights along the two valleys, with big spots of light where the filling stations and shopping centers were, and the darker spots between that meant trees and fields. It was a half-cloudy night, and maybe time for the moon to come up, but the moonrise would be at my back. In the dark, far off, you couldn't see the hotdog stands and billboards that I knew were making a mess all along those roads. I was beginning to smell sweet clover. With the valley lights below and a few stars among the clouds above them, you could almost believe Carolina City was what the advertisements claimed.

But out on Beaver Valley Pike, just when I thought to be easier in my mind, another commercial caught up with me:

> Handy-Pandy Kitchen Komfort
> Fine and dandy Kitchen Komfort
> Give yourself a break
> Broil a T-Bone steak
> In a Handy-Pandy, fine and dandy Kitchen Komfort skillet.
> Hurry up and fill it!
> Kitchen Komfort's all the style.
> Kitchen Komfort makes the housewife smile, smile, smile.

Good God, it was like a ha'nt following me, dogging me with the jig-slap of the auto tires and the pat-pat of the motor, all the way to MacGregor's place. I couldn't drown Handy-Pandy Kitchen Komfort out of my mind till I rolled up the avenue, braked to a stop, and turned the ignition key. I was out of the car in one motion, not bothering even to roll up the windows, and I made for the light in the cabin where, I knew, Mrs. Parsons had a late supper waiting for me.

I felt better right away.

Country ham—from my own place. Stringbeans right out of the garden. Little young beets. Potato salad, made the old-fashioned way. Hot biscuits with red-eye gravy. More hot biscuits and butter—Mrs. Parsons' butter—with some of her new-made blackberry jam and some of her last year's pear preserves—that was dessert. Plenty of coffee.

Light streamed on the white tablecloth and the sparkling glass dishes of preserves. Mrs. Parsons rustled softly back and forth to bring me hot biscuits. Old Man Parsons sat in his corner, feeling his beard and striking his stick on the floor to hammer his arguments. That was the way we planned my barbecue—the last part of the planning. We'd already been over the first part.

"Did you find the Japanese lanterns, Mrs. Parsons?"

"Yes, Mr. MacGregor, they was right where you said—in that old trunk in the attic. Five dozen of 'em, lackin' three that was tore too bad to use. Hit's been many a year since I laid my eyes on Japanese lanterns."

"They're all right to use, then?"

"Good as new. All that's needful is for you to tell us where you want 'em strung up, and furnish the candles."

"Well, I think all along the front porch and on both sides of the walk up to the gate. There ought to be enough wire out in the barn, but you'll have to string 'em fairly high to keep 'em out of the folks' way. Around among the trees and bushes too, if you have enough. But if it rains, I don't know what we'll do. Put 'em all on the porch, I reckon, and in the hall and rooms."

"Hot and dry. That's what the weather will be," said Old Man Parsons. "The weather's settin' in to be hot and dry. Dog days. Grass is already burnin' a little, snakes are seekin' the water, cattle the shade of trees. Moon is just past the full."

"I looked at the almanac," said Mrs. Parsons. "The almanac says hot and dry."

"The truck will bring the folding chairs and some tables tomorrow," I told them. "And if the meat gets here early Saturday mornin', that will be soon enough, won't it, Mr. Parsons?"

"There will be time if the folks are comin' late Saturday night, like you said. I will start the fires early. The pits are dug. I have good split wood of dry hickory and ash ready stacked, by God's blessing. In *that* matter, the Lord is good to us."

There was something about the way he said "in *that* matter" that made me glance up from my plate. The old man was looking far off.

Mrs. Parsons gave a little chuckle. "Alex, he'd ruther be a-slaughterin' your own beef and mutton. That's what he used to do when it come to barbecuin' meat. He don't like store-boughten meat. Alex don't hold with packin'-house meat or any store-boughten thing."

"Mrs. Parsons," I said, "these folks will never know the difference. You and me would, but they won't. Hit'd be a waste to slaughter our good money-makin' cattle for 'em. Besides, I don't want to work you that hard. You've got enough to do, even with the help I'm gittin' for you."

"I could do it." Old Man Parsons nodded stoutly. "I could do it, and hit would be better. For the Good Book says: *The lambs are for thy clothing, and the goats are the price of the field. And thou shalt have goats' milk enough for thy food, for the food of thy household, and for the maintenance for thy maidens.* And that means that a man should eat and entertain from the yield of his own land. That's the way God planned it. But the cattle butchered in droves in the great city far off and carried abroad on ice in the trains and the trucks, that is what man devised and is not accordin' to God's plan. And thereby the blood and bone of the new generation is made weak."

His stick thumped three times on IS—MADE—WEAK. Then he went on. "But we'll do what you say. Lula and me—we'll barbecue the meat you bring us. Them that's roamin' about the world, always movin', they can't raise their own breadstuff, nor their meat; nor withouten a field or a

218

household they can't hev goat's milk nor cow's milk, nor maid or wife to churn and make butter. There's many sech in the world today, and they are livin' somehow, but they are not livin' accordin' to God's plan. In His good time the Lord will teach them, but first His Hand will fall heavy on them, as it fell on the chariots of Pharaoh, and on Sodom and Gomorrah in their day of evil. But now there's no help for it, and I won't live to see the end of the buyin' and sellin' of the souls of men, their immortal souls for money at the bank and credit at the store. The Bible says, *The goats are the price of the field*. That means a field is somethin' money can't buy, that's the true meanin'. For God made the field, and money never made any field, and you can't put a price on what God made."

Old Man Parsons slowly rose and straightened up.

"Still, hit's a good thing to have your friends here, and a barbecue for the pleasure of the young folks. Barbecue is the best cookin' there is. Fire in the open earth, and hit good wood, and the taste all runnin' through the air, ever'body bein' together, and the girls and boys eatin' off one another's plates. Well do I know it, and Lula and me know how to butcher beef or mutton or pork, how long to let the meat hang, and how to keep good coals, not to let the meat scorch and yet it be all cooked through. The turnin' and the bastin', the right seasonin' and sauce, and to keep ever'thing hot till the company comes. We was raised to hit."

Old Man Parsons was reaching for his hat. He was going to take his walk.

"You'll have to let us know when you-all will be here, so we can have it hot to serve and not cooked too much," said Mrs. Parsons.

"It'll be nigh on to midnight, I reckon, Mrs. Parsons. Might be sooner if we are lucky, but I don't think so."

I put down my coffee cup and called to the old man.

"Mr. Parsons, have you seen any strangers around here lately? Anybody asking about me? Or jest lookin' around?"

Mr. Parsons' eyes glittered as he turned.

"No strangers but the men on the delivery trucks." He took a couple of steps toward me and raised his stick. "But now that you name it, there was somethin' I meant to tell you. Last night an autymobile woke me up, and the dog barkin' too. Must have been 2 or 3 o'clock in the mornin'. I looked out to see. They didn't have their lights on. They stopped a minute, then turned around and went off down the hill before I could get to the door. I could see they turned on their lights at the gate. They druv off towards Carolina City."

"Might have been some teenagers," I said—but I wondered if that was right. "If you hear anybody tonight, shoot off your gun, and I'll come runnin'. That's the quickest way to let me know, and it'll give any prowlers a scare."

"I'll watch out," said Mr. Parsons. "If the autymobile noise don't wake me, Old Shep will. I'll put the gun by the door."

August nights are sometimes coolish, even in dog days, out at the MacGregor Place. I could feel the chill setting in when I stepped out. The moon was over the roof of the MacGregor house, and I walked towards it, thinking deep. Somewhere in the dark of the fields the old man would be walking, and would soon be back to read his Bible, and maybe I would hear him singing. What could I be singing? I didn't bring my ballad books, but my guitar was handy. I rolled up my car windows, and pulled the guitar out of the case. I touched the strings, letting my fingers stray on the frets, letting the moon and the dark old house tell me what to sing. They had more to say than I did. I would listen to their tune and play it.

That was the way it started. Something took hold of me. The tune begun to shape up—something like the one that came to me before, only better. I don't take much credit for it. I played what I heard on the mountain air—the tune first. Then the words begun to come along with it like they'd been waiting all the time. Like something I had always known and just now remembered:

> As I came down the mountain road
> A-fearin' roads must part,
> I set my mind to choose but one
> And follow my sweetheart.
> But everywhere I stopped to ask
> I heard the old folks say,
> "It's easy come and easy go;
> Young man, you better stay.
> She's gone to seek some other one
> And love will pass away."

—And maybe (I thought) it is something I'm just remembering. If it is, somebody else will remember it, and I better not try to pass it off for new. But my Grandma never sung me that song or anything like it. Nor any soul I ever heard sing. It's something that came to me right out of the MacGregor Place tonight, and I'm entitled to claim I made it, for nobody but the MacGregor Place will ever know better.

—But it's not a hillbilly radio song exactly. It's more like some of the old songs Cissie's been a-teaching. But it's not a ballad either. It's betwixt and between, the way Danny MacGregor is betwixt and between this very night.

220

It's MacGregor and nobody else, that's what it is. The tune, I think it's all right—in fact it's pretty good. But what am I going to do for the second verse—and there may be something a little bit wrong with that first verse?

—I'll have to think about it some more. I'll go to bed and sleep on it.

With that, I put my guitar back in the case, got my flashlight and my bag, walked up to the house, lit a fire and hummed the tune over a few times, then went to bed.

Soon as I hit the bed, the ring-around-the-rosy started. The Handy-Pandy Kitchen Komfort jingle jumped me first, with me tumbling and tossing, throwing off the covers and pulling 'em back. To drive off Handy-Pandy, I tried to think of my song and start a second verse, but I couldn't hit the tune, even though I had played it and memorized it an hour before. If only I had had Cissie and her tape recorder, I thought, then I'd have it, but now I've lost it. But what would Cissie think, anyhow, of me making up a song like that? Maybe it's a rotten song, and I'll give up trying to finish it. Next thing, I begun to worry about all our plans, and how everything was going to turn out. I went over every little detail, acting it out in my mind, and I couldn't see much wrong with it *if* everybody lived up to his promise.

But that was a big "if." It all depended on how Cissie would take it, when you came right down to it. There's an old saying that there's no rule for a mule, a pig, or a woman. It was a shame to bring Cissie under that rule. But she might get upset, somewhere along the line. When a woman gets upset, there's a strong chance that she'll blame everything on the one she loves the best. If things went wrong, wouldn't she wind up by blaming me, even though everything I was doing, and the whole crew was doing to help, was all for her sake?

And that would finish me with Cissie—and with everybody else. It would be ruination. Trouble set solid in my mind like a fence post in concrete, and I wouldn't budge away from it. The words of the ballad took over, the one we were all going to sing together at the end: "What have you there to entertain me on, To keep me from slavery." And the other two lines: "I do not weep for gold, she said, And I do not weep for store."

Well, what was she weeping for? I was making good money, working for Rufus, with some on my own, besides. Enough for Cissie and me. Together, the two of us could make a lot more. If the Grand Ole Opry proposition opened up, then we really would be in the money. I hadn't told Rufus yes about it, and I hadn't told him no. But he was counting on me. If I didn't go along, like he figured, that would mean a break. I would lose some mighty good friends. I would be on my own. What then? Could I risk it?

But if I went along with Rufus, how could I hold on to Cissie? Now I knew how she happened to get set on ballads. Nothing I had in hand, nothing that Rufus or even Grand Ole Opry could do would come up to ballads—at least to what Cissie could do with ballads and that kind of music. But suppose I joined up with Cissie and tried that line, what kind of living would it be? Could I ever pay out on the MacGregor Place and have a real home there?

Sing any old thing that ketches on, whether you like it or not—and make money—and lose your girl—and to hell with the money—but then you had to be sure of getting the girl! Was I sure? Was Cissie just fooling me along?

She was weakening a little bit on ballads. There was some tough digging and pizen-snake ambushes on that side of the row, too, and Cissie was just finding out about it. And Rufus, on his side of the row, was wondering if the potatoes would hold out.

Exactly what was the choice?

If I could figure out, for sure, what Cissie wanted, then I could figure out the choice. But every time I thought I had the answer to what Cissie wanted, I bumped into a big question mark somewhere. Maybe it came down to the plain fact that I didn't count one bit in what Cissie wanted. Maybe I jest wasn't good enough—or she didn't trust me—or anybody. I couldn't believe it, but I couldn't quite deny it either. I would roll over from one side to the other, and grab the pillow, and imagine Cissie standing right there before me, like she might be the girl in the song—

> Last night as I lay in my bed
> As I lay fast asleep,
> I dreamed that my true love stood at my head,
> And bitterly did she weep.
> She wrung her hands and she tore her hair
> Crying, "Oh, what shall I do?
> For they say that the love that the men-folks bear
> Dries off like the foggy dew."

The fire was dying out in the fireplace, and the shadow of the trees was shutting off moonlight from the windows, but I could bring her there in my dream-thinking almost like a little ghost, and she was saying how could she trust me, or any man, and I was pleading with her in my dream-thoughts, as if I might be saying it out loud: "I've served you hand and foot, Cissie, all the years. I've carried the loads you said carry. I've stood in the corner and waited when you said wait. I've shut my mouth and bit my tongue when you praised old Buck Kennedy, and watched you keep company with him when I wanted to kick him down the steps, and maybe ought to a-done it. You low-rated my singin', and I took it from you because I loved you and thought you would learn better in time. Now I'm trying' to untwist you from a tangle, and takin' the risk, along with some other good men that are all on your side. And what do I get out of it? No man that's any part of a man would stand for it forever—and I won't stand for it—it's got to stop somewhere—so make up your mind, girl."

But no sooner had I thought it than I knew it would never do to make that speech to Cissie. Even if it was all true, I better not say it . . . I had to have that girl . . . I had to keep going . . . I must have made a mistake somewhere . . . But if it hadn't been one mistake, it would have been another . . .

Somewhere along there I must have dozed off. I remember a little breeze fingering among the leaves and rattling the windows. The door stirred on the latch—a sleepy sound—and at last I was sleepy.

Then I had a real dream, but not about Cissie. At least everybody will say it was a dream, but if you say that, I'll say I must have dreamed with my eyes open. I saw it plain. I saw my Grandpa.

The fire blazed up till the whole room was light, yet the light didn't seem to come from the fire only. The walls gave off light, somehow. But I remember thinking it was the fire woke me.

My Grandpa was standing by the fireplace, shaking his head as if to say Danny had been careless. I saw him, plain as I ever saw anything, reach down for the poker and tongs and shove back a stick that had fallen on the hearth, all the time grumbling under his breath, though I couldn't make out what he was saying. He had pulled on his trousers over his nightshirt and I could see where his black galluses crossed, but over his shoulders he had a shawl—an old green shawl like Grandma used to have and sometimes would spread over the old man's shoulders when he was sitting in the breeze on the porch and she stepped out to the back to get supper on the table.

Grandpa raised up, after he fixed the fire to suit him, he raised up slow with his hand on his back like I remember. He turned around, pulled the shawl tighter around his shoulders, then looked straight at me across the bed.

"Danny MacGregor!" he said. "Danny MacGregor! Take keer of your own, Danny MacGregor!"

Just those words. No more. Shook his head at me. Then walked out the door like a natural man.

I found myself out of the bed in the middle of a dark room, with hardly any light at the windows, stumbling about, all turned around, not knowing which way was which.

I grabbed for my flashlight, knocked it off the table, and it rolled off in the dark. I felt for matches on the mantel and struck a light.

The bedroom door was standing wide open. A strong gust of air rushed through it and put out my match. I struck another one and located my flashlight. The fire was out, but there were dead coals and ashes on the hearth where a half-burnt stick had fallen out, and the stick, still smoking a little, was only an inch or two from the edge of the floor.

Then I heard the shot outside—and feet running hard—and Old Shep barking—and Old Man Parsons' yell—

"Danny MacGregor! Oh, Danny MacGregor!" And another shot!

I slipped into my pants and shoes and ran to the sound.

My flashlight picked out Old Man Parsons on top of the stile. Shotgun in hand, he was peering down the avenue. The dog rushed at me, growling.

"Hush up, Shep. Come here, Shep," he called. "Hit was too fur for a shotgun to reach, but I mought a-peppered 'em a little."

Far down the avenue a car door slammed, and a car engine started with a roar. They were gunning it hard. They put on their headlights as they turned through the gate. At high speed the lights cut the valley road towards Carolina City.

"Who was it, Mr. Parsons? Did you get a look at 'em?"

"There was several of 'em, but they was in the shadow of that big tree where your car is parked and I couldn't get a good sight of 'em. One was a pretty big man and one a little fat feller, I think. They must have walked up mighty quiet through the grass on the other side of the oak trees because Shep didn't bark at first. But something called me out of sleep. I went to the door. I could see somebody with a flashlight working at your car. I fired the first shot to call you. The second one at the men. But hit was too fur for a shotgun to carry."

"I better look at my car."

"You better be keerful. They were doin' somethin' to your car."

The door was standing open on the driver's side. The lever that locks the hood was out of position—released.

I checked the inside of the car first to see whether any wires had been tampered with. Nothing wrong there, it seemed. I crawled underneath with my flashlight—and everything looked normal—except there was a big puddle of water. I lifted the hood—very slowly—and put the flashlight on the starter—the plugs—the distributor—the drain-cock.

Everything that could be pulled loose by hand had been pulled loose. The spark plugs disconnected—the radiator cock opened—the radiator cap off—the distributor cap off, but at least it was still there.

224

"They might have been starting in with a wrench when you fired at 'em, Mr. Parsons. You leveled at 'em just in time."

I checked to see whether anything else was loose. There was nothing else loose so far as I could tell, but I thought I could see where they had begun to work on the starter wires. I replaced the connections and shut the radiator cock while Mr. Parsons brought water to refill the radiator. At first we couldn't find the radiator cap, but it turned out they had just dropped it in the grass and hadn't thrown it away. Somebody had started to prize loose the ornaments but hadn't got very far with it.

"At least they didn't plant any dynamite on me, this time," I said, more to myself than to Mr. Parsons. "It's just meanness—just some of this vandalism."

"Now who would a-wanted to do all this to you? You've got enemies, Danny MacGregor."

"Well, I don't know . . . They might have me mixed up with somebody else, or they might be after me. But I think it's jest meanness."

There was light now in the cabin. Of course Mrs. Parsons would be up to see what all the shooting was about. I heard the door open, and she called out: "Air ye all right, Mr. MacGregor?"

"We're both all right, Mrs. Parsons. Jest some foolishness goin' on around here."

"I'll make some coffee if ye say so. Hit's near daylight, and maybe you'd like some breakfast."

"Thank you, Mrs. Parsons. I'd like a cup of coffee, and breakfast whenever you are ready."

It might be near daylight, but I couldn't see much in the way of daylight on the mountains, or in Beaver Valley, or anywhere about MacGregor Place. In my head, it was all dark. Buck Kennedy was mean—mean enough to mess up a man's car, or get somebody to do it. He wasn't mean enough to plant dynamite in it, if that was what they were working up to. Buck cared too much for his own hide to take that risk. But he might have got tied up so tight with the Art's Grill crowd that he told 'em some big tales—and they drew their own conclusions. And there was Mr. Picture Shirt, and Wallace's funny ideas about him. Maybe they thought I was messing in their business. Maybe somebody was—and they picked me for the man. Still, it didn't look like a gangster sort of job. It was more like a prank, maybe. I began to think back, and I remembered about Chubby and the college boys that Buck was furnishing. We might be getting in their hair . . .

"What's that on your gatepost yonder?" Mr. Parsons pulled my sleeve and broke up my thinking. I had passed by it in a rush, and we had been too busy with the car to notice it.

We walked back to my gate, and I put the flashlight on it. It was a sheet of paper, stuck on with thumbtacks. The dew had softened the paper, and the ink had run a little, but it was plain enough:

FIRST AND LAST WARNING
Keep Your Damn Fingers where they
Belong You Damn Hillbilly Dope and
Stay Out of Other Folks Busness
This Means YOU
Next Time you Get the Works
K K K

I laughed out loud when I saw that paper. No whiskey-running gang would be using a nice piece of looseleaf notebook paper, with ruled lines and punchholes at the side, like I had in my own notebook. In fact, no gangster would be fool enough to write out something like that and stick it on the gatepost, though he might wake you up at 2 A.M. with a wicked phone call from a booth. Or so I figured. I begun to think some more about Chubby and his pals, and how Buck Kennedy could have put 'em up to it. Of course they'd want to be stagey and highfalutin' about it—that's the part they would enjoy, and especially the K K K part. Still, it went all over me to think anybody would hate me that much. Hate me enough to sneak up in the dark, tack a paper on my gate, and mess up my car.

Mr. Parsons came close and put his hand on my shoulder. "Air ye all right, Danny MacGregor?"

"I feel fine. But I'm madder than a hornet."

"I could see it teched you some, and well hit mought. Air ye goin' to call the Sheriff?"

I pulled out the tacks, folded the paper, and tucked it in my pants pocket.

"If it was any other time but this—I might. Maybe I'll let the Sheriff know later—after the big singin' and our party."

"I never was one to call the Sheriff, myself. Hit's a bother to be a-goin' to court."

"It might be somethin' bad, but I think it's jest foolishness. We'll wait and see. There's plenty of trouble in the world, and mean people. And I did have a peculiar experience tonight."

I told him about my dream—if it was a dream—and my Grandpa.

"Hit was the power o' God workin' for you." Old Man Parsons clenched his stick and pointed it at the still bright stars. "Him that dwells on high—it was Him that sent you a vision like to the men of the old times. The sperit of your grandfather, sent by God Almighty to warn you and to bless you.

God is showin' you the way, young man, and the power o' God is in you, like I told you, to see visions and dream dreams and make songs and music in God's Holy Name."

Again he laid a firm hand on my shoulder, a knotted old hand with a grip in it that would make a stump leap. "And to cast down the wicked—and the mighty from their high seats—and they shall fall into the dust."

After his thunder Mrs. Parsons' voice was little and sweet. "Breakfast is ready," she was calling through the dark. "You-all come on—before the biscuits git cold."

It was coming on daylight. I could hear the robins starting their chirrup in the treetops and the redbirds shaking out some bugle notes. I jumped into some clothes and went to breakfast before full daydawn, like the MacGregor Place was a real farm and I the farmer.

After breakfast Mr. Parsons and I walked down to the main road to see what we could see. The first thing was that they had heaved my big front gate off the hinges and flung it in the ditch. We found where they had backed and turned their car in the grass—the cigarette butts where they waited—some beer cans. Then one whiskey bottle—a pint, empty. A label, but no sign of revenue stamps. It might be some of Buck's stuff, but how could I be sure? All the same, the thought kept boring in that my visitors might be some of Buck's customers.

But in broad daylight, after I had walked around the place a while, the whole thing didn't seem to matter. It was Friday now, with Saturday coming on. I telephoned Wallace and got him out of bed. He waked up fast when I told him I wanted to see him in an hour for a strictly confidential talk.

While I was getting ready to go, my song begun coming back to me. The tune was better than I had first thought. Some words begun to shape up for the second verse. I hummed them over to see if they would stand daylight.

They would.

I had to get to ballads class and see about a thousand things, not forgetting the Turkey Hollow Boys' regular Friday night show with a studio audience. But at ten o'clock I would see Cissie. I rolled towards Carolina City, singing the MacGregor Song:

> As I came down the mountain road
> A-fearin' roads must part,
> I set my mind to choose but one
> And follow my sweetheart.

22

THAT FRIDAY

I can remember that Friday just about perfect—all the way around the clock.

7 A.M.—AND A HOT MORNING, TOO!

I was having a cup of coffee with Wallace Exum while he ate breakfast at the Deep South Cafe. At first I couldn't get much more than sleepy-eyed grunts out of Wallace. He had the *Carolina City News* propped against the sugar shaker and was swallowing headlines along with orange juice while I was trying to tell him about my car. (I decided not to bring my Grandpa into it.)

"We want to prevent violence if we have to bloody some noses to do it. That's where the football players come into it. But first I want to get some idea how everything connects up—about my car, and so on."

Wallace said "Um-humph" and drank orange juice.

"It's your project, ain't it? To find out whether Buck Kennedy's back in town. And whether Dr. Hoodenpyl is here. And what about Chubby and his pals? And the Art's Grill people? And Mr. Picture Shirt—if he's followin' folks around?"

"It connects up all right," said Wallace, and all that kept him from yawning was bacon and eggs. "It's got to."

I tried to get him awake. "They could a-planted dynamite in my car, if they knew how. But I jest don't think it was experts, do you? What have any expert criminals got against Danny MacGregor? Look what I found on my gatepost."

Wallace's eyes began to open. "Does look sort of amateur," he admitted. "But it connects up."

He turned the *News* over to read the lower half of the front page while he took a sup of coffee. The coffee cup stopped, halfway to his mouth. He set it down slowly, not looking, and almost missed the saucer.

"Here's the proof—here in the paper. Two 2-column headlines at the bottom of the front page, one on each side. Maybe you *are* just lucky. They could have decided to blow you up."

I grabbed for the paper, but Wallace jerked it back. "No, let me read it to you. See if you know how to read a newspaper. Try this one first."

He began to read—and this is exactly what it said, because I checked it later on. (Cissie kept the clipping.)

Noted Figures to Attend College Folk Song Meeting

Prominent folklorists and noted figures in the radio and folk song reproduction field will attend the folk song festival which is to be held here tomorrow night under the joint auspices of Carolina City Teachers College and West Carolina Folklore Society.

Announcement concerning the eminent visitors was made by Mrs. Georgia Eccles, President of the Folklore Society and Program Chairman of the festival.

Among those expected to be present are: Prof. E. Y. Goodenow, emeritus professor American literature, University of Pennsylvania, and recently visiting professor at Fenimore Cooper School of Music, New York; Eli S. Muradian, Vice-President of American Music Features, Inc., of New York; N. Josef Poradowsky, of the Archives of American Folksong, Library of Congress, Washington. Ballad scholars from the English departments of the University of Virginia, Duke University, the University of North Carolina and other institutions are also expected, Mrs. Eccles said.

Prof. Goodenow is the author of *Ballad Heritage, Melodic Patterns of American Folktunes*, and other standard works. He is known as a pioneer in the study of the "Americanization" of traditional folk tunes inherited from English and Scottish sources. Through his recent work at the Fenimore Cooper School of Music he has brought many young American composers into touch with the musical possibilities of our native folk song.

I broke in there: "I can connect that up. That's some of Cissie's doin's. Mrs. Eccles never would know a thing about that man unless Cissie told her."

"Don't interrupt. Listen to this one."

While in Carolina City, Mr. Muradian and Mr. Poradowsky will be the guests of J. Chauncey Hoodenpyl, Professor of English at Teachers College.

"Wait a minute. I think I see a connection. That's the muscle gang, ain't it? Rufus was tellin' me about somebody musclin' in."

"Pretty good, Danny. All the station managers and disk jockeys are beginning to find out about Muradian and his American Music Features.

Maybe it isn't exactly a racket, but he's got the muscle all right. It's like blockbooking in the movies, he's trying to crowd everything off the air in the popular music line except what has a contract with AMF. But I don't know about this Poradowsky. Hold on a minute—continued on page 2 . . ."

"Bet he connects with Buck Kennedy—you said Library of Congress."

Wallace turned the page.

"Well, I don't see . . . This next is just about the program and the singers . . . Oh, yes, here's something maybe. Buck Kennedy gets a special plug—"

> Mr. Buck Kennedy, of Beaver Valley community, has just returned from Washington, where a special recording of his songs was made at the Library of Congress for the Archives of American Folksong. Arrangements are being made, Mrs. Eccles said, to tape-record the festival program on the spot.

"The hell you say, Wallace. Let me see that paper. Arrangements are being made . . ."

"Well, that's all—that's about all except the usual stuff about the time, and where the singin' will be, and so on."

I felt glum. "Arrangements are being made," I said. "And who is makin' 'em? I am the arrangements man. Is there anything in that news story about Cissie—anything anywhere?"

Wallace ran his eyes over the paper. "I read it to you, didn't I? Not a word about Cissie. Not a word."

"Now ain't that a devilish shame? Cissie's doin' all the hard work, and she don't git a line of credit. And they are fixin' to steal her stuff, I'll bet. That's why Hoodenpyl brought the Library of Congress man . . . I can see it all clear."

Wallace slapped the table. "I pretty nigh forgot," he said. "Cissie wants you to call her right away. She called me and said she'd been telephonin' all around." I started for the telephone. Wallace shook the newspaper in my face. "You better glance at this front page police story first. It connects up."

CITY 'LEGGERS BELIEVED "MOST WARNED"
OF ANY GROUP OF LAWBREAKERS

> It is doubtful that any group of lawbreakers received as much warning before they were hit as did local bootleggers prior to last night's "surprise" raids by state police.
>
> State police raids, beginning early in the evening and continuing till midnight in this and adjoining counties, seized only small amounts of liquor at various popular "clubs" and small establishments.

Asking not be to quoted by name, one well-known bootlegger said: "The big clubs were called up and warned to clean up before police arrived. They didn't give some of us small operators a warning."

City Police Chief Roscoe, however, blamed previous stories in the *Carolina City News* for the alertness of bootleggers to danger of arrest. "If the newspaper spills all the information in advance," he said, "what can the police do?" Chief Roscoe disclaimed all knowledge of any warnings and stated that his officers were cooperating with state police.

County Sheriff Looney stated that his office was advised as to the raids but was not asked to take part. He said that the sheriff's office was ready at all times to cooperate with other enforcement agencies.

See Related Stories
Wrecked Car Abandoned Near Campus, p. 5
Drunk While Driving Arrests Increase, p. 5
Current Crisis Invites New Consideration of Steps to Curb
Gangsters, Corrupt Officers, Officials—Editorial, p. 4

A midnight check by *News* reporters revealed that, despite raids and warnings, certain night spots were operating full blast, and were not visited by police. Among these were: Art's Grill, 1421 Cummington Ave.; Larry's Drive-In on Greenville Pike.

"So they didn't touch Art's Grill," I said.

"No, but that means Buck Kennedy will be wise, and he won't be passing out any pints on the campus tomorrow night."

"What's that story about the wrecked car?"

Wallace turned the pages. "Here it is."

The story said that residents, awakened by a crash shortly after midnight, called police, and the police found a car had run into a utility pole and been abandoned. The car had a campus registration parking sticker.

"That couldn't have been the crowd that came to MacGregor Place," I said.

"No, I'll talk to my pipelines and see what is goin' on. I think they are more afraid of the Sheriff, this big liquor outfit is, than they are of the state police or the city police. Because the Sheriff is on the other side, politically. That's why they might be watchin' you, because they know you went to the Sheriff. But that stuff out at your place—now that might be Buck Kennedy, puttin' college boys up to mischief, just for spite. Or it might be the liquor gang. I'll find out."

"You find some football players, too."

I left Wallace and went to the coin telephone.

I dialed Cissie's house and she answered the 'phone.

"Bad news, Danny," she said. "Bad news, and more trouble for you and me. Some good news, too."

"I saw the morning paper. Hawks and buzzards comin' to town. Sure will steal your chickens if you don't watch out."

That put her in a good humor. She laughed, and I tried to think of her eyes crinkling at the corners, and Cissie looking up sideways at me.

"And one eagle on our side. That's the good news. He might help keep the hawks and buzzards off."

"Who's the eagle?"

"That's my old teacher—Dr. Goodenow—at the music school. Don't you remember? He's the one that really got me started right. I sent him a program, but didn't have any idea he would come. Now he's here. He'll be at class this morning, and I want you to meet him if there's time. Of course it complicates everything to have these guests coming in, but it makes me feel better just to have Dr. Goodenow around."

"All right. What's the bad news?"

"Well, they are still piling things on. I hate to bother you, but I thought I'd better call you right now. Dr. Hoodenpyl 'phoned, and this friend of his from the Library of Congress is going to tape-record . . ."

"That's in the paper."

"So you'll have to put that on your list. I just hope there are enough outlets in the chapel for his machines . . ."

"We'll rig up somethin'."

"I don't know what it all means, but anyhow, Dr. Goodenow wants to see my thesis right away. He'll check it over while he's here, and I think he'll help me get it published, no matter what Dr. Hoodenpyl does."

I couldn't say anything to that but "Hooray," and then I heard paper rustling against the phone.

"Now let's check our lists once more," she said, "and make sure who's going to bring who tomorrow."

She began to call the names. But she didn't call Buck Kennedy's name.

"What about Buck Kennedy?" I asked. "O.K.?"

Cissie starched up her voice. "Mr. Kennedy came yesterday with Dr. Hoodenpyl's party. They drove from Washington in Mr. Muradian's Cadillac. We don't have to worry about him."

I felt like she wasn't smiling. Eyes cool, not crinkling at the corners. "I hope you are right, Cissie. See you at class."

That was what I wanted to know. Buck Kennedy was in Carolina City some time on the day before. Hoodenpyl—Muradian—Poradowsky—Kennedy. Some combination.

10:00 A.M.—EAGLE IN OUR BALLADS CLASS

Everything was buzzing and excited like blackbirds in a cherry grove. Wallace came in late and gave me the high sign. He was frowning. Miss Blue Eyes and Miss Black Eyes bracketed me with some fast chirruping, one from the seat in front, one leaning over from behind, almost chinning my shoulder. Cissie came in like a summer cloud drifting with the breeze, and with her a very nice-looking old man, white hair and dark eyes, tall and thin, with a high forehead and fine good-natured nose. I wondered how he could be an eagle. I soon found out. First we went over all the arrangements for the festival, where the class was to sit, and when we would sing, and how Buck Kennedy would lead, and we tried over "The House Carpenter" once with Cissie leading at the piano. That didn't take long.

Then Cissie introduced the nice-looking old man. He was Dr. Goodenow, her revered teacher and guide, she said, and knew more about the music of ballads and folk songs than anybody else in the whole United States. And she turned over the class to him.

Right away we knew he was an eagle. He took us on his broad wings and rode the air. In five seconds we were a mile high, proud to see what the world looked like from above, full of the pure ozone, goosepimples breaking out all over, but not once afeared of falling.

First he praised Cissie to the skies. Said she had the gift. Said Cissie had her fingers on the harpstrings of heaven and could teach us more in an hour than we could dig out of library books in a year. It all came from the deep memory of our foreparents going back for a hundred generations of living and loving, working and playing, sailing and settling, and fighting for what we truly believed. We all had the deep memory, but just neglected it, and didn't use it, but Cissie could tell us how, by the studying and the singing, most of all the singing. Said he ought to speak with some authority because he was born down in Edgefield County, South Carolina, and floated on the deep memory without knowing it all the days when he lived amongst the old folks, ploughed his old white mule in the cotton fields, or hunted and fished in the Savannah River bottoms. Then he went to school and lost it, studying books too much and forgetting with his mind what the heart remembered if he only had listened to it. Said he didn't get it back till late in life, living and teaching in the great cities of the North, but thank God it wasn't too late, for then something sounded like the judgment trumpet up there on the banks of the Hudson River among the skyscrapers and he cast his eyes back to his own country and felt the sweetness of it rising up in his heart. It was not till then that he knew what he was really studying, and he would tell us what it was.

Oh, said Dr. Goodenow, it runs like an underground river through all our lives, and we don't know what is carrying us, and so it is dark to us and we are blind to it, till the moment comes and it turns into a river of light bearing us into a fair country.

He said folk song and tale-telling was that river, always the same through the ages, but always a little different wherever you dipped into it, and it had ten thousand creeks and branches and lakes and sometimes—he would have to admit—some stagnant ponds where it got dammed up.

But mostly it was rippling and running and shining with life, Dr. Goodenow said, and he would show us how it kept running and changing, yet always kept the same. "Now here's an old Irish and Scotch tune," he said, "and no telling how old." In a good baritone voice he hummed us a tune that sounded familiar to me but I couldn't place it. "And here it is, in a slow time, a little twisted around, but the same melody—a sacred tune." And he sung "Amazing Grace." "You sing it with me, the way the old folks sing it," he called out, and we all slipped right into it, and I could hear the twirly little old-fashioned notes and slides working into it, while we floated on it together, the tears crowding close up to the eyelids—

> Amazing grace, how sweet the sound
> That saved a wretch like me.
> I once was lost but now am found.
> Was blind but now I see.

That was a solemn sweet minute, when we rested on the ebb of "Amazing Grace," blind but beginning to see. "It's being Americanized," he said, very quiet-like. "I might say Southernized, because we sing it most in these parts. It's ours." Then he went on to tell how that kind of music, both the ballad kind and the sacred kind, was flooding up into opera music and orchestra music, and some of the new composers were beginning to dip at it in little spoonfuls and cupfuls, to ease the dry, dead, squawky throat of American song music and take out the Tin Pan Alley bang and the European la-de-da.

He'd give us a little sample, Dr. Goodenow said, from an excerpt tape he had brought with him. He glanced at Cissie, and she, bright-eyed, began to warm up that old machine I had toted over the hills and hollows. Dr. Goodenow mentioned a foreigner name Kurt Weill who had made something out of "Birmingham Jail" and called it "Down in the Valley"; and a couple of New Yorkers, Copland and Gershwin, I think he said. But what he wanted us specially to notice was a piece by a young Tennessee fellow named Charles F. Bryan—"White Spiritual Symphony." It went at our old music the right way—from the inside. The other men—well, they were good composers but were not raised to the old music, not born with it on their mouths like Charlie Bryan. The hillbilly singers were born to it, too—but that was another lecture.

He signed to Cissie—the music began.

Most of it was away over my head, especially that Copland and Gershwin. That "Down in the Valley" thing—nothing much to it. Turkey Hollow Boys could have sung it better.

But that "White Spiritual" piece! Away over my head, too, at first. But soon I begun to get my chin above the ripples and float with the music. It was a creek I had swum in. "Amazing Grace"! Something flashed into my head. A fair Sunday morning, a road through a city, and us setting out on a journey home, with a river bright below the bluff. And from some church steeple the slow chimes begun to spell it out: "Amazing Grace, how sweet the sound, That saved a wretch like me." Folks all in their Sunday best, walking to church, the children running ahead, pigeons swooping over the roofs, and the round mellow notes drifting through the air: *A-a-a-ma-zi-i-ing Gra-a-a-ace.*

The back of my head tingled. My neck stiffened. Cissie's eyes drew mine across the rows of blonde and dark heads. A full long look telling me *yes—yes—yes.* The music stopped, but the chimes kept ringing while Cissie slowly turned away.

Dr. Goodenow was saying: "Let down your buckets into that river. Draw up the living music."

The bell was ringing for the end of class. Cissie was suddenly introducing me to Dr. Goodenow with students crowding all around.

"We may be seeing you tonight," she was saying. "Dr. Goodenow wants to hear Rufus' show."

I had things to do. I was thundering down the steps with the other students. Wallace braked me to a stop and put his mouth to my ear.

"One bit of news. The rumor is that Chubby's been to the doctor to get some birdshot picked out of his hide. No real harm done, but he's fiery mad."

"For the tenth time, Wallace—be sure to have them football players lined up for tomorrow night. Some of 'em will have to stay outside and miss the ballad sing."

"Fine," said Wallace. "They'd ruther fight than sing, anyhow."

I decided to get a haircut and freshen up before our 12:30 program. There wouldn't be any other time for barbering before Saturday night.

Luckily the Friday trade hadn't piled up too much and I got into Ed's chair without having to wait very long.

"How's courtin'?" he asked as he pinned the cloth around my neck.

"Still at it and the end not in sight!"

"She's still layin' on the punishment, ain't she?"

"Laid on some more this very day. Tape-recordin' the festival."

"Well, good! That's a good sign. Like I told you, the more a woman lays on the punishment, the more sartain you kin be she loves you."

Ed made a few dashes at the back hair with his clippers.

"But that don't mean you have to set and take it. Somewhar along the line, you got to turn it back on her. Think up some way of foolin' her. Women don't mind bein' fooled if they r'aly love a man. They'll love him all the more. Now there was Jack Doster and the Flighty Gal. I don't reckin you ever knowed him, did you?"

"No, and I'll bet my socks you never did either, and I can't stand another courtin' story. I'm up ag'in the real thing."

I hated to stop Ed Cooley, but I wanted to shut my eyes and think while he cut my hair. In fact, I didn't hush him up completely.

"Well, it won't hurt my feelin's none if you don't want to hear a good story. I'll jest tell you the endin'. It might help you some."

I said nothing and hoped Ed would stop. But he went on.

"There was three hard jobs that the Flighty Gal set for Jack Doster, like she set for all the men that tried to marry her. And Jack was the first that did 'em all. They was: to break and ride her Pappy's mean sorrel stallion—that was the first. And second, to yoke her two white bulls and plow an acre with 'em. Lastly, to break up the eagles' nest in the giant cypress tree. But he didn't r'aly git nowhurs till he fooled her. Not ontil he sont a boy to ride to her house and tell her, 'The tree fell on Jack Doster and he won't last more'n ten minutes!' That brought her a-runnin'. She fell right on his bosom. But he was jest *playin'* dead."

I said nothing. Ed snipped away a little awhile longer, then stopped his razor, and sopped lather around my neck and ears.

"That's the way to do it, Danny. Grab her when she can't argue. Maybe play dead, like Jack Doster."

Ed finished with the razor, blew with his blower, combed my hair, slicked me with lotion, powdered me with powder, and twitched off the cloth before he said another word. I didn't say a word either. He twirled the chair so I could look in the big mirror. I looked at my red hair, and I looked at Ed Cooley. Then I opened up.

"Cissie ain't got no sorrel stallion, and no two white bulls, and no tall cypress tree with eagles in it. She's got a tape recorder and a thesis and a head full of notions."

Ed nodded and grinned at me in the mirror.

"But you could *bait* her somehow, couldn't you? You'd make a purty good Jack Doster."

"There's somethin' in what you say. But we've all got a lot to do."

Ed's face changed. His mouth got hard. He put his lips to my ear: "We've got a watch on Buck Kennedy, ever'whur he goes. We'll give you a report."

I eased out of the chair. "See you tomorrow, then."

12:30–1:00 P.M.—NEWS ALONG THE GRAPEVINE AND ALL THE OTHER VINES

It was our Cute Cookie and Mixie Marvel program. Knew it all by heart but had to grit my teeth to sing it:

> Cute—cute—cute—cute!
> No more achin' when you're bakin'.
> Like a heap o' lovin'
> Toastin' in your oven.
> No more tricks with cup and spoon.
> You'll hum, "Yum-yum!"
> Easy as a lovin' tune.
> Package full of Cutie kisses,
> Never any misses.
> All fixed, ready mixed.
> Cute————Cookies!

Mostly that kind of commercial, with some of our regular numbers chopped in between.

But Rufus was feeling good. I could tell by the way he wiggled his ears and grinned at me.

"Don't take it so hard," he said when we got through. "Don't act like a buzzard was peckin' at your liver. We are goin' to have visitors at our Studio B program tonight. You'll be surprised!"

"Can't surprise me. I've done been vaccinated for it." I started out, but he tagged me.

"Hold your 'tater and let me tell you! Brewbaker is here from Nashville. He wants you and me to eat supper with him at the Piedmont. Be there at 6:30. He tried to get Cissie, but she's tied up."

Rufus breezed along without looking back. I *was* surprised, after all, but before I could really feel it Wallace stepped out of a telephone booth and snagged me.

"Elvira can't pick up anything at the Sheriff's office," he told me. "Sheriff has pulled down the iron curtain, and my pipelines are all dried up. Just one thing—Buck Kennedy is having lunch with Hoodenpyl and the Muradian fellow—in a private room at the Piedmont. I tried to plant a waiter on 'em, but it may not work."

I begun to fear that Wallace was off on sidelines.

"Too much shenanigans!" I said. "You'll cut your own finger with all this cloak-and-dagger stuff. We've got to get that Old Chapel ready, this afternoon. I want that crew of boys you promised. And you better 'phone this Poradowsky man about placin' his tape recorders. Tell him to come over and show me what he wants."

Wallace was pulling at his ear in a fretful way.

"All right," he said. "But I think I better tell you that Cissie may be gettin' suspicious. Maybe she has picked up some information."

"What! About our plans, you mean?"

"She might be doin' some good guessin'. But anyway, she's heard *somethin'* about what happened to your car. I reckon Chubby or some of his crowd talked, and the news spread along the grapevine. She's all on fire about it. Maybe we ought to tell her . . . you know what I mean!"

I was on fire, too, in a proud way. Yet even while I was saying, "Bless her heart!" to myself, I was anxious. If Cissie took some steps of her own without telling me, we might get crossed up.

To Wallace I said: "I know what you mean, but the plan is to keep Cissie out of these doin's. If last night's pranks are all she knows about, it don't matter. Keep your ears open."

1:00–2:00 P.M.—MUST HAVE BEEN MY COFFEE BREAK

2:00–5:00 P.M.—I WAS WORKING FOR MY FLIGHTY GAL

Heavy work at the Old Chapel, unloading and arranging some extra seats, rigging the stage, and all that. They were a good lot of boys that Wallace sent to me. We moved the grand piano, put our screen high up on the wall next to the stage, placed the projector in the back, and tested it. We checked the switchboard and the stage and house lights. I worked out my signals with the two boys that were handling the projector and the switchboard—and most particularly a white handkerchief signal for the most important moment. I went over the seating arrangements with the ushers and made sure they understood. They were all boys. I didn't want the girls for that job. They could look pretty and hand out programs. We had some trouble rigging a spotlight, high up, for my special purpose. That took some climbing on high ladders. The Old Chapel was never made for a theater, though the college used it for that.

The boys worked like beavers and asked no questions. I didn't explain *why*, about anything, because Wallace had passed the word to them, and they were a picked crew.

We had just finished a sort of little rehearsal and got the ladders out of the way when the Poradowsky man finally came in with a fellow that he introduced as his sound engineer. They looked the place over, noses in the air, as if they thought they'd got into a stable by mistake. Poradowsky said he would have two big tape recorders and three or four microphones to hook up. He was a little stooped-over man with thick black whiskers like a picture of a dwarf in a storybook. His sound engineer was a high-cheeked, chunky blonde with a wide face and a kind of flat nose. They talked to one another for a while in some foreign language, then began to give me orders. I couldn't hardly understand their brogue, and they didn't seem to understand me any better. It turned out they wanted two microphones on the stage and another one somewhere else; they couldn't decide where. I tried to explain that they couldn't count on the singers singing right into the mikes, but Poradowksy brushed that aside. They both seemed to take me for some kind of janitor, and maybe I looked like one. Finally I made out that they would put the stage mikes near the footlights, no matter what, and the main thing they were after was to locate the floor outlets where they would plug in, and to measure how much extension cord they would need. I wouldn't say they weren't polite. Polite enough they were, but with a sting in it. I could see the boys looking at them curious, out of the corners of their eyes, but they kept mum until the foreigners left. Then they busted out laughing.

"It's all one world, so they say," said one boy.

"Hands across the sea—and put somethin' in the hands," said another.

I cracked down. "Shut your big mouths. Those nice gentlemen come from the Library of Congress at Washington where the government keeps its folk songs. They are experts."

"Experts in Vodka!" said a boy.

"Pull, brothers, pull!" a voice sang out.

"I see an angel comin'!" said another.

I heard a tap of high heels and looked over my shoulder. It was Cissie carrying a big tray full of sandwiches. Right after her came a drugstore delivery boy with a bucket full of Coca-Cola bottles on ice.

She was a whole band of angels, and in a heavenly good humor as she passed around the sandwiches and drinks. She called the boys by their names, thanked them for helping, and praised them to the skies while they grinned and watched her with worshipping eyes. Somebody raised a tune, and they all joined in:

> She called up her merrymaids all
> And she dressed them all in green,
> And every city that she rode through
> They took her to be some Queen.

Then they changed the tune and sang "Rose of Alabama" in fast time. A couple of boys did a dance step. But Cissie twitched my sleeve and said, "Let's check the fixin's while the boys are havin' fun. I've got about ten minutes."

Coca-Cola in one hand, sandwich in the other, I followed Cissie around the Old Chapel. She made me change the angle of the grand piano a little and showed me where she wanted to sit, with the ballads class at the left front. "Right by this side exit, back of the piano, and I want you in the seat next to me, the whole time." Then she counted the seats I had reserved at the front for special guests. A little frown settled on her forehead. She pulled a paper out of her purse and frowned harder, studying the paper.

"That's too many reserved seats," she said, and gave me the full effect of the frown, but with mischief in her eyes. "We won't have that many special guests."

"Better be over than under. There's no tellin' who'll turn up at the last minute. Besides . . ."

I couldn't say more without saying too much. I hadn't counted on this check-up. Maybe I ought to pitch in and tell her the whole thing, I was thinking. "I wonder how much she knows . . ."

Cissie read over her list again, her lips moving. The frown went away. She was smiling at me over the top of the paper, and teasing me with her eyes. "You must have asked some special guests yourself." She made it halfway a question.

"I might have."

"Then why didn't you tell me?"

"Precious little chance I get to tell you anything."

"Oh, it don't really matter, I reckon. Ask anybody you want to."

"If you'll jest step outside a minute—"

"I've got to run. But I'm having Dr. Goodenow at our house for dinner tonight, and I want you to come!"

"Cissie, Rufus has shanghaied me to take dinner with that WSM man—that Mr. Polka Dot Tie—I'll 'phone and call it off, right now."

"No, you don't! I *want* you to talk to that man." She tapped my shoulder with the paper. "It's important. Don't get crossways with Rufus. Anyway, I'll see you tonight at the studio show. I'm bringing Dr. Goodenow."

She was gone with a whirl of skirts and a wave of her hand. Her hair made a bright spot against the dark of the side exit, then the late sunlight framed her for one quick moment. I could hear her heels tapping. She was running. And mighty pleased about something. I wondered what.

5:00–6:30 P.M.—INTERMISSION. I HAD TO DRESS UP SOME

6:30–8:00 P.M.—ALMOST LIKE MULE-TRADING BUT IT WAS MUSIC

Rufus was waiting in the Piedmont Lobby and said he would take the elevator to Mr. Brewbaker's room. He punched me playfully in the stomach and gave me a big wink, but I was like a farmer's dog visiting city kinfolks and walked stiff-legged through the whole thing with my back up a good part of the time.

Mr. Polka Dot Tie shook hands with us at the door as if the single bedroom was a hundred-year-old plantation house and he was Ol' Marster. A waiter was already setting a table in the room, white cloth, silver, and everything. Another waiter whipped out menu cards big as a Sunday newspaper, but Polka Dot Tie didn't let us waste any time wandering amongst the fancy names. "We all want steaks, don't we?" he said, and ordered the biggest sirloin steaks on the menu with shrimp cocktail to start off. "And we'll have a little snifter while the dinner's comin'," he added. I looked at Rufus to see if he would break his rule.

"Being as it's you, I'll take a little one," said Rufus, and winked at me again. "Bourbon."

"The same," I said.

On the dresser was a quart of Jack Daniel No. 7, Black Label, and beside it a fifth of Scotch.

Polka Dot Tie slopped four or five fingers of the Jack Daniel into tall glasses, added ice and water, and handed the drinks over. "Never hurt a soul," he said. "Pure juice of the pure Tennessee corn." But he poured himself a little drink of Scotch and put the soda to it. I didn't want to get crossways with Rufus, but all the same I hoped the waiters would be quick about that dinner, for I didn't want to knock myself out. I wondered if I could slip into the bathroom and pour some of that tall drink out, but decided to follow Rufus' lead instead.

Close up, Mr. J. Theo Polka Dot Tie Brewbaker was more like a preacher than a horsetrader, with a long fine-shaped nose and big wide thin-lipped mouth that curled up at the corners in a dry little funny twist, so that even when he wasn't laughing he seemed to be getting ready to laugh. He had a good-sized Adam's apple, and his bow tie, just below it, was blue with red and yellow dots. But his brown eyes were honest, almost anxious.

"Well, here's to our plans!" he said, and lifted his glass. Rufus took a little sip, and I took a little sip. "I'm sorry Miss Timberlake couldn't join us," he continued. "I asked her but she had a previous engagement."

"It's her busy day," I said, to be polite. Then a thought struck me, and I added: "But you did talk to her?"

"Oh, yes, we had coffee together this afternoon."

In my stomach that sassy little sip of Jack Daniel met up with a big knot of bad temper, all of a sudden. They began to chase one another round and round. So Cissie had had time to talk to this man, maybe right after she saw me at the Old Chapel and was so sweet. I started to take a bigger drink out of pure cussedness, but luckily Polka Dot Tie said: "We might as well look over these bookings right now." The corners of his mouth were working. "Take seats and get comfortable."

He took some papers out of his grip. He handed one to Rufus, one to me. Rufus put his drink down on the floor by his foot. I did the same. We went at the papers. I soon saw that now-or-never was right in the palm of my hand.

It was a list of bookings for the Turkey Hollow Boys on Grand Ole Opry, starting in October. Grand Ole Opry at Nashville. And some other places, too. A lot of traveling. As I skimmed along, Cissie's name caught my eye, and mine was with it, at two or three places. The typed lines ran together as I gazed, all in a fog.

"I started to write you about this," Polka Dot Tie was saying, "but I knew I was coming here and thought it would be easier for us to go over it together. Of course it may not work out exactly like this. It's just tentative. We can make some adjustments to fit your home arrangements, but we can't wait long to hesitate. And I'll explain what's happening."

He took a drink and set his glass on the smoking stand by his chair. Rufus seemed to be fumbling for his glass, down by his foot. I was sure he tipped some of his drink onto the hotel carpet before he raised it to his mouth. "I'm a-listenin', Mr. Brewbaker," he said.

"These Southern Textile people have got religion at last," Mr. Polka Dot Tie continued. "They've decided they need our kind of advertising if they are going to meet this new Japanese competition that's knifing into their sales. They want a real, honest Southern program like the one you put on. No singing commercials at all. Some dignified patriotic talking— Southern, but not too much Dixie in it, no moonlight-and-magnolias. Propaganda, but it won't seem like propaganda—that's what they want. Only, they didn't know they wanted it till we talked them into it. I played their advertising man some recordings, and I want to get some more tonight."

He held the list in his lap, rolling it and unrolling it. Rufus was saying nothing but *yes* and *um-humph*, going over the bookings with his finger, line by line.

I ought to have felt good. If it had happened the year before I would have been all hallelujahs. Now I was like a medium-good baseball pitcher that the clubowners were selling for the profit on the deal. I had no say in all this—unless I got out entirely. I felt sick all over.

"Excuse me a minute," I said. "Go right on talking." I took my glass with me to the bathroom and watched Jack Daniel No. 7 drain slowly down the washbowl till the glass was half empty. I wondered if, after all, Cissie had signed up.

The voices came through the door. Polka Dot Tie sounded more and more like a preacher, but not a hellfire preacher. He was just dragging Rufus up the Golden Stairs by the hand, in a fatherly way. And Rufus was kicking at the steps a little as he got dragged along.

"It looks good," said Rufus, "but I've got to think about the future too. These New York people are tryin' to move in on us. My boys all live around here. This is their home country. We've built up a lot of good will that I don't want to lose, and I don't want to lose any of my band. I've got to hold 'em. Otherwise it won't be the same."

"If you think it's too big for you to handle, we might cut down on these bookings some. But it's the chance of your life."

"Yes, it's a chance—and it's a risk too." (Is Rufus just trading, I asked myself. Or does he really mean it?) "But we can handle it." He called to me. "Ain't that right, Danny?"

I had to come back and look Polka Dot Tie in the eye.

"Turkey Hollow Boys can handle anything from pitchin' horseshoes to ridin' bulldozers. Of course I know my Old MacGregor Place won't run itself. And I shore think this Muradian man is up to mischief—and this Dr. Hoodenpyl."

I thought Rufus was winking at me again. "Danny here, he's enlisted for ballads and a lot of old stuff. You'll have to help me argue with him, Mr. Brewbaker." Polka Dot Tie figured that Rufus was trading. They were both having fun at it, and took for granted I was, too.

"I'll come to the ballad part later," said Polka Dot Tie. "The point is, Mr. Whitthorne, that you can't fight those New York people by yourself. You've got a good thing here, but they are too big for you. It's war all along the line. This new crowd means to cut in on the popular music field and everything else. They'll do it with this new Rock-and-Roll stuff and every kind of jazz. They're after the teenagers and the college crowd. All of us country music people have got to stand together and hold the line. That's what I say. And once you start cuttin' records at Nashville, you know what that will mean."

The waiters came in with the shrimp cocktails, and he broke off. From then on, through the steak and French fries and the dessert, it was shop talk. By the time we had our second cup of coffee, it began to be an argument about hillbilly music and where it was going to land.

"You've got to level up or level down." That was Polka Dot Tie's argument. "Can't stay in the same place. My notion is, it's more and more leveling down. The bigger it gets, the more it levels down."

"Turkey Hollow Boys can stick somewhere in between." That was Rufus' argument. "Danny there—and Cissie—they keep levelin' us up, every time we slip down. Every now and then they pull my hair jest to see if my neck will stretch another quarter inch."

"Better do that than be pullin' your leg." That was my argument.

"Didn't I tell you?" laughed Rufus.

"Mr. Brewbaker," I said, "what ever happened to Renny McClain? I thought he was good when I first heard him down at Macon. But I wouldn't walk around the corner to hear his latest."

"Ain't it a shame?" Polka Dot Tie hardened his lips into a tight line. "It was a woman. I don't mean a love affair. It was a woman manager that ruined a good boy just so she could rake in a big commission and switch around in a mink coat. That boy drove to my place, one bitter January day, to do a little private singin' for me. Drove up to ninety miles an hour, he said, coming from St. Louis, to keep the appointment. First two or three songs were good, extra good. A real folksinger, he was, and had made up a song of his own just about like folk song. Fine voice. Really could play a guitar, not just thump a few chords. But I could see his woman manager didn't like it that way. 'Oh, Renny,' she said. 'That isn't what Mr. Brewbaker wants to hear. Give him that corny one we were working on.'

"It wasn't my job to tell him what to sing. He looked at the woman like she was Mamma, and he had to be a good little sonny-boy. He lit into a common honkytonk sort of blues piece, jazzing it for all he was worth. He didn't know any better than to do what she said, but it was like Katherine Cornell deciding to go in for striptease. I knew what would happen, but I signed him up all the same. Of course the woman was right if you want to look at it that way—the straight money angle. Now he's got money and success, and that woman has got money. But it's a shame. She ruined a fine singer."

Nobody seemed to want to talk for a minute. I had never seen Rufus so quiet. He looked at his watch.

"We've got to run on over to Studio B," he said. "I'll talk to the boys about it, and Cissie and Danny can do their talkin'. We'll get this all settled before you leave town."

Polka Dot Tie didn't seem to hear. He sloshed his cold coffee and stared into the cup as if he could see the future there.

"Now my side proposition is another thing entirely. I've been workin' on it. It's not connected with Grand Ole Opry, but they might be interested if we put it over. It's that whole big question of levelin' up or levelin' down, and how long country music can last if it levels down too much. There's television, comin' on fast. And there's this big grab for power in the radio music business. We've got a lot to think about. One thing is sure: we can't level up very much with the kind of radio audience we are reaching now. We've got to move a little higher. Anyhow, reach a different group. Now I have some friends that are interested in backing an experiment. I'll call it a pilot project. It'll be country music still—but at a higher level. Maybe a Sunday afternoon program, to start with. Something that might do for television later on. Now I realize some of your band members might be reluctant to go all the way on the first proposition. Let's say they are serious musicians. They need the money, but don't want to put in all their time leveling down."

His anxious brown eyes were on me. Rufus was standing up, and grinning. "Tell him, Mr. Brewbaker, but be quick about it."

"We might make it a package deal. Would you be interested in a pilot project, Mr. MacGregor—if we can interest Miss Timberlake too?"

"You mean ballads—that kind of thing?"

"It could be that, but you'll have to—well, you can't do it for a show the way the country folks do it. You'll have to popularize it some."

"The first and second propositions are the package, then? Can't take the second proposition by itself?"

Rufus lost his grin. He was walking to the door. "You don't have to decide now, Danny. Come on."

Polka Dot Tie stood up and patted my shoulder.

"I wouldn't put it that way. It's like I told you, the first night I heard you sing. There's such a thing as being too damned good for these ordinary commercial programs. All the same, we ought to be able to find a place for the people that are too damned good for the ordinary line. That's why I'm here. I'd be a fool to come all the way over here for a common ordinary hillbilly radio singer. But it might come to a point where you might have to choose."

"Choose between what?"

"I think you ought to know."

Rufus was in a sweat to get away. We made our thank-you's. I did know, like he said, and he knew that I knew. There was only one kind of song that would win Cissie over. At least that was what I thought I knew at 8:17 P.M. on that Friday. I remember looking at my watch as we left.

Rufus stopped me with a jerk in the hall.

"You remember we're puttin' on our Double-A, Three Star program tonight? No Grade B stuff."

"Yes." I had forgot, but I remembered when he reminded me.

"I may want to make a little change. What was that old ballad song we had the row about, some time back?"

I hesitated. It was a long time back.

"Come on, Danny! If you can't remember it, what else like it kin you sing?"

I saw Rufus' eyebrows rising to his hairline, and I remembered. "You mean 'Gypsy Davy'?"

"That's it. Sing it tonight. You can, can't you? You ain't forgot it?"

"Couldn't forget it, once I git started on it."

"Sing it then. Or if you've got somethin' better, sing that. Put your best foot forward. Right after the Cottonbale song. I've got to stop here and telephone. Git over to the studio."

I got right on over—soon as I could.

8:00 P.M.–9:00 P.M.—CHANGED TO MY CREAM-COLORED PANTS

9:00 P.M.–9:30 P.M.—FRUITBASKET TURNED OVER

It all goes to show what a fool a man can be when he thinks he has a woman all figured out.

The first surprise was when I drove into the WCC parking lot. Two men were standing there in a dark place. One of them stepped out and motioned to me.

246

"O.K., Mr. MacGregor," he said. "Put your car in this space."

"Who are you, and what is goin' on?"

The man lifted his coat and showed a shiny badge. He was a city detective—a plainclothesman.

"Special orders," he said, "to watch these cars and yours in particular."

"It's an honor and a help. But what *is* goin' on?"

"Don't know. Maybe we'll find out. I think Headquarters got a tip. Has somebody been trying to plant dynamite in your car?"

I told him no, I didn't think so, it was only teenagers prankin'. It was no use to ask him who gave the tip. I thought I knew where to do the asking.

The second surprise was when I walked into Studio B and saw the size of the crowd. Usually we think we are doing well enough if the place is better than half full. People would rather sit at home and listen. This night, every seat was taken. People were lining up along the wall. I guessed why, when I stepped onto the platform and got my third surprise.

The third surprise was Cissie in her old regular place with the Turkey Hollow Boys—waiting for the show to start as if she had never left it, and giving me our old secret sign with her pretty fingers. Quickly I answered back and slid into my seat next to her.

"So you've done gone and changed your mind?" My heart was flopping 200 to the minute.

"Changed my mind about what? I told you I would see you here."

"But I never thought—" I didn't finish. Bob Greenhow, the announcer, was in front of me with a script, checking. "Danny, you know about the little change in the program?"

"I know I'm supposed to sing 'Gypsy Davy' or somethin'."

"Yes." He frowned and added, "There are some other little changes, but it won't matter to you." He hurried to his place. We were tuning up. Over my guitar I saw Rufus, smug as a fox, and winking again. Ozro was laughing. All the boys were feeling good. It was going to be a big night. The electric sign flashed STAND BY. The program manager was in his place, getting ready to point his finger. In the front rows I got glimpses—old Dr. Goodenow, Mr. Polka Dot Tie with his same notebook—students everywhere—Cissie's class! Just before we went on the air I saw three men squeeze through the crowd at the back and stand near the center aisle. Dr. Hoodenpyl, Buck Kennedy, Muradian . . . Then the sign said ON THE AIR, and we came in, our regular way.

Regular except for Rufus' special announcement. Almost the first thing he put in a plug for Cissie's folk festival. Told everybody to come—and pass the word along.

"Right here in Carolina City at our own Turkey Hollow college! Maybe you didn't remember we have a college. But we're like everybody else. We believe in eddication, up in Turkey Hollow. All but my old Dominecker Rooster—and he's a hard case! Says he ain't ag'in eddication so much, when you come right down to hit. Whut sticks in his craw is *co-eddication*. Says it ain't the thing for young pullets. Puts notions in their heads, and when they come home on vacation they begin to squawk about these ol' dustbaths bein' unsanitary. And when are you goin' to put runnin' water in the chicken house? And why cain't we have a radio, too?

"But hit don't do him no good to object. The hens and the pullets all gang up on him and say they ain't a-goin' to raise up *their* chillun in no dirty old-fashioned chicken yard. They're a-goin' to hatch 'em out in electric incubators—and save all that labor of settin' for three weeks on some nasty ol' straw! Goin' to raise 'em on nice clean wire and have plenty of good food with plenty of vitamins in it, all furnished by the governmint. Not have to scratch around for bugs and worms any more.

"Oh, my ol' rooster gits red around the gills and tries to answer but it ain't no use. Then my ol' Turkey Gobbler swells up and says: '*Whut-whut-whut-whut the heck you goneter do about it?*'

"And that ends it.

"Now about the folk festival. This is our own Cissie Timberlake's show. She's the boss and the manager. And I'm proud to say she's back again with us tonight as guest singer, for old time's sake. Tell us a little about your program, Cissie."

Cissie stood up to the mike.

"There's two kinds of country music," she said. "The kind that keeps everybody tuned in for the Turkey Hollow Boys and the good old-fashioned kind that you've known all your lives if you were raised in these hills. The two are not so far apart as some folks think. But tomorrow night it'll be the good old-fashioned kind and I hope you'll come. We'll have some real folksingers that many of you already know. There's Aunt Lou Watkins—and Emmett Core—and Buck Kennedy—and—" (She named them all.) "And a square dance with old-fashioned fiddle-playing at the gymnasium afterwards."

"Turkey Hollow Boys will be there too!" said Rufus. "And proud to be in the audience for a change—not on stage. Tonight we are goin' to give you some of *both* kinds. The new and the old. Start with the new—Ozro!"

Ozro took over with one of his best songs—and we went right along, nothing unusual, except that we had plenty of steam and I suddenly begun to feel excited, the way I used to, before I studied ballads.

Then it was time for "Ridin' on a Cottonbale."

Rufus said: "We are doin' this one by special request, and I want you to know it's a college professor that asked for it, and he's right here tonight. I believe he was Cissie's teacher once." I thought he was going to name Hoodenpyl, but I was wrong. "That's Dr. Goodenow, from South Carolina and New York. You take over, Cissie!"

I was like the Petrified Man, solid rock, frozen to my guitar. Cissie touched my arm and whispered, "Stay right with me—do the regular stuff." The applause went up. One minute the fire ran through me and the old guitar felt sweet under my fingers. Next minute I had the cold shudders. I couldn't believe what I was seeing with my own eyes, and was pretty nigh ashamed to look.

Cissie was at the mike, with Ozro's bull fiddle. Ozro, grinning like a big he-coon, was sidling up close to her.

"This is Rufus' song," she was saying, "as you all know. And I'm proud to salute him as author of one of the best songs in all the history of country music. Ozro wants me to be his 'stand-in' tonight. I can't wear his big brogan shoes, but maybe I kin knock out a tune on his old bull fiddle." Ozro was at the mike. "I always likes to see a woman do my work." He let off a big long horse whinny and slipped into Cissie's chair. The crowd cheered.

We hit the chords, and they swept me into the music. Cissie knocked out the bold bass tune, all like I remembered, hair tossing, fingers flying, till we came to the umpa-umpa and Rufus started the song:

> Oh-h-h, the times was hard and the market kind o' rotten,
> But I always believed in Southern cotton,
> And the banker said it would do no harm
> To stake me to a loan on my one-horse farm.

We put in some farm noises—rooster crowing, turkey-gobbling, hee-haws, whinnies.

> So-o-o, the bottom and the hillside, all one crop,
> Hit looked purty good when we started in to chop,
> Till along come the rain, and up stepped the Devil,
> And he made me acquainted with Mister Boll Weevil.

Moaning and crying with the fiddles, groaning in the bass.

> Oh-h-h, I looked to the East and I looked to the West,
> And still I vowed that cotton was best.
> Mister Banker he said, "Yore crop will fail";
> "Oh, no, Mister Banker, I'll make one bale."

So-o-o I picked my cotton and I proved it true,
But my ol' woman she shore felt blue:
"No meat in the smokehouse or flour in the barrel,
Empty skillet and the chillun in a quarrel."

Cissie did that part in a squawky old woman's voice, and we made the chillun cry.

"Honey, jest wait 'twel I haul to the gin.
I'll sell off my cotton and I'll borrow ag'in.
Banker will smile when I pay off my loan,
And we'll eat might pretty when I git back home."

We did that part faster.

Came to a hill and I couldn't git it up.
Tried a little cussin' and I tried my whup.
Got off my waggin, but I couldn't turn a spoke;
Saw it wan't nothin' but the axle—BROKE!

We broke it.

I stepped to the woods and I cut me a pole,
Worked on my waggin till I made her roll.
"Oh, you'll never make it," the neighbors was sayin',
But I never pay attention to a jackass brayin'.

There was the jackass—Ozro.

So I dragged towards town through the mud and muck
'Twel I come to a swamp and my horse got stuck.
Lifted him out with a ten-foot rail,
And he tore off through the bushes with my cottonbale.

Come to the river and I couldn't find a boat.
Well, I cain't fly but cotton will float.
So I hitched me a rope to an alligator's tail,
And I rode the river on my cottonbale.

We did that last verse slower, with lots of oomph.

You could hear the people shouting when I floated into town,
"Old Carolina's up though cotton is down!"
So I sold my cotton and I told my tale,
And I rode to glory on a Southern cottonbale.

My heart was on fire, but my sweat was dripping cold. I had what I had wanted, yet didn't want it when I got it. It was like something I dreamed, and in fact had dreamed it the night we quarreled, the night before Cissie went to New York. It was done fifty times better than I'd dreamed. Yet the dream come true was more like a nightmare. Off and on, out of the corner of my eye, I could see Cissie's fingers flying on the bull-fiddle strings. It was perfect. But the marrow of my bones cried out against it. In my head I knew that Cissie's fingers and voice, and all the beauty of her, had raised Rufus' song to the highest heaven a country song can reach; but the red blood in my heart kept drumming *No—No—I won't have it—There's something wrong*.

But I must be, I thought, the lone man in that place that could hear his bones making objections. The crowd would hardly stop shouting. But now Rufus was up at the mike and my time had come. I felt Cissie's eyes on me but didn't dare to look at her. Should I listen to my bones? Should I take it with my head? I could hardly catch what Rufus was saying—about Danny MacGregor . . . the right man to sing a good old timey song. I remembered Old Man Parsons' voice: "Young man . . . the power of God . . ." The eyes in my head saw the faces lifted up before me, but I could sing only to the girl that was sitting close by me. For better or worse, I touched my guitar and sung to Cissie Timberlake my very own song—

> As I came down the mountain road
> A-fearin' roads must part,
> I set my mind to choose but one
> And follow my sweetheart.
> But everywhere I stopped to ask
> I heard the old folks say,
> "It's easy come and easy go;
> Young man, you better stay.
> She's gone to seek some other one
> And love will pass away."
>
> I followed her on mountain roads
> And many a city street
> And all the people turned to look
> Where stepped her wandering feet.
> And young men all who know love's rule,
> I heard them grieve and say,
> "Oh, hard to win is best to keep,
> And love, it knows no stay.
> Her mind is but to try your heart
> If love should pass away."
>
> Oh, years have come and years have gone
> On all the roads that run,

But now I know, of all the roads,
True love can choose but one.
It leads by mountain water
Where first I took my way,
The rocky road, the lonesome road
Where love can meet no stay,
For love that keeps us on that road
Can never pass away.

There was a lot of applause, but I couldn't bear to notice what was going on. For me, the rest of the show was all mechanical. I knew it was going fine, and I did my part, not caring about the big hand they gave me, or what Rufus might think, but only about one thing, and that was *What am I going to say to Cissie?* And *What is she going to say to me?*

I didn't get much chance to say anything. Nor did she. We met once in the break-up after the show when a hundred students were mobbing us. There were people all around, shaking hands. Old Dr. Goodenow came up and put his arm around Cissie. She turned and looked at me. I thought maybe she was crying. I caught her for a second and said, "That was fine, Cissie, but I wouldn't have thought it of you. I'm starting right early tomorrow to take care of those singers."

Cissie gave me a strange glance as if she didn't know what I was talking about, and said, "Oh, yes." Then, "You were wonderful—yes, take care of the singers. Take care of yourself."

The crowd closed in. I could see only that her cheeks were flushed and she couldn't seem to get her hair in place.

When I went to take the elevator, the receptionist girl signaled me. "Lots of calls and messages for you already," she said, "and here's the first message that came." She handed me an envelope.

The writing was strange and hard to read. A big scrawling handwriting. I made it out finally:

> Ten thousand congratulations on your superb art. May I see you tomorrow and make an appointment for you to meet Mr. Muradian and me for a little conference? Thanks infinitely.

There wasn't any yes-yes it in, but it was signed "J. Chauncey Hoodenpyl, Consulting Editor, American Features, Inc."

I tore it up and threw it in the wastebasket.

23

MORE AND MORE SITUATIONS

That Saturday, it was a fair day in August, coming on hot at sunup, with hardly any breeze, but we had had rain a while back, so that corn wasn't hurting, and the cotton liked it, and the tobacco didn't mind. Not so good, though, for folks sweating away in classrooms. I was glad to be off campus, rounding up singers and fiddlers for the big jamboree. I was invited to the dinner the College was having for the singers and big bugs, but I had to telephone the Dean I couldn't come. It would be all I could do to haul our loads and manage our tricky arrangements.

While I shaved, I looked myself over in the mirror once more, the way I'd been looking at myself all the mornings of that summer—gaunt as ever, not taking on weight, the face with red hair topping it, and the cowlick staring back at me between the ballad things-to-do on the right and the hillbilly things-to-do on the left. There were checkmarks right down to the end—and doublechecks at some places.

"MacGregor," I told that face, "maybe this winds it up. Maybe you can throw them lists in the wastebasket and walk out of this old apartment forever."

I thought about my song, and hummed it for another try, with a razor scrape for accompaniment.

It sounded good. "But the whole point is," I said to my face, "did *Cissie* like it?" And I went on saying: "If she don't like it, and if things don't go right, where will *you* be, MacGregor? Right on the bottom of the pile, with maybe Buck Kennedy sittin' on top! Or maybe you'll start your car some morning and that'll be the last time you'll ever start anything—"

The telephone rang. I guessed it would be Wallace. It was.

"Reportin'," Wallace said, "for Ed Cooley and me. Everything checks. Sheriff has his cues. So does Rufus. Also student ushers—football players. Don't worry."

"That's right," I said. "This is a one-shot affair. No chance to practice. We hit or git hit. Anything else?"

"At Art's Grill, I passed 'em your question, but they ain't talkin' much. Only word I got was, 'Do anything you want about Buck Kennedy; we ain't interested!' "

"What's goin' on?"

"The Federals are breathin' down their necks. I think the gang are skippin' out of the state."

"Are the Federals after Buck Kennedy?"

"No, I think only the big boys. I don't guess Buck had much real connection, after all, with the Art's Grill gang. But he's scared. I was doin' a little snoopin' last night at the Grill. Everything was quiet as Sunday School. Buck drove in some time before midnight. A man stepped up and whispered to him. Buck jumped in his jeep and burnt the wind gettin' out. I reckon he's been out of town and hadn't heard about the Federals."

"That's good," I told Wallace. "Cissie will be glad that Buck's chair won't be vacant when she calls the roll for the jamboree."

It was a fool thing—to talk about vacant chairs. But I was feeling good. Pretty soon I was in my car. I started it, and it didn't blow up. I made off to the mountains before the sun was very high.

I got back with my last load, which was a couple of oldtime fiddlers, just about half an hour before sunset, and dropped them at the women's dormitory, like Cissie had told me. It's a nice, handsome building, with a big front porch and tall pillars and a circle driveway right up to it. I didn't see Cissie anywhere around, though there was a lot of cars already, and a lot of folks on the big porch. So I had to drop off too and see if I could find Cissie, and turn over my fiddlers.

There was a fat man in a white tuxedo sitting on the porch among the folks. I didn't recognize him till he called out my name.

I looked again, and it was Dr. Hoodenpyl. He was the same as ever, except that he was wearing that white tuxedo, and he was holding a baby on his lap. The baby was crying. On one side of him was an old woman dipping snuff, and on the other side was a young mountain girl, right pretty she was, with a split hickory basket in her lap. She was chewing gum and rummaging through the basket.

"Just a minute, Mr. MacGregor," he said, "till the emergency passes."

The old woman was handing her snuffbox across, right over his head.

"Drafted into service, you see," said Dr. Hoodenpyl.

254

"Whyn't you take it?" said the old woman, waving the snuffbox in front of Dr. Hoodenpyl's face, and I saw that she was Aunt Lou Watkins, so dressed up I hardly knew her. The baby was crying all the time.

"Just hold your 'tater," said the young woman, "till I find my cigarettes."

She found a pack of cigarettes and lighted one, still chewing gum. Then she took the baby from Dr. Hoodenpyl, opened her blouse, and started to nurse the baby. Dr. Hoodenpyl looked relieved and absquatulated, all in the same look. The young woman put her cigarettes back in the basket, took the snuffbox and put it there too, then sort of relaxed, chewing hard, blowing cigarette smoke, and having a good time, her and the baby.

Dr. Hoodenpyl got up, gave his tuxedo a brush or two, and shook hands with me. He was a little red in the face, and for a minute he didn't say anything. His coat was a good tight fit, and I can't say it improved his looks. He brushed it a little more, then finally seemed to pull himself together.

"Well," he said. "Yes-yes. This is the way the world goes 'round."

"I see you been gittin' acquainted with our folks."

"Yes-yes, let me introduce you. Mrs. Watkins, do you know Mr. Mac-Gregor?"

"I mighty nigh raised him," said Aunt Lou. "Hidy, Danny." And she got up and spit over the edge of the porch. "Nothin' like a dip o' snuff to quell the appetite. Looks like they ain't never goin' to have supper."

"And this is Mrs.—Mrs.—?" He looked at the young woman.

"She's my youngest granddaughter," said Aunt Lou. "Effie Lou's gal. And spoiled by goin' to school, jest like her mammy."

"Mrs. Hardacre. Mrs. Joe Bill Hardacre," said the granddaughter, smiling as if she didn't give two figs for her grandma. "And that's Minnie Ruth's Joe Bill, and not Elora Mae's Joe Bill, you know, Danny. And this is my youngest." She pointed at the baby with her cigarette. "The other younguns are over on yan side the porch." She pointed her cigarette the other way. She was fair-haired, and her breast as white as snow. The baby was fair-complected too.

I looked where her cigarette pointed. The porch was full of folks, standing and sitting. I could see Dean Bronson and the President, talking to Mrs. Eccles, and a lot of country folks. And right nearby was a bunch of four or five children, all sizes, and every one of 'em towheaded. The others were sort o' huddled up, gazing hard at Mrs. Eccles. I couldn't see Cissie anywhere.

"We thought we might as well bring the family," said Aunt Lou. "There's more of 'em, around somewhere, with States Rights. We left the dogs at home."

I could feel Dr. Hoodenpyl pulling at my coat sleeve.

"Let's step aside for a moment," he said, and I walked onto the grass plot with him. "It's quite stunning, isn't it? Yes-yes, quite stunning. The unselfconsciousness of the folk. The singing, dancing throng. Increase and multiply."

I could only half ketch on to what he was saying. But somehow I knowed he didn't mean it for a compliment. He wasn't bubbling any more. He just stood there in his light coat and dark pants, picking at his little moustache and looking at me hard, the way a farmer looks at a mule he's thinking of buying but don't want to pay too much for.

"They are fine folks, I want you to know." That's what I told him. "I've known Aunt Lou Watkins since I was weaned. And I wa'n't weaned off no bottle neither."

"Yes-yes," he said. "I have no doubt. Excuse me, Mr. MacGregor, for lapsing into pedagogical terms. I am primarily a research man, of course. I seldom have an opportunity to take my folklore in the raw, you see. Always in the libary, and that sort of thing."

"What worries me," I answered him, "is how Cissie is going to feed all them chillun. I know she didn't expect 'em."

"Yes-yes. That will be a problem. But really she is quite capable, don't you think?"

"Do you know where she is? I got to see her. Pretty quick."

"I believe that Miss Timberlake went on some last-minute errands. To meet the bus—and go by the college post office. Luckily Mr. Kennedy and his jeep were on hand, and he offered his assistance. I'm sure they'll rejoin the grand assemblage without much delay."

He was still looking at me as if he was studying me, and he was fiddling with his moustache, and not cracking a smile.

"I can't wait long," I told him. "I've got things to do. If she don't come soon, I'll jest have to turn them fiddlers over to you. And you can turn them over to Cissie."

I pointed out the fiddlers to him. They weren't hurting any, to tell the truth, them two old fellers. They were hunkered down on the grassplot with some of their friends, smoking and chawing and passing the time of day, like the college might be a country store. But I wanted to get Dr. Hoodenpyl off my hands and rush over to the chapel.

For the first time Dr. Hoodenpyl looked pleased, more like the man I'd known before. He put his hands behind his back and rocked back and forth on his heels, pushing out his stomach like he was something in a circus.

"Now that, Mr. MacGregor, is a truly unexplored realm, both of folklore and of musicology. I should be pleased to have you turn over the fiddlers to me. I might ask them about certain features of their tuning. Yes-yes, I should really like to. The whole thing is purely traditional art. Untainted, absolutely untainted. A most remarkable phenomenon."

He got out a cigarette and begun to tap it on his wrist. He didn't offer me one.

"By the way," he said, in a kind of confidential tone, "I think we have that engagement at Harvard for Miss Timberlake and Buck Kennedy."

I was sorry to hear it, but I said, "Ain't that fine!"

"It's not absolutely fixed, but I think we have it. As to the other engagements planned—our little project, you remember—they are still in a somewhat indefinite state. But we shall see. Yes-yes, we shall see."

I didn't answer him, and he went on in an even more confidential way. He pushed his face right up close, and I could look down and see exactly how his little moustache was planted.

"But on the other hand, Mr. MacGregor, I have begun to have certain doubts. I have begun to wonder whether that is a perfectly ideal arrangement. Not that Mr. Kennedy is not a unique, a highly distinguished singer, and, I am sure, eminently responsible. But folklore in the raw, you see! Ha-ha! There might be—there might arise, don't you know—"

"Situations!" I blurted out. "You mean there might be situations that a young attractive woman would not—could not—?"

"Exactly!" He poked his finger right at my chest. "The precise word! Situations! We don't want any situations, do we? Not of the awkward kind, oh no! And so I have been thinking. Now don't let me detain you too long. But I have been thinking what a whale of an idea it would be to—" He broke off and looked at me closely. "Did you get the message I left for you last night, by the way?"

I hated to lie to the man, straight-out. But I was caught. So I put on a face and stalled: "Message? What message?"

"It doesn't really matter—since I can speak to you now. You will receive it later. I want to congratulate you on a superb performance. What you and Miss Timberlake did was absolutely convincing—absolutely—to me, and I might also say to my friend Mr. Muradian. And I wish to make an appointment—yes, an appointment. Now Mr. MacGregor, I am speaking to you in utmost confidence—which I am sure you will respect."

He put his hands behind his back, bent close to me, and lowered his voice:

"I have certain contacts in New York. That is the unvarnished truth. But you will appreciate that this is not something I have—er—you might say—er—emphasized publicly. In fact I do a little scouting, you might say—and not such a little either—for certain interests in the—er—entertainment industry. They are on the outlook—yes-yes—on the outlook for fresh talent. Such talent as you and Miss Timberlake have, for example. There might be openings. In fact, I am instructed by Mr. Muradian to approach you and Miss Timberlake about the matter."

"Openings for what?"

"Well, not for folklore in the raw, Mr. MacGregor. Other types of entertainment in the raw, but not folklore, you see. Yes-yes, Broadway won't quite take that. Neither will radio. And not quite the hillbilly music either. But if we could work out a combination, something in between, don't you know? The best elements of both, as you and Miss Timberlake so admirably exemplify them. It would be a new thing, but you would of course need connections. You would have to put yourself in professional hands, so to speak. Don't you see?"

"No, Dr. Hoodenpyl, I shorely don't see."

"It would be a unique thing," he went on, almost in a confidential whisper. "Unique, whether on stage or radio. And by the way, don't forget that television is coming along—it may take over. And with you and Miss Timberlake as a start— I had once thought of Mr. Kennedy, but now I see the complications, or as you so happily said, the situations. We will have to—ah—well, his is a different talent. But we could—though it would be a shame, wouldn't it?—if we could perhaps tempt you and Miss Timberlake and one or two of the Turkey Hollow Boys. Ozro, for example. We could form a singing group of a new sort, but somewhat like the Hutchinsons and others of old-time fame—a family group, you see. 'The MacGregor Family.' "

The man was winking at me. Teetering back and forth on his heels, with a silly grin below his moustache, and winking.

"And how did you ever git such an idea as that, Dr. Hoodenpyl? What makes you think we would want to leave Carolina?"

"Yes-yes, I realize—I realize—to pull up your roots. It might seem confusing at first. But my friends would make it worth your while, Mr. MacGregor. I did not fully develop the idea, Mr. MacGregor, until I studied the score of that alligator song. Yes-yes, the alligator song."

"So you got that arrangement from Cissie, after all?"

"Well, I have discussed that with her, Mr. MacGregor." He began to look a little puzzled. "But of course I asked you for it first, Mr. MacGregor. I hope you don't object—it is beautifully scored, by the way."

"But I'll bet you didn't say nothin' to Rufus!"

"That hardly seemed necessary. The record is on the market, and any good musician could . . ."

He hesitated when he saw how hard I was looking at him.

"But Miss Timberlake is an exceptional musician of course, and I am proud to have her as my student. This was just a phase of her advanced studies—an exercise, you might say—but also a favor to me."

I knew the man was lying, but I thought I better pass it off somehow. But I'd give him one lick.

"The pore little thing is already worked to death," I said. "And I don't see why you damn perfessers keep pilin' stuff onto her, but maybe if I can stick around here a few more days I'll find out."

Dr. Hoodenpyl stepped back as if I had really hit him, and got red in the face. Then he calmed down. "There she comes now," he said.

The jeep was rolling up to the porch steps, and Buck and Cissie were in the front seat. Buck ran around to the door and helped Cissie out. She was in a yellow dress, with some white around the neck and sleeves, and I thought she had never looked sweeter.

"Think it over, Mr. MacGregor," Dr. Hoodenpyl whispered in my ear. "If we could just see you for a few moments before we leave for Washington—maybe after the project tonight?"

I had my eyes on Cissie, but I turned around and looked at him one more time.

"Jest pure friendship, I reckon, and wantin' to prevent situations? That's damned nice of you, Dr. Hoodenpyl, but what do you get out of it?"

He turned red again. "That should not be a factor in your decision. That would be taken care of."

"I see what you're drivin' at. But for tonight, I'm hangin' on to ballads, like I've done told Cissie to do."

That was when Cissie spotted me. I wondered if she would, or if I would have to chase her. She came running up, and she looked worried about the eyes.

"Did you bring the fiddlers?"

"Right yonder on the grass."

"Oh, Danny, I'm relieved. At least we'll have them."

She began to walk along the porch, and me right with her.

"What's the matter, Cissie?"

"I'm afraid old Emmett Core is letting us down. We just met the bus, and he wasn't on it."

"Don't worry, Cissie. He probably caught a ride, and is eatin' at some hamburger stand, this minute."

A bell begun to ring, and the folks begun to move through the door.

"Danny, how are you goin' to get anything to eat?"

"Don't worry about me. Worry about all them Hardacre chillun. Jest look."

She looked, and all she could say was "Oh, Lord." She started away from me, then turned around and whispered, "Buck Kennedy's been drinkin'. He's already half drunk."

"He'll sing all the better, Cissie. Don't worry. He could kill a quart and never stagger. And I'll be right there."

The blue eyes were anxious, but she tried to work up a smile: "Just like Carlos B. Reddy, you are always ready, ain't you, Danny? Do I look all right to go in to this awful dinner?"

"Perfect—but you won't believe me till you check. Let me see now— you've got on a pretty dress—and your slip ain't showin'." I begun to walk around her. "And you are all zipped up and hooked in the back."

"I'll check the rest."

Cissie opened her big purse and fished out her compact. She started to check. Four or five letters slid out of the purse and hit the floor.

"That mail," she said. "I thought I'd better get it before the office closed. But I won't have time to open it, much less read it."

I was picking up the slick envelopes. My eye fell on one. "You've got a letter from the Dean! And look here, so have I! Whut's the Dean doin', sendin' my mail to you?"

The letter was marked CAMPUS MAIL and addressed to me in care of Miss Cecily Timberlake, Box 105.

"Maybe the Dean wanted to reach you right away and knew I'd see you."

"Maybe the Dean has caught up with us at last. Anyway, I'm in your care, all right!"

"Ain't you goin' to open it?"

"Ain't got time to fool with readin' letters now."

"Good! We'll open our mail later. Here—take the whole lot and stick 'em in your pocket. They're a nuisance in my purse. But don't forget you have 'em."

All of a sudden Cissie gave my hand a big squeeze and looked almost ready to kiss me to boot. Then she ran to ketch up with the crowd, and I was there all alone, hungry enough, with no supper in sight, but it wasn't the kind of hungry that any dining room you ever saw would satisfy.

24

THE BIG BALLAD JAMBOREE

People started crowding into the Old Chapel before it was good dark—almost before I finished giving my last check to the lights and stage and the projector and the ushers. The ushers were all on hand early, like I told 'em. You might have thought them country boys had been studying with an undertaker, so well did they steer that crowd. Without any trouble much, we kept the crowd out of the seats we had reserved at the front—and the two most important ones at the righthand side of the front row, convenient to an emergency exit. There were four rows at the left front, near the piano, for the ballads class, with the special seats for Cissie and me next to the exit on that side. At the right front we held some rows for the special guests—the President of the college and Dean Bronson, and the officers of the folklore society, and some faculty folks—and I don't remember who else except that all the preachers in town had been invited. The center section was left to the general crowd except for ten seats in the front row. The boys had strict orders to keep them for Rufus and the Turkey Hollow Boys, who would stay in the back of the house until the right minute.

It was Ed Cooley's and Wallace's special job to be in the two seats at the right-front until the time came, like we had planned, for the Sheriff and his deputy to act their parts. The spotlight was rigged to turn there first, when I would give the signal, and then it would shift to front center. But nobody knew about that except the boy at the switchboard in the balcony, and Ed and Wallace and me. And Cissie knew nothing whatever about all this, except that the Turkey Hollow Boys would be on hand, like Rufus had said.

I saw Wallace's red head darting through the crowd. He slipped up close to me and reported.

"We've got the jeep spotted," he whispered. "Buck parked it on the street this time, right where the steps go down from the campus."

"That's convenient. Well away from the crowd. We can stop Buck there, and neither Cissie nor anybody else will know."

"I noticed Muradian and Hoodenpyl came together, and parked right next to the jeep. It's a big new Cadillac with a New Jersey license."

"And you've got that other deputy spotted?"

"Behind some bushes, close by. And a couple of football players for good measure."

"Where are the others?"

"Well, Chubby's crowd are hangin' around outside, and we thought some of the football men better watch the cars—the Sheriff's and yours."

"They already parked?"

"Sheriff's car is already there, and Rufus will be comin' along. I've got a boy to show him."

"I haven't laid eyes on Ed, so far."

"He's here."

I looked over the heads of the crowd, and Ed was in his place, one of the boys sitting beside him. Ed raised his hand and grinned, and I waved to him.

"O.K.," I said. "I reckon we are all set. It's a danged complicated thing, but it ought to work."

"Buck Kennedy has been hitting the bottle. He's jittery."

"Cissie told me."

"And well may he be jittery. Federal officers have just closed in on the whiskey-runners. They got it on the ticker, over at WCC, just as I left. It'll be in the morning papers."

"Did they get the whole gang?"

"Some arrests still to be made. Art's Grill is already padlocked, with the Sheriff's office cooperating. Officers walked in at the dinner hour."

"Did they get Mr. Picture Shirt?"

"I don't know. I couldn't tell from the names."

"Well, I hope they get old Picture Shirt, and I hope them that's still on the loose don't mess us up."

"They won't be hanging around here."

"Maybe not, but it looks like everybody else is."

Wallace walked over and sat down with Ed. The boy that was holding his seat came and took his place with the ballads class.

I went over it all in my mind one more time. The ticklish point was for Buck to make his break and run for his jeep at exactly the right minute. It would be terrible to spoil the show by throwing our scare too soon, and I almost wished we had thought up some other scheme. But it would certainly rouse Buck when he laid eyes on the Sheriff and his deputy, right at the end of the last song on the program. Especially if he had any pints of stuff in that jeep. And we would drive the hint home with our fake "warning" that a boy would bring—a note from a "friend" to say the Sheriff had a warrant for him. We knew which way he would run—and being Buck, he was bound to run. We had him hemmed in, and we could chase him if he broke through, even though the Sheriff didn't like the idea. Yet you never can tell about these old ballad singers. Folklore in the raw—that's what gave Dr. Hoodenpyl his surprise. It ought to have been a warning to me.

It was a hot night. Hot as August in dog days can be in this country, in the first part of the night before the cool drifts in from the mountains. There was more people fanning themselves with their programs than was reading 'em, though Cissie had got up the programs mighty pretty, with that picture on the cover and a lot of interesting stuff about the old songs on the inside. I stood up to take a good look at the audience. Sheriff Looney was there in the back, as he promised, his spotted head shining like a patch of cotton in a hayfield. Buck would not see him on the last row, when the house lights went off and the singers came on the stage.

The ballads class were all fluttering their programs and talking. Miss Blue Eyes and Miss Black Eyes both switched by, close to me, just to pass the time of day of course, and both of them made motions to take the seat I was saving for Cissie. "Teacher's orders," I had to tell 'em. "Got me for her sideman tonight. But you look mighty pretty." The seats for honored guests were filling up with high-falutin' folks—the folks that belong to everything and are always getting their names into the newspaper. I saw the Methodist preacher and his wife—the short-haired thin woman that's always getting up youth groups and talking about youth and the modern world. I saw a couple of Presbyterian preachers and their wives, but I didn't see Dr. Stokeley, the pastor of the First Baptist Church, and I wondered a little till I remembered that he would be on the stage with Mrs. Eccles and the singers. He would open with prayer, no doubt, and then introduce Mrs. Eccles, who would be the chairman and introduce the singers. So of course Dr. Stokeley would be at that dinner with the singers and the big bugs. It's a way Mrs. Eccles has, to line up the preachers and big businessmen. They can't back down, once she goes after them. Soon as she walks in, they start nodding their heads—so folks say.

It was getting on to eight o'clock and time to start the show. We were going to run ten or fifteen minutes late, I could see. But finally the President and Dean Bronson came in and took their seats. They had their wives with 'em, and there was old Mrs. Rountree too, right between the President and the President's wife. She had hardly taken her seat before she got up, went to the side exit, then came back, and I wondered if she was dipping snuff like Aunt Lou. Poradowsky and his sound engineer were at the front, warming up their recorders. I could see Dr. Hoodenpyl's bald head not far away, and with him a slick-looking, dark-complected, sportily dressed man that must be Muradian. And Dr. Goodenow . . . and Mr. Polka Dot Tie, craning his neck around. I wondered if I ought to go over and speak to him.

That very minute Cissie came through the side door and eased into her seat. Right away I knew she had been crying.

"What's the matter?"

"It was terrible," she whispered back. I could feel her trembling. "Danny, I don't know how we ever got through with it."

"Buck Kennedy misbehavin'?"

"Buck Kennedy had been drinking, but I can put up with that. It was a lot of things, but mainly it was old Mrs. Rountree."

Underneath the big buzz of talk she told me about the big dinner, pretty near sobbing it into my ear. The first trouble was to find places for those children and other unexpected guests, and not keep the big bugs waiting. In spite of everything, Buck Kennedy disappeared at the last moment, then turned up with a stout breath. But the real disaster was old Mrs. Rountree. First she said she wa'n't comin' to supper because her stomach was upset. Then she changed her mind and said if Ike was a-goin', derned if she could be kept out, but they'd have to feed her bread and milk and nothin' else. And Cissie promised she would do that.

She is a notionate old woman—Ike's third wife, she is, and they say she married him for his pension money. No sooner did they get settled at the dinner table than she remembered she had forgot and left her purse and a paper sack in the ladies' room. So Cissie had to get up and fetch the purse and the paper sack. Next thing, the waiter brought her the bread and milk as Cissie had told him. But the bread was lightbread, and she flew into a huff.

"She actually picked up the piece of that bread and sniffed it," Cissie said. "Then she said right out loud that it wa'n't fitten to feed hogs, but she had brought a piece of cornpone along. She reached into her paper sack and brought it out, all wrapped in newspaper. She unwrapped it and offered the President and Mrs. Eccles some, but they refused. She grumbled all through dinner, but instead of eating just bread and milk, she took something of whatever the waiters brought, including both hot coffee and iced tea. I was so mad I nearly died, but there wasn't a thing I could do except try to look pleasant. The dining room was too hot, and the President kept asking me polite questions across the table. All the time Mrs. Rountree was telling Dean Bronson that Ike was a big fool to get up and sing because he had never been to singing school like she had and didn't know the rudiments—didn't know Fa from La."

"I'll bet she's right at that," I put in.

"But Ike knows some wonderful ballads," Cissie said.

She told me how things went along that way till the dessert was brought. Then Buck Kennedy knocked over his iced tea glass and the tea ran down into Mrs. Eccles' lap. Cissie had to jump up with a napkin and mop off Mrs. Eccles while the waiter was mopping the table. But the tea left a big spot, and so Mrs. Eccles rushed out of the dining room, and the President and the Dean rushed out after her, and Cissie rushed after the three of them.

"That was when I nearly broke down," Cissie said, right tearful. "Danny, you just don't realize what I have to take from these people. Mrs. Eccles had to race into her dormitory guest room and change her dress."

"Is that why we are a little late startin'?"

"That's it—except that old Mrs. Rountree wouldn't let the waiter take any of her dishes away. She made him put the apple pie and lemon pie down by her plate. She took both! I could hardly get her to leave the table. If they had brought more food, she would be eating yet. The President's wife finally took her off my hands, while I was leading the singers around backstage."

It was around eight-fifteen when at last the stage lights went on and the house lights off, and the performers began to file on, Mrs. Eccles leading them and nipping 'em into place like a big old sheepdog herding sheep to the shearing. Cissie began to sit up and take notice. Her eyes fell on the vacant seats.

"Danny, why are those seats still vacant, there in the front center?"

"S-s-h!" I said. "Hark to Dr. Stokeley."

It was lucky for me, right then, that the Reverend started asking the Lord's blessing on our assembly and these our friends from our beloved Carolina hills.

"Danny, I'm scared," Cissie whispered, after the prayer. "I really don't know what will happen."

"Whatever's done started, hit can't be stopped."

In the dark of our corner of the front row, while Mrs. Eccles was saying "Ladies and Gentlemen" and complimenting the President of the college and naming and thanking the sponsors of the festival, and enlarging the grand old traditions of Carolina and the mountains, and working around to introduce Emmett Core for the first number, somehow our hands just naturally come together. There we sat, amongst all those people, as it might be on the old front porch, a long time before.

But everybody was looking to the stage of course, looking and listening. Except for Buck Kennedy, I don't reckon there was one amongst those old folks that had ever sung in public before or been on any kind of stage. I'll have to say they did right well. Their voices squeaked a little at first, and they hemmed and hawed at some places when they forgot a few words. But once they got warmed up, you might have thought they had been singing in college all their lives.

In fact it was as natural for them to sing as it was to talk, and so being up on that stage didn't make no difference much. I reckon the crowd and the excitement, too, helped 'em out more than it flustrated 'em. Then there is something about the old songs that just carries you along anyhow, especially if you've sung 'em since you was a youngun. The old songs come through, riding on the tune, and pick you up to ride with 'em, and you go loping along with the best of the tune until you arrive safe home. If you happen to forget a word or two, you put in another one that will do just as well, and go right on, it don't make no difference much, but you can't hardly forget the words because the words remember easy, and the story helps.

I had fixed things the way Cissie told me: the chairs for the singers in a kind of half-circle, with Mrs. Eccles in the middle of the line, against the back drapes where there was an exit, and Buck Kennedy right by her in one place of honor, and Dr. Stokeley also was honored on the other side. Mrs. Eccles would announce the number, and the singer would come and stand by a little table at the front of the stage that had a water pitcher on it and some glasses. Poradowsky's mikes were pointed at that table, and on the far right from me, by some steps that mounted to the stage, I could see the reels of the tape recorder glinting as they turned, and the sound engineer tending the machine.

I kept thinking how fine it would be if Cissie could be up there doing the talking in Mrs. Eccles' place, because Cissie was the one that had done all the hard work, and it would have been a pretty sight. Mrs. Eccles mainly just read off Cissie's program notes when she introduced the singers, or else talked like something out of a book. Sometimes she would put in things that she made up herself, like "our rich community life," or she went on about how old-fashioned we were until, to hear her tell about it, you might think Shakespeare and old Walter Raleigh had been the first settlers on Beaver Creek and had raised their chillun on poke sallet, sidemeat, ballad songs, and not much else. Of course, not being raised in the woods like Cissie and me, she didn't know any better than to talk that way. Still, Mrs. Eccles is a mighty woman to push things along, and you had to admire her. When she pushes, something has got to move. Things moved that night in more ways than one.

Cissie had the program arranged so that the oldest songs came first—like "The Devil's Nine Questions," and "The Miller's Two Daughters." Then it came on along to the real love stories, and so to some light songs like "The Quaker Courtin' " and "They say that the women are worse than the men." At least it was supposed to.

At first the crowd was just polite and nice with their applause. You couldn't be sure whether they liked the songs or was just showing respect. But pretty soon the old songs began to work on 'em, as the old songs always do. You could tell the crowd was warming up to the songs, and the singers warming up the crowd, and they were getting hot together, inside and outside both, with the sweat running down everybody's face from the outside heat and the hearts stirring up more heat inside from what the songs said.

When Buck Kennedy sung "Lord Thomas and Fair Elender" and came to the end where it says, "All true lovers that go together, May they have more luck than they," old Mrs. Rountree was so lifted up that she shouted "Amen!" like she was in church. The crowd had started to clap. When that "Amen!" rung out, they hushed in a startle for a second, and I heard somebody giggle. Next thing, the crowd was clapping for old Mrs. Rountree, and some of the boys in the back hollered "Amen!" and "Hallelujah!" to keep her company.

Cissie was wiggling around in a nervous fret. I told myself things might suddenly slide out of control. After Aunt Lou had sung "Lonesome Valley," Mrs. Eccles begun to explain how the song was sometimes called "Bamboo Briars" and how some famous poet took the story and wrote it into a poem because he was in love with a girl named Fanny Brown. That's what I understood her to say, but it didn't connect up. The more Mrs. Eccles tried to explain, the more tangled and twisted she got. When she stood up to speak, she had left her program on her chair, or mislaid it somehow. So she made a wild stab at what was coming next and called on Aunt Lou again, out of turn.

"Oh, Lord!" Cissie groaned in my ear. "What is goin' to happen next?"

"It'll be all right, Cissie." I poured it on her, just for fun. "You know Aunt Lou knows some wonderful songs—her and Buck Kennedy."

Aunt Lou don't always hear too well. All she caught, I reckon, was "Bamboo," and she thought Mrs. Eccles said "Dew." So up she stood, as sassy as she really is, and sung 'em "Foggy Dew." Not the nice, polite one, but the other one—the one they never would let you sing over the radio. Every verse of it to the bitter end. And every time she came to the chorus— "All I did was to hold her in my arms, And to keep her from the foggy, foggy dew" she grinned like a she-bear and put all the meaning in it that's supposed to be there. To make it worse, she put in some comment. "She ought to a-tuck warnin'!" said Aunt Lou. "He must a-been a fair-spoken man." And she started in giving the girls her regular advice, "Beware of a fair-spoken man!"

Dr. Stokeley, caught there on the stage, put on a silly smile like he hadn't noticed any harm, but his nose was as sharp as a thistle. The boys in the back yelled and stomped and called for more, and before Mrs. Eccles could take hold of the reins and bridle Aunt Lou back into her seat, she was giving 'em an encore. The ballad she picked out was "Little Matty Grew."

"What will the Parent-Teachers Association think about *that* one?" Cissie had passed the crying stage. She just asked the question like it was a question in class.

"I think maybe you are a ruined woman!" I answered, like I was a real scholar. "But you may as well set back and enjoy the show, like me."

Aunt Lou sung right on through all the wicked parts of that story as if she was reciting her Sunday School lesson and she didn't care who was a-listening. That crowd sure was listening, and I'll bet the preachers, even, didn't put their fingers in their ears. Up on the stage I could see Buck Kennedy leaning forward and his eyes a-sparkling, and I knowed for certain that he wasn't aiming to be outdone by no old woman when it came to that kind of singing. The old singers were whetting one another up to no telling what kind of mischief, and the crowd, especially the young folks, was whetting up the singers.

Aunt Lou came to the verse that goes:

> How do you like my blankets,
> And how do you like my sheets?
> And how do you like my pretty lady
> That lies in your arms and sleeps.

She just about brought down the house with that one and with little Matty's answer and the big fight at the end where everybody gets cut up including the old lady. They were laughing, though, when they ought to a-been crying, because it is a sad story and I don't know why folks think it's funny. But anyway, the rafters shook with the clapping and yells when Aunt Lou finally sat down. Dr. Stokeley looked like he had been drinking sour milk, but there wasn't a thing he could do or any other preacher could do, right then.

Then Mrs. Eccles made her big mistake. Instead of going on with the program as if she didn't notice, she got flustered and begun to cover up and apologize.

"Those of us who know our Shakespeare," said Mrs. Eccles, "will realize that Mrs. Watkins' interesting ballad is in the tradition of *Othello* and *All's*

Well That Ends Well. And after all, the story of Richard Wagner's most famous grand opera is a story of—of—"

She hesitated, and I wondered what might come next.

With her lips close to my ear, Cissie prompted savagely: "Illicit love! Plain old adultery!"

But Mrs. Eccles didn't say that. She caught herself and went on to make the best of it.

"Of the tragic fate of star-crossed lovers," Mrs. Eccles said, and put a lot of volume into "star-crossed." "Though the phrase," she went on, "is Shakespeare again, I believe. And Mr. Kennedy, who is a product of our historic Carolina frontier, is very close to the Elizabethan tradition. I believe it is time now for Mr. Kennedy to sing us a sweet romantic love song. Mr. Kennedy will now sing . . ."

Mrs. Eccles stopped, because she still didn't have her program. She had forgot to look for it. From where I was I could see it, a-lying underneath Preacher Stokeley's chair where it had slipped down. But the singers didn't see it, and if they had seen it they wouldn't have helped. They just sat there like boiled owls and looked straight ahead.

Cissie rushed to the corner of the stage and tried to hand a program across the footlights. Either Mrs. Eccles didn't notice her or didn't want to notice her. She was bound and determined to risk her memory.

"Mr. Kennedy will sing the old song about Barbara Allen as our final number," announced Mrs. Eccles. "And Miss Timberlake's ballads class will join in, as a special feature."

That wasn't right or anywhere near it. Cissie was there at the footlights waving a program, and almost jumping up and down with excitement. But Mrs. Eccles was sort of bowing to Buck Kennedy and smiling in a stiff way, and the crowd was applauding. Cissie laid the program down on the stage floor and came back to her seat. The ballads class was fidgeting and whispering all back of us.

Cissie just put her face in her hands and bent over as if she couldn't bear to look.

"What are we goin' to do? Do we sing this with him?" A girl was hissing into my ear from behind.

'Twas no use to answer—but I passed the word to hold everything. Buck Kennedy had tuck the bait. He was a-running away with the hook, and nobody to check the line.

"I'll come to the singin' in a minute," said Buck Kennedy. He had his thumbs in his belt and was talking proud. "Us folks up in Beaver Valley leads a purty rough life. We ain't much on Shakespeare. But when hit comes to lovin' and marryin', or even to lovin' and *not* marryin'—that's somethin' we air good at, as good as the next un."

Buck's face was red, and he teetered the least bit as he stood there all a-swagger.

"I could prove the marryin' part by Sharp Snaffles. He got his capital and his woman by snaggin' ten thousand wild geese and the biggest b'ar hide and the most tree honey ever heard tell of from here to Table Rock Mountain. He was a Beaver Valley boy. I knowed him well."

That was a lie, of course. All of us country boys and girls had heard of Sharp Snaffles, but he must a-been dead and buried more'n a hundred years.

"But hit's a long story," Buck went on. "Too long to tell. So for tonight I'll take the lovin' and *not*-marryin' part and sing you a song along that line. The gal in this song wa'n't no Barbary Allen—by no means."

The house was quiet as a cemetery. Not a rustle or a cough. Buck took one step back from the little table, raised his chin, put his hands behind his back, and let go. It was a rowdy song, and I had heard it several times before, but not quite like Buck begun it.

> A gallant London prentice
> Came to his love by night.
> He came up to the window
> Where she had put a light.
>
> He stood beside the window sill
> And tapped upon the pane.
> She quickly rose and let him in
> And went to bed again.

Buck stopped for a minute and looked down, like a man that sees a sinkhole in front of him and wonders how to get around it. There wasn't any sinkhole, but only that crowd of dressed-up folks, frozen to their seats and waiting for Buck to take the next step. I heard Cissie gasp and ketch her breath. I could see a baldheaded preacher mopping the sweat from his scalp. The sweat was popping out on me too. It was folklore in the raw, sure enough, and I almost reached for my handkerchief before I caught myself. I thought I knew what was coming, and I wondered if Buck would go on.

He would. Buck cleared his throat, rolled his eyes, and stepped off into the sinkhole. But I could tell he was getting sober—fast.

> The streets are cold and rainy,

he sang;

And people walk about.
Oh, take me in your arms, Love,
And blow the candle out.

I knew then it was going to get worse before it could get better.

Your father and your mother
In yonder's room both lie
A-hugging one another,
Then why not you and I?

So let us talk no further,
Or have no fear or doubt,
But—

Buck stopped again. He even looked a little scared. I knew what the next line had to be. It was something about that girl taking off her clothes. Was he going to sing it? No, he was playing forgetful. He coughed behind his hand. Then sort of choked and said, not singing, "Well, she blowed the candle out!" and sat down right quick. I could hear people whispering, "What'd he say?" I could feel constarnation rising from the ranks of the respectable like greasy smoke on a hot skillet. There was a snigger or two. Then a boy busted loose with a big "Haw-haw!" and the explosion came in a big ripping laugh.

I was so relieved to think they would laugh like that, and maybe pass it off, that I clean forgot where I was and what I was supposed to do. I snatched out my handkerchief, and begun wiping my face. But Good Lord, that was the signal we had agreed on, and I was waving it too soon.

Pat as Old Nick, the boy at the switchboard turned on the big spotlight. And into the spotlight marched Rufus and the Turkey Hollow Boys, their instruments bright in the glare, and took the empty seats at the front. Ozro whinnied. The crowd laughed again in a big roar and clapped hard. In the middle of it all, here came Sheriff Looney, his calico head shining and a deputy right with him. They took the two front seats that were left.

"What are you up to?" groaned Cissie. "This isn't on the program."

"But watch the crowd eat it up," I said, and needed to say no more, for Mrs. Eccles was on her feet again. This time she had a program in her hand and had caught up with the procession. She is a stubborn woman, with plenty of grit, and she was bound and determined to set things right.

"We will return to the evening's program," Mrs. Eccles said, as if nothing whatever had happened. "Our concluding number will be 'The House Carpenter.' We will flash the words on a screen so that the entire audience can join Miss Timberlake's ballads class in singing this fine old ballad. I am also glad to welcome Mr. Rufus Whitthorne and his group, and I hope they will join in too. And I think I will ask—"

That was the minute when a lot happened in a flash. I don't know when Cissie slipped out. It must have been when Mrs. Eccles started her little speech, because I caught a faint murmur of Cissie's voice saying something like "Can't do this to me," but I was watching the stage. I felt a breath of air and looked, and Cissie's chair was empty. I looked back at the stage, and Mrs. Eccles was sort of half-turned, as if to introduce Buck Kennedy once more. But his chair was empty, too. He must have eased out, between the drapes at the back, when Mrs. Eccles stood up in front of him.

It flashed through my mind that Cissie had run out to look for Buck, and get him back on the stage. Now she *would* do that, I told myself. But there was no chance to think. Mrs. Eccles was covering up, like a veteran used to situations.

"I think I will ask," she repeated, "our good friend Mr. Danny MacGregor to start the song for us."

Now it was my turn to cover up and be quick about it. Luckily the switchboard boy had cut the spotlight, and the audience couldn't see much of what was happening in the front rows. But as I hustled across, toward the stage steps, I caught a glimpse of Rufus and the Sheriff slipping towards the exit on that side. Poradowsky's sound engineer was smack in my way, bending over his machine. I couldn't wait. I put my foot in the middle of his back and made it to the stage floor in two big steps. I heard the man grunt, and it did my soul good.

I faced the crowd. There was no Cissie at the piano, but I could see Ozro had the Turkey Hollow Boys on the alert, and they knew what to do.

"I'm proud to be here," I said, "and start any kind of song. But 'specially this one right now because the Turkey Hollow Boys are going to play and Miss Timberlake's class is goin' to sing, and we are all goin' to j'ine in and put the old country music and the new country music together. I want you to sing every verse, and sing it all over again if you feel like it. And when it's over, Mrs. Eccles will take charge and tell you about the square dancin' and everything at the gymnasium."

I waved my hand to Ozro, and with a fine big sweep of fiddles, guitars, and bull fiddle we went into that song. The ballads class pitched right in, and the crowd caught it right now as if they'd practiced:

> "Well met, well met, my own true love."
> "Not so very well met," said she.

"For I am married to a house carpenter,
And a very fine man was he.'

"If you'll forsake your house carpenter
And come along with me
I'll take you there where the grass grows green
On the banks of the sweet valley."

It would have done me good to stay and hear it, if Cissie had been there and the situations all in hand. But the situations were all out of hand. The switchboard boy had turned off the stage lights when the song started. I left Mrs. Eccles and Ozro to handle the rest and dodged for the side exit, heading back of the Old Chapel and down the slope of the campus towards where Buck had parked his jeep. Two white spots caught my eye on the grass. I scooped them up without hardly stopping. Cissie had kicked off her high-heel slippers and was running barefooted after old Buck Kennedy. And back of me I could faintly hear the song still going.

She had not sailed six weeks on the sea,
Oh, no, not more than three,
Before this fair lady began for to mourn,
And she wept right bitterly.

25

THE VALLEY AIR WAS FLOWING SWEET

At first, when I got to the side entrance and saw Buck Kennedy's jeep, I thought we had him stopped. The jeep was there on the street, all alone, and nobody in it. Nobody around. "They are givin' Buck the works," I thought.

Then a voice called out of the darkness, up the campus walk: "That you, Danny?"

It was Wallace. When I answered, he said, "Hurry, the Sheriff's startin'."

I ran to catch up. Wallace was there with the deputy and a big football player. They were breathing hard and moving fast. In the dim light I saw the deputy was dabbing at his face with a bloody handkerchief. Wallace's shirt was torn.

"What happened?"

"Buck got away in the Cadillac," said Wallace.

"He knocked me down before I could pull my gun," said the deputy. "He can hit hard."

"Two goons jumped out of the Cadillac and held us off," said the football player.

"There were two more men in the Cadillac," said Wallace, "but I couldn't see who they were."

"Where's Cissie?"

"Up there—with the cars. She's all right." Ahead of us the red light on the Sheriff's car was winking. A late low moon was showing. I could still hear the singing in the Old Chapel.

"Chubby's crowd tried to move in on the cars up there," said Wallace. "That drew us off. We didn't have enough men down here to stop Buck."

I ran ahead towards the cars and the arguing voices.

"Honest, Mr. Sheriff, we were just going to sit in the cars and drink a little beer." That was Chubby. A sharper voice cut in: "I ought to take you to jail—or to the City Police." That was Sheriff Looney. "But maybe you've had enough punishment for one night."

A bunch of people were huddled in the glare of the Sheriff's big headlights. The football players were holding Chubby and two of his pals, arms pinned behind their backs. They looked considerably mussed up.

"I'll keep your knives that you were goin' to slash tires with," the Sheriff continued. "And I've got your names to give the Dean. Turn 'em loose, boys, and let's get goin'. I want a couple of you big fellows in my car. I'm deputizing you—and you—right now."

"Where's Cissie?" I gasped out.

"Get in Rufus' car," the Sheriff said, without answering. "Tell him to follow me close. We'll ketch those devils time they reach Beaver Valley. The city traffic will slow 'em up."

The huddle broke. I saw Cissie at last. She was opening the door of Rufus' car. Rufus was gunning the motor.

"No, you don't, Cissie! Keep out of it. This ain't no place for a woman." I pulled at her arm. She pulled right back.

"I know all about it." Her purse was on her arm and she was calm and steady in her stocking feet. "You can't keep me out of it. Thank you for the shoes."

I had forgotten the shoes were in my hand. Cissie grabbed them and scrambled into the car.

"Sheriff's startin'," was Ed's voice on the front seat.

"Git in! Git in!" That was Wallace.

I was inside, on the back seat with Cissie, slamming the car door as Rufus' tires screamed with the quick start. When we reached the street, the Sheriff turned on his siren. "Sheriff said to tell you to keep close," I yelled at Rufus.

Behind the wheel, Rufus yelled back. "Keep close yourself, you two. I'm drivin'."

It was good advice, and I took it, while we zinged through city traffic that froze as we passed. I put my lips close to Cissie's ear.

"Right back where we were. Only chance to talk is in an automobile at 60 miles per hour. But you ought to be back there managing things."

I could feel Cissie's breath, warm on my ear and cheek. "I couldn't bear to stay in that place another minute. I've had enough. I'd rather be here."

"What good can you do here?"

"What do you think I've been doin', all the time? Lookin' after you, Danny MacGregor. Keepin' you out of trouble."

"Oh, no, it was the other way. I was keepin' you out of trouble."

"That's what *you* thought." Cissie gave my ear a tweak and laughed. I moved up a little closer, but she pushed me away.

"You watch the road. I'm goin' to change my stockin's."

"What?"

"I always carry a spare." She was opening her purse.

Already we were five or six miles out in the country. The Sheriff's big headlights, and Rufus' right behind, rolled the dazzling highway towards us at airplane speed, the Sheriff's top light winking in the middle like a big star just above the three dark heads on the front seat. We shot past a late mule wagon, the scared driver whipping his team into the ditch, and paralyzed a few pickup trucks and slow Saturday night cars full of country folks. But I could see no Cadillac taillights on ahead. I looked to the left, with a shy glimpse at Cissie, bending over her white feet. The mountains were looming higher, their ridges hardly touched by the thin moonlight, and in the shadowy bottoms along the creek millions of lightning bugs were winking their little taillights back and forth in chorus. We were getting into Beaver Valley, near my own place. Suddenly I remembered something and yelled at Rufus, "That bridge over Kennedy's Creek—it's no good. How are we goin' to warn Sheriff?"

Not moving his head, Rufus answered: "We've done told him. But he already knew."

Ed Cooley's head said: "We've fixed up a trick."

Now we were on winding road, the old hairpin turns in the high part of the valley, and were slowing down a good deal. I thought I glimpsed red taillights ahead, but I wasn't sure. Cissie was curled up in her corner, bracing at the curves, but almost falling over when the car banked steeply. Mountain air, sweet and cool, was flowing in. The siren was cut off. Cissie began talking, low and confidential.

"You didn't have to do all this tricky stuff tonight, Danny. Buck Kennedy would be out of our hair anyhow, after tonight. But I'm glad you did it. Makes me feel good—makes me proud of you."

"So you caught on to Buck Kennedy?"

"Long ago."

"I wondered if you had. And what about Hoodenpyl?"

"He's a fat old fraud."

"Does he have the music to that alligator song?'

"No, I have it. That was how I caught on to *him*. Practically had to hire a lawyer to make him give it back."

"Has he been after you to join the big time?"

"Yes."

"Are you goin' to?"

"I haven't answered him yet."

"Well, I did!"

"Oh," she said in a surprised voice. We rounded another sharp curve, and Cissie was thrown over against me. She didn't straighten up, this time. "You ought to know," she whispered, "what my answer would be."

"Looks like all they want is to get something out of you, don't it?"

"Yes," she said, and put an edge on her voice, "just make an advertisement out of you!"

"No matter whether it's the hillbilly music—"

"Yes."

"Or even ballads?"

"I'm afraid so—yes!"

"Now I've got you started sayin' yes--and I want you to go on sayin' it when I ask the next question. The only thing for us to do is to be independent—to go ahead and get married right now. Isn't that so?"

"I'll give you my answer before this night is over."

We held together as the car slewed and skidded around the last sharp turn. Then it straightened out on the level creek road. I thought I could see taillights far ahead.

"How did you manage to find out about our doin's, Cissie?"

"Don't worry. Nobody taddletaled. I could read your face. I did happen to find out about your car—and those boys—and—"

The jolting road flung us back and forth. Cissie was holding me tight.

"What is all this in your inside coat pocket?"

"Letters."

"I remember. We still can't get time to read our mail—just—hold on—to them." The car was bouncing hard.

"I'll do that. We'll read—our mail—on the way back--when we settle—this—business."

We were right at the bad bridge and the hidden ford below Buck's house. Now the cars rolled slow and easy through thick grass and weeds.

"Watch it, Sheriff!" I couldn't help saying it, and bracing my feet for a crash.

The siren was screaming again. It seemed louder than ever. Rufus braked to a stop.

"That will scare him good," shouted Ed. "This will scare him better." He jumped to the ground and fired his pistol in the air three times. "All out!" he shouted.

"No!" cried Wallace. "Stay in the car!"

"Stop that shooting," called the Sheriff. He was out of his car, talking to Rufus. "That little won't hurt. But no more! Back up your car, Rufus, and take the ford. It isn't as bad as it looks. We are close behind 'em. I saw their headlights going up the hill. Those in my car stay behind. We'll give Buck a chance to clean up a little. You can handle him till I get there. I'll give you fifteen or twenty minutes, then we'll follow on foot. No gunplay, now."

As we took the ford, I could see that the Sheriff had put his front wheels as near the old bridge as he could get—like he might be stalled there. Up the rough road we screeched, weeds slapping the fenders, and piled out at the top of the hill. A big car was standing there, deserted. The hot motor was making cooling-off noises. Buck's house was dark. Below, at the old bridge, the Sheriff's red light was winking, and the siren was wailing and wailing like the ghosts of all the dead Indians in the country.

"Rufus, you and Ed watch the house," I told them. "Wallace and me will look into the corncrib. He'll be wherever his stuff is hid."

"All right," said Rufus. "You take the back door, Ed, and I'll take the front. Whistle if you find him."

"You get back in the car," I told Cissie.

"Don't talk crazy," said Cissie, and kept right up with us as we dashed across the dry grass. Buck was nowhere in sight, but inside the corncrib I could hear a considerable rustling sound.

I peeped through a crack in the logs. A pocket flashlight was propped among some cornshucks, and I could see Buck Kennedy. He was on his knees, filling a bushel basket with pints of whiskey. He was laying ears of corn amongst the bottles and over the top. What Buck thought to gain by all that, I didn't know and didn't care. He was my meat.

"Buck Kennedy! Oh, Buck Kennedy," I called through the crack. "Why don't you bring that stuff out here where you can see to work!"

He came out quick, not with the basket, but with his hands over his head, facing us in the moonlight, expecting guns.

"He thinks it's a movie," said Wallace scornfully. Cissie just looked.

"Put down your hands, you fool," I told him, "and bring that basket of corn here quick!"

"I thought you was the Sheriff!" Buck said, all distracted, and glancing around wildly. "Whose car is that?"

"Sheriff's car is stuck, down at the bridge. He made a mistake. But he's comin' right up the hill, and a bunch of deputies with him. You bring that basket. That's Rufus' car, and I think he'll let you put it in his trunk."

Buck hesitated a second. No doubt he thought it might be a trap—or a bluff. "Miss Timberlake—" He started to appeal to Cissie. I cut him off.

"You don't deserve it, but we aim to git you out of this mess—and the mess you got Cissie and all of us into. We followed the Sheriff's car. We took the ford and got here jest in time to salvage your remains. Now git that basket!"

In one long screech, the siren stirred up the echoes again. Somewhere in the backyard an old hound dog was howling. Buck fetched his basket.

"Is this all you've got on the place?"

"Hit's all, before God," Buck groaned.

"You ain't makin' it on the place?"

"Lord, no!" said Buck. "And this is the last."

Cissie spoke up. "I'll run ahead and get the trunk open," and went away like a deer in the brush.

"You run too," I told Buck. "Run like hell." And I whistled to Rufus.

With a grunt, Buck heaved the basket to his shoulder. One on each side of him, Wallace and me, we ran to the car. It did me good to hear Buck wheeze. Without a word Rufus locked Buck's load in the car trunk. And there we were in the late moonlight—Cissie in her yellow dress, with her bright hair glinting a little--and Rufus—and Ed--and me. We had Buck Kennedy backed up on the tall steps of his porch where all the trouble started. It was time for me to preach my sermon, but first I told Wallace to run down the hill a little ways, and whistle when he heard the Sheriff coming.

"Oh, no," said Wallace violently, "I want my lick at this old bastard."

"You do what I tell you! Run!" And he ran.

"Now, Buck," I said, "you are in real hell-fire trouble this time and no foolin'. If it wa'n't for Cissie here, I'd jest let you burn and be damned. But for Cissie's sake we'll try to pluck you from the burnin'. What have you got to say for yourself anyhow?"

"About what?" He spoke a little too peart to suit me.

"About what I'm goin' to tell you, and there ain't much time to tell it. All we got to do is to lift the lid of that trunk when the Sheriff comes—"

"I knowed it was a trick—but go on and tell me."

In the August moonlight Buck didn't look so handsome any more. He was still panting a little, and he sagged all over. From wherever Buck had tied her up, that old hound bitch was howling. It was a mighty mournful howl, and it went with the proceedings.

"Now the first thing is that Cissie here got you started and built you up, and yet you caused her all this shame and trouble. You've acted worse than that old hound dog younder, and whut are you goin' to do about it?"

"U-lulu-lu-lu!" went the old hound dog.

Cissie broke in. "That isn't really necessary, Danny. Just call it quits and we'll try to fix things with the Sheriff for old time's sake and forget about all that trouble."

"Don't take up for him," I said, though I really was beginning to feel just a little sorry for Buck. "He ought to crawl on his belly."

The hound dog gave another quavering howl that ended in a distressed bark.

"I don't know whut come over me tonight," Buck said, wiggling his hands nervously. "That woman got me mixed up. I'm sorry I done it."

I wasn't satisifed. "You've got to do better than that. You've got to make some promises. Promise that, as long as you are booked to sing in this neighborhood or anywhere around here, by Cissie Timberlake or anybody connected with her affairs, you'll not make or sell a drop of liquor."

"I kin promise that all right."

"Then promise it and swear to it."

"I swear to it."

Cissie wanted her word and she put it in.

"*And*, Mr. Smarty Buck Kennedy, always to sing or say *only* what's put down on the program for you."

She shook her little fist in his face. Buck dodged back, caught his heels on the steps, and sat down hard.

"I'll shore God promise that!" said Buck in a weak voice, looking up at Cissie. I thought for a minute that Cissie was going to slap his jaws for good measure.

But Rufus spoke up in his dry way. "Seems like some other folks ought to be promisin' the same—about programs."

They busted out laughing, all but one. Then Wallace whistled and came running back. "They are close on the way," he called.

I stood closer to Buck. "There's one more thing. We've been seeing too much of you, Buck Kennedy. It'll be better for you if you make yourself kinder scarce."

He stood up and clenched a fist. "This is my place, and there's no MacGregor goin' to give me orders about my goin' and comin'—nor no Cooleys or Exums either." He suddenly spat towards Ed Cooley. I grabbed at Ed and Wallace as they lunged for him—but I couldn't have held them long. The Sheriff's cool voice stopped them.

"Wait a minute, boys. No brawlin'!" With the football players and deputies, they looked like a regiment coming.

"Buck," said the Sheriff, "I have a complaint ag'in you for suspicion of bootleggin', and I'm goin' to search the premises. I have a search warrant here if you want to listen to it. You want me to read it?"

Buck sat down on the steps again. "Go on and s'arch, Sheriff, and welcome to hit. You'll find no likker because I ain't got none."

"We'll see about that." The Sheriff told off his deputies with his finger. "You take the corncrib and barn. And you and me'll take the house." He took a flashlight out of his pocket and paused with one foot on the steps, as if he'd just noticed us. "Quite a party you're havin' here tonight. I don't see how all you folks got here ahead of me after the singin'."

Rufus sat as if he never hoped to rise again. The Sheriff turned on his flashlight and climbed the steps.

Rufus called to him. "We chased out here to get those cases of Coca-Cola that Buck promised for the dance. Let us know if you find 'em."

Buck opened his mouth—thought better of it—closed his mouth—scratched his head.

There we stood with nothing to do. Rufus said, "Let's start a song," and eased over to me to whisper, "We planted the Coca-Cola—brought it with us." Then Rufus raised his chin and said, "Danny wants to sing 'Be Honest with Me!' Let's go." So we struck into it. It was one of the older hillbilly songs we used to sing on the radio. Buck stood up and seemed to be feeling better. When we changed and swung into "Live and let live, don't break my heart," he even put in a little bass, and I could hear Cissie tuning in on that one too. It sounded fine there with the moon overhead and the valley lying out before us. But the old hound dog was barking strong, hearing the deputy on the prowl.

Buck put out a mean snigger. "Maybe I better ontie that dog."

"She ain't got near as good alto as you have bass," said Rufus, "but it's a shame to waste a voice."

The Sheriff and a deputy came back, carrying something.

"Not a drop of liquor did we find, Buck. But there were some cases of Coca-Cola in the kitchen, for a fact, and here's a couple of them." They set the Coca-Cola down on the porch. Mouth open, Buck stared at it. Then he got the point.

"That's all you'll find. I forgot to take it to the college."

The other deputy came around the corner of the house and reported. "Nothing in the barn, nothing in the corncrib. But I owe this old devil a lick for the lick he gave me."

Before the Sheriff could catch his arm, the deputy landed a smacking right that rocked Buck's head. Buck staggered, recovered, put a hand to his ear.

"Hold on, Charley," said the Sheriff. "We'll handle this peaceable. Well, Buck, it does seem like you are in the clear on the big count this time. But p'raps you can explain to me how the Dean of the College, a l'arned man like him, could be so misinformed as to send me out here on a wild goose chase."

THE VALLEY AIR WAS FLOWING SWEET   **281**

"Yes, I kin explain," growled Buck, then caught himself and said, very polite, "No, Sir, Mr. Sheriff, I mean I don't know nothin' about it." He was still putting a hand to his ear, very tenderly.

The Sheriff looked at him hard and turned to Rufus. "Maybe I ought to search your car, Rufus. If I was sure I could find an explanation there, maybe I *would* search it."

"Whatever you might find there, Sheriff," answered Rufus, "it wouldn't be an explanation about a Dean. And how could you have a warrant to search for an explanation?"

"Maybe so, maybe not. But anyhow, there's one thing that ain't so easy to clear up. Buck, you assaulted an officer of the law tonight." He took out his handcuffs. "I reckon I'll have to take you in after all."

He was swinging his handcuffs, sort of pleasantly, not yet moving, when we heard a scrambling sound under the house, and somebody said "Ahem!" in a voice that seemed familiar.

They crawled out one by one from under the steps.

The white tuxedo—that was Hoodenpyl. The dressed-up, sporty character—he was Muradian. Number Three was a stocky-built man I didn't know. But I knew Number Four, even with his coat on—he was Mr. Picture Shirt. Slapping at the dust on their trouser knees, they stood before us in a draggly line.

"Great Snakes!" was what Ed Cooley said. We would have been less surprised if they had been a bunch of chickensnakes. Next to me, hand over mouth, Cissie was choking back the giggles. It was like something in the funny paper.

Dr. Hoodenpyl straightened up and bobbed his head. "Pardon me if—yes-yes, pardon us if we seem to have been eavesdropping. It was purely accidental—I might say unpremeditated. Yes-yes, we hardly—uh—expected—"

"Professor," drawled the Sheriff, "jest drop all that talk and tell us what you were doing under Buck Kennedy's house, this time o' night."

"Yes-yes, Mr. Sheriff. Yes, indeed. But it is important to—please allow me to introduce—you know me of course. And this is my good friend Mr. Muradian, Vice-President of American Features—and his secretary, Mr. Angelo Forunato—(that was Picture Shirt)—and—uh—his—uh—chauffeur—Mr.—ah—Pappadoupolos."

"Very interestin'." The Sheriff motioned to a deputy. "Go over them, Charley, and see if they have any concealed weapons."

Charley reached for Hoodenpyl, but the Muradian man stepped forward angrily.

282

"Thees ees most insulting!" he spluttered. "I protest! I demand my r-r-rights! Thees ees not ceevilized!"

"Git back into line!" the Sheriff shouted. 'Hold up your hands, all of you!"

They reached for the sky. I wouldn't have taken a million dollars for the sight, as that deputy went down the line, emptying their pockets and patting them all over. But the Muradian man kept on screeching: "Thees ees an outr-r-age! I demand my r-r-rights! I will r-r-repor-r-t thees to the Depar-r-rtment of Justeece!" The Sheriff ignored him. It was music to the rest of us. Buck Kennedy watched, sitting on the steps and thoughtfully puffing a cigarette, chin in hand. His ear was swelling fast.

The deputy found nothing until he came to the stocky chauffeur. "Those three are clean," he said, "but this feller carries a blackjack" (he yanked it out of the man's pocket) "and brass knucks" (in another pocket) "and an automatic in a shoulder holster."

"We'll take that hardware to my car," said the Sheriff. "And now rest easy, you men."

Soon as they took down their hands, all four men began to scratch wildly—on their legs, under their arms, and in other places. I wondered if Buck would bring on the Flit, but he didn't move.

The Sheriff looked at his watch. "It's gittin' towards eleven o'clock, and I promised Elvira I'd come to the gymnasium without fail. See the dancin', maybe dance a set or two myself. We'll wind this up quick. Now, Mr. Muradian, down here in the South we always make allowances for strangers, and I'm not sayin' that I'll place charges against that chauffeur of yours, or you. But if you want to take up the matter with the Department of Justice, it will naturally be my duty to appear in Federal court, if it comes to that, and give my testimony. And I'm sure the Court will be interested in the business, whatever it is, that makes it seem advisable for you to come among us with a thug for a guard, carrying concealed weapons."

Muradian found another place to scratch and said nothing.

"Dr. Hoodenpyl," he continued, "go on with your lecture. I'll give you one minute to finish." He still had his watch out.

"Yes-yes," said Hoodenpyl, rather weakly. "Yes, indeed, Mr. Sheriff. I merely want—I simply intend to explain—it is just a little embarrassing perhaps. But actually, you see, Mr. Sheriff, my friend Mr. Muradian was so kind as to—uh-uh—offer transportation—uh-uh—to the airport—for Mr. Kennedy and me. The—uh-one o'clock plane. We have engagements in Washington and New York. Is that not correct, Mr. Kennedy?"

"Signed up today," said Buck. He was beginning to swagger a little.

"I see." The Sheriff's voice was cold. "You all came away out here just to take Mr. Kennedy to the plane. But that don't explain what the devil you were doin' under Buck Kennedy's house!"

"No intention to eavesdrop, I assure you, Mr. Sheriff. But we heard the siren, Mr. Sheriff—and what sounded like—uh—gunfire. It seemed discreet—we did not want to be in the line of fire—a police raid. It was not brave, perhaps. But under the circumstances, you understand . . . we thought . . . it was entirely innocent . . ."

"In other words, you were scared as hell." The Sheriff paused solemnly. "You should have remembered your Bible. For the Bible says, don't it, that 'the wicked flee when no man pursueth.'"

He turned quickly. "Buck, since you are leavin' town, I won't bother to take you to jail tonight. I want to git back to that dance. But if you or any of these mugwumps you run with are in Carolina City twelve hours from now, I'll place charges."

"One moment, Mr. Sheriff, please." Hoodenpyl sounded real earnest. "If I might just speak to Miss Timberlake privately—if you will kindly . . ."

The Sheriff nodded and waved his hand. "Come on, boys, let's get off that bridge." They laughed and set off. Hoodenpyl whispered something in Cissie's ear, bobbed his head once or twice, and mounted the porch steps with his partners. We watched the back of his white tuxedo, now well seeded with spiderwebs and trash, as he faded into the shadows. And that was the last I saw of Dr. Hoodenpyl.

And now old Buck Kennedy was stepping into the shadows too. Rufus yelled his farewell. "Don't forgit you owe Johnson's Grocery for four cases of Coca-Cola. They are charged to you!"

From the top step Buck threw us one backward glance. It might be he was grinning. It might be he was showing his teeth one last time. "Tell him to send the bill"—he paused to let it sink in—"to my New York address."

It was a pleasure now to walk the grass, and no dew on it, to Rufus' car, and I told him, "It's a pleasure, Rufus, to be ridin' back with you."

"The pleasure's all mine," said Rufus. "All aboard!"

"Well done—it was well done," said Cissie, yawning a little. "But I'm glad it's over."

"You ought not to have let him have the last word," said Wallace.

"Let him lick his wounds," said Ed Cooley, "like any other yaller dog."

"They'll be half through the dance," said Cissie, looking at her wristwatch.

"But the night is young, and my barbecue's waiting," I answered.

She grabbed my coat and begun to feel in my inside pockets. "Those letters! The Dean will be at the dance. We better read the letters before we see him. Have you got a flashlight, Rufus?"

"Get in the back seat. You kin sit close and read 'em while we ride."

We were rolling back, on the same old road, but taking it easy.

"Maybe we ought to have the weddin' in a automobile," I told Cissie. "It would seem real natural, wouldn't it?"

"Ridin' in the automobile comes *after*, not *durin'*, the wedding."

"What was it that man whispered to you?"

"Oh—just that he might not be back soon and he wanted me to know he had *already* signed my thesis."

"Thoughtful, ain't he?"

"Don't think I didn't remind him. Turn on the dome light and we'll open our letters."

They were short and to the point. The Dean wrote Cissie that he wanted her to know, before the Folk Festival started, how much he appreciated her good work, in the Festival and everything else, and that he was recommending her for an appointment as Instructor, beginning with the fall term. He mentioned a pretty good salary, for just a teaching job. Since Dr. Hoodenpyl's place would be vacant, he said that Cissie would take over the ballads class and some other work that he would discuss with her later.

The letter to me began about the same way, but was shorter. The Dean said he was recommending me for a special temporary assignment as consultant in audio-visual education—which however could not begin until January when the new building and equipment would be ready; and he hoped I would accept. At the bottom of the typed page he had written with a pen: "Thank you for taking care of 'situations.'"

I switched off the dome light. We were riding smooth, and pretty soon we would be passing the MacGregor Place.

"Are you goin' to accept the Dean's offer, Cissie?"

"You wouldn't want me to refuse, would you—darling?"

"No, darling," I said. "I don't think I would."

"And are you goin' to accept, Danny?"

"Well, I think I'll tell the Dean that this takes care of a lot of situations. Between now and January I can help out Rufus on this Grand Ole Opry proposition, and that'll go a long ways towards payin' off my mortgage."

"You owe it to him to help. We both do."

"Maybe you could figure to run over to Nashville, week-ends, and we could both try out Polka Dot Tie's new pilot project."

"Maybe I could, sure enough. But not give up our own pilot project."

"You mean the MacGregor Place—our independence?"

"Yes—and our own songs, the old and the new. Our own songs—your songs and mine—our own folks."

"It's all country music—the good country music, both the old and the new."

The valley air was flowing sweet upon us. In the cool dark I could not see Cissie's eyes, but I felt in my heart she was smiling consent to all I was thinking.

The time had come. I tapped Rufus on the shoulder.

"When you come to my front gate, stop and let us out."

Slowing down a little, Rufus turned his head, but kept one eye on the road. "What! Not goin' to the dance?"

"You make our excuses. Tell 'em we are tired. Tell 'em anything you want to. But pass the word to our friends that we stopped off at the house to get things started and we are expectin' them soon for our big barbecue. And be sure to remind the Dean that we are expectin' *him*."

Rufus pulled up at the big front gate. "Don't you want me to drive you up to the house?"

"No. No, thank you, Rufus. Thank you for a lot. You'll be back soon, won't you?"

"Oh, we'll give you lovers some time to yourselves. We'll be back soon enough. I'll bring your guitar, and I want to hear you sing that new song of yours, right on your own front porch. It's country music."

"I can purty nigh taste that barbecue right now," said Ed Cooley. "In fact, I can smell it on the air."

Above the dark ranks of oak trees on the avenue, the MacGregor House stood up, lights in the windows, softer lights of lanterns marking the porch; and as we looked, another lantern, and another came to life, where Old Man Parsons and his wife were making ready.

"We will sing the moon down tonight. And I want you to rest easy in your mind, Rufus, about everything."

I helped Cissie out of the car. Back of the windshield we could see those three faces, all pleased, all smiling. They seemed to be waiting for something. So with my arm I turned Cissie toward the gate, and she leaned towards me.

"I think it's a good night to be walking up the avenue, under the oak trees, to our own house, don't you Cissie?"

"It's the finest night in all time, Danny. Yes. Yes."

Afterword

BY CURTIS W. ELLISON AND WILLIAM PRATT

Those who know Donald Davidson only as the Fugitive poet, the Agrarian essayist, the author of a widely-used composition textbook, or the much-revered teacher of literature and writing will no doubt be surprised to learn that he also wrote a novel. The man who taught creative writing for over forty years at Vanderbilt University in Nashville, where he encouraged such budding novelists as Robert Penn Warren and Jesse Stuart, knew how to write fiction as well as how to teach it. Though it mysteriously failed to be published during Davidson's lifetime, *The Big Ballad Jamboree* is one of the best novels ever written about an abiding instrument of American popular culture, the country music business.

Actually, it is fitting to discover that Davidson wrote a novel linking southern literature to country music, considering his long interest in the English lyric, in oral tradition, in balladry of the southern mountains, and in the vernacular art of sacred harp singing. There were other connections as well, involving geography, timing, and cultural history. Vanderbilt, where the Fugitive poets and Agrarian writers were centered, is located in the same southern city that nurtured key institutions of country music. In fact, by the time *The Big Ballad Jamboree* was being written in the middle 1950s, the Vanderbilt campus and country music's 16th Avenue recording studios were adjacent neighbors.

Furthermore, in the late 1920s and early 1930s, at the same moment when academic culture's Fugitives and Agrarians at Vanderbilt were praising the South's agricultural past as an antidote to modernity, a parallel event in popular culture was taking place just across town. There, "The Solemn Old Judge," George D. Hay, was creating a stylized string band music dedicated to "old time tunes" with "a delightful little folk strain that brings us all back to the soil." This music, derived mostly from rustic styles of the rural southern past, was being broadcast by station WSM on country music's most influential radio voice, the Grand Ole Opry. The Opry was destined to become the world's longest-running radio program, and the musical tradition popularized there was to be the focus of Donald Davidson's only novel.

Nashville's academic poets shared with the city's commercial music entrepreneurs an understandable impulse to imagine an agrarian past more hospitable than the southern present. Between 1920 and 1960—a period corresponding with Davidson's tenure at Vanderbilt and with the rise of the country music business—traditional southern agriculture fell to modernization. In the Appalachians, the setting for Davidson's novel, seasonal cycles of family farming were replaced by the industrial economy of coal mining, textile mills, railroads, highways, national parks and hydroelectric projects. These changes brought cycles of economic depression and unemployment, as well as aggressive government programs aimed at improving domestic life. In this same period, southerners were experiencing the social dislocations associated with fighting a world war, and they left the region permanently in record numbers.

Judge Hay and other country music promoters responded to these circumstances by marketing emotions that would appeal to a fractured society—sentimental longings for extended family, domestic harmony, spiritual salvation, and romantic love. The Agrarian writers, especially Davidson, usually presented a more defiant face to the New South. They were certain that industrialization would bring cultural ruin by displacing both natural communities and the social function of the arts.

The Big Ballad Jamboree, a novel about country music by a Fugitive poet, crosses the boundary between academic and popular culture in its characteristic southern objection to modernity. Sentiment for the past and defiance of the present both appear here. A direct critique of modernity is well represented in Mr. Parsons, and a humorous spoof of it is captured deftly in the commercial jingles sung by Rufus and the Turkey Hollow Boys. Country music's sentimental impulses toward the southern past surface in the stage performances of Danny MacGregor and Cissie Timberlake. The novel's resolution suggests that one of the Agrarian movement's most formal critics of the New South found in country music a commercial art worthy of appreciation.

Donald Davidson's interest in vernacular music of the rural South began at least in the early 1930s, when he was infatuated with the sacred music collection of his Vanderbilt colleague George Pullen Jackson. Jackson published *White Spirituals in the Southern Uplands* in 1933, and the following year Davidson observed a sacred harp singing in Marshallville, Georgia. He wrote about it in an essay that first appeared in the April 1934 *Virginia Quarterly Review*. This item was condensed for popular circulation in *Reader's Digest* the following month. Here Davidson described "shape-note" or "fasola" singing as "an intense personal experience" signifying an older, rural authenticity that confronted the modern world as only "poetry and religion united in music" could. Styles of stage performance and audience response were important to Davidson in this early essay. They would continue to be eighteen years later when Davidson and Charles F. Bryan, professor of music at Nashville's Peabody College and a composer of classical works drawing upon folk music, wrote a folk opera, *Singin' Billy*, first produced at Vanderbilt in 1952. Its hero is William H. Walker, compiler of *The Southern Harmony*, an 1835 collection of vernacular sacred music standardized to a shape-note system for teaching part singing in evangelical singing schools. Anticipating Davidson's novel, there is an assertive female singer in this story whose interest in the song collector has romantic overtones, and a comic resolution where Billy betters his detractors in a climactic public singing duel.

In *The Big Ballad Jamboree*, Davidson for the first time in American fiction presents a contrast between the sentimental folk songs of the Grand Ole Opry, written and marketed for wide appeal, and the older folk ballads passed down from generation to generation by mountain families who cultivated among themselves, for no commercial profit, the songs they had heard from their forebears of Scottish or English or Irish descent. In his courses at Vanderbilt he liked to use Francis Child's *English and Scottish Popular Ballads* (in George Lyman Kittredge's condensed edition), recorded straight from the lips of border Scots or English singers, just as Cissie Timberlake, the heroine of this novel, does when she makes it into her "ballad Bible." During his classes in the English lyric, students might be startled to hear Davidson sing aloud, with no accompaniment, songs he had heard while growing up in the country villages of Tennessee. Though he was a serious poet, Davidson was not above attending performances of the Grand Ole Opry in the old Ryman Auditorium in downtown Nashville, where professional country music had found its home, and *The Big Ballad Jamboree* proves that he was interested in the popular commercial ballad as well as the oral mountain ballad.

This novel also shows Davidson to be a master of the colloquial narrative tradition first brought to perfection by Mark Twain in *The Adventures of Huckleberry Finn*, and *The Big Ballad Jamboree* is a significant addition to that major genre of American fiction. The narrator is Danny MacGregor, a country singer courting his childhood sweetheart, Cissie Timberlake, whose story he tells sympathetically, while also telling his own, describing how he kept the old MacGregor Place from being sold to the government—as Cissie's family's had been—to become part of the Great Smoky Mountains National Park. Danny, who is practical enough to take up commercial folksinging and guitar playing and to become a member of the Turkey Hollow Boys, now finds himself in a dilemma. The genuine oral tradition in which he was raised has no monetary value but is a link between generations of his family, while the kind of country music promoted by his band leader, Rufus, meets his need to make a commercial profit.

Cissie Timberlake, who had once performed with Danny and the hillbilly radio band, has been to New York City to study folklore and is returning to collect ballads and to teach a course at a state college in the southern Appalachian mountain town of Carolina City, North Carolina, where the story is set. Exposure to formal learning has caused her to have reservations about using traditional music for commercial gain. Davidson's story pursues a reconciliation of Danny's hillbilly enthusiasm with Cissie's ballad scholarship through a series of live performances. It is also a love story with ironic turns that elaborate Davidson's critique of modernity in sometimes unpredictable ways.

Danny, for example, has "old" domestic values that focus on rescuing his family home in the mountains, marrying Cissie, and living a peaceful farm life, yet he is also beguiled by modern music, stage performance, and touring. In Cissie, Davidson reverses Danny's temptations. A thoroughly modern young woman who wants to have an academic career, she also intends through the work she does—collecting ballads in their purest form— to preserve remnants of the disappearing rural past.

On stage, Davidson's scholarly heroine has other qualities. In a practice session when Cissie plays the "bull fiddle," with her "high heels scotched well apart, skirt up to her knees, yellow hair flying" and puckering her mouth "to make the notes come better," we see the overtones of sexual encounter that are often implicit in popular musical performance. "The more she puckered," Danny observes, "the more I twanged all over." But Cissie objects to performing publicly in this provocative manner; she wants authenticity. Authenticity, however, has its own price. Cissie's "great discovery," Buck Kennedy, "a perfect example of the true folk singer" who is "unspoiled by civilization," turns out to be a bootlegger who sells liquor on the campus where Cissie teaches.

Issues of authenticity haunt Cissie and Danny throughout the story. The question of musical originality, evoked in renditions ranging from mountain ballads and bawdy songs preserved in oral tradition to string band tunes written for radio to country music and commercial jingles that aim for broad popularity, is a central theme of the novel. Davidson shows, for example, that the older folk ballad tradition was more explicitly bloody and bawdy and supernatural than its commercial counterpart, in which musicians used language carefully so as not to alienate the public. That this strain of prudery was present in popular country ballads and absent in the more realistic old folk ballads is an important difference emphasized by Davidson.

The degree of performing authenticity attributed to the novel's characters also varies. Most authentic in Davidson's view, no doubt, is the sacred sincerity of Mrs. Parsons. With her dulcimer, she could "lift us up to where we could look down on trouble." The bawdy "loving songs" performed by Aunt Lou Watkins as well as versions by Buck Kennedy, who sings from his mother's handwritten collection of mountain songs, appear to be variations of authentic folk expression. The country music played by Danny and Cissie, derived from traditional ballads but written for popular appeal, is shown sympathetically. Although Rufus and the Turkey Hollow Boys play compellingly, they are ultimately governed by commercial interests. The popular Cowboy Copas and his band, with their steel guitars "pouring on molasses notes," probably appealed least to Davidson.

When he looks for authenticity in the academic study of country music, Davidson finds it mostly lacking. Although Cissie did have one admirable teacher, Dr. Goodenow, who tells her class that mountain music represents the "memory of foreparents" that runs "like an underground river through all our lives," her thesis advisor, Dr. Hoodenpyl, is an academic fraud. His study of the "Frank Sinatra curve" brings him grant money "for making charts of what everybody already knows." He is also "cashing in" on his position by cooperating with shadowy business figures who hope to establish an exclusive rights arrangement with radio artists. At his worst, Hoodenpyl tries to steal Cissie's work for his own publication and self-promotion. A classic example of an exploited graduate student, she is afraid to challenge him.

The theme of authenticity appears satirically in Davidson's depiction of politicians and civic leaders. New Deal Congressman Carlos B. Reddy sees both economic and political opportunity in promoting folk songs; he describes them as "the richest crop we grow." Mrs. Jethro Z. Eccles, an "enthusiastic booster of folklore" with aspirations for a Carolina City folk festival that would rival a famous one at White Top Mountain in Virginia, makes herself the center of attention at the novel's culminating event in the Big Ballad Jamboree. She cannot, however, prevent the embarrassment of local clergy at the "raw" performances of real mountain people, and her public befuddlement there is one of the story's most amusing moments.

Like many movies, biographies and novels depicting country music entertainers that were to follow it, *The Big Ballad Jamboree* reveals key meanings of its story during scenes of live performance. Eighteen of the novel's twenty-five chapters include performances, and at least three give detailed accounts of musical events. When Danny, Cissie, Rufus and the Turkey Hollow Boys play for the Future Farmers, we are treated to a portrait of country music as "picking and singing for fun." Yet performance can also have an emotional power that goes "right to the marrow of the bone"; when Cissie sings "White Roses on My Mother's Grave," her voice "was a white rose growing right up out of the guitar music." Later in the novel, after Danny's appreciation for "old" mountain music has deepened, he is able to blend the ballad and hillbilly traditions to find his own authenticity. When Danny steps forward to sing "MacGregor's Song," Davidson shows us a celebratory public moment that reconciles traditional with modern music to imply an accommodation between the rural past and modernity.

On the way to this achievement, Danny MacGregor is drawn as a characteristic country musician—he is at once an untutored vernacular stylist inspired by conventional values and evangelical religion, a humble, adoring fan of other talented but untrained singers, and an emerging star driven by ambition for public success. Although he is adored by fans who write to him from across the nation, Danny experiences the physical and emotional fatigue typical of country music touring. Davidson uses this common complaint of country entertainers to create an anticommercial, antimodern image. In Georgia with the Turkey Hollow Boys, Danny complains that the musician's road life "wore me out." "I could hear the adding machines clicking underneath my guitar frets," he adds.

In the comic resolution of Davidson's novel the two young people will enjoy, it seems, the best of both folk and commercial worlds. Cissie will go on teaching the ballad to her college classes, after earning her master's degree by collecting American versions of the old border ballads, and Danny will be her audio-visual assistant, while they will both continue to sing with Rufus and the Turkey Hollow Boys to make money. They will even have an opportunity to tour as stars of the Grand Ole Opry. Thus, Davidson artistically draws together two differing factions: ordinary people who sing original folk ballads at home for pleasure, and country music stars who sing adaptations of them in public for profit. Danny and Cissie will "put the old country music and the new country music together" to carry on traditional as well as derivative forms of American popular music.

The posthumous publication of *The Big Ballad Jamboree* may lead readers to wonder why Donald Davidson departed so far from his usual practice as a writer, and why, having written a novel, he was unable to find a publisher for it in his lifetime. We may never know complete answers to these questions, but we can make some educated guesses thirty years after his death, based on information in the Davidson papers now in the Special Collections of the Jean and Alexander Heard Library at Vanderbilt University. In a letter to his editor at McGraw-Hill, who was eager at one time to publish the emerging novel, Davidson suggested that the American country music scene already—in the 1950s—offered a prime subject for fiction. His intuition about the marketability of such a subject indicates just how much in touch with America's popular audience this supposedly elitist writer really was. Davidson's textbook, *American Composition and Rhetoric*, was at the time used in Freshman English classes across the country; it dominated that high-volume market for three decades, serving as a sort of McGuffey's Reader for a generation of American college students in the period after the Second World War when enrollment in American higher education was exploding. Thus Davidson proved he could interest a wide audience of teachers and students even before entering what was for him the uncharted domain of American fiction, with its potentially wider audience. Furthermore, he had found a sympathetic editor in New York who gave him every encouragement to expand his fictional treatment of country music from a short story into a novel, and who was eager to see the revision that Davidson eventually produced.

What happened to keep the novel from being published at the time probably had much to do with the vagaries of American capitalism, which Davidson as a southern Agrarian fully understood: the book became the victim of an economic system committed always to profits first. While Davidson was revising his novel, the trade department of McGraw-Hill fell prey to economic forces and was summarily abolished. But there is no reason to doubt that when Davidson wrote this novel in the 1950s—dating it "1949" to make it a piece of contemporary history—he knew what he was doing, and he had found a New York editor who agreed that he was onto something he could handle effectively. The poet who could write "Sanctuary" and "Hermitage," memorable poetic descriptions of the southern Appalachian region where his ancestors had settled, could, as a novelist, take fictional measure of the oral tradition of the Blue Ridge and Great Smoky Mountains area, one of the original sources of American country music. Fortunately, his heirs preserved the finished typescript.

The Big Ballad Jamboree makes a notable contribution to the social history of country music. In its broad exploration of authenticity in popular entertainment, its sensitive depictions of country radio and stage performances in the 1940s and 1950s, and its examination of sources of inspiration for a country music star who is able simultaneously to earn financial success, personal peace and romantic love, Donald Davidson's novel illuminates themes that remain important in the 1990s. *The Big Ballad Jamboree* also reveals Davidson's gifts for comic and satirical writing that are not conspicuous in either his poetry or nonfictional prose. Here he uses those gifts to extend his long critique of modernity and at the same time to embrace a modern popular music that had been playing near his Vanderbilt doorstep for at least thirty years. This achievement deserves the attention of anyone interested in the complexities of American life.

Donald Grady Davidson was born in Campbellsville, Tennessee, in 1893 and died in Nashville in 1968. He spent most of his life as a teacher, like his father, and became widely known as one of the Fugitive poets and Agrarian essayists at Vanderbilt University. He received a classical education at Branham and Hughes preparatory school in Spring Hill, Tennessee, and then as an undergraduate at Vanderbilt met John Crowe Ransom, who had returned from a Rhodes Scholarship at Oxford to begin his career as a teacher. Both Ransom and Davidson were officers in France in the First World War; both came back to Vanderbilt and resumed the informal discussions which in time led to the literary movement known as the Fugitives.

Davidson received his master's degree from Vanderbilt in 1922 and began a long and distinguished teaching career. *The Fugitive* magazine was published from 1922–25, with Ransom and Davidson as principal editors and contributors and with strong support from Allen Tate and Robert Penn Warren, who were invited as undergraduates to join the Fugitives. Davidson published his first book of poems, *An Outland Piper*, in 1924, and he helped edit the 1928 volume *Fugitives: An Anthology of Verse*. In 1930, he contributed to a book of essays called *I'll Take My Stand: The South and the Agrarian Tradition*, which launched the Agrarian movement led by the four principal Fugitive poets.

In 1931, Davidson began a long association with the Breadloaf School of English, buying a house in Vermont near the school where he did much of his later writing. He taught there every summer until his death. In 1939, his textbook, *American Composition and Rhetoric*, was published and widely adopted for English courses in American universities. He published the two-volume history of *The Tennessee* in the Rivers of America series in 1946–48. In 1952, his ballad opera, *Singin' Billy*, with music by Charles F. Bryan, was performed at the Vanderbilt Theatre. A volume of his essays, *Still Rebels, Still Yankees*, was published in 1957, and a second volume, *Southern Writers in the Modern World*, came out in 1958. His long service as book page editor for *The Nashville Tennessean* was commemorated in 1963 with the publication of *The Spyglass: Views and Reviews, 1924–1930*.

Davidson retired from teaching in 1964, and a comprehensive collection of his poetry, *Poems: 1922–61*, was published in 1966. After his death in 1968, new editions of his poetry and prose were issued, but his only novel, *The Big Ballad Jamboree*, has remained unpublished until now.

4/97